SONG OF WAR

BY APRIL ADAMS

THE NEW WORLD

TABLE OF CONTENTS

I. FISHING

"There," Noga said, pointing.

The Crommags did not have to sight along Noga's outstretched finger to know what, or who rather, he meant. There was nothing but snow and ice for miles in all directions, broken only by stunted trees that had long lost all foliage. The hulking Crommags were half-crouched behind a group of such shrubbery. Peering through the barren branches, they could see a curl of smoke rising before a hut made of wood scavenged from the warped trees and covered with animal hides frozen stiff and covered with frost.

The hut, looking for all the world like it was cringing down from the cold, sat on a flattened bank of the Ice Floe. The entire landscape was so completely covered in drifts of snow that the land was only distinguishable from the frozen river where the line of stunted trees ended. There, the land became a smooth white road dividing the world of the Crommags from the world of men and elves.

The Crommags, self-proclaimed the Great Men due to the weaker species that lived south of the Floe, were gruesome creatures. Most stood eight feet tall or more, corded with muscle and packed with fat to keep them warm throughout not just the winter but all year round in the brutal climate in which they lived.

Had lived.

Now there was a promise of spring. One that would last the whole year through.

Their heads were narrow at the top and wide at the bottom.

Eyes that were beady and close-set stared out over humps of bone that served as a nose. Their lower jaws jutted out and thick lips covered rows of interlocking fangs. But it was Noga, the brother of the Chief of Great Men and the leader of their small expedition, whom the other Crommags found hideous.

The Crommag was a runt, saved at birth by his brother when their father meant to hurl the misshapen babe off the nearest cliff. Not only was Noga small, but his face was flat and his hide was as thin as a film of ice on the first day of autumn. His eyes were too far apart and a pale and ghastly shade of green.

Yet his brother, the massive leader of the Great Men, claimed he was cunning. Higa was a member of their tribe and had come to learn this over time. Dolf was from the clan of the Walrus Men, but he was learning the same. They both had a begrudging respect for the ugly runt.

Together, the three watched in silence, their breath fogging in the ice-cold air. Something was moving about in front of the hut. Finally, a figure detached itself from the hide-covered shed and moved towards the snow-covered river. Its snout was tipped with a black nose and its arms ended in long claws that flopped about the lanky body.

"Are you sure that is a human?" Dolf asked doubtfully. It looked larger than any human he had ever seen, and he had never seen one so covered with hair. "It looks like a scrawny bear."

Higa snorted and looked over an immense shoulder at the Walrus Man. "Have you ever seen a bear with an axe?" he asked. "Or make a fire?"

Dolf frowned, his heavy brows drawing together over his close-set eyes as they looked back to the figure that had moved out onto the frozen waterway and was now chopping at the ice with his small tool, not with his claws but with mittened hands. He nodded slowly, realizing that it was indeed just a man, wearing the hide of a bear. These Great Men of the Bite were wise indeed.

Noga smiled and both of the other Great Men looked away. Not only was he ugly, but he had disfigured himself horribly. Noga cared not what they thought, he knew he had chosen them well. Higa would follow him, he knew. Dolf was slow, but of quicker wit than most Great Men, and showed promise.

Noga turned his mossy eyes back to the figure chipping away at the ice that had formed in the night. The man-thing had dug a hole the previous day in the giant waterway that separated the world of elves and men from the lands of the Great Men – the Ice Floe.

In the spring the Floe cracked and broke as the air warmed, grinding and moaning like some prodigious tortured beast. Eventually bergs of frozen water would begin to shoulder one another on a slow moving but an ever-increasing rush to the sea. By the summer it was a torrent, but as fall deepened it grew colder and colder. At the onset of autumn it would frost at the edges and grow sluggish. Temperatures plummeted until the Floe froze completely on the surface, a white road that meandered its way between the Bite and the Siber Massif. In the winter it was not just a road to the sea, it was a road across.

The Great Men thus far had lived in the Bitterlands, mountains to the north of the Floe that were covered in snow and ice all year round, divided into clans. It was Ayala, a mountain of a Great Man and Chief of the Bite, that had brought all of the clans together. He made speeches. Big talk of leaving the mountains where only two babes in three survived the cold, and only one of those survived the winter starve. More were lost to accidents, predators, and fights amongst each other.

A few, very few, knew that it was the runty yet cunning brother of the Great Ayala that had inspired the speeches, the plans, and the stimulus to unite the clans and move them to an easier life where they might not only survive but thrive.

Noga, since he was child, had watched from his frozen waste the lands of the south as they turned green every year and then gold before the winter took them under her blanket once again. His mother had been down the mountain many times before and told him stories of warm rivers jumping with fish and animals so fat that they just lay around until the slaughter.

"Why don't we live there?" Noga had asked once. Even as a child he could grasp that it was senseless to live in the harsh climate of the mountains if there was a much better alternative so nearby. His mother, who had been scraping meat from inside the skin of a goat with a sharpened rock, did not look up as she spoke.

"Because," she told him, "these lands are the lands we know. Besides, the men down there hate us and we hate them." Her crude knife slipped and cut her arm but she did not stop her work. Noga moved to help her by holding down the corner of hide that once covered the goat's leg.

"Why?" he asked, peering at her curiously with his curious eyes.

"Men, even Great Men, fear what they do not understand. And, more often than not, they hate what they fear."

Noga had pondered that statement while he watched his mother finish her work and for long after.

I would not be afraid, he had thought. *I would make those lands my own.*

He recalled that moment now, knowing that he was on the brink of making a childhood thought a reality. Not just for himself, but for all his people. He crouched between the two other Crommags, watching the human lower a metal hook tied to a thin rope into the hole he had made in the ice.

"Remember," Noga said, "don't kill him."

Dolf grunted. He was not sure how one was supposed to subdue an animal without killing it. Higa grinned at him, showing a set of interlocking fangs that were mostly intact but decidedly yellow.

"Hit it on the head," he advised the other Crommag. "Just don't use your club. It's not a walrus."

Noga snorted and turned his attention back to the man squatting by his hole in the Ice Floe, the thin rope wound over one of his gloved hands.

Dolf shifted his great weight from one huge foot to the other. "When do we get him?" he asked.

Noga's smiled widened. "When he gets a fish."

⚜

Asger's eyes, green as summer grass, looked out onto a world of white. Across the frozen river crouched the Bitterlands – a frozen range of mountains that never thawed. To the west loomed the Siber Massif, glacier high and choked with snow. His own lands had been iced over for a month. A fishing shack had been erected on the edge of the Ice Floe by others long ago and he had fortified it with skins that were now hard as boards and dusted with snow. The frost covered the land and river, the trees, his clothes. The white was almost blinding in its brilliance and everywhere the eye could see.

His clothes were stiff with rime and made a cracking sound as he sat down on the largest chunk of wood that he now owned and contemplated the phrase *colder than an ice fisher's ass*. He gave a grunt of appreciation for the term and used his free hand to pull his bear-skin cloak tighter around his broad frame. The head of the skinned bear was whole, cured and dried with teeth and all, and sat atop Asger's own head. The rest of the pelt hung down his back and over his arms, yet the chill still pervaded his bones. The young Vikeman knew that bears stayed warm not just because of their fur-covered skin, but from a great amount of fat under that skin. Fat that Asger did not have. At seventeen he was tall, very near seven feet, but very lean. Not nearly enough fat to keep him warm. He wanted to stomp his feet but he knew it would scare away any nearby fish.

His gloves were better since they were lined with rabbit fur. One of his gloved hands had a line wound around it and he gave it a little jerk, hoping a fish would see the wink of metal or smell the eye of the squirrel he had slid on the hook.

A fish would be good. Asger was getting tired of eating dried goat meat but he was not about to pack up and go home. He had only been out on the Floe for a week and he was determined to stay at least a month, unless he brought down some big game. He would be ridiculed if he went back so soon. Not by his mother or sister of course, but the other young men of the village would raze him. The older men would not be as coarse, but they would mutter to each other and nod, their eyes squinted against the cold air and full of cold judgement.

Winter was just setting in, the temperature only a few degrees below freezing, and there should still be plenty of fish to be had since the river was only frozen a good two feet down. He aimed to catch a fish today and maybe hunt tomorrow. Asger's brother had been a great hunter and it was his bearskin that Asger wore now. Algot had killed the bear when he was seventeen but died just a year later from the ice flux. His death was hard on Asger as well as their family and even their borough, which seemed to be dwindling of late. There had been whispers of packing up and joining a larger borough to the east. But those were just rumors. Roskilde Borough was too proud to do such a thing.

Asger twitched the line again and thought of his brother. Algot had been a great man, even as a boy. When their father had died, Algot stepped into his boots though he had only been a boy of eleven at the time. He hunted and fished and taught Asger and their little sister how to raise goats. He encouraged their mother to stop sewing for other women and instead make nets for fishing, which brought more money to the family.

The young Norseman shifted on the chunk of wood, pulling

the bearskin cloak tighter. It helped to keep him warm. But
it also helped to muffle the sounds around him and blocked a
good part of his peripheral vision. He did not hear the mutters
of the Crommags as they watched him from behind the stunted
trees and he did not see them as they began to edge their way
closer.

Algot, like Asger and their sister, had hair the color of honey
and eyes the color of grass. He had been liked by all in their
borough. There was a girl in Roskilde that he was going to
marry once he knew his little brother could step into his shoes
and take care of the family. He never hesitated to help anyone
in need. Asger tried very hard to be like him, but he felt that he
was not as liked as his brother had been.

His dark thoughts fled as he felt a tug on the line, then a
downright *pull.*

Asger was on his feet, but only for a second. The rope,
which had gone slack for a moment, gave a jerk so hard that he
lost his footing and went sprawling on the ice. The line began
to slip off his glove and Asger promptly regained his wits. He
tightened his grip on the line and yanked it back, winding
it around his gloved hand one more time. He knew he had
hooked a big one. Really big.

The next time the fish pulled, it pulled hard and dove
deep. Nearly seven feet of young Vikeman, belly down on the
ice, followed. He saw the hole rush towards his face and for a
second feared he would be dragged down into the river. Asger
rolled over and turned his body as it slid along the ice just in
time for the bottom of his boots to crash into the far side of the
hole he had dug. He locked his knees, grabbed the line with his
other hand, and braced himself.

The fish hauled on the line and Asger was pulled forward
so far that his head came down between his braced legs and
his gloved hands were nearly in the water. The hole was not
big, but it was big enough for him to slip through. Visions of
being pulled under flashed through his mind. He knew if that

happened there was a good chance he would drown or freeze to death while he searched wildly for the small hole he had dug. For a second, just a second, he was flooded with fear and almost let go of the line. Then his teeth came together with a snap and he pushed with his legs as he yanked on the rope.

As the line came from the water, ice crystals formed immediately on the fibers of the rope. The fish dove again and again nearly pulled him into the hole. He guessed the fish to be at least fifteen kilos and a great deal of muscle and meat, but it was no match for a two hundred-pound Vikeman, flooded with adrenaline and testosterone.

Asger hauled back the line, this time hooking it with his elbow. He grabbed the rope with his other hand and pulled it in until he could grasp it in the first. Then he repeated the movement, hooking the rope around his elbow and then pulling the rope into his hand, winding the line around his forearm. The bearskin cloak fell from Asger's shoulders and his breath misted in front of his face, leaving crystals of frost around his lips and under his nose.

The rope seemed to be twice as long when hauling it in rather than dropping it down and as the fish cleared the water and emerged into the icy air it seemed twice as heavy and fought him twice as hard. With his legs braced and the cords in his neck standing out, Asger lugged the fish from the freezing water, and then lugged out some more. He recognized the black and gray scales that marked it as a taimen trout, but he had never seen one so big. The thing was a monster, bigger and heavier than one of his own thighs.

With a final heave upon the line, the taimen came clear of the water, its tail and body thrashing wildly. It flopped on the ice and slid towards him, trying to take a bite out of his calf.

The young Norseman gave a yelp of surprise and kicked the fish in the head, stunning it. Digging his heels into the snow-covered river, Asger backpedaled, dragging the gigantic taimen along with him. The stunned trout was quickly regaining its bearings and already beginning to thrash and bite at his legs. Fetching up against the bank of the Floe, he groped around his gear until his hand closed around the handle of his adz. He swung the tool over his head in an arc that ended on the skull of the fish, crushing it.

It thrashed one final time and then was still.

Asger gave a shout of victory to the gods as he turned his body and raised himself up on his knees. He jammed four of his gloved fingers into its gills and tried to lift the thing off the ice but it was too heavy. He laughed, elated. Each breath was heavy and made a cloud of arctic fog around his face. The young Norseman knew he would have to skin and gut the monster where it was. It would provide all the food he needed for a month of hunting.

Or, he thought, looking down at the giant fish, *I could haul it up onto the sled and drag it home.*

There would be no need to stay and hunt. Not now.

It began to snow. Fat flakes came down in drifts, making the world of white even whiter. And smaller.

I can always hunt next week, Asger thought as he unwound the line from his hand. His heart was still beating hard from the struggle and now thrummed with excitement. *There is plenty of time before winter sets in for good. Besides, this scaled beast is prize enough and will feast us for weeks. If I don't take it back to the borough now then no one will believe how colossal....*

Then something heavy smashed into his head and turned the world of white into a world of black.

"Got 'em!" Higa shouted triumphantly.

Dolf squatted down and peered at the human that had shed the skin of a bear, squinting. "How do you know it's still alive?"

Higa looked hard at the Walrus Man and then pointed. Dolf sighted along Higa's finger to where it ended at the face of the human that lay sprawled upon the ice. At first he did not understand, then realization dawned as he saw the cloud of vapor form around the man's mouth each time he exhaled.

"Ah!" Dolf exclaimed. Then he stooped low, scooped up the seven-foot human as if he were a sack of grain and threw him over one of his massive shoulders. "What is next?"

"Take him back to camp," Higa instructed, omitting *you imbecile* from the end of his instruction to Dolf.

Where did I learn that word? Higa wondered as Dolf grunted and turned, gallantly trudging away. Noga clapped him on the shoulder, reaching up to do so.

"Good job," the runt told him with a smile.

Though the smile was macabre, Higa felt a rush of pride at the praise and wondered at that as well. Noga laughed, reading the expression on the bigger Crommag.

"And bring that fish," the runt added, jerking his oddly round head towards the giant taimen before he turned and followed Dolf.

Higa grinned and retrieved the gargantuan trout, hooking it in the gills with three calloused fingers before slinging it over his right shoulder. He turned and followed Noga, realizing that he not only respected the runt, but he liked him as well. Ayala had been right, there was a lot to be said for cunning. Higa decided that there might be a bit of cunning within himself.

He liked that, too.

Smiling, he shifted the weight of the taimen on his shoulder so it would not slip off, and followed Dolf and Noga back to their camp. A camp that comprised almost the entire population of Crommags that had migrated down out of the Bitterlands under the leadership of Chief Ayala. Great Men that meant to make war on the lesser men and the elves that lived to the south – taking their green lands and wiping them from existence.

2. MAJOR CONCERNS

The sound of bootheels made a hollow ringing sound on the stones of green-veined marble as Sir Dellion ran up the stairs in the south tower of Castle Song. The sound rebounded off the curved walls and echoed deep into the castle.

Five, ten, fifteen, twenty... Dell counted the steps by fives as he wound his way up and around, around and up. The entire castle seemed hollow and echoey to Dell, Praetorian Guard to the royal family of the Skye Elves. He served as well as Captain of the Jägers, an elite force of elfin hunters, and had recently been made Major of the Elfin Army.

The more titles I get, he thought testily as he climbed the tower steps, *the less time I have.*

Clothed in drab gray and green like a shadow of the forest, his face was ageless despite the fact he had seen the dawn and dusk of over three hundred years. High, arched brows perched over dark eyes that were never still.

Those dark eyes flicked about to the stone walls on either side and then up ahead once more as he ascended. The air grew colder the higher he went and Dell made a mental note to ask the housekeeper to start keeping fires going in a few empty rooms before the whole place turned into a giant icicle.

The castle had been built for Addison and Ilse Song, the parents of Queen Elyse, when the elves had arrived in the New World. When Ilse died, Addison soon followed. Servants were sent to other posts and much of the furniture was removed. The castle became a shell.

Castle Song had remained empty for the next four decades until Dell and his royal charge had both returned from separate journeys, each with warnings of an impending invasion of the beasts from the Bitterlands – the Crommags.

Now, and quite in totality, the castle had become a single monstrous war room. The rooms on the lower floors served as armories, storing weapons that were being made day and night. Bows had been carved and strung and then neatly hung on racks along the walls while fletchers still made arrows by the score. Mule-drawn carts arrived every evening from every smith in the elfin city. Some carts were filled with weapons, others with chain mail and plate armor. All of it was accounted for and carefully stored.

The second floor was dedicated entirely to logistics. Maps were hung on walls and spread out upon tables. A multitude of rooms were designated as departments where appointed officers engaged in plans for supplies, food, and weapons. The castle grounds had become training fields where the elves sharpened their archery skills and learned hand to hand combat. Lists were made of the male elves that had enlisted to fight and where they stood in their training.

During the day the air was full of brisk commands, the ring of boots on the marble floors, and the song of steel in the courtyard. Yet, as the sun went down, officers and enlisted alike drifted back to their homes. Only the castle's lone resident remained, and as darkness crept across the land the fortress became still and ghostly, a near empty shell once more.

Dell reached the top of the staircase where the finely chiseled marble steps ended on a broad landing a few feet from a heavy door made of golden oak, dried and cracked with disuse, but recently polished to a high shine. New iron bindings and hinges stood in sharp contrast against the gleaming yellow wood and the Praetorian thought it looked like a room where one might lock a crazy man. He snorted softly as he paused for a second before the closed door, thinking it was not far from the truth, and then rapped on it quickly. His entrance was demanded from within and the Jäger turned the new iron handle as he pushed on it. The door swung open easily to reveal an apartment that took up the entire top floor of the tower, the bedchamber of Castle Song's only current occupant, as much a shell as the castle itself.

There were as many maps here as there were downstairs, littering desks and tables. Another table held a tray of food that appeared to be untouched. The fireplace held nothing but ashes, as cold as the meal upon the tray. A large four-poster bed, inviting with piled blankets and pillows, also looked unused. A solitary stuffed chair faced the cold fireplace. Over it was slung a strap fitted with a quiver and two six-inch hilts of carved and polished bone capped with gold protruded from leather sheaths on either side.

A figure, tall and lean, stood looking out an arched window that had been opened to the cold. A pale gray linen shirt hung on his frame like laundry on a line and a shag of tousled curls, drained of color by the twilight, fell to his collar. A vest of darker gray draped his broad shoulders and buttoned down over his thin chest. His doeskin breeches were the color of damp ashes and tucked into a pair of black leather boots. A sword hung from his left hip. He turned from the window as Dell entered, the rays of the setting sun painting his face in light and shadow.

"My Lord Prince," Dell greeted.

Traejanale Royce, second son to King Rowland the Great and prince of the Skye Elves, smiled at his guardsman. It was a gentle smile, yet it made his gaunt face look eerily skeletal.

"Dell," he scolded softly, "how many times have I dismissed the need to call me such, especially when we are alone?"

The Jäger blew a burst of air through his nose. His respect, like any elf, ran deep. But he had served as the Praetorian Guard to the elfin prince for over a century and sometimes his patience was whipped.

"You look like the Specter of Death, should I address you as such?" Dell asked.

The smile on the prince widened into a grin as if he had been complimented, then his face turned back to the open window and his expression tightened.

"What brings you here, my friend?" he asked.

"It is the solstice," Dell stated.

"So it is," the prince agreed.

"The festivities will start when the sun has set."

"They always do."

"Aren't you coming?"

The corner of Traejan's lips twitched. "I don't have anything to wear."

Dell's chest swelled with air as he controlled his ire. "Shall I fetch you a dress?" he asked, his impatience growing.

The prince almost laughed at the jape. Dell was getting bolder, something that would have brought a sharp reprimand or even dismissal by some of the other royalty, but Traejan did not care. "I am needed to train soldiers," he informed his Praetorian. "Not to dance at festivals."

Dell's arched brows drew together. "War may be on the horizon, but our people still hold to their traditions. The sun sets and we celebrate a new turn as the shortest day of the year is put behind us. It would be well for you to be at the festivities."

"You sound like my mother," the prince remarked. "Did she send you?"

The guardsman felt the muscles in his jaw flex and tighten. "No, you did."

Traejan, his arms crossed over his lean chest, turned at the waist to peer curiously at his Praetorian. "I did?"

"Yes, when you made me a major."

"I only did that so I could call you a major pain in the ass."

"You put me in charge of the captains," Dell continued as if he had not heard, "who are in charge of our troops. Elves that you are training, training to go war, yourself included. Those elves need to see you tonight, proud and strong and confident."

A smile ghosted Traejan's gaunt face. "But confidence is the one thing I lack," he told his guardsman, his voice soft. Dell's stiff form stiffened further.

"Confidence in your men?"

"In myself."

Dell shook his head. "Then be there for *them*."

The prince turned his gaze back to the window, fighting an internal battle. The sun was almost gone, the orange light a streak over the trees. "A hundred days," he said softly, the orange glow bathing his face in demonic radiance.

"I beg your pardon?" Dell asked.

"It has been one hundred days since I saw her last," Traejan said. It was an effort to keep the sorrow from his voice.

Dell's only movement was in his throat as he swallowed. The memory for him was clear as a chuchbell chime. Just last summer he had led a team of Jägers on an expedition to either confirm or dispel the rumors of an invasion of the Northlon. As they returned, Dell had gone to meet the prince who had just spent two seasons of weapons schooling with a legendary mercenary known as the Roshan Simorgh. As the Praetorian arrived at the meeting point he was shocked to his very core upon hearing the prince pledging marriage vows to his mercenary teacher. Dell had never spoken of it and prayed that the prince had done the same.

Traejanale had returned to the elfin homeland of Tuar Ceath with his Praetorian to confirm what Dell and his Jägers had discovered. The beasts of the Bitterlands were moving south. Not due to weather, plight, or plague - but for war. Their exact destination had not been discovered but the elves, being the first race in the path of their southerly direction, would be the first ones hit.

The prince, after delivering this news to his father and his brother, had done three things. First, he had locked himself within his personal chambers. For days on end he took no visitors, food, nor drink. When he finally emerged, dehydrated, hollowed out, eyes rimmed with red, he moved into Castle Song. From there he called the elves to arms and began to train them.

The quickest of hand and mind he made swordsmen, and worked with them every day until he had a squad of captains. From dawn to dusk he instructed them, singly and in groups, working tirelessly to teach them every form of close combat that he himself had so recently learned. When Traejan felt they had learned enough, he had them teaching their own groups while he supervised.

Others were marshalled for archers or horsemen or stewards or squires. The Jägers, the group of elite elfin hunters, were divided. Most were put into scouting teams but a few were made Captains. He put Dell in charge of them all.

Now, Sir Dellion of Kren, an elf of barely three hundred summers yet Captain of the Jägers, Praetorian Guard to Prince Traejanale Royce and the newly made Major of the Army of the Elves, straightened his five-foot form. He had hoped that time away from the human woman would help the prince forget her. But time, even a hundred days, appeared to have only made him worse.

"And do you think you will ever see her again?" he asked boldly.

Traejan's face, gaunt as it was, snapped to the left and caught his Praetorian with eyes that were once soft brown but for the nonce blazed bright blue.

"I *will*," he assured his guard.

"And how do you expect to find..." Dell began to say but, as the expression on Traejan's face began to change, he ended his sentence with a sigh. "You already know, don't you?"

A smile quirked the corner of Traejan's lip and he turned his gaze back out the window, looking south. It did not take but a moment for Dell to piece it together.

"Xander's messengers," he said through his teeth. "The elves that your brother sent out to warn the other races about the Crommag invasion, you hired them on the sly."

"There was nothing sly about it," the young prince informed his guardsman. "After Xander gave them his instructions, I told them to afterwards inquire of the Roshan Simorgh and bring me any word. It was surprisingly easy."

Though Dell knew quite well that it was none of his business, he could not help but ask. "And where is she?"

"In the Redlands," the young prince replied, staring out of the window as if his elfin eyesight allowed him see all the way down into the Southlon, "training men for the Crimson King."

Dell drew a breath deep into his lungs and let it out again slowly as he digested the information. Then he continued, plowing ahead brazenly in a way he had never dared to imagine when he had first come into the service of the royal family. "And when you do see her, would you like for her to see *you* - as you are now?"

The prince gave a jerk as if poked in the back. Dell's question, though simple, ran though him like an arrow. Though the Praetorian could only see a part of the younger elf's face, he saw his expression go from drawn pain to chagrin. A moment later it settled into resignation.

"No," he answered. "Not even for a second." His broad shoulders sagged as he sighed and then he turned just enough to give his Praetorian a ghost of a smile. "Better get me a dress, then. But not one of yours, it would be too short."

The corners of Dell's lips twitched at his joke, then he bowed to the prince and took his leave, closing the door behind him. The Praetorian hurried back down the stairwell in a race to find something suitable for the prince to wear. Though it was no matter for the Queen, Dell decided to seek her out. Undoubtedly delighted at Traejan attending the celebration, she would have all that he needed delivered to Castle Song, along with a horde of attendants, within the hour.

The young prince, alone in his room once again, listened to the fading ring of Dell's boots on the stone as he turned back to the window. The sun was gone and all that remained was just a bright pink glow that was fading expeditiously.

As always, without a task before him, his mind wandered to what *she* might be doing at the exact same moment.

Was she fighting? Training? Nursing a wound?

Was she asleep? And, if so, was she sleeping soundly somewhere safe or was it a broken doze with only her beast of a Night Stallion to stand as guard?

Was she gazing out of a castle window with her gem-like eyes, thinking about him?

For the short time they had spent in each other's arms they had whispered words such as *love* and *forever* and *always*. Had those only been words to her?

She had found new employ – had she found new love as well?

Did she still care for him?

Had she forgotten him?

The questions came faster and faster, each more bleak and despairing than the last, swirling through his head like a cyclone. Finally, with an effort, he banished the dervish from his mind. He had become quite used to doing so.

One hundred days, he mused, this time without sorrow or self-pity. He thought of the elves he had trained over the past mad season. He had worked tirelessly, but it was from his desire to keep the thoughts of his love from his mind and drive the ache from his heart. His men had labored tirelessly out of love for their people and the kingdom they had built.

Contemplating it made him cringe.

They have a warrior's responsibility already, he realized. *Where mine has been sorely lacking.*

His hand dropped to the hilt of his sword and tightened around the pommel, ashamed and angry with himself. He had been training the men, yes, but his heart had not been in it because his heart was somewhere else. Somewhere it had no place being while his people were facing a war that could mean their annihilation. He had been going through the motions like a Gnomin steam-machine.

Traejan turned from the window and left his room.

One hundred days past, when his Roshan had left him physically incapacitated and emotionally butchered next to a burning fire, he could hardly believe it. For the entire trip home, the disbelief was so real that he thought she might come riding up at any moment - or at least send a rider with a message.

Return to the haus in a fortnight, it might read. Or, *I will see you on the next turn of the moon.* He could not believe that she would really leave him.

But a day passed as he travelled northward with Dell and his Jägers, and another. And another. A few more and they were riding into Tuar Ceath. Traejan's soul felt as if it had been wrung out like a wet rag. She was not coming. She had not sent for him. His soul became dry with despair.

After a short and awkwardly empty reunion with his family, he had locked himself in his rooms under the pretense of exhaustion. He spent four sleepless nights staring at an empty fireplace, as his eyes leaked like the roof of an inn long condemned, wondering if it would be different had he been born into another family. A less prominent family surely would have less problems with social expectations. Traejan knew that he would trade being a prince with being a woodcutter if it meant he could be with the woman he loved.

He held endless conversations with her in his mind, pleading his case in every way he could think, promising her anything. He held similar imaginary discussions with his family that he never dared broach aloud. After bargaining mentally with everyone he knew and to no avail, he left his rooms and did what he knew he must. He moved from his family's royal castle, not wanting them to see him in such a state. Then he began to prepare his people for war.

After moving into Castle Song, the young prince was busy from an hour before sunrise until the sun went down every day. Every second of daylight was put to use and he was secure in every task before him. But in the dark, cold and alone, the winds began to blow through his soul and the cyclone of grief and doubt would begin to build. The result was an interspersion of depression and anger. When depression had the upper hand, he could do no more than lay on his back in the murky gloom, hot tears leaking from his almond-shaped eyes down towards his pointed ears. When anger found him, he would stare into the fire for long hours, hatching plans on how he would act when he saw her again. He decided the cruelest would be to turn his back on her and walk away. He felt it was the one she deserved the most.

Now, as he raced down the South Tower stairway, Traejan felt something different. Someone experienced with the stages of grief could have told him what it was. It was acceptance.

I will see her again someday, he thought, taking the stairs two at a time. *And when she sees me she will be proud of what I have done, of who I am. If she can be patient, how could I be any less?*

The young prince left Castle Song through the front doors rather than through the kitchens or a side door as he normally did, heading for the royal castle. He knew it would be more efficient to get ready there, or to simply go as he was. Finery did not matter. What mattered was that he was *there*, in heart and soul rather than just in body.

He crossed a stone bridge over a bubbling stream, fed by one of the many waterfalls that served as the backdrop against the Mountain of the Moon. Torches were being lit in the deepening twilight and Traejan breathed deep the cool mists that gathered there. He came upon a group of young men and he hailed them with a heartfelt salutation.

The young men, four of whom he had been training for the better part of the past three months, were surprised – both to see him and at his warmhearted address. The prince banished the guilt that wanted to rise within as their expressions quickly turned to those of delight and they greeted him enthusiastically in return. Each person or group of persons that Traejan encountered along his way was met with the same genuine geniality. As the groups grew larger their responses grew in kind and by the time he was at Castle Royce it was a cheer that rose in crescendo at his passing.

The prince had finally come home.

One hundred more days passed.

3. THE PRINCE OF TIDES

"The Titan Saturn, or Cronus as he was called by the Greeks, was known to devour his children!"

The group of young Atlanteans, most aged two to seven years old, drew back and gasped, chubby hands bolting up to cover mouths that were wide in wonder and tremulous terror. Gathered in the Solar of the Scallops, they sat upon the steps of the dais, listening to Marea tell them the ancient tales.

The room was round and brightly lit by sunlight that streamed in from the shafts above. The curved walls were inlaid with thousands of pearly-white scallop shells, uniform in size and trimmed out in neat, tight rows. A thin curtain of water slid down over the lines of shells to gather in a low berm of seashell mortar that ran the length of the curved walls.

"Zeus escaped, and aided a few of his brothers and sisters to do the same. But when Rhea gave birth to Poseidon, she hid him among a flock of lambs and told Cronus that she had given birth to a colt and the titan seized the colt and devoured it instead."

The children gasped again, this time taken aback as much by the devouring of a young horse as they had an infant.

"Why?" one of the younger children asked. "Why did he want to devour all his children?"

"Because," one of the older girls answered, "Cronus was foretold that one day he would be overthrown by one of his own children, so he ate them all when they were born!"

The Atlantean children gasped again and held a collective

breath before turning their attention back to Marea who sat at the top of the dais. Her silver braid was draped over one shoulder and fell all the way to the waist of her blue toga.

"Now," she said, continuing her story, "Poseidon fathered many children, but his first was Triton. He lived in a golden palace and was the royal messenger, often called the Hermes of the Sea."

"Hermes was the messenger of the Gods," an older boy told the younger children, his blue eyes lighting up with excitement. "He was also the god of sports, athletes, travelers and thieves! He was so fast that even his sandals had wings!"

The children *ooohed* and Marea smiled at his enthusiasm, waiting patiently until he was finished. "Indeed, Hermes was fast - as was Triton, who had the legs of a man or the tail of a fish, whichever afforded him swiftest voyage." The children all nodded for this was well known, even to them. "One day, Triton was feasting with Thor in the Halls of..."

"Who is Thor?" one child asked.

"He is a God of the Norsemen," an older girl with long brown curls and large dark eyes whispered, a dreamy look on her face.

"Indeed," Marea agreed, "and both Gods became quite drunk and began to make boasts about whose men had the best horses. Each God upped their claims on which beast was the strongest, the fastest, and so on until the boasts became a wager. Triton gambled a chest of gold and pearls while Thor wagered his mighty Warhammer." Marea leaned forward and lowered her voice, "But the real stake, as always when boasts are made by God or man, was pride."

The older children nodded sagely while the younger ones waited, mouths half-open.

"'Name the time and place!'" Thor thundered as he held high a great tankard of ale (and, to the delight of the children, Marea did the best she could to mimic the God of Thunder).

"'My steeds will grind your trifling horses into ponies!'" Marea continued:

"Atlantis on the morrow!" Triton roared back, holding high a tankard of salted mead. "A chariot race on the island of my son, Atlas! The race shall begin on the beach, and end at a chest of pearls so rare and gold so fine that your men will rename their steeds after oysters and ore!"

The mighty Thor had boomed laughter as they clanked their steins together and quaffed their godly ale.

On the same-said morrow, the God of Thunder arrived on the shores of Atlantis as the golden sun rose over the waters of blue. His horses surrounded him, gigantic beasts that were as dark as a stormy sea, tipped with a foamy white on their noses and fetlocks. One, a monster among the giants, pulled the God in a chariot of hammered gold with wheels of tungsten and rimmed with shining steel.

With his cloak of crimson billowing in the morning breeze, Thor's dark blue eyes searched the throngs of people gathered on the sand for long moments before he spotted Triton. The Herald of the Sea motioned for the other god to join him in the surf where he waited in the shell of a giant conch, tethered to a single mammoth seahorse.

"There!" Triton shouted with a grin, pointing out to sea when Thor's chariot pulled near. "The chest is a mere league away! You have the honor to start the race, but take care that your beast does not crush the coral as he founders!"

The throngs of people on the beach bellowed laughter as Thor glowered at Triton, realizing that he had been fooled. He tugged at the reins on his monstrous equestrian, knowing that the beast, already wallowing in the deep sand, could not swim under the water.

"Very well," the handsome god acquiesced as a grin of his own surfaced, "you win." He then pulled his mighty Warhammer from where it was strapped to his back, held it out, and let it go. It dropped with a mighty crash and the sound it made was like a tidal wave of stars hitting a planet of rock. The Norse God laughed and his horses leaped into the air, making like the wind in sound and speed for the nearest bank of storm clouds and whisking him away.

Meanwhile, the sand around Thor's mighty hammer trembled and shook. The entire island shuddered, squealing like a reef-struck galley. The quaking grew and spread until the whole island began to list, and sink. Triton moved quickly, turning the people into merfolk and fishes as the kingdom of Atlantis was quickly claimed by the sea – sunk by the Hammer of Thor.

Marea sat back as the children oohed and aaahed and talked excitedly about the tale.

Tristan Greenwater, passing by the Solar of the Scallops, caught part of the legend and found himself smiling. It had been one of his own favorites, and he had heard the tale many times. He could have told the youth that was obviously taken with Hermes that the messenger god had also been known as a trickster. In that, as well, he and Triton were alike. Triton had tricked the Norse god Thor, but had paid the price. Centuries later, Triton had played a similar trick, and paid thrice the price.

Having deceived the god Apollo, Triton fled to the edge of the Solar System and hid from his wrath. He hid behind his father's planet, Neptune, but (ever the trickster) took up residence with his people not on Triton – the moon named for him – but the dwarf planet of Eris. He named the new kingdom Atlantea, in honor of the original Atlantis that had been sunk so long ago. Yet Atlantea, it seemed, had no better future.

Apollo found Triton and in his fury pulled the sun so far from the miniature planet that the watery domain froze within a day, trapping the Herald of Poseidon and all his people within.

In that ice they remained, even as men from Earth (Thor's men if truth be told and god be poked) and elves from Andromeda came to take up residence upon the ice where it had begun to slowly (oh, so slowly) melt. Triton and his people, however, remained frozen in the hopes of forgiveness or some unforeseen cataclysmic event.

In the worlds of gods, a cataclysm was always expected yet seldom welcomed - certainly not as welcomed as the one that hit the world of Eris, especially since forgiveness was much less likely.

The cataclysm melted so much of the ice in such a short time that most of the world was awash with floods, and Triton and his people freed. The kingdom of Atlantea was restored to much of her former glory, though half of it remained within the waters of the Sabado Sea.

Tristan now walked steadily downwards, his long strides taking him through soaring halls made of marble blocks and seashell mortar as he made his way from the land to the sea through his father's castle. The halls were supported by great fluted columns crested with molds of orange seahorses and the walls were hung with heavy tapestries that depicted sea life in grandeur. One side showed a number of scenes done in brilliant blues, woven illustrations of dolphins jumping the waves and plumbing their depths. The opposite side of the hall displayed tapestries depicting a sea-turtle migration in countless hues of green and gold.

Water, of course, was everywhere. Fountains adorned the walls and everywhere in between. Both salt and fresh water bubbled in pools or simply streamed down the walls as it did in the Solar of Scallops. To Tristan, the sound was always a comfort – murmurs and giggles and whispers of safety. He supposed it was because it was the sound of his home, from his nursery as a babe to his bedchambers as an adult. He never guessed that it was because, as a son of Triton, it was in his blood.

The prince strode down steps taking him below the tide. Here, the blocks of white marble that made the castle walls were tightly mortared with both seashells and magic to keep the sea at bay, literally. Still, the water seeped in, trickled and murmured. The murmur became louder with voices as he approached the great hall, then washed over him like the tide as he entered.

The room was oval-shaped, ringed with white marble benches where toga-clad humans lounged and chatted. The center was reserved for entertainment that ranged from wrestling matches to acting performances. Currently, it was occupied by a trio of naiads playing harps.

Those close by rose to their feet and many greeted him with a great cheer, their voices rolling around the length of the great hall to where his father reclined on a giant throne of copper medallions that had long since gone a crusted patina of green. The arms of the throne were adorned with golden sand dollars pecked out with diamonds and crystalline sea stars stippled with rubies.

The Sea King himself wore a short toga over his barrel chest and sandals that laced over his thick calves. His wrists were covered with wide bands of gold. He had flowing white hair and beard, with an easy smile on his lips for the maiden that was speaking to him. Hearing the small commotion over the music of the harps, his ocean-blue eyes rose up and spotted his son. Triton's face was timeless and handsome, but it lit up with joy at the approach of the prince.

"Tristan!" he boomed in greeting, rising to his feet and descending from his throne.

"Father," Tristan greeted politely. He began to bow but found himself encircled by the king's bulging arms in a powerful embrace.

The king released him and held him at arm's length. "It is good to see you down here! You so rarely come below the waters!" Triton knew that his son loved the water, but spent much of his time roaming the lands, especially the forests.

"Likewise," Tristan said. "I was hoping to speak with you."

"Certainly!" the Sea King exclaimed. "Sit down," he invited, shooing the maid to the side with a wave of his hand.

"Thank you, but I would rather stand."

Triton, who was seating himself back upon his throne, lost his easy smile. "I am not going to like this," he said. "Am I?"

"The beasts from the north," Tristan said, "are moving south to make war with the elves."

Triton waved a dismissive hand. "I have already been informed, thank you. But it has nothing to do with us."

"I have reason to believe the Roshan Simorgh might fight with them."

"The mercenary hermit from the west?" the Sea King asked making a face. "I still do not see how that involves us."

"If she does, I plan to fight with her. My men as well."

The ocean-blue eyes of the Sea King filled with furious indignation. "Absolutely not!" he declared. "I forbid it!"

Tristan's own eyes widened. His father was protective of him and he expected some resistance, but not so much as this. "She saved my life, and the lives of my men. I owe her a debt of honor. I owe her my life."

Triton frowned deeply. He had many children, but only three sons. If the prophecy was true, as they most often were, Tristan would be his last. Plus, his mother had been special, and held a special place in the king's heart. Tristan was precious to him beyond measure. He could not let him risk his life. Yet if this mercenary had saved his life, and the lives of his men...

"Your men may fight," he conceded. "You may not."

The Prince of Tides bristled. "I swore to her an oath. You would make me go back on my word?"

The Sea King hooked a finger over his white mustache as he pursed his lips and thought, his white brows drawn together. The entire room had gone quiet, the only sound being the gentle babble of the streams and fountains, interposed with the distant roll of waves from above.

"You may aid her, and the elves," Triton finally announced, making the prince beam. "But!" he added, pointing a finger at his youngest son, "you must do so from the water, where you will be safe!"

Tristan's lips pressed together, displeased at the condition, but he bowed respectfully. "Thank you, father," he said.

The king was known for his wily nature and, though he might obey the terms of an oath, he knew how to write his own terms as well. In this case, the shell did not wash far from the ocean.

"I heard that Mikos and Mallack are going to arm wrestle today," the Prince of Tides said.

Triton grinned and brought his large hands together in a mighty clap. "Now you are talking!" he boomed. "Send for them now!"

A cheer went up as the tension was broken and replaced with an air of celebration.

Tristan smiled and kept his plans to himself.

4. FLYING HOME

The girl, who was no longer really a girl, awoke to find her master sitting on a hill near their campsite, watching the sunrise. He wore a belted tunic and breeches, both the color of golden saffron, and so loose that they could easily be mistaken for robes. A gnarled, leafless tree stood guard over his slight form. Her clothes were those of any country traveler – a dusty brown blouse and pants that were tucked into high leather boots.

She knelt on the cloak that served as her bedroll and ran her nails all over her head, shaking out hair that rivaled the color of the rising sun. The master knew she was awake but kept his gaze upon the landscape as it illuminated the countryside in shifting rays of blood and gold. They had left their home a fortnight past and were now almost to the coast. Almost to his destination.

The girl rolled up their beds and tied them tight to her pack before walking up the hill to the master. She edged around toward his front, looking intently at his face. He had been acting so odd these last few days. What she saw made her take a step back. Tears rolled down his cheeks and his countenance was brimming with both anguish and joy. She had never seen such a look in all her life, and never expected to see the like of it on him. He turned his eyes to the girl.

"We must hurry," he told her.

She bowed quickly, lost for words, her eyes not leaving his. He struggled to get up, using his staff to aid him. The girl stood by, knowing that trying to help would only get her shooed away, possibly with the staff. Once he was up she bolted down the hill and shouldered her pack, scattering the ashes of their fire from the night before.

She looked up the hill as the master hobbled down. *Slow. So slow.*

When he reached her she helped him slip his stick-like arms through the straps of his own pack. Years back she tried to tell him that there was no need for him to carry a pack at all, she was more than able to carry their things when they traveled. What she had really thought was he was becoming too frail to do so, but she dared not say such a thing. He had insisted that he most certainly could and *would* carry his own pack. Since then, the girl simply began putting a little more in her bag each time and less in his. Now it was no more than a sack with straps that held a round of hard bread.

"Come on now," he chastised when it was settled over his narrow shoulders. "We have to hurry."

She fell in step beside him as they crested a rise and took the road they had been following the day before.

"Why?" the girl demanded.

"I fear I have less time than I thought."

"Time for what?"

"We must reach the village before tomorrow," he told her without answering her question. "Maybe before moonset tonight."

"Why?" she demanded again. This time he did not answer at all. He just smiled, his eyes fixed on a road that was barely more than a rutted trail. The girl clenched her fists in frustration. He could be stubborn beyond compare.

They were descending a gentle decline into a long valley and the blushing light of dawn painted the landscape pink and gold. Acres of flax turned the valley into a rosy sea, the young stalks undulating gently. It looked to the girl like they were waving at her. Here and there, small trees stretched their leafy branches as if awakening from slumber.

The girl watched the old man silently as they plodded along. He would plant his stick and then shuffle along. Plant and shuffle. Plant and shuffle. It was as if he was trying to ferry across a sea with nothing but a pole. The air was full of morning birdsong as the sun rose, warming his bald head. He smiled as he shuffled.

"Why don't we have horses!?" she demanded. The old man laughed, a dry rattle in a hollow chest.

"You haven't asked me that for a long time." His face was dry but his eyes still held tears and that look of pained happiness. The girl, normally as cool as a midnight breeze, was unnerved. Still, she tried to remain patient and calm. And quiet. For an hour she succeeded.

"What is this woman for?" she finally asked. "Why are we going so far to find her?" The old man smiled without looking at her. The girl knew this meant he would not answer. Normally she would be angry, but for once she was too worried.

The trail divided and they took the right fork, angling east. Before long, they could hear the cry of gulls and smell the sea. Within a few minutes the beaten path gradually curved due north once again, taking them along the cliffs that bordered the Sabado Sea even as it progressively yet gently slanted down towards a delta.

The girl could make out the humped shape of a long line of villages at the bottom of the valley, but they were far.

Plant and shuffle. Plant and shuffle. The sun rose higher and beads of sweat formed on the man's bald pate before forming rivulets that gathered and ran down the sides of his face. Plant and shuffle became plant and hobble as the master pushed on, leaning more heavily upon his staff.

They nibbled on bits of food at midday as they walked. The old man did not want to stop, though the girl urged him to rest. As the sun began its descent his look was that of bleak resolve, yet he pressed onward. Just before dusk it was one of saddened disbelief and as sunset settled over the horizon it was near desperation. They would not make the village by moonrise. *He* would not make the village by moonrise. The old man sighed and nodded towards a copse of trees just off the beaten track.

"There," he said. "I will rest there." He stumbled coming off the path and the girl who was no longer a girl reached out instinctively, unable to help herself. He did not chastise her or push her away, but gratefully leaned on her for support. It was the first time he had ever done so and, also for the first time, she began to be afraid.

She helped him lean his back against a solitary tree at the edge of a small grove and pulled his cloak from her pack and wrapped it around him, though the air was not cold. He took a deep breath to steady himself and then took her hand in his own. His grip was like iron.

"Go to the village," he told her. "Find the Shama. Bring her to me. Quickly." When she hesitated he waved her away. "I will be fine. These are peaceful lands, and I am not as feeble as I look. Now go!"

The girl turned and was gone. Even after walking all day, she ran like a deer – light and fleeting in the twilight as it gathered in a blanket over the land – a shadow among shadows. As the land dropped down, the cliffs she ran along began to diminish gradually until she ran along a rocky shore.

Finally, she reached the most south-easterly village of Trigo. Ramshackle buildings of weathered wood dotted the south side of the delta as well as out over the rocks on piers that reeked of tar and fish. It was now full dark and stars were winking high above.

She slowed as her boots traded land for planks and she swayed slightly, feeling as if she had stepped onto a boat, before she pressed on in a hurry once again. The first person she questioned in the village showed her where to find the Shama and the girl breathed a quick sigh of relief. Her master had said that there might not be a black elf in the village at all and they would have to take a boat to The Dabs, a blight of rocky islands off the coast. The girl knew that there was no way he could make even a short voyage on the sea, not in his current condition.

The girl pounded on the door of the woman's home, not knowing what to say and hoping she would not have to force her to come. Not knowing what or whom to expect, the girl stared curiously as the door swung open.

The Shama was an elfin woman with pointed ears and skin as dark as a moonless night. Her dress was the bright blue of a sea in sunshine and her black hair was twisted into a hundred coils that fell down her back, adorned with small shells. She was obviously just sitting down to her meal but saw the desperation in the girl's eyes and grabbed a light cloak without a word.

They left the village on foot and headed south up the hill under a blanket of stars, the shells in the Shama's hair clicking together with every hurried step. The girl pressed the woman as much as she dared – silently cursing the world for the seeming lack of horses, cursing herself for leaving the old man alone. The moon began to peek out, slowly swelling as it rose, casting its reflection on the water below. The girl began to think of wolves and cursed herself again.

When they reached the copse of trees the old man was nowhere to be seen. The girl felt panic rise like hot bile in her throat and forced it down. The emotion was raw and unfamiliar which only increased her distress. Her master had trained her well, but not for this. She looked right and left and was ready to bolt toward the trees when the Shama wrapped a hand around her arm.

The girl jumped at the sudden touch but followed the woman's gaze. The Shama pointed to a small form lying in a huddle on the ground under the trees, obscured by starlight and shadows. The girl rushed to the man, exhaling in relief as he opened his eyes, turning his face towards her.

"I needed a little rest," he said, almost apologetically, as he read her expression of exasperation. He moved to rise but struggled to do so. The girl helped him into more of a sitting position, leaning his weight back against the trunk of the short and gnarled pine.

"What is happening?" the girl demanded. "Are you sick? Will this woman heal you?" The old man smiled.

"My spirit is preparing for a journey," he told her. "And my body is acquiescing."

"You are in no shape for a journey," the girl that was no longer a girl scolded. "You have gone far enough."

The old man let out a soft chuckle that shook his slight frame. "You are more right than you know." He smiled at her frown. "I am going to see your mother," he told her. "I have missed her so much, these many years. I have longed to see her, have yearned for her with so much pain, but now that I am to be with her again I feel a longing and a sadness for leaving you, my dear."

"Hush," the girl admonished. "It is wrong to cling to such musings."

He laughed his hollow laugh. "I have taught you well. *Too well,* I am afraid." He laughed again. "It was foretold on a day long ago but it is one I can remember with perfect clarity... the sounds of hawkers and the smells of sawdust and sugar and roasting meats. The quality of the light..." The master's voice faded as he brought forth the memory but the girl, as impatient as ever, even at such a time, cleared her throat in a loud and obvious manner. Brought back to the present, the old man continued. "A teller assured me that I would be torn between two women. I thought it was nonsense. I was dedicated to my craft and could not picture myself overcome by one woman, much less two."

The girl that was no longer a girl frowned, not understanding. She had never seen her master have even a passing interest in any woman or, like he had said, much less two. She feared he might be sick with fever. If so, she hoped the Shama was there to help.

The old man smiled at her confusion. "I miss Hope the way I would miss my heart if it had been carved from my chest. Yet, I know I made the right choice. Maybe because it was her choice."

The girl, so quick of both hand and wit, stared at the old man as she tried to puzzle out his meaning. It took her long moments to realize that her mother was one of the women of which he spoke. She herself was the other.

"Yes," the master told her, seeing her confusion. "You are a woman now."

"I don't feel like one," she confessed. This time his laugh was no more than a rattle of breath. The Shama moved around, clearing the brush away from them, humming and lighting some sort of twig.

She obviously knows more about what is going on than I do, the girl thought. *Maybe the smoke will stop that rattle in his lungs.*

"But you are a woman," the master affirmed. "And a warrior trained, with a warrior's responsibility. You must pass on what you know, and find your destiny in this world."

The girl scowled, a line between the brows on her young face. "What is my destiny?" she asked.

"You must find that out for yourself."

The Shama moved around them, chanting. The girl could smell incense, strong and sweet.

"What is going on?" the girl persisted. The old man smiled and stroked her straight red hair.

"I am going to see your mother," he said softly.

The girl looked at him, her heart skipping a beat within her chest. "My mother? Where is she?"

Again the rattling breath of a laugh. "I wish I knew."

This time his words sank in. She knew he was going on no journey afoot.

"You are dying?" the girl asked, incredulous. The master smiled.

"I am moving on."

"Is my mother dead?" the girl whispered.

"That I do not know," he said, wistful. "I hope not. I like to believe that she is somewhere, cursing at someone in the same way you do." Again came the faint shake of laughter, now barely more than a tremor. His almond-shaped eyes shifted away and the girl followed his gaze to the Shama.

The black elf laid a slim-fingered hand upon his arm.

"Where is it that you want to go?" she asked. It was the first time the girl had heard her speak and was taken aback by her voice. It was deep and mellifluous, like a musical instrument.

The old man looked at the Shama. "Send me to the dragon," he told her. "From there I can find her, or she will find me." The Shama nodded. He looked back at the girl that was now a woman and found her hand. *I love you so much.*

The girl held on tight, so tight, and his body clenched as it was wracked with indecision once again.

Tears leaked from his eyes as he thought of Hope, of how much he had missed her. Her eyes, her touch, her laugh. The lessons she would teach him though he was so many years her elder. The way she would make *him* laugh until he thought his sides would rupture. The feel of her smooth skin under his hardened fingers. The joy she had taught him. The child they had made together.

He looked at the young woman now, deliberating if she was really ready to be on her own.

Has she learned enough? he agonized. *Will she be happy? Will she be safe?*

He realized that the black elf who had foretold his future at a galaxy fair long ago had been right more than once as the formerly Zenarchist monk was torn again between the same two women.

Hope! he cried out silently in anguish as he stared into the gem-like eyes of the now-grown child. *What would you have me do?*

The Shama held the stick of incense close to his mouth as he drew his last breath.

"The dragon?" she queried, noting his keen stare upon the young woman with hair the color of dying flame.

Hahn nodded as a fresh pair of tears trickled from his dark almond-shaped eyes.

The Shama leaned close as his last breath came out, drawing his spirit into herself. She seemed to hold it forever, placing her jeweled hand upon his thin chest, searching out his heart and his desires, before releasing it into the warm summer sky.

A deep silence settled over the already quiet land as the stars above flickered, as if blinking out tears.

The girl that was now a woman kissed the hand that was in her own, closed her master's eyes, and then wiped the damp from his face before kissing one cheek and then the other.

"I love you, too, Father," she whispered. Then she buried her face on his chest and wept. The Shama touched the young woman's hair in sympathy and farewell and left her to her grief.

From a branch on the gnarled tree, a nightingale sang.

◌◈◌

Leagues to the south and many decades later, in a sumptuous room in the long gallery of the castle of the Crimson King, Ember L'chiross jerked awake. She was covered with a glimmer of perspiration but that was not unusual, the short and barely cool winter had come and gone like a promise on the wind. One month till spring and already the air was warm enough to keep the temperatures elevated in the dark hours as well as the light.

"Roshan?" a voice asked a second before a gas lamp was turned on, revealing eyes that were dark and seductive. "Are you alright?"

"Yes," Ember replied, giving the young man that hovered by her shoulder a disarming smile. "I am fine."

He turned up the gas on the lamp, driving the shadows closer to the walls of ochre stone. Her face was framed by her hair, red as blood. A few strands clung to her forehead and neck. His dark brows drew together in concern over eyes that were black as ink. "Bad dream?" he asked.

The Roshan's smile turned into a smirk as she pushed herself up slightly to recline on her pillows and gave her head a small shake. "No, just a dream. Go back to sleep."

His dark eyes, full of apprehension, regarded her for a moment longer before he extinguished the light. Ember sighed and rolled onto her side, a slight frown marring her darkened face.

She had not had that dream in a long time.

Why now? she wondered, though the answer was before her straightaway.

Because I was full of questions, and touched by fear. She thought of Traejanale Royce, the elfin prince she had schooled in combat less than a year past, and knew that she would be seeing him again. Soon. *And again I am full of questions, and touched by fear. That is why the dream came.*

The Roshan closed her eyes of green and amber and gold,

pushing the fear from her heart and the questions from her mind. She had gotten through her grief once before, she could do it again.

The cycle of loss ebbed and flowed for the elfin prince for a hundred days and a hundred days more. The Roshan was well-schooled in loss and could have told him well about the stages of grief. It had ruled her own person for almost a hundred years.

# 5. STRANGE ACQUAINTANCES

Gerta lay on her side on her bedmat, her arms clutching her body as she tucked her chin to her chest and coughed. She did not know if she was truly ill, or if her misery was manifesting itself in her body, making her physically sick. A knotty hand reached out and caressed her coarse blonde curls.

"Gerta?" Gunta asked. "Are you alright?"

No, Gerta thought, despondent. *We should have been married by now. Celebrating like none had since reaching the New World. We should be safe within the Coil, warmed by fire and drunk on ale, making a baby. Instead we are here, prisoners of beasts in the dead of winter, tortured and starving and afraid! Most of all afraid!*

"I am fine," Gerta whispered as she continued to stare straight in front of her, her blue eyes not moving to meet his.

The hand jerked back, as did Gunta's body. The strange and sudden action was enough to make Gerta turn and look up, startled. Gunta's face was scrunched in anger and he turned it towards her, his own blue eyes wet and glistening.

"No!" he whispered hoarsely. "You are not! None of us are!"

His eyes rose up to scan the threadbare tents and the desolation within. The other Gnomin, normally stout and robust, were now small and thin as they wasted away. It was a good thing that they all wore suspended trousers, or else they would have been without pants. A few of those that had been captured by the Crommags had died. More had been dying lately, but Gunta was sure that it had from been from despair.

Gnomin, as a rule, were astoundingly tough.

Gerta watched as the man she still considered her fiancé, gaunt as the rest of them, breathed deep. Under his suspenders his checkered shirt was torn and dirty and did not fit well on his shrunken frame, but it billowed gallantly as he puffed out his chest in steadfast resolve.

"Enough!" he growled. He took two more of those great breaths of air before turning quickly back to Gerta, taking up her hand in his own. "I have a plan!" he exclaimed in the same hoarse whisper.

Gerta, who still had the egg of engagement he had offered her months ago hidden in her bedmat, smiled. It was the first time she had smiled since they had been taken by the Crommags.

"I have never known a plan of yours to fail," she said.

Gunta's hard expression softened and he ducked down to kiss her cheek. "I'll be back," he assured her, then rose and left just as quick. The eyes of the other Gnomin followed him as he walked resolutely through the tent, pushed aside the flap, and stormed out. Gunta looked around and spied a Crommag, sitting on a rock while eating a haunch of meat. There used to be two sentries, armed and alert, but the months had shown that the Gnomin needed very little guarding.

The Crommag looked up and frowned as Gunta stalked over to him and stood near his hulking form. His people called the Gnomin, women included, "metal-men." A band of Crommags had rounded them up and taken them from their homeland last fall to work the metals they had scrounged from the Northlon into weapons. They found the Gnomin to be less threatening than sheep, but were still concerned they might make a break for it – hence the sentry. Even that concern diminished as the weeks passed.

"I want to speak to someone in charge!" Gunta demanded.

The Crommag did not understand, nor did he care. He

grunted and pointed back to the tent.

"I want to speak to someone in charge!" Gunta repeated.

"Little metal-man!" growled the Crommag. "Go!" he commanded, pointing to the threadbare tent. Gunta did not speak Crommag but he got his meaning well enough. Still, he did not budge.

"I want to speak to someone in charge!" he repeated.

The Crommag repeated his own response but when the little man did not go he reached out a massive hand towards the thing's small face.

Gunta found his head engulfed by enormous fingers and for a terrifying second he thought the giant meant to crush his skull. Then he found himself rolling like a hedgehog towards the tent. When his body came to a stop, he stood up and dusted off his shirt and trousers – more from habit than anything else. He had been thrown by explosions plenty of times before. He marched back up to the Crommag.

"I want to speak to someone in charge!" Gunta insisted, stomping his foot. "My people are getting sick!" A second later he was rolling again towards the tent. The scene repeated itself until the Gnomin was stumbling and dizzy. Still, he persisted.

The Crommag, losing what little patience he had, finally stood. He knew he was not supposed to hurt the little creatures but he wanted to finish eating and go back to the fires for more meat before it was gone. Grunting, he reached out and picked the Gnomin up and tucked it under an arm before he lumbered away.

Gunta, terrified, held very still as he was toted through the campsite. Not much later, his captor stopped in front of another tent and began grunting and jabbering in such a way that could only mean he was arguing with another Crommag. After a few more words, the tent flap was pushed aside and the Crommag took Gunta inside and deposited the Gnomin on its feet, grunting and gesturing at him.

Gunta looked up, his blue eyes taking in the strange scene. A man sat at a table with another man that was much, much larger. With them sat a small and most peculiar-looking Crommag. The tent was now silent and all eyes were on him and Gunta realized they were waiting for him to say or do something.

"My people are getting sick," he said with all the force he could muster. The Crommag and the giant human looked at the man and Gunta recognized him as the one who was there on the day his people were captured. He had spoken Gnomin to them then, and again as they were put into the camp, giving them instructions on what they were expected to do. Gunta remembered seeing him around for a few days as their work area was set up, but not since. The man had looked gaunt and haggard back then but now looked strong and healthy. He was obviously being treated better.

The man's face turned to the small Crommag and spoke a few words in the human tongue and, to Gunta's amazement, the Crommag replied in the same language. The man's face turned back to Gunta. "How many?" he asked in Gnomin.

The displaced miner was almost too astounded to speak. Here was a Crommag that spoke in the tongues of man and a man that spoke Gnomin. How did that come to be? And why? And what were they doing in this tent? Gunta shook his head, trying to clear it and make sense, but all that came to him was the image of Gerta curled up in misery on her bedmat. His blue eyes sought out the eyes of the man.

"Uh...ah...all of them," he told him.

The man translated and the Crommag looked sharply at Gunta, making him tremble. It was his plan to ask for better treatment in the hopes that the Crommags would be afraid of losing all their Gnomin. They wanted weapons and the supply of metal was still plentiful. The abducted miners and metal workers had been careful to work diligently but not quickly. They knew what fate awaited them once they were of no use.

"We need better food," Gunta said, pressing on, "and clean water. We need blankets and fire."

The man translated and the Crommag looked hard at the little prisoner through narrowed eyes.

"If we don't," Gunta continued, "we will all be dead in a month." He doubted this was true, but he knew that this could be his only opportunity to try and prayed it was worth the gamble.

The man translated again and this time there was a flicker of concern in the Crommag's strange, mossy eyes. Not for the Gnomin, to be sure, but for his own plans. He spoke to the man who looked back at Gunta with a smile.

"I will come find you in the morning," he told him, "and see what I can find for you."

The little metal-man gave the strange trio a low bow and then exited the flap, making his way back to the Gnomin tent, on his own legs this time. The sentry that had brought him watched him go, but did not follow. Another sentry would be along soon enough to guard the metal-men.

Gunta went quickly, keeping his face pointed straight ahead, but his eyes were everywhere. The Crommags obviously did not see them as a danger and, in their current condition, they were anything but. He would see to it that their condition would change. And then, their circumstances. The miner, forming a plan, kept the smile from creeping onto his face until he was safe inside. He supposed he should be grateful for the drafty tent. Before the snows came, the Gnomin had been kept in pens like animals.

Back in the Crommag tent, sturdy with animal hides to keep out the elements and fires in braziers to banish the cold, Noga sat with what the other Crommags called his "pets." Noga did not care. Most were cretins. Ayala understood. So did Higa, with whom Noga was beginning to share a mutual respect.

The man's name was Tyler, the Vikeman was Asger. Noga

was fascinated by them.

Noga had taken Tyler from a farm the Crommags had been raiding. He spoke a few words of the human language and needed to learn more. The tricky part was finding one that spoke Gnomin.

Afterwards was just as tricky.

At the raid, Tyler was trapped with three females in a barn on a farm close to the Mountains of Blood. He had been ready to fight to the death with an axe he had snatched from a woodpile, pushing the shrieking and terrified women behind him. Noga had stepped forward and swatted the axe away.

"You come," Noga had stated, pointing at Tyler, "women live." He then pointed at the females, crouching down behind their brother, sobbing.

Tyler had dropped the paltry weapon and surrendered immediately, eager to come with the Crommags when he was offered the chance to save his sisters, but had fallen into a funk shortly after and was not eager to communicate. Noga had gnashed his teeth in frustration but kept at it, trying to learn more of men and the world they ruled. Tyler had helped in the capture of the Gnomin and gave a listless attempt at helping Noga learn the man language. Worse, he was despondent and continued to lose weight and the Crommag feared he might get sick and die. To his eyes, the man looked horribly frail to begin with and was getting thinner by the day.

But when Noga had brought back the Vikeman, he got better. Much better.

The man seemed not only pleased to have someone that could speak in his strange native tongue but someone that he could *care for.* Noga had been enthralled at his behavior and watched closely as the man had become engaged once again. The Vikeman was now the one afraid, trying horribly not to show it, while the man brought him food and assurances of well-being that Noga found amusing.

To demonstrate it was safe, Tyler started by stuffing food into his own mouth and encouraging the Vikeman to do the same. The Vikeman was unwilling at first, but had not eaten in almost twenty-four hours. Hesitantly, he took one bite and then another. Soon, he was wolfing down the plate of hard bread and boiled potatoes. Tyler had then beckoned to Noga and the small Crommag had joined them, smiling broadly.

He sat with the two men and tapped his chest.

"Noga," he said.

The Vikeman had recoiled, staring at the strange creature, finally tearing his gaze away to stare at Tyler. The man kept his own gaze on Noga but spoke to the Vikeman.

"I know," he said, "at first I didn't think it was a Crommag."

"It's not," Asger said, swallowing hard and looking back at the strange creature.

"What do you think it is?" Tyler asked, giving Noga a disarming smile.

"I don't know," said the Vikeman, "but it's not a Crommag."

"Crommag," Noga had said, tapping his chest again. "Man," he said, pointing to Tyler. "Vikeman," he said, nodding his large head towards Asger.

"That's right," Tyler agreed amiably.

Noga was pleased to see his man-pet behaving in a completely different manner. "Eat," he instructed the two, pointing to the food. Asger started eating again, not taking his eyes off of the thing in front of him.

"What do they want with us?" he asked between bites. "Why haven't they killed us?"

"I'm not sure," Tyler admitted, "but he has been trying continuously to talk with me. I think he wants to learn to speak Anglicus."

"Why?" Asger asked, incredulous.

Tyler shrugged and took another bite of food. "I don't

know, but I guess it wouldn't hurt to try. They haven't killed us yet and have treated me fairly well. If we can learn to communicate better, maybe we could ask."

Asger was skeptical but Tyler proved to be right. As the weeks passed, Noga proved to be an eager and apt pupil. As his skills increased, he told the other two that many Crommags were migrating to better lands where they would farm. It made perfect sense since the Bitterlands were such a harsh climate and Noga's camp was a reasonable size. Of course he needed to learn how to speak if he was to communicate with the people to the south and acquire suitable farming lands. Neither man nor Vikeman asked how he planned on acquiring those lands. Noga told them he would set them free in the spring, when the snows in the passes melted and the Crommags began their journey.

Tyler was uplifted, thinking that he would see his family again. Asger as well, knowing that he would have a tale that might be sung in songs and someday become legend. They stayed mostly within or quite close to the large tent that Noga had made very comfortable for them. The air outside was frigid and the other Crommags were still terrifying. But not Noga, who spent so much time with the two that he became as normal to them as if he were one of them – especially as his Anglicus improved. By mid-winter he was speaking so well that he began to mimic Asger's strange accent, making the other two howl with hilarity and he joined in their laughter. Sometimes he would sneak in some grog and they would all three get drunk together.

It was not lost on Noga that these two strangers had accepted and befriended him in such a very short time and in a way that his own people never had. Except for his brother, whom he missed sorely and thought of often.

Ayala had spent the winter crossing the Floe and moving their people as far south as they could. Now they were gathered under the Siber Massif, weathering the brutal winter until the spring thaw. Most of those in Noga's camp would join the others then, but Noga and his pets had another route to take.

As the winter wore on, the runty Crommag began to look at the men and hope that he would not have to kill them. He would, of course, if it was necessary, and without a second thought. He could not and would not change who he was. He was a Crommag on the inside, despite how he looked on the outside.

6. SMALL REINFORCEMENTS

Dawn bloomed over Tuar Ceath, the kingdom of rainbows. The stones of the city, from bridges to castles, were mostly white quartz, flecked with sparkles of color. Others were marble veined with gold, or shimmered silver, or any single color or all of them together.

Tall poplars with golden leaves mingled with elfin maple, their spreading branches covered with pink and purple foliage. Weeping willows grew against the banks of streams, their green leaves dipping into the gentle current of blue water where white swans swam in graceful patterns. Pastel-colored shrubs were clustered near flowerbeds bursting with lilacs and bluebells.

The backdrop to the kingdom, anchored against the mountains, were the royal castles. The rising sun threw golden beams onto their façades and towers, making them sparkle. Around them, lesser buildings flickered with a myriad of iridescent hues. Behind them, waterfalls poured from varying heights and the sunlight sent prisms of color dancing from their swirling mists in all directions.

One hundred more days passed for Traejanale Royce and brought to the elves the Spring Equinox. It was traditionally even more celebrated than the Winter Solstice, but this year a pall hung over the entire elfin population. Festivities were planned and feasts were abundant, but smiles were forced upon faces that were drawn and tense.

In a land that had only known peace, where the elves had

taken refuge to escape the conflicts of races that included their own, war was imminent. People that had once been forbidden to make weapons (much less carry them) wore bows and blades and guarded expressions. Even at the Spring-Day Dance and with the enemy still far from their lands, almond-shaped eyes darted restlessly during conversations that were clipped and hands were curved around the hilts of swords.

The only ones unaffected were the children. They laughed and shrieked as they ran across the verdant grass in the normal manner for children at a festival. They were the only bright light at the celebration and brought an occasional smile to the adults. After the morning bruncheon, a pair of girls - chasing a pair of boys with a garland of pink flowers - ran by the only two adults that seemed as unaffected as the children.

One was Acqtraejale Royce, once ruler of the elves and named the Battle King for the hundred wars he had fought in the old lands. Though still handsome for an elderly elf whose white robes matched his white hair, those wars of long ago were still plain upon his face. The lobe of one pointed ear was missing, a scar cleaved one white eyebrow in two, and the left side of his jaw was blemished by a weapon that did not exist in the New World save for in memory.

Next to the Battle King stood a female elf, tall and stately with ebony skin. Her ears were long and pointed like those of the former king, though she had both earlobes and each sported three gold rings. She wore a dress of bright green silk, striped with turquoise and cloth of gold, in honor of the Equinox. A matching silk headband held back a hundred braids, shining like polished jet. They poured down her back, their tips beaded with rows of silver shells.

The pair smiled at the children as they ran past. They sipped brightly colored nectars from glasses shaped like flowers as they were approached by another pair of elves that were much younger than themselves, but far from children. Traejanale Royce, the Battle King's namesake and second son to

Rowland the Great, smiled and nodded to everyone he passed – an encouragement to the elves to liberate themselves from worry and enjoy the celebration.

The young prince had filled out again and had an air of good health. His thick hair, the color of golden sand, had been freshly cut. He had forgone his usual drab clothing and instead wore a woven linen shirt of robin's egg blue, covered with a long vest of crushed velvet in soft sage, debossed with the leaves of his house. His doe-skin breeches were tucked into a pair of leather boots that had been shined until they glowed like polished wood.

At his elbow was Sir Dellion – Praetorian to Prince Traejan, Captain of the Jägers, and Major of the Elfin Army. As they reached the black elf and her kingly consort, Traejan motioned for his guard to continue on towards a small group of Jägers who were talking softly at the edge of the Great Lawn watching elfin maidens wind streamers of yellow roses. Dell paused before the stately pair.

"Your Majesty," he greeted, bowing deeply. "My Lady," the elf continued, dipping just a little lower.

"Bah!" the Battle King spat, motioning for Dell to be on his way. He had as much hold to formalities as his grandson. Dell smiled broadly as he straightened and turned to make his way towards the Jägers.

Karamine laughed, a sound that tinkled and merged with the musical sound of the shells in her hair as they clinked and chimed. "Did you hear that?" she asked. "He called me a lady!"

Traejan bowed low in Dell's wake. "My Lady, Karamine," he greeted as he swept up her hand and gave it a kiss. He gave her a long look before giving the Battle King a much less formal bow. "Grandfather," he said with a smile as Karamine laughed and tried to swat him with a long-fingered ebony hand.

The elfin prince was quick to touch Karamine in any appropriate manner every time he saw her. As a black elf, she had the gift of foresight and Traejan always hoped she would divulge any images she saw in his future. So far, all he had gotten from her was knowing smiles. It was maddening.

"What kind of mischief are you two up to?" he asked when he saw he would get nothing but another smile.

Karamine laughed again. "He is wise for one so young!" she intoned, leaning towards the former elfin king.

"Gossip," his grandfather confessed, "the worse kind of mischief!"

"Would you care to indulge, Young Prince?" Karamine asked.

Traejan shook his sand-colored waves in the negative, though his smile shone. "Certainly not," he told the pair, "yet I doubt that is the worst sort of mischief."

"Maybe not the worst," Karamine admitted with a wink, "but certainly the most wicked."

"But enough of gossip!" the Battle King declared. "I would have news, and I would have it from you."

Traejan bowed his head respectfully. "Well," he began, "it is the first day of spring…"

"You don't say!" Acqtraejale resounded as another group of children ran by, screaming in delight. He looked at Karamine, his white brows raised high, and she looked around in mock surprise.

"I had no idea!" she exclaimed before taking a sip from her tulip-shaped glass. The elfin prince blew air from his narrow nose in exasperation.

"Are you done?" he asked, his eyes flicking from one to the other. Karamine gave him a broad smile of teeth that were perfectly white and even, despite the fact she was nearly of an age with the Battle King.

"For now," she told the prince.

His eyes went to his grandfather who gave him a nod to continue. He did so, giving the pair a look of good-natured mistrust. "You two well know that it is normally a day of promise for the elves, but today, spring brings a promise of war. Spring is what the Crommags have been waiting for – the snow will melt and let them through the mountain passes of the Siber Massif, allowing them into the Northlon."

Karamine frowned at him over the rim of her glass as she sipped her drink. "But spring has not started that far north," she said, lowering her glass and then using it to motion to an area high up and beyond the prince. "The snows have not yet begun to melt on the Mountain of the Moon, they certainly could not have begun to melt in the passes so close to the Bitterlands."

The prince nodded in agreement. "Probably not for at least another month, and it will take a good month or more after that before they are passable. The Mountain of the Moon, in fact, will serve as a good indicator on what to expect. Like a giant hourglass, as the snow melts more and more, it will number the days we have until the Crommags are on the move. Though that day is months to come, today marks the start of the countdown."

The former king and black elf nodded in understanding as they sipped their nectars and looked up at the mountain range that ringed the northern and western borders of the elfin homeland. To the west rose the largest mountain in the chain, the Mountain of the Sun, green and gold with sugar pines and bigleaf maples, boulders of quartz winking back at the sun like the wings of giant pixies hiding amongst the trees. To the north, connected by a double ridge of peaks of lesser height and grandeur, were a series of alps thick with blue spruce and long firs. Some alps were dotted with snow and ice while others were covered completely. Above them all rose a glistening white spire that was the Mountain of the Moon. Even now, the snows at its base had begun to melt, streams feeding the brooks that would gather and feed the waterfalls of Tuar Ceath.

"This is common knowledge to every elf in the kingdom over age twenty," Acqtraejale remarked, his voice gruff as he turned his almond-shaped eyes back to his grandson. "Tell me of your plans."

"Certainly," Traejan acquiesced as his own eyes narrowed, "but surely Xander and my father have…"

"Bah!" the Battle King cursed. "Like a prize truffle, they keep me in the dark and feed me shit!" Karamine's dark hand came up quickly to cover her mouth, keeping her latest nip of nectar from coming out. "I hear but a bit," Acqtraejale continued, "and that bit is of *their* doings. I want to know what *you* are doing these days."

Traejan dipped his head in understanding and respect. "My father, as I am sure you know or at least would expect, has sent heralds to all peoples, warning of the threat and requesting aid." His grandfather nodded and waved a hand to acknowledge that it was both known and expected. "Xander has, of course, dispatched units of men to guard the passes, both our own and those of the Siber Massif. They will return on our swiftest of mounts to give us as much warning as they can." Acqtraejale grunted and motioned for him to continue. "I dispatched three parties of Jägers to the Northlon," he told him, his eyes darting to Karamine for a second before going back. "They evacuated what farmers were still there to the far west, sending with them all the provisions they could carry and driving their livestock before them. The Jägers in turn brought back what else they could." Traejan drew a deep breath and pressed on. "They burned everything else, food and structures both, under my orders of course."

The young prince straightened, mentally prepared for shock and a reprimand and possibly worse. Burning crops and homes was such a primitive thing to do, such a waste to living things. His grandfather, however, nodded sagely.

"A wise choice," he said.

Karamine reached out, her green silk robes rustling softly,

and grasped Traejan's arm. "But a difficult decision," she sympathized.

Traejan gave them a trace of a smile and nodded his thanks. "The Crommags will get through the mountains only to find the shelter and provisions they had expected are gone. That should slow them even more."

"And of the word that was sent to the other lands?" the Battle King asked. "What response have we had? Can the elves expect help from any quarter?"

Traejan shifted his weight and rested a hand on the hilt of his sword and his dark blonde brows drew together slightly over his soft brown eyes. "As of yet, none. Not that we expected an army to be delivered to our doorstep..."

His grandfather sipped his nectar and looked at a group of musicians that had begun tuning up. "But we should have had riders by now, bearing messages from the other kings as well as the leaders of the larger towns in the Southlon."

Traejan nodded in agreement, his brown eyes moving to the musicians and then to Dell and the small party of Jägers that stood in a line, speaking to one another from the sides of their mouths with loose grips on the handles of the daggers they wore.

"And how does the elfin army stand," Karamine asked, "if it must stand alone?"

Traejan's lips pressed together into a line. "The fact that we have an army at all is the first step but, unfortunately, it is a small one. We are outmatched in size, strength, and numbers. But our riders have come across travelers headed towards Tuar Ceath, mostly from the Midlon, riding singly and in pairs or small groups."

"They know that they too cannot stand alone against an invasion of Crommags," Acqtraejale mused aloud. "But we will need more than piecemeal reinforcements."

Traejan nodded. He had wanted to question those riders.

Had they seen a woman, all in black, riding a monstrous Night Stallion? Traveling alone, or with a Vikeman perhaps?

He was sure that Ember, by now, must have finished the employment she had taken for the Crimson King. He hoped that she would finally be joining him. He felt that she would. If she truly loved him, she must.

Softly, the music started, filling the warming air with sounds of sitars and lap-harps. Later in the day, they would be replaced with drums and fiddles and the dancing would begin. The young prince smiled, thinking about what it would be like to hold Ember and move slowly to music. His brown eyes lifted and focused, brought immediately from his short reverie as he spied a runner coming from the direction of the castles, quickly closing the distance to the Great Lawn and heading for Dell and the clutch of Jägers.

The group turned as one, long before they could have heard the elf, watching guardedly as his swift gait brought him to their Captain.

Dell's eyes darted to the young prince as the runner was delivering his message and Traejan's heart began to beat faster. The Praetorian was about to motion to his charge but the prince was already sketching a bow to his grandfather and Karamine. "If you will excuse me?" he asked, but did not wait for an answer. He strode quickly, his heart in his throat, to where Dell awaited him with the messenger. Traejan recognized the elf as one of Xander's emissaries to the Southlon.

It's her! he thought, trying to stem his excitement and slow his heart. *She has come at last!*

"My Lord Prince," the herald said, bowing deeply. Traejan gave him a nod as he straightened, encouraging him to continue. "Your brother and your father, King Rowland, request your presence at Castle Royce."

"News from the Southlon?" Traejan queried, unable to constrain himself.

The messenger, an elf of Dell's stature but more fair of face and hair, shook a head of heavy blonde curls. "No, my lord, from across the Echo Sea."

"The Echo Sea?" Traejan asked, frowning. "But were you not sent to the south?"

The elf bowed again and rose. "I was, my lord. Shane and I returned just yesterday. It is Vis and Yen that have just ridden in from the Crook. They are with your father and brother, who request your presence as soon as seemly, my lord."

Traejan felt his heart drop back to where it had been, perhaps slightly lower. He dipped his head once again. "Of course," he acquiesced. He should have known that someone who had so soon arrived on horseback from a hundred leagues away would not have been sent to deliver a message on foot. "Please let them know that I will be there forthwith."

The runner bowed again and then turned and ran back in the direction he had come. The prince followed, motioning for Dell to accompany him. His guard fell into step next to him and together they crossed the Great Lawn, drawing looks of concern from many eyes. Traejan nodded and smiled reassuringly to everyone that he could, not speaking to Dell until they had passed through the hedgerow and turned up High Street towards his family's castle.

"The Echo Sea?" he asked as they walked quickly, their boots clicking on the cobbled street. "You said there were no villages there, no farms."

"There isn't," Dell reaffirmed. "Unless there are hermits hiding in caves of sand. Nothing will grow there."

Traejan nodded, trying to tamp down his disappointment. *She will come,* he assured himself. *She must.*

The streets were empty and quiet, mostly everyone having already made their way to the Great Lawn or to private parties. The pair crossed an arched stone bridge over a rushing stream fed by the waterfalls behind the triad of castles, the largest of which now loomed before them. They passed through a curtain wall, made for aesthetics rather than defense, bedecked with climbing yellow roses. Where a fortified castle would have a bailey, there were cutting gardens and manicured hedgerows.

As the prince and his escort entered the castle proper, they found themselves greeted with music and laughter, amongst a party once again. This one was much livelier than the one they had left. They were met with cheers and toasts by each group they passed and politely refused invitations for drinks and dancing as they made their way through the great hall. Dell knew that the upper and royal classes did not worry less about the impending war, they had just been at the mead and nectars a bit longer.

Traejanale and his Praetorian passed through the gallery and finally entered the atheneum - a spacious apartment in the castle which resembled a library more than an office or a reception room, though that was exactly what it was used for by the king. He was already there with his counselors and Xander.

Xander, Crown Prince to the throne, was a stocky elf - serious nearly to a fault yet with the same head of dark curls that crowned his father. He had his own attendants but Traejan was surprised to see Zephyrn, their younger brother, there as well. Zephyrn was the polar opposite of Xander, tall and slim with blue eyes, blonde hair, and a perpetual grin that bespoke mischief.

Their Praetorian Guards stood under one of the high, arched windows in the atheneum talking softly as they kept unremitting watch over their charges. Dell gave them a nod from across the room but stayed close to Traejan. As the Major of the Elfin Army, he was included in all news that pertained to the war unless dismissed by the king or any of the princes.

Traejan bowed quickly to his father and brothers, eager for news. His father acknowledged him with a nod as he finished his conversation with one of his counselors but Xander and Zephyrn paused their conversation to greet their brother.

"What news?" Traejan asked softly, keeping his excitement at bay.

"There are two riders approaching from the west," Xander informed him. "More are following on foot just a day behind, seventy-seven, the Jägers claim."

"Farmers or fighters?" It would be the largest group to come to Tuar Ceath since word went out of the coming invasion.

"Gnomin miners on foot," his older brother answered, his voice flat. "The two riders are on donkeys."

"We may win this war yet!" Zephyrn quipped with mock cheer.

"Gnomin?" Traejan asked. "On donkeys?" Most would have shaken their heads in dismay or consternation but the young prince felt a surge of hope.

"Yes," his father answered, dismissing his counselors with a wave of his hand as he joined his sons. "One might think they seek refuge, which we would not deny, yet we wonder why. They would certainly be safer within their mountain."

"There is only one way to find out," Zephyrn offered with a smile and his father gave him a look that expressed great patience.

"Of course," King Rowland said, "we will send an envoy to meet them. Causis has left to find someone that speaks Gnomin."

"I speak some Gnomin," Traejan informed his father. "I would be glad to accompany the envoy."

Zephyrn looked at him with surprise while his older brother and father exchanged a quick glance. Traejan did not tell them that his Gnomin was limited mostly to numbers and curses.

"Should we send something more formal than an envoy?" Xander queried of his father. "This is the first offer of aid, if that is the case, we have received."

"An envoy is what is proper to receive a group of that size," his father informed him, "and Traejan will be a proxy of the royal court. It will suffice for seventy-seven Gnomin."

Xander gave his father a respectful nod, though Traejan did not miss the quick and impatient exhale from his nostrils as he turned to face him. "Then, by all means, accompany the envoy," he instructed his younger brother. "They will leave by the south gate at noon."

Traejan bowed to his father and brothers, as did Dell, and took his leave. "Should I send for your horse?" the Praetorian asked once they were clear of the room. The young prince shook his head.

"I'll take Zeph's."

Dell nodded and motioned for a servant, a young elf that hurried to his side and then hurried alongside the prince and his guard while he took instructions for securing their mounts.

"I want paper and pencil in my saddlebag," Traejan told him, producing a questioning look from his guard. "In case my translating skills fall short," he explained.

Dell, his already high eyebrows arching even higher, said nothing.

The pair avoided the crowds of revelers this time and left through the kitchens.

"Is it my imagination," the prince asked as they left the castle proper and entered the bailey, "or is my brother trying to fill my father's boots a little soon?"

Dell's sharp eyes glanced about and, though he saw no one, he knew that ears were always open. Especially elfin ears. "It is not my place to say, Your Highness."

Traejan threw him a look of impatience. "But you know your history, as well as I, if not better. A king should serve for a thousand years, yet my father has only served half that. What's up Xander's ass?"

Dell repressed his smile the best he could. "Again, it is not my place to say, Your Grace."

Traejan gave a quiet grunt and let the matter drop. By the time they reached the stables, their mounts were saddled and ready. The prince and his guard were astride a pair of palfreys and headed for the south gate as the sun was headed for its zenith. They met with the envoy and headed south, hugging the mountain chain and circling the elfin kingdom as they made for the Echo Pass.

Two hours later, as they were approaching the edge of the forests east of Amherst, they encountered two Gnomin riders upon donkeys. One was obviously a male and one a female, though their age was indeterminate to the elves. Their hair was coarse and thick, and they both wore checkered shirts under suspended canvas pants that stopped below their knees. High woolen socks padded stout boots made for working rather than riding.

The separate envoys of the different races stopped short once they saw one another and, after a moment, both dismounted in a fashion that was both cautious and formal. Six elfin riders faced the two Gnomin silently, waiting. There was strict protocol for royal emissaries, which the young prince completely disregarded.

Traejan approached the female Gnomin with a grin nearly splitting his face in two and embraced her. "Gatha!" he exclaimed, lifting her off her feet.

The normally stoic Gnomin woman could not help but grin as well as she hugged the young prince, giving him hearty pats on his back, her face buried in his shoulder.

After Traejan introduced Gatha to the others, the male

Gnomin introduced himself as Otto. He was more swarthy than most Gnomin, with hair of dark brown and hazel eyes of brown and green. The elves were quick to offer the pair food and water and a chance to rest and refresh themselves. Dell found a clearing that had perceptibly been used often as a campsite and the small group sat themselves on logs and rocks while one elf minded the horses and the donkeys.

Otto spoke Anglicus, saving Traejan from having to translate and Gatha, who was mute, from having to scribble. He offered the elves cold potato patties, which they politely declined. Otto nodded as if he had expected as much and wrapped them back into a piece of checkered cloth and tucked them away into a satchel. He climbed and then perched upon a rock large enough to bring him eye level with the elves and Gatha stood next to him, keeping her feet on the ground. With the formalities dispensed of, as far as he could tell, the Gnomin male planted strong hands on his knobby knees and leaned forward.

"We know the Crommags are coming," he began, "headed for human and elfin lands. We know the elves mean to fight them. We plan to help."

Traejan was grateful that he was with trained men, and that they had met the Gnomin riders in the woods rather than at court. None of them so much as cracked a smile, much less laughed aloud.

"That is a very generous offer," Traejan replied. "We will gladly take any help you can give."

Otto squinted at the prince and then scowled at him. "Don't patronize me, young elf!" he scolded and the frozen expressions on the elves began to soften. The corner of Jaden's lip twitched up ever so slightly. "The Gnomin mean to aid in the effort and, believe it or not, war is something we know a thing or two about. We can make weapons, raise tents, plan battlefields, dig trenches and cook food. We don't mean to fight, we know we are no match for the Crommags, but fight we will if it comes to that."

Traejan dipped his head in respectful understanding, his sand-colored curls falling around his pointed ears. "Help that will be gladly and gratefully received," he said.

Otto straightened. "The Crommags have been raiding our lands for years, but last year was the worst. We lost people by the score in the late summer, their bodies never even found."

Traejan glanced at Dell and their eyes met. The Gnomin did not miss the look that passed between them.

"What?" Otto demanded, looking from one to the other. The young prince gave his guard a quick nod and Dell turned his face back to the Gnomin where he was scowling once again from his seat on the boulder.

"We came across the Crommag encampment last year," Dell informed him, "and they had many Gnomin with them."

Otto clutched at Gatha, one burly hand grabbing a fistful of the shoulder of her red-checked shirt. She did not seem to notice. Her blue eyes had grown as wide and round at this news as Otto's hazel ones.

"Alive?" he asked Dell, his voice harsh with desperation and hope.

Dell nodded. "Captives, for sure. Enslaved."

Though it might be expected for the Gnomin to take this news poorly, they both smiled.

"Alive," Otto whispered, his eyes far away until they focused suddenly back on Dell. "Do you know how many?"

"Thirty?" Dell ventured. "I could not say for sure, since there were tents. No more than twice that, I would guess."

Otto said something to Gatha in Gnomin and she nodded quickly. "Our missing miners," he said in Anglicus to the elves. "We will have to rescue them."

"Whoa," Traejan said, holding his hands up, palms out. "One thing at a time!"

Otto scowled at him once again and waved a thick hand in his direction. "I don't mean now, I'm no fool! The Crommags will certainly bring the miners with them. They do not know how to work metal, make weapons, even shoe a horse."

"If they are smart enough, they will keep them alive," Jaden said, speaking for the first time, "but the Crommags are not known for their wit."

"If they have the wits to capture Gnomin for their metalwork," Otto answered, "they should have the wherewithal to keep them alive. The wits of the miners should serve to make up the difference."

Gatha nodded her approval of the idea and Traejan took her endorsement to heart. "Very well, then we can plan a rescue for once they are here with the Crommags, if that will suffice."

"It must," Otto insisted. Gatha asserted the same with a vigorous nod of her dark blonde curls.

"Alright," Traejan acquiesced. "We will offer what aid we can when the time comes. "Until then, will you join us in Tuar Ceath?"

Otto considered the offer and then shook his head. "We will wait for the others, and then continue with them."

"How many are in your party?" Traejan asked.

"Seventy-five, not counting Gatha and myself."

Traejan nodded. "We will see what kind of accommodations we can prepare," he began but Otto shook his dark head once again.

"Don't waste the time. Have you a map of your kingdom? The surrounding area?"

Traejan looked to Jaden but the small elf was already moving towards his horse. The Gnomin hopped down from his rock as the Sylvan procured a roll of parchment from his bags and spread it out on the forest floor. He placed small stones on the corners to keep it flat while the others gathered round the map and hunkered down for a better look.

"Here," Otto said, tapping the map with a thick and calloused finger, "is where they are most like to enter your lands."

The elfin prince nodded. "We surmised as much, though we will have scouts posted at the narrow passes of the mountains, just in case they are that foolish."

"We could only hope!" Otto grunted. "And, in case we are that lucky, our miners can rig those passes to collapse on top of them."

"That would be good," Dell agreed. "We would have to leave less men guarding the passes and have more amassed at Morgan's Vale."

"Good, because that is where they will come," Otto said, his eyes still moving across the map. "I'd bet my hose on it."

Dell looked at the Gnomin, his arched brows raised over his brown, almond-shaped eyes. Traejan laughed softly.

"His pants," he explained to his Praetorian. A few others chuckled as Otto moved his hand, his finger dropping to an area between Morgan's Vale and Tuar Ceath.

"These are forests?" he asked. Dell nodded assent. "And here," Otto asked, moving his finger slightly north, "these are cliffs?" Again, Dell nodded. Otto grunted in approval. "Good. This is where they will camp," he said, pointing to the forests south of the Vale. "Here," he said, moving his finger, "is where we should camp. The first, and undoubtedly the fiercest battles, will be fought here."

Every pair of eyes stared at the spot he marked.

And so, Traejan thought with a chill, *the battlefield is set for the First War of the New World. Not by generals or opponents, but by a Gnomin squatting on the forest floor.* Yet the young prince did not doubt him in the slightest.

"I will direct our company to head to the top of the bluffs and make camp," Otto said, glancing at the elfin faces that huddled around him. "From there, we can send an envoy to the elfin kingdom, or you could send one to us." His hazel eyes looked questioningly at Traejan, who dipped his head in response.

"Sir Dellion is the Major of the Elfin Army," he replied. "I will trust in whatever you two deem best." He bowed to Otto and his guardsman and turned away, pulling Gatha along gently by her elbow as Otto questioned Dell about water supplies. For the young prince, the ancillary matters of the war were trite. He had been dying inwardly to speak with the Gnomin woman. He stopped when he thought they were a safe distance away and turned to face her, his hand dropping from her elbow to hold her loosely by the wrist.

Gatha took a deep breath and drew herself up, ready to face the questions she knew he would ask. Her blue eyes bored into him, ready and waiting. Because the hearing of elves was so greatly heightened, the young prince spoke in the Gnomin tongue, as best he could.

"It is good to see you, Gatha."

The Gnomin woman smiled at both his words and his horrible accent. She dipped her head of dark blonde curls to assent to the same.

"Have you heard from her?"

Gatha became so still that for a second she appeared to be made of stone. Then she nodded.

Traejan grinned, unable to help himself. "Did she give you a message for me?"

Again, the Gnomin appeared to be frozen before she slowly shook her head back and forth.

The young prince tilted his head, his expression crestfallen. "Is she back at the haus?" he asked.

Gatha shook her head slowly.

A crease formed between the dark blonde brows of the prince as his soft brown eyes narrowed in consternation.

"Did she know you were coming here?" he asked.

Gatha nodded gently.

"And she sent no word for me?"

Again Gatha turned her head slowly from side to side.

"I see," the young prince replied, drawing a look from the Gnomin woman so sorrowful that his heart broke twice within his chest. "The elfin people cannot thank you enough for your assistance," he said, switching back to Anglicus and a more formal demeanor.

Gatha, uncharacteristically, embraced the elfin prince and held him tight. Traejan lowered his face until it rested on top of her dark blonde curls.

She is not coming, his heart whispered.

The elfin prince fought back a moan of pain even as his sense of responsibility hardened around his body like a shield.

His mind was already racing, thinking of where to put the Gnomin as well as the troops they would no longer need in the mountain passes. He calculated the area they would need for the elfin infantry. He estimated what he could reserve for the farmers and villagers that would undoubtedly join their cause. He knew that he needed a plot for Vikemen as well, he could undoubtedly count on at least a small company of the gigantic Norsemen.

The mind of the warrior raced. The heart of the elf wept.

She sends no word for you. She is not coming for you.

7. SOUTHBOUND FORCES

Ayala roared with such force that Borg was sure he could feel the very mountains quake. The chief of the Great Men turned sharply, looking for something to smash to pieces in his anger but saw nothing but ashes and scraps. He roared again, his meaty fists clenched, thinking that if he could not throw or slam anything, it would suffice to tear something, or someone, apart. His guards saw the thought flash in their leader's close-set eyes and all took a step back. They were wise to do so.

Ayala was a mountain of man, even among his own kind. Over eight feet tall he stood, even when his feet were bare, which was always. His back and chest were bunched with muscle and his arms so large that he could not touch the top of his own head, even if he had wanted.

Stupid elves! Stupid small men! he raged inwardly. *I'll rip them all to pieces! I'll tear the legs and arms off every one of them! I'll...I'll...I'll....*

The giant Crommag wanted to roar again, to stomp his feet and pound his fists, but was just wise enough to restrain himself. The cords in his neck stood out in the attempt at control and a vein pulsed on the side of his narrow forehead. He gnashed his mighty fangs in frustration.

Anger is expected, he told himself, *but a childish tantrum is not.*

The voice in his head sounded exactly like his brother, Noga, and Ayala clung to it.

What would you do? he lashed out silently. *Better, what*

would you tell me to do? Eyes that were dark and beady looked back over a shoulder humped with muscle, back in the direction Noga had taken before Ayala had led their people through the passes of the Siber Massif.

Take action, his brother's voice advised wisely. *Take command.*

Ayala heard his brother and, as always, agreed. A small smile made his beady eyes narrow to slits.

"We will camp here!" the chief thundered to those around him and the word was passed back throughout the masses, echoes upon echoes of his command. He motioned at two of his guards, Borg from the Cave Bear Tribe and Ipa from the Polar Bear Tribe. Both men were even larger than Ayala, their new chief, almost like bears themselves. "Raise my tent," he ordered, "and have grog for me when I return."

The two giant Crommags gave him a nod and turned to do as they were bid.

"You two!" Ayala ordered, motioning to his other guards – one from the Ice Walkers and the other from the Snow Leopard Clan. "Come with me!"

The two dipped their own ugly heads and moved to follow the Great Chief as he stalked away over the charred ground. All of his guards served him faithfully and well, but Pel and Yon were by far more intelligent. They had begun to serve as occasional advisors in Noga's absence. Ayala stopped when he was some distance away from where his people were now busy erecting tents and looked back over the land.

They stood in the middle of a vast prairie and the plains stretched around them for miles in all directions. Forests were distant, just greenish-blue blurs on the eastern and western horizons and completely non-existent to the south. In the north loomed the colossal peaks of the range they had passed through into the lands of the lesser men.

The ground upon which they stood was blackened. Most

had been vegetation, but there were chunks of charred wood in small heaps and piles that together outlined what must have been a number of structures.

Ayala crossed his arms over his massive chest and surveyed the scorched earth, a scowl in his heavy brow.

"Do you see what they have done?"

Yon, a hulk of a Crommag from the Snow Leopard Clan, frowned. Confused, he looked at the masses of people that were setting up camp. Pel, however, nodded sagely. He reminded Ayala of his brother. He had the same cunning in his eyes as Noga, but that was where the resemblance ended. His eyes were dark, not that strange color of winter moss. He was slim for a Great Man but still huge - a member of the Ice Walkers, as tall and looming as death.

"The men have burned their own settlements," Pel said.

Yon's enormous head swung around again to reassess the scene and this time he understood. "The food and the shelters!" he surmised aloud.

Ayala nodded. It was the third burned farm the Crommags had encountered on their journey south from the mountains. "The first I thought was accident," he told his guardsmen. "The second left me confused. Now, especially with what you see, I know for sure."

The two nodded as they resurveyed the scene, proud that they were not just as smart as the Chief, but that he considered them so as well. The thought made Yon hesitant to speak, lest he be thought a fool, but he felt *someone* must ask it.

"Have we brought enough food to sustain us until we reach the elfin lands?" he ventured.

Ayala shook his great head slowly, his dark eyes angry. "No. We counted on what Noga and his men left behind on their raids last summer."

"Do you think all the farms he left waiting for us will be burned like this one?" Yon asked. "Would they really burn them *all?"*

"We have no way to know, until we get there," Ayala replied, clenching his fangs. "But we must assume *yes!*"

After a moment of silence, Pel spoke. "We are not without. We have enough to maintain all of the people for three weeks, a month if we ration."

The chief, his face tight and angry, nodded in agreement. His people were not strangers to having food rationed – some winters were longer and more bitter than others. It was a price one paid to survive. At least here they need not fear the cold. Every step they took south led them to warmer and warmer lands. Most of the ground, the miles that had not been blackened with fire, were sparse and barren – still frozen even after the snows had melted. Here and there were dormant plants and sprigs that were slowly coming back to life. Tiny leaves on bushes and an occasional blade of grass brave enough to push through the hardened ground. Ayala and many of his men had been raiding the lands south of the Ice Floe for decades and knew there was only more to come. For most of the Crommags, however, the still barren wasteland was a display of the most verdant spring they had ever seen.

Ayala reached into the crude vest he wore and pulled out a scrap of goat hide that had been dried and cured and beaten soft. He unrolled it and held it out as the other two stepped close to observe the crude map that had been drawn on it with a burnt stick. There were no words, for the Crommags had no system for writing letters. There were small drawings, however, depicting a few mountains and forests and rivers.

"This is the Massif?" Pel asked, pointing a huge and grubby finger at a large section of triangles near the top of the map. Ayala nodded and Pel's large digit drew a slow line down and stopped. "We are here?" he asked. Ayala nodded again and Pel moved his finger southwest to where a circle had been drawn. "And the lands of the lesser men," he surmised aloud. Ayala grunted his assent.

"To the west," the Great Chief growled, "a river cuts south. It has fish, and the surrounding lands have animals that are easily hunted. But it is not the direction we want to go!"

"Forests surround the lands of the elves," Yon observed. "A forced march through the drylands might bring us there in time to replenish our stores."

A forced march was exactly what Ayala wanted. It would bring them there faster than they had anticipated, possibly catching the lesser men unaware. Less prepared, that was certain. And he was itching for a fight. A fight that would make his people the dominant race of the world, as they should be. The spring was going to be long enough, he did not want to make it longer.

Yet pushing women and children on such a trek could prove fatal for many. Even the men would arrive exhausted and hungry, maybe unable to fight. Noga had warned that going would be slow across the dry lands and that they would most likely have to abandon their wagons there if they became stuck in the thick sand.

Ayala felt driven with urgency, but he did not want to bring his people to the promised land only to have them starve to death within sight of it.

"We can send hunting parties in both directions," Pel suggested, "and bring food to the people as you lead them south. But it would slow us by days, maybe weeks."

Ayala was so full of rage that he wanted to tear the map into pieces. He forced himself to stay composed and his hands begin to tremble with the effort. By sheer force of will he made his entire body still. As he did, a sense of calm washed over him and, with it, a sense of clarity.

"Both ideas are sound," he agreed, his beady eyes on the map as if seeing it for the first time, "but I want to keep the people together. If we all head west, we can follow the river south, fishing and hunting as we go. We will avoid the drylands altogether, and by doing so, save our wagons and make up time when we are ready to travel east." It was all he could do not to shout the last few words in triumph of his own discovery.

"If we could keep the wagons, we could carry more food," Yon observed, frowning at the map. His scowl melted as he shifted his small eyes to the Chief. "We would arrive fed, and could bring stores of game as well."

Pel nodded in agreement, his eyes going from one Crommag to the other. "And we would not have to carry our weapons upon our backs."

"Nor our tents or tools," Yon agreed.

"We would be more rested and fresher for battle," Pel finished.

"A good plan," Yon attested.

"A better plan," Pel propositioned. "It will serve our needs, and our people well."

Ayala flashed his huge and fearsome fangs in a grin as he straightened, his barrel of a chest rising and swelling. "Let the tribes know. Then we will rest and feast. The next part of our great trek will begin at dawn!"

His Crommag guards nodded, their approval glinting bright in their normally dark eyes as they moved off to do his bidding. Later, they would rejoin the Chief in his tent and feast on roasted goat and strong grog.

Ayala watched them go and then turned his massive head to the south. It felt good to have made a strong decision. Noga would have cracked wise, as was his wont, but he would have been proud.

His fangs still bared in a grin, Ayala headed to where his tent was being prepared and shouted for a stein of grog.

⊂⊃⊂⊃

On the same day the Crommags cleared Tannlinn's Pass,

Traejan stood in a pass the elves called the Crook. This gap was much smaller than the one that linked the Northlon to the Bitterlands, full of switchbacks and in some places so narrow as to permit but a single horse and rider, but it was still a viable entry point for the Crommags to enter the elfin lands. The constricted pathway was almost equidistant from the Mountain of the Moon and the Mountain of the Sun, wedged in the middle of the range that separated Tuar Ceath from the Echo Sea.

A team of Gnomin workers, led by a young miner named Wilhelm, escorted the prince along the floor of the narrow valley in the bright spring sunshine. The sky was a startling and cloudless blue and the air was warm with an occasional breeze that was extraordinarily cool. The mountains rose to either side of the small party, jabbing at the blue sky in majestic audacity. The peaks to the south were green with grasses and blooming with a myriad of hues from springtime flowers. To the north, the ridge rose higher in rocky alps that were still crested white with snow.

Wilhelm was tall for a Gnomin, almost five feet with his boots on, and had a reddish tinge to the downy blonde beard that covered his full cheeks. "Got a bit of the Vikes in me!" he would jest when he had downed a bit of hard cider. He stood in his work boots and woolen socks and hooked his thumbs under the straps of his short, suspended trousers. His linen shirt was a solid color (green) rather than checkered and marked him as a mining team leader.

"There!" he exclaimed, pointing high onto the face of a cliff. "And there!" His hand swept from an outcropping of rocks on one side of the pass to a similar ledge on the other side of the valley. Traejan's brown eyes followed the movement of his hand, his elfin eyesight picking out the grouping of stones. "Those are rigged with an explosive charge," Wilhelm said, proud. "The charge will tumble the stones, which sit above slate -a very unstable rock. The slate, in turn, will crumble and slide, starting an avalanche. It will bury anyone who stands where we are now, all the way back to the last bend, making further travel for any survivors quite difficult, if not impossible." The Gnomin grinned at the idea, the sunlight glinting on his beard of red and gold, as he rocked back on his heels. "Since this is the last of three similar traps we have set along the pass, it is doubtful they would even get this far. But still, we prepare."

"Thank you, Wilhelm," Traejan began but the Gnomin waved him away with a hand of stubby and calloused fingers.

"It is nothing!" the stocky man interrupted. "Child's play! And, please, call me Wil."

"Thank you, Wil," Traejan acquiesced with a smile. "With this we can focus our efforts towards Morgan's Vale, where your people have been equally beneficial to us. We cannot thank you enough for what you have done."

Wil gave another dismissive wave and the smile melted from his typically jovial face. "The Crommags have been the bane of our existence for as long as any Gnomin can remember. We would be crazy not to help you." His smile returned, lighting up his broad face. "We cannot very well sit a horse and swing a sword!" The Gnomin hooted with glee at this suggestion, his stubby fingers clasped around a belly that had been growing steadily wider the last few years.

Traejan smiled and clapped a hand upon his shoulder. "As you wish," he agreed. "But perhaps I can invite you to lunch?"

Wil's bright expression brightened even further. "Gladly! I've developed a taste for that honeyed ale of yours," he admitted, giving his belly a pat. He turned and called out to the others in his party. Traejan understood enough Gnomin to know he was giving commands to clean up and return to camp. The team leader turned back to the prince and gave him a nod to show he was ready.

Together they made the short walk to the eastern end of the valley where it opened up to the kingdom of Tuar Ceath. There, Dell waited for them with Traejan's palfrey, Peg, and his own slender mount. Nearby was a corral of donkeys the Gnomin used for riding and hauling and Wil selected one of these and slipped a halter over its long nose as the elves mounted their horses. He pulled himself onto the back of the animal with surprising agility and gave it the heels of his work boots and the three of them made the short trot back to the cradle of the elfin kingdom.

The lands south of Tuar Ceath had changed much since the arrival of the Gnomin. The small city remained a glistening jewel, cupped by cliffs to the south and ringed by mountains to the north and west. Guarding the east, all the way to the mountains in the north, was the Elysian Forest - a vast expanse of enormous silver-trunked Linden trees. The forest was cleaved by the Saranac River. The Saranac was wide and, in some parts wild, as waterfalls and snowmelt fed into the waterway that led all the way to the Sabado Sea.

The royal castles, with the mountains at their backs and the city built into the woods to the east and west, were fronted with acres of grassland. Closest to them was the manicured greensward of the Great Lawn that gave way to Fosse Meadow, a beautiful but empty stretch of grasslands that ended at a long cliff.

Now, the edge of the meadow was a hive of activity. A camp was being erected and quickly developing into a small village the Gnomin called Kriegslager. A hundred yards before the land dropped down into Morgan's Vale stood row upon row of smart tents made of heavy green canvas. They ranged in size - the smallest able to house sleeping quarters for half a dozen men. Corrals had been built for the horses of the Elfin Cavalry but, as of yet, were empty.

The tents, also empty for the time being, would serve as the barracks for the elfin army and the few dozen humans that had joined them. The current plan was to move them all into the camp a fortnight before the Crommags were expected to arrive. Jäger scouts had been posted along every possible route, ready to ride ahead with plenty of time to warn the homeland.

East of the tents, three buildings had been erected. There had been much discussion at first – the Gnomin had planned for four buildings yet the elves had quietly insisted, with no explanation, that three would be better. The Gnomin, with little consternation, had relented with a collective shrug and simply joined the two middle buildings into one large structure. North of the structures, nestled against the trees of the Elysian Forest, were the tents set up by the miners for their own use, and here they had stayed while they worked and built and prepared.

A hundred yards of grass stood between the line of tents and the edge of the bluff that dropped eighty feet down to the vale. East of the buildings was a natural grade just under fifty yards wide that gave easy access to the meadows below. Past the slope, space had been left for more tents but, as of yet, none had been erected on that side.

A wide prairie was at the bottom of the slope, stretching out between the face of the bluff and the Elfin Greatwood. It was there that the elves and Gnomin expected the Crommags to wage their first battle, the battle for Tuar Ceath.

As the two elves and the lone Gnomin rode over a stone bridge towards Castle Song they were met by two things; the ring of steel upon steel from the practice yards, and an elfin rider from Castle Royce. The rider, a young elf of almost pure Seleucian blood, was one that Traejan had secured for the sole purpose of bringing him news of any comings, goings, or messages of import from the royal castle. His brother was not often speedy sending his own messenger and it irked Traejan to no end. The messenger reined his horse hard, making her turn and prance in agitation. His pale blonde hair whipped around his long, pointed ears and his bright blue eyes searched for those of the elfin prince.

"My Lord Prince!" he greeted, dipping his head in respect.

Traejan edged Peg closer and nodded in return. "Niall," he greeted. "What news?"

"A party approaches Tuar Ceath from the east."

Traejan felt his heart sink an inch. He was hoping for news from the south. *She will come,* he told himself. *She must come.* "From Bayard?" he asked. It was the largest village to the east, a fishing town on the edge of the Sabado Sea.

Niall shook his head, still trying to steady his mount. "A party of Vikemen. Twenty of them. Your brother is planning to ride out to receive them."

Traejan felt his heart lift. Ryen. Ryen could be with them. She could be with Ryen. He wanted to ask if a woman rode with them. A woman with hair the color of blood and riding a beast as large and as black as night. Instead he asked, "Did my brother send word for me to join him?"

Niall shook his head again. "Not as of yet, my lord."

"Typical," Traejan remarked caustically before dismissing his own feelings and turning to where Wilhelm waited patiently upon his donkey. "I am sorry, but I feel that I must go," he explained to the Gnomin miner. "You are welcome to sup without me - Niall can accompany you if you wish."

"Don't be silly!" Wilhelm exclaimed, waving him off with a gnarled and calloused hand that was missing the tip on his right pinky finger. "I will not detain your messenger. I am quite acquainted with your kitchen staff and they with me."

"Thank you, Wil," Traejan said. "I will catch up with you this evening, or on the morrow."

The Gnomin gave him a nod and put his heels to his beast. The donkey jerked and then hurried off in a jostling trot, bouncing the miner along again towards Castle Song.

"Thank you, Niall," Traejan told his messenger. "You may return to your post."

"My Lord Prince," he said, bowing his head. "Sir Dellion," he said next, by way of farewell, dipping his head towards the Praetorian.

Both the prince and his guard did the same in return and the elf turned his mount and spurred her back the way he had come. Traejan and Dell followed at a slow trot.

"My Lord Prince?" Dell asked as they headed for the main gate of Castle Royce.

"Yes, my Lord Major?" Traejan asked, a smile sneaking across his face.

Dell sighed. "It is not my place to say…"

"But you are going to anyway," Traejan interrupted. "Then by all means," he encouraged, "please continue."

"I know a friction has been growing between you and your brother," he ventured, to which Traejan gave a snort, "but I would advise not to make it apparent." The smile slipped away from Traejan's face as Dell continued. "It is not good for morale, even in peaceful times."

The elfin prince flinched, and his guard braced himself for a scathing reply, but Traejan looked at him with somber eyes. "That is good advice, and advice that I will follow. Thank you, Dell." The Praetorian looked at him, his dark brows raised high above his dark eyes. "Don't look so surprised," Traejan told him with a smile. "You are right, and I have no problem admitting that. But I will still complain to you."

Dell grinned. "Of course you will."

The horses increased their pace as they smelled the horses that were gathered near the main gate of Castle Royce. Traejan and his guard fell in beside Xander and his escort just as they were moving out. The young prince broke away from his guard to join his brother, talking the place of the rider on Xander's right.

"Do you mind if we join you?" he asked, his tone overly light.

"Of course not," Xander replied with a sidelong glance at his younger brother. "As long as you can restrain yourself."

"Restrain myself?" Traejan asked, surprised by both his brother's suggestion and his mocking tone.

"I was told of your behavior when you were sent to greet

the Gnomin envoy."

"My behavior?"

Xander's dark brows came together over his dark brown eyes. "I was told that you embraced one of them." He glanced askance at Traejan and his expression softened into one of humor. "Though, I can only suppose that you would not do the same to a Vikeman!" Xander gave an uncharacteristic chortle that was echoed by his closest guardsmen.

I guess they did not give him the same advice that Dell gave me, the younger prince surmised with a scowl. *And if the Roshan Simorgh is with them, he is going to be more than a little put out at what I might do.* The thought melted his scowl into a smirk that Xander did not fail to notice.

The elfin envoy traveled southeast, mostly in silence as they skirted the city and entered the Elysian Forest. They crossed a massive stone bridge over the Saranac and Traejan hoped with every step of his horse that Ryen would be with the Vikemen, and Ember with him.

They rode for just over an hour and Xander was ready to call for a rest when their elfin ears caught the sounds of horsemen. The crown prince signaled for a halt as they came into a clearing in the forest. The horses became as still as their riders and, five minutes later, the sounds grew and grew until movement could be seen through the trees. Finally, the Vikemen emerged into the clearing.

Dressed in leathers banded with studs of brass and draped with furs, the Vikemen were the largest race of humans in the New World. They rode khusars – equines larger than any human warhorse or plow ox. Broadswords hung from their belts and axes were strapped to their wide backs. All, but one, had beards and most had hair that was long and thick. Some wore braids in their hair or in their long mustaches, held by silver bands carved with runes.

Traejan was amused to see that they rode in a column, if but a loose one, four riders wide and five deep. He was more than pleased to see a familiar face, that of Ryen Glace, though the young prince was inwardly crushed to see that Ember was not among them.

She will come, he told himself. *She must come.*

The six Vikemen nearest the front of the column dismounted, the smallest of them standing just under seven feet tall. Xander dismounted and, flanked by four guards – two on each side – approached the gigantic men from the north.

One of them, the only one that Traejan recognized and knew, stepped forward with a smile he could hardly restrain and offered the crown prince a hand as large as the paw of a bear. He had ice-blue eyes, rose-gold hair, and a short-clipped beard to match.

"I am Ryen Glace," he told Xander, who had also offered his hand in greeting only to have it swallowed by the hand of the Vikeman that stood over a foot above him. "And we are here to offer the elves what aid we can."

Xander did not know the population count in the Vikes, but he knew it should afford more than twenty men. He swallowed his first choice of words for another time and another audience.

"The elves are grateful for any help you can offer," he responded, but his tight expression was not lost on the Vikeman.

Ryen Glace gave him a grin. "It was intended that the four boroughs each send nine men, but a few…ahh.. fell short."

Ryen looked over his shoulder to the other five Vikemen that had dismounted with him and the first stepped forward. He was by far the largest, over seven feet tall with a chest like a bull, and the only one that did not sport a beard. His square chin was clean shaven and his hair was the color of golden flax.

"I am Crag," he said, bowing low to Xander, "of Roskilde Borough. Since we are the closest township between the Vikes and the Bitterlands, our village elders thought it prudent to keep most fighting men at hand in case there is an attack from that direction as well." Xander nodded in understanding, knowing that it was a logical decision. Crag saw his veiled disappointment and grinned at him, a fearsome sight on such a sizeable countenance. "But don't worry!" he assured the crown prince. "I have the strength of *ten* Vikemen!"

Xander could not help but smile at the man towering over him. "And you are welcome! Thank you, Crag." The enormous Norseman dipped his head in response and stepped back as the next man stepped forward. The sides of his head were shaved and tattooed with letters and marks. The hair that ran down the middle of his scalp was dark blonde and woven into a braid that fell down his back. He was lean, compared to Crag, but still loomed over the crown prince.

"I am Kamut," the man said, bowing low, "of Copen Borough." He straightened and Xander could see golden hair glinting in the man's bushy beard, showing that he might hold common ancestors with Crag. Yet he seemed to be lesser in conversation as well as stature, stepping back without another word.

"I am Haldor!" the next man boomed, stepping forward. He was larger than Kamut, though nowhere near as large as Crag, with a luxurious, if tangled, mane of hair the color of a burnt orange and a long beard to match. But, like the flax-haired man from the Vikes, seemed more inclined to smile. "My name means *the rock*. The man looming behind me like a henge is my brother."

"Halvar!" the Vikeman, who was indeed looming behind Haldor, announced. "It means, *defender of the rock*!" Halvar was of the same image as his brother, though his dark orange hair was brushed into waves with a pair of braids on each side to keep the wild locks from his face. His beard was cut short but his carroty mustache was long and braided.

"We," Haldor continued with a grin, "along with two of our cousins, represent Borough Oslo."

The last of the Vikemen stepped forward. He was the

closest in girth to the giant Crag, though he was half a head shorter - making him looking stocky in comparison, even at seven feet tall. He had black hair that flowed from a widow's peak on his forehead to well past his shoulders. His black beard and mustache were thick, but clipped close to his broad face. He had a handsome, hooked nose and deep blue eyes. "I am Yasgir," he said, "from the Hamburg Borough."

This time it was Xander that bowed. "You are well met, men of the Vikes, with much gratitude. Please accompany us to Tuar Ceath, and give us news of the Vikes along the way, if you are so inclined."

"We are so inclined," Ryen claimed, jovial. "But, first, I must say hello to an old friend." He looked over Xander's head of dark curls to where Traejan stood, holding the reins of his palfrey. He gave the crown prince a nod and then strode past him. A second later he was embracing the younger prince in a bone-crushing hug that lifted the elf's boots off of the ground.

"Ryen!" Traejan exclaimed, breathless, clapping the Vikeman on his back as the Norseman set the prince back down upon his feet. He kept his clasp on the big man, holding him at arm's length. "I am not old, nor is our acquaintance, but it is good to see you!"

"And you as well!" Ryen boomed, his icy blue eyes a twinkle.

Xander cleared his throat, making the pair turn to him. Traejan thought the smile on his brother's face looked painfully forced. "I am sure the Vikemen have traveled far and could use both rest and refreshment."

"Indeed!" Ryen agreed with a bow. "Though we can wait until we reach your homeland." He turned his head and whistled for his khusar. The great gray gelding plodded up to him with his head held high, blowing bursts of air from its nostrils as it neared Peg. The white palfrey whickered in return, dipping her long white nose to greet the beast.

Those standing on the ground remounted their steeds and followed Prince Xander as he led the party back west.

Ryen rode by his side as the prince told him all that had been happening in the Northlon since the last fall of autumn. The other Vikemen followed, a looming rearguard at their backs.

Traejan and Dell found themselves riding abreast with the brothers Haldor and Halvar, both to whom Traejan took an immediate liking. He enjoyed their conversation and reciprocated well enough in the bawdy spirit he had learned from his short time with Ryen, but his brown eyes still searched out the loquacious Vikeman that rode alongside his brother. He wanted badly to talk to the Norseman in private.

The ride to Tuar Ceath seemed to last forever to the young prince, and forever twice again for Xander to show the newcomers around Kriegslager.

"We intend for the elfin infantry to occupy the west side of the buildings," the crown prince informed the Vikemen from astride his horse. "We, or the Gnomin, would be glad to erect tents on the east side if you wish."

"Thank you, but we can raise our own tents," Ryen said, drawing a snicker from a few of his fellows. "And the sooner, the better. It will be good to be settled down for a bit, even if it is to prepare for battle."

"Very well," Xander granted, "but will you join us for a dinner in your honor tonight at Castle Royce?"

"Certainly," Ryen agreed, his khusar stamping and snorting, anxious to be unsaddled. "We will never turn down an offer for feasting!"

"Very well, my brother can bring you and your men when you are ready, or you may send for an escort."

Ryen dismounted and bowed to the crown prince and the other Vikeman followed suit. Xander dipped his head in acknowledgement and turned his horse north, finally leaving the Vikemen to a few moments of rest and respite. He glanced back over his shoulder at his younger brother, his dark eyes full of warning.

Traejan dismounted, his smile forced and his brown eyes patiently fixed so they would not roll in exasperation. He lifted a hand in goodbye to his brother and turned back to the Vikemen as they were suddenly confronted by a dozen Gnomin. The scene was almost comical as it appeared for a moment that the giant Norsemen might be under attack by people that stood only a head higher than their belts.

Before they could voice a word, much less unpack or unsaddle their worn mounts, the Vikemen were set-upon by the camp's Gnomin kitchen staff - brandishing armloads of twisted bread and pressing steins of hard cider into any empty hand. The broad-chested giants ignored their weapons and bedrolls for the nonce to accept the steins and cheer the stout men and women that were nearly half their size. Those same men and women echoed their cheer, quaffing their own ciders in nearly half the time. There was an uproar of approval and festivity from all and the Gnomin refilled the steins from large clay jugs they had carried in over their shoulders.

Friends were quickly made between both races and the drinking and boasting began in earnest. Ryen motioned for a few of the younger Vikemen to take care of the horses and Crag spoke to a few others about staying sober enough to attend a royal dinner. Both received responses that were reluctant but compliant.

Finally, Traejan Royce stepped in front of Ryen Glace and caught his eye from behind a stein as it was being emptied. "Might I have a word?" the prince asked as the Vikeman lowered the vessel.

Ryen grinned. "By all means!" he agreed, wiping his mouth with the back of a hand as the two of them turned from the small crowd. The prince motioned for Dell to stay with the impromptu celebration, though he knew his Praetorian would hear every word. He also knew Dell would actually try not to listen – his guard was already loathe to know about his feelings for the human woman.

"Have you seen her?" Traejan queried immediately. "Have you spoken with her?" When the Vikeman hesitated, puzzled, Traejan pressed. "Ember!" he cried out softly, as if an explanation should not be necessary. "Have you heard from her?"

The icy blue eyes of the Norseman went from slightly puzzled to outright surprise. "Ember?" he asked, his face quickly splitting into a grin. "And just when did you become on a first name basis with her majesty, the Roshan?"

Now it was Traejan's turn to be taken aback.

He doesn't know, he realized and then, with disappointment on the tail of that realization, *he has not seen her.*

"Yes," he said, the single word exhaled in what was almost a laugh. "I'm on a first name basis with her."

The Vikeman cocked his head, smiling but not understanding.

Traejan lifted his chin. "We were together," he told Ryen. "Closely, after I saw you last." His voice trailed off on his last sentence, softer with each word. And, with each word, the face of the Vikeman fell a little more until it hardened completely.

"When I left you both in the woods above Goldensword, it was the last time I saw either of you."

"And you haven't heard from her since?"

Ryen shook his head. "Not personally. She sent a rider with a message, about the impending invasion, asking if I would address the Norsemen." The elfin prince looked away, thoughtful while the Vikeman's light brows drew together. "And just how long," Ryen asked, "were you...close with her?"

Traejan's brown eyes locked back on the Vikeman. "We only had two weeks," he told him, "before I had to return home." He decided not to relate the details of their parting.

Ryen's expression softened and he gave the prince a conciliatory smile. "Two weeks do not a marriage make," he replied. "Lucky for me – I would have more wives than Triton!"

The Norseman laughed heartily at this suggestion.

Traejan did not laugh but returned his smile with a look of knowing. "It might in this case." Ryen's countenance fell as the elf continued. "And you were wrong about her, Ryen. Her heart might not have walls, but it does hold love."

The Vikeman bristled visibly, drawing himself up. His blue eyes narrowed at the prince. "And you have not heard from her since your training?"

"No."

Ryen seemed to relax a little, and then a little more. "You must know that you are not the first student she has...she has been...close to, as you put it."

Traejan stiffened. "But I will be the last. She loves me."

The Vikeman cocked his head and gave him a small smile. "Traejan..." he soothed, his voice so gentle that the young prince recoiled.

"Don't patronize me, Ryen," Traejan warned, his voice low.

"I'm not trying to patronize you, elfin prince," Ryen said, his blue eyes darting around to see what sort of ears might be close by. For the moment, Traejan did not care who might be listening, but had the awareness to speak quietly.

"Our time together was short, I will admit, and not by my own doing, I can assure you. But that time was meaningful. Neither of us will ever be the same, and never whole for as long as we are apart."

Ryen looked as if he thought different, or maybe hoped different, but nodded instead. "If you say so," he acquiesced. "But come!" he announced, changing his tone and demeanor in an instant. "Let's have some more of that Gnomin cider, toast to our Dark Lady, and hope that she joins us soon!"

"I will at that," Traejan agreed, his own jovial demeanor obfuscating his own feelings.

He loves her more than he has ever let on, the young prince thought. He tried not to let it concern him, but it did. Along with the knowledge that the Roshan had been close with just not Ryen or himself, but other students as well. He could not help but wonder how many, or how often.

But it was different for me, he thought. *It is different for me. She loves me.*

She will come. She must.

He wore an ersatz smile through a welcome supper with the Northmen, meeting and greeting them all personally.

The Gnomin helped the Vikemen set up their camp on the far side of the large wooden structures, past where the land sloped down into the valley. Five gargantuan tents, which the Norsemen called yurts, housed them all.

In turn, the giant men helped the Gnomin in their tasks as a week passed, and then another.

All the while, the elfin prince kept to his mental mantra.

She will come. She must.

8. NORTHBOUND FORCES

Three days after the Vikemen had raised and settled into their yurts, a rider arrived at Castle Royce. He was a Sylvan rider, a small elf named Lorn on a small elfin horse, carrying big news.

Traejan had been showing Ryen around Castle Song and, by the time they arrived at the royal castle, the messenger was leaving. He hated being last to know, but Traejan knew that it would be ridiculous to ask his father to wait on him before receiving messages from his scouts. Besides, it often worked out in Traejan's favor. Especially when he had questions he did not like to pose around his father and brother.

Lorn, his face sweaty and blonde hair disheveled, was in the royal stables when the young prince, along with his Praetorian and the Vikeman, arrived on their own mounts. The Sylvan elf looked more like a boy in from a hard day of playing in the woods, rather than a grown elf after a hard day of riding. He turned from his calypso, a breed of small fast horses favored by Sylvan elves, and bowed.

"My Lord Prince," he greeted as Traejan slid from Peg's back and dipped his head in return.

"Lorn, it is good to see you. Have you been offered rest and refreshment?"

"I have, thank you, my lord."

"You have already been inside to speak with my father?"

"Yes, my lord."

"Do you mind if I detain you a moment longer to receive your news personally?" Traejan asked. *And in private,* he thought.

Ryen swung down from his saddle and joined the prince. Dell had dismounted, but hung back, his hands grasping the bridle of his horse. He knew where Lorn had been scouting so he had a good idea of what was coming next.

"I am at your service," Lorn assured him with another bow for the prince as well as a nod to Dell and the giant Vikeman. Ryen's great size made the Sylvan look even more like a child, a very small child. "An army," the elf informed then, "albeit a small one, crossed the rivers at Trigo just yesterday."

Traejan felt his heart skip a beat and return to its normal rhythm. If an army was crossing the rivers then it was not men from Atlantea.

"From the Southlon?" he asked.

Lorn nodded vigorously. "From the Redlands," he affirmed. "Two hundred men afoot, another hundred on horse."

"A small army indeed," Ryen mused aloud, "but an army nonetheless."

"And the largest force of supporters we will have received," Traejan said, "if that is what they are."

"Did you make contact with them?" Ryen asked.

The Sylvan gave his head a shake, his blonde locks clumped together with dried sweat. "I made haste for the king, as I had been instructed."

"I am sure they are coming to offer aid, but we will know soon enough." The prince glanced at the Vikeman before looking back at the small elf. "Was there a woman riding with them?" he asked. *Beautiful and terrifying? With a mocking smile and hair the color of blood?* "Riding a Night Stallion?"

"Aye," Lorn agreed. "That beast would be impossible to miss."

For a moment the prince thought, with a jolt of hilarity, that the young rider was referring to the woman rather than her horse. Still, a chuckle escaped his lips even as his heart began to beat a little faster.

She's coming, he thought. *She's coming.*

"Two weeks?" he ventured, estimating the time it might be before he saw his love again and glancing at Dell for confirmation. Dell gave him a nod to concur his estimate and the prince looked at the Vikeman. Ryen paused before giving him a curt nod as well.

"Possibly ten days," he admitted. "Depending on how hard she drives them."

"Ten days," he whispered, relishing the idea that it could be so soon. He placed a hand on Lorn's shoulder. "Thank you, Lorn," he said earnest. "Is there anything else you need? Anything I can do for you?"

The young messenger gave him an impish grin. "I doubt you want to give me a bath, my lord, and that is all I need right now."

Traejan chuckled and gave the Sylvan a hearty clap on his small shoulder. "You bring good news, young elf, but not that good. But you do have my leave to restore yourself as needed."

The messenger gave the prince and the others one last bow before pulling himself into the saddle of his calypso and departing through the stable gates at a smart trot.

"Do you still wish to confer with your father and brother?" Ryen asked as they watched the small elf ride away.

"No," Traejan replied. He took a deep breath and then sighed. "But we must." He gave the Norseman a sidelong smile. "Care to join us?"

The Vikeman gave the prince and his Praetorian guard a grin and a quick shake of his head. "I think I will pass, if you will allow it. I feel a family argument on the horizon, of which I want no part. I would rather partake of Gnomin cider and bawdy jokes than a royal elfin court."

"I would rather as well," Traejan admitted. "But, for me,

there is no choice."

The Norseman laughed and grabbed his khusar by the reins and stuck a booted foot into a stirrup before he pulled his mighty bulk up and into the saddle. "There is always a choice, young prince. You can always choose your fate, even by the moment, for that is when and how all fates are decided."

Traejan felt his heart catch at his words and watched him depart through the postern gate. Ryen had been much more jovial when they had first met, nearly a year ago. He was still blithe, but his demeanor towards the prince had changed. It could have been due to the impending war and the fact that the lives of the Norsemen as well as his own were now at stake, but the young elf doubted it. The change was slight, but it wasn't there before Traejan had told the Vikeman of his short affair with the Roshan, and his insistence that she loved him.

The young prince shrugged off the feeling of gloom that wanted to descend upon his shoulders and left the stable with Dell by his side. He thought about how he would be seeing Ember in just two weeks. Less, if Ryen was right. He could not keep the smile from spreading across his face as they crossed the bailey and entered the royal castle through the kitchens. He passed through the sculleries, oblivious to the sounds and smells as the preparation for dinner was underway, thinking about what he would say when he saw her again. It was a scene he had played a thousand times in his mind but in every mental depiction they had been alone.

The prince and his guard skirted the Great Hall and took a side passage in silence and Traejan was suddenly vexed about his first meeting with Ember after so many months apart.

It doesn't matter, Traejan decided as they made their way to his father's offices. *I am finally going to see her again,* he thought, his heart beating faster. *Smell her, touch her.* The ideas bloomed into memories and his mind was full of the scent of wild roses and leather and iron. He recalled perfectly the feel of her skin beneath his hands, the feel of her lips pressed against his own. He paused, suddenly lightheaded, as they reached the atheneum. Two guards stood on either side of the doors and one moved quickly to open the door on the right. The prince took a second to gather his thoughts and emotions before he entered. *When the time comes,* he decided, *I will follow her lead.*

Unable to keep the grin from his face, he and Dell stepped into the room just as Zephyrn came running down the hall, breathless, to enter right behind them. Traejan turned his smile to his younger brother and Zeph drew back, almost into the arms of his own Praetorian, Dirk.

"Whoa!" the younger prince cried, flipping a thatch of blonde hair away from his face, his blue eyes full of surprise. "Your..."

"Traejan!" their father called, "Zephyrn!" Both turned as one. King Rowland, flanked by Xander on his right and his counselors on his left, was bent over a map with his palms flat on the table. He beckoned to his younger sons as he stood upright.

Drustin, a counselor to Acqtraejale Royce and veteran of many wars from long ago and far away, stood close across the table. Acqtraejale himself, Traejan's grandfather, stood slightly apart from the group, peeling an orange. Dirk remained by the door while the other three hastened to join the others. King Rowland dipped his head towards Dell.

"Sir Dellion," he greeted.

Dell bowed. "Your Majesty."

Traejan, flanked by his guard and his younger brother, approached the others gathered around the table. Drustin stood aside for the prince who looked down at the map and recognized it in a glance. It was one of Kriegslager and the surrounding lands that went all the way south to the three rivers that separated the Northlon from the Midlon.

"You have heard?" the king asked. "That a small army from

the Southlon is on approach?"

"I have," Traejan affirmed. Dell concurred with a nod.

"I as well, Father," Zephyrn agreed.

"Good," the king acknowledged. He pointed at the map, a slender finger with a heavy gold ring indicating the Elfin Greatwood to the south of Kriegslager. "If they continue on the same course outlined by our riders, they will come through the woods here."

"Trampling a path for the Crommags," Xander said with no small amount of disdain, "should the monsters take the same course." Traejan bristled and opened his mouth to object but someone spoke for him.

"Or," the Battle King interjected from where he was listening, dropping orange peels onto a golden tray, "they are purposely getting a look at the land the Crommags are sure to occupy. And getting a good measure of our defenses." He gave Traejan a wink and popped a segment of the orange into his mouth.

Traejan grinned at him before giving a nod to his brother and father. "He is right," he agreed. "They will be seeing our defenses from the viewpoint the Crommags will have when they get here. Our last report said they should be here no later than midsummer. The Southlon troops should be here in as little as ten days. I think all we need to decide right now is whether I should ride out to meet them with a platoon of our own soldiers or ride ahead with a small party of Jägers to..."

"You?" Xander asked with a soft chuckle. "You will not be riding out to meet them, not with anyone."

Traejan looked at his father, his brown eyes full of disbelief, and the king gave a nod to the affirmative. "We were just discussing how this should be handled when you and Zephyrn arrived. We do not think..."

"That I should be the one to receive them even though I know..." Traejan interposed only to be interceded by his older brother.

"You should not interrupt the king!" Xander scolded, a deep furrow between his dark brows.

"And you should not interrupt me," Traejan retorted, keeping his voice even. "You are not the king. Not by a long shot."

Though they did not yell at one another, the animosity of their exchange was apparent and the silence that fell was thick. Glances were exchanged between the others around the map.

"Traejan!" King Rowland admonished. "Xander!" His sons continued to glare at one another from across the table and he looked from one to the next until they relented their stares and met his eyes with their own. When they finally did, both looked down, chagrined. Rowland's face and voice both softened. "We will follow royal protocol in this case." His eyes went to Drustin.

The elf was gray of hair and eye, scarred and battle-seasoned eons long past. He had been put in charge of the elfin cavalry and was called upon for every council that concerned the approaching war.

"We will take thirty soldiers, all on horse, to meet the troops from the Redlands," he told the others as his gray eyes scanned their faces. "Plus the king, his sons, and their Praetorian." He looked down and tapped the map. "Our company will halt here. The crown prince will ride out from there to parley with their leader. He will be escorted by four Praetorian guards. The king will stay with the main party, also with four Praetorian soldiers." His eyes glanced up and found Traejan. "You and I will be at his left flank, with ten swordsmen and a platoon of your best archers."

The young prince knew that such a large party demanded attendance by the king, and saw the military logic to keep the elfin king at a safe distance until they were sure that the oncoming army was indeed friendly, but logic was all but nonexistent in matters of the heart.

"I think I should be with Xander," he advised, "to ensure his safety. Or better, to ensure everyone's safety, I could ride for Amherst with a small party of Jägers to meet the oncoming force and ascertain their intentions."

"How noble of you," Xander said, though his tone and expression did not match his words. "But Drustin's plan is the one we will use."

"Dell can..." Traejan began but his father cut his argument short.

"Sir Dellion will be by your side and you will be by mine!" the king growled. "You two command our military, you will ride with our military!" His words were delivered in a tone and force than he had never used until now and it made all present draw a quick breath.

"Yes, Father," Traejan said bowing his head.

Dell, who had been silent the entire time, bowed his head as well.

"I will stay here and guard the castle," the Battle King offered in hopes to break the tension.

King Rowland straightened and his expression softened by fractions. "I think that is an excellent idea," he agreed, tugging down on his doublet as his eyes shifted to his father before taking in the others. "You are all dismissed. We can discuss more details as they arise. For now, I would like to speak with my sons."

As the others bowed to the king and took their leave, Traejan turned to Zephyrn. "And just where will you be for all of this?"

Zephyrn gave his brother a charming smile. "Next to you, of course. I am dying to know what is actually going on with you."

Traejan's brows went up over his soft brown eyes. "What do you mean?"

Zeph's smile widened. "When we came in here, your eyes were blue," he said. Traejan's brows went up even farther though he could not say that he was surprised, recalling what his thoughts had been when they had reached the atheneum. "And," Zeph added, "I have the feeling it wasn't the first time."

⊂ဒ⅋⊃

To the west of Tuar Ceath, past the mountains and the Echo Sea, a storm blew down from the Mountains of Blood, unleashing torrents of rain upon the river lands of the Northlon. The tribes of the Great Men that had come down from the Bitterlands sulked inside their tents and eyed the shimmering curtains of water with suspicion.

The leaders of the clans had told them that it was only snow that had melted, which made sense, but snow had never come down with such ferocity. Snow did not soak tents or clothes the way this falling water did, making an entirely new kind of misery. It seemed more likely that it was the wrath of some god that was displeased.

It seemed even more likely in the morning. All of the wagons were hopelessly stuck in the mud.

"Should we try to pull them out?" Pel asked.

"They would only become stuck again," Yon said.

"Should we leave them?" Pel asked. "Carry what we can?"

"What should we do?" Yon asked. Both Great Men looked to their leader.

"Give me a few minutes," Ayala instructed. He was about to duck back inside his tent when movement on the horizon caught his eye, making him freeze. It was far away and disappeared back into the trees like melting ice. Ayala growled. They had been plagued by ethereal figures in the distance that would appear at times only to vanish. Ayala knew they were elfin scouts, reporting on the movements of the Great Men. "Go find a Walrus Man," he instructed Yon, "ask him how to trap a walrus."

Yon raised a brow that was thick and flat but left to do as he was bid as the leader of the Great Men went back inside his tent.

What to do? What to do? Ayala agonized over it. He decided then that the hardest thing about being the Leader of the Great Men was making decisions. Odd, he did not remember it being so difficult in the past.

I always had Noga with me then. Did I let him make the decisions? Ayala wondered suddenly. But the answer was no. *I made the decisions, but Noga helped me. How did he help me?* The Great Man listened to the drip of the water from the leaves off nearby bushes and trees. It seemed as if even the drips and drops were questioning him. *How did he help me?* Ayala thought. *That is the question.*

The question.

He asked me questions. My answers led to my decisions. A broad grin spread across the Great Man's gruesome face as he made the realization.

I can ask myself questions.

But what do I ask? The Great Man laughed at his predicament and then heard Noga speak in his head. It sounded so like his brother that he jumped.

What do you want most? Noga asked.

I want to get there quickly, Ayala answered immediately. *As soon as possible.*

Well, what is slowing you down?

Moving with so many people. And now those damn wagons! And I hate those damn elves, spying on us!

I think you have your answer.

Ayala realized with a shock that he did. He felt proud that he had done it on his own and was already looking forward to telling Noga about it when he saw him next, which he guessed would be no more than a week now. Something else to be glad about. He had missed his brother more deeply in the past weeks than he would ever admit. He shouldered his way out of his tent just as Yon was returning.

"We are going to separate into groups," he told them, and proceeded to tell them his plan on how many groups and how many men. "We will leave the last group behind with the wagons. Once the land dries, they can follow. We can take the handcarts, they are lighter and they will roll over the mud without getting stuck."

"We can move much faster in small groups, and without the women and children," Pel said with a grisly smile.

"We will get there even sooner than we had anticipated," Yon admired aloud.

Ayala gave a quick nod at their praise. "What did the Walrus say?" he asked.

"Goo goo g'joob," Yon answered and all three broke into laughter. The joke never failed to crack them up. Yon continued when the chuckles died down. "He said you don't trap a walrus, you hunt it with spears. But, he said, you can trap seals."

Ayala grinned, showing all his fangs. "Good. Tell him I have some little seals for him to trap."

◯ℨ℞◯

Towards the middle of camp, in a threadbare tent, Gunta squatted on the wet floor with another miner named Karl. The living conditions for the Gnomin had improved slightly, but not much. They were dirty and gaunt. Their hair and beards were matted.

The march south had been long, but being in air that was their natural climate rather than the freezing weather north of the Siber Massif had done them a world of good. Plus, they were now allowed to have fire, which meant they could cook whatever scraps of food were thrown to them by the Crommags.

They were still malnourished and miserable, but no one else had died.

Gunta had brought Karl to the side of the tent furthest from the flap and squatted down with his back to it, though Crommags were not known to go into their shelter. Still, it was better to be safe. Gunta flipped over a piece of cloth on the floor and revealed an object with a long wooden handle topped with curved blade that was flat on one side and pointed on the other.

"A really big axe?" Karl asked. He looked up as Gerta kneeled down next to them, handing them wooden bowls full of steaming soup. It was thin, mostly made of boiled goat bones and some purple root the Crommags carried, but it was hot.

"Thank you," Gunta told her with a smile before she moved off, then turned his attention back to Karl. "It's called an adz," he told him. "It is what the those tall and creepy Crommags wanted. But I made a little adjustment."

Karl watched as Gunta picked up a small hammer and, turning the handle of the adz, struck a near invisible pin towards the top. He hit it again and most of the long handle fell away and Karl grinned. "Now it's an axe," he said, pleased.

"And if you turn it this way?" Gunta asked, flipping the now much smaller tool easily in his hand.

Karl sighed. "It's a pick."

Gunta nodded, his blue eyes gleaming in his thin dirty face. "Eventually, these monsters are going to stop. And when they do, we are going to dig ourselves out."

Karl looked at the other miner with tears in his hazel eyes and then blinked them away as he had an idea. "Have you put those hidden pins in anything else?"

Gunta shook his head. "Just these, so we can use them when the time comes."

"We could put them in the weapons as well," Karl suggested. "In the swords, where the hilt meets the blade, or the maces, just about anywhere. If we knock the first pin out, the next time the Crommag swings the weapon – or maybe the second time – that other pin will come loose and the weapon will break."

Gunta grinned at Karl. "That is a good plan."

⋗⋖

Twelve days later, Traejan sat astride Peg, gentle fingers of air rifling through his sandy curls and caressing his stern face. Though spring was nearly done in, the elfin kingdom was still part of the Northlon - it would not be truly warm until midsummer (and then only during the day) before cooling again after just a few weeks, melting into an early autumn.

Dell was to his left, astride his own mount, and to *his* left were thirty more elves on horseback. The ten elves in front were swordsmen, ready to ride to the aid of the crown prince, if need be. Behind them were twenty archers, ready to cut any threat to pieces.

In front of them, mounted on the swiftest steeds in the elfin kingdom, were Xander and Garamond, flanked by two more of Xander's Praetorian. To Traejan's immediate right were Zephyrn and Dirk. Beyond them was their father and their father's Praetorian guards as well as Drustin and another counselor, Duncan. Like Drustin, Duncan had served the Battle King in the wars of old. The elf was as gray as the other and bore the ghost of a slash on his left cheek, along with another scar that extended from the outside corner of his right eye to his temple.

The entire group was gathered where the crumbling cliffs at the edge of Fosse Meadow softened into a slope. Below them all stretched the grasslands the elves called Morgan's

Vale - where, if they were correct in all their suppositions, the battle for Tuar Ceath would be fought. Beyond the grasslands rose the Elfin Greatwood, miles of spruce and soldier pines that stood between Tuar Ceath and Goodman's Bay.

The Gnomin and Vikemen alike had been notified of the approaching army and had been asked to keep a low profile while the elves rode out to meet them. Xander was bound and determined to keep everything as formal as possible.

Zephyrn's mount danced sideways to the left, and then back again. "Do you think..." the youngest prince began to say but then stopped himself, suddenly sensing what his horse had picked up on two seconds ago. The breeze shifted, bearing the sounds from so far that they would only be detectable to elfin ears. Other horses on approach. Zephyrn's pointed ears twitched amid his light blonde locks of hair and in the distance he could hear more than just horses.

The scrape of stirrups against the girth straps of the saddles whispered through the forest beyond. The soft clink of metal bridles and fastenings. The creak of leather, the minute rattle of swords in their scabbards.

The sounds, for the elves, preceded the riders by minutes.

Their ears could distinguish the sound of horse's hoofs from the march of soldiers. They could discern that the riders and marchers alike had been divided, if only slightly, suggesting the formation of columns.

The whispers and murmurs of tack and weapons became a soft clank and clatter to the ears of those that waited upon the ridge. Still, no rider or soldier was yet to be seen.

Finally, shadows among the trees followed their sounds. Moments later, six riders emerged from the forest. Foremost among them was a small rider on an unholy and enormous mount unlike any horse outside of the Spawning. It was covered in smooth black skin; its only hair was a great tuft upon each fetlock and a rippling mane of black silk. In place of teeth it had fangs that dripped with foam and red eyes stared wildly from their sockets.

The rider of the Night Stallion was a woman, dressed in dark ashen pants and blouse and a black cloak that trailed over the rump of her stallion. Her hair was the color of blood streaked with honey. It poured from her head like an autumn sunset to the nape of her neck where it was twisted into a braid that fell over her left shoulder. Traejan felt his heart stop within his chest.

She wears her hair down now, he observed, breathless. *Or she wears it down for me.* When he first met her, over year ago, she had continually tied her red tresses into a knot on the back of her head. The result, to him, looked like the nest of a small animal. His chest swelled more with every breath. Zephyrn looked askance at his brother and, seeing his eyes, a knowing smile spread across his young face.

The riders, except for the woman in black, all wore shades of red. Burgundy riding pants and loose crimson shirts. None wore cloaks. They stopped when they spied the elves and the Night Stallion stamped the ground with massive hooves, pulling up grass and clods of earth in consternation. Behind them, only shadows among the trees, Traejan could see two columns of mounted soldiers.

After a momentary pause, knowing that the time was upon them, Xander and Garamond put their heels to their mounts, urging them down the slope. The riders below conversed quickly and commands were called out over their shoulders before they too rode forth over the grasslands, leaving their troops concealed amongst the trees.

"Six riders for our four," Dell said softly to Traejan. "Would you like me to send another pair of swordsmen?"

The young prince shook his sandy curls. "If she means to kill him, twenty more swordsmen would make no difference, much less two." His remark was made without so much as a glance at his Praetorian. King Rowland, however, did not miss his words and looked sharply at his son.

"She has chosen her captains well," Zephyrn observed aloud. "They look young and strong."

"If she truly is the one that commands them," Duncan replied, "which I still find hard to believe."

"And young and strong they may be," one of Rowland's guards commented, "but none look wise or battle hardened."

Traejan gave his dark-golden head a barely perceptible shake and stifled his own remark. *None among the elves save for Duncan and Drustin and the Battle King himself are battle hardened, you fool.*

They watched as Xander and the others reached the bottom of the slope and reined in their horses, waiting less than a minute for the approaching riders to cross the field. When they did, both sides observed one another for a moment before the Dark Lady swung down from her colossal mount and dropped to the ground. The other riders with her followed suit.

Zephyrn was correct, they did look young and strong. All five were dramatically handsome and unique in their looks, but it was the one who had ridden next to the Roshan that drew Traejan's eye.

He was human, as the other four appeared to be, with a square jaw and narrow chin. He had raven black hair and eyes as dark as ink in a well. His skin was deeply tanned, though not quite dark enough to be brown. Traejan could see the outline of round muscles under his crimson tunic. Unlike the other four, who remained with the horses, he stayed as close to the Roshan as if he were her shadow. He was as tall as a man, standing half a head taller than her, but his face was smooth and unlined.

"He can't be more than, what, twenty-eight?" Traejan queried softly.

Dell's dark eyes followed his line of sight and shook his head. "Younger. Twenty-three, maybe four."

Who is he? Traejan wondered with a growing unease. Then

his eyes were drawn back to Ember, approaching the elves where they had stopped at the bottom of the slope. The young man moved as if tied to her with a string.

The Roshan called a halt with just a whisper and elves and humans eyed each other for a moment before the elves dismounted without a word.

Xander's party left their horses and slowly crossed the space between. They stopped with a good three feet still between them and appraised each other in silence for long seconds. From his vantage atop the bluff, Traejan could clearly see Ember and her men. He could discern the faces of his brother and his guards, but only by a fraction. He could not see their eyes.

Finally, the dark-clad woman bowed low to Xander. When she rose, the breeze pushed tendrils of red hair from her face and Traejan felt his breath hitch in his chest. Though she was down the slope and a good fifty yards away, he could see her eyes with perfect clarity - bright brown, edged with black and shot with green and amber and gold.

"I am Ember donnis L'chiross," she told Xander, "and I come on behalf of the Red King, Marco Trapoya. I am here to offer what services I can, what men I can, and any aid I might be unto your people."

Xander's chin dipped the slightest bit in acknowledgement before there was a pause, a stillness of breeze and breath, and Traejan realized what she meant to do next.

The Roshan Simorgh threw back her cloak and the young prince felt his hands curl into fists around the reins of his horse, holding back the words that screamed within his mind.

No no no no no no no no!

Xander stood, straight and proud, waiting his due.

Don't do it, Traejan prayed silently. *Please! Do not! Do not kneel! Do not kneel before my brother!*

Peg, sensing his turmoil, danced nervously beneath him.

Traejan jerked reflexively on her reins as he watched his teacher, *his love*, sink to one knee before his older brother. It took all the control he had not to rush to her side and yank her to her feet, ungraciously but happily kicking Xander into the dirt in the process.

She bowed her head and her red braid fell forward like a rope of blood. Then his eyes caught her face, and saw what no one else did. Her smile. Her crooked, mocking smile that told him she bought into none of this. Ember L'chiross may sink to her knee, but she would not prostrate herself before anyone. There was no obeisance, no deference, and certainly no defeat. She was there for reasons of her own. His hands relaxed as he watched her stand. The raven-haired young man stepped forward quickly as if to help her to her feet and then stopped short as she rose, hovering just behind her shoulder.

Traejan's brows pulled together and his hands clenched back into fists. Beneath him, Peg snorted and tossed her white mane.

"Your help is not only accepted, but gladly welcomed," Xander told the Roshan warmly. "I believe you know my brother?" She nodded once, but did not look away from the crown prince. Xander smiled knowingly and Traejan, catching a glimpse of it, wondered exactly what he knew. "He can show where we have made camp, and introduce you to a few of the captains. Garamond will see that you have everything that you need."

One of Xander's Praetorian guards stepped forward and bowed.

"Thank you," she said, "but I believe we have everything that we need, I just need to know where you want us."

Xander nodded, pleased. "Garamond will see to that, then. After you are settled, it would be our pleasure if you would join us for dinner. Our captains will be there and it would be an opportune time to meet and even make some preliminary plans. Unless, of course, it is too soon. You have traveled far and if you need more time to rest and refresh yourself, it is more than understandable."

The Dark Lady gave the crown prince a shark-like grin. "It is never too soon to plan against an impending danger, my lord."

Traejan flinched, hearing her address his brother in such a way, but it was only to be expected.

"We have accomplished much," Xander informed the Roshan, "but there is still much to do. My brother, Traejan, will serve as a liaison between our combined forces - but should you ever desire to speak personally, or if there is anything you need, please do not hesitate to send for me."

The red-haired warrior bowed to the crown prince again, making Traejan's skin crawl. Xander gave her a nod and took his leave. Both parties returned to their horses and remounted. Xander's party, save for Garamond, turned their horses to climb the slope. Garamond joined the emissaries from the Redlands as the dark commander issued orders. Two of her riders wheeled their mounts and returned to the columns. Three remained, including the one that hovered at the Roshan's side.

Traejan frowned as Xander and his guards rejoined him and the other elves atop the slope. It deepened into a scowl as Xander put his horse between his brother and the riders in the vale. He fought the urge to move Peg so he could see around him and instead met his brother's eyes with his own.

"I will escort father back to the castle," Xander told his brother. "You and Sir Dellion are to escort the officers of the Red King to Kriegslager and see them settled."

"I remember," Traejan said. It was one victory he felt he had scored. The job had been originally designated to Alastair and Nevin, two of Dell's former Jägers that had been promoted to captains in the elfin army, but Traejan insisted it should be himself along with Dell. Since they were both prominent leaders in the army, his father had relented.

"Afterwards, meet Halloran in the white cabin," Xander instructed him, "with the captain of the crimson troops, if she is not too fatigued. He will be going over preliminary plans with the Vikemen and it would be better if everyone could be there at the same time."

Traejan held back a sarcastic remark. "I understand," he replied, keeping his voice even and respectful.

Xander gave him a look that said he thought otherwise but gave his brother and Sir Dellion a nod. He put his heels to his mount and moved quickly to join his father's party and escort them back to the royal castle.

Traejan pulled sharply on Peg's reins and her hooves danced to the left, turning quickly, and there she was.

She was nearly halfway up the slope, every step bringing her closer.

"I can see what had you in such a fuss," Zephyrn remarked under his breath.

Traejan shushed him and waited, his heart kicking in his chest. In a matter of moments, she was finally there.

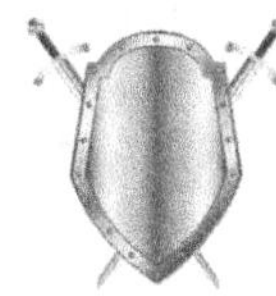

9. THE GRIZZLED COMMANDER

The black-clad commander sat astride her giant Night Stallion, a beast so large that it put her eye-level with the prince, though he was taller and on higher ground. Dell's mount wanted to shy away from the horse, if it could be called that. Its great size, demonic eyes and foam-flecked fangs were enough to strike terror in any man or beast. Peg, however, was quite familiar with the monster and wanted to move forward to greet him. Both the prince and his Praetorian held their horses still.

Next to the red-haired warrior, on a slim roan that danced nervously from side to side, rode the young man with deeply tanned skin. Up this close, Traejan could see even better his strong jaw, full lips, and dark eyes. More than handsome, he was strikingly beautiful. He remained close to the Roshan as if charged with her protection.

Discomfited, the prince's gaze darted to the two others that flanked his former teacher. Mounted on barrel-chested bays, these men were also remarkable in their looks. Both were tall and lean and young. One had a sharply squared jaw, light brown hair, and eyes that were the color of honey. He was more broad-shouldered than the other, who had a pointed chin and hair like summer wheat with darker brows over eyes that were a startling blue and framed by dark lashes. Traejan disliked them all instantly, but none more than the black-haired youth by the Roshan's side.

The Roshan. Traejan's eyes found her, and found her penetrating gaze staring straight into him. Her eyes were like strange jewels, mostly brown but shot with green and amber and gold. Traejan knew without having to be told that his own brown eyes were turning blue just looking at her.

"My Lord Prince," she greeted, bowing from her seat in the saddle. He expected her to smile at him as she straightened, or to laugh at the formality or senselessness of the whole charade. But her face remained straight, and quite relaxed.

"Roshan," he greeted with a nod, just as formal though he was troubled inwardly.

"These are two of my captains," she said. "Gavan…" and here the young man with brown hair and golden eyes urged his mount a few steps closer "… and Rhys." The handsome youth with blue eyes and dark lashes gigged his horse closer and bowed his head of thick flaxen hair. She did not introduce the man at her side.

Traejan was careful to keep the consternation from his face. He also noticed that while the two captains each wore two swords, one long and one short, the young man by her side wore only a long knife. *What in the Seventh Circle?* the young prince wondered as he bowed his head in recognition to the entire group.

"This is my brother, Zephyrn," Traejan said by way of introduction, motioning to the youngest son of the king.

"My Lord Prince," the dark commander acknowledged, bowing deep from her seat on the Night Stallion.

Zephyrn gave her a mischievous smile, his blue eyes bright. "My lady," he greeted with a nod of his blonde head.

"His Praetorian, Dirk, and I believe you are acquainted with Sir Dellion?" Traejan asked without so much as a glance at either of them.

"Yes," the Roshan agreed, "though only by letter." Still, she gave a small but formal bow to the elf who responded with a prolonged nod of his dark curls.

"If you would let me escort you," Traejan continued, "I can show you where we have made camp in anticipation of the

Crommags. And where you might wish to bivouac as well."

"Certainly," the Roshan agreed, urging her Night Stallion forward to accompany the prince as he turned his palfrey at the top of the slope. Peg whickered a greeting to the beast and it gave her an amiable snort in return as the other riders fell in around them.

The elfin prince led the way, full of strife and confusion. *Don't be a fool!* he told himself. *She certainly cannot leap into my arms in front of her own troops and mine.* Still, he was wracked with doubt. There was no hint of a smile, no conspiratorial wink, not even a glint of light in her eyes that was just for him. His chest felt constricted, as if squeezed by a giant hand.

"Your training is serving you well?" she asked with the same nonchalance one would use in a parlor asking about the weather. Her eyes were everywhere as they approached the camp, everywhere but on him.

"It is," the young prince replied. "Thank you."

"You have been responsible for training your troops?"

"The infantry, yes."

"I have been responsible for our company of archers," Zephyrn piped in, leaning forward over the horn of his saddle so he could see past his brother. "Along with Alastair, of course," he added.

Ember looked past the young prince towards his younger brother, smiling at her, then back at Traejan, an auburn brow arched in silent question.

"Alastair is the captain of our archers," he informed her stiffly as the horses neared the camp. He glanced at the Roshan but her eyes were running across the newly inhabited meadow, taking in everything in a single sweep.

They were almost to the three large wooden structures. To the left of the buildings were rows and rows of orderly tents made of uniform gray-green silk. Five larger tents of canvas and hide were on the right side of a wide path that, if followed in the opposite direction, would take them back down the slope.

"This was well-planned," she said, eyeing the forestlands behind what were clearly Gnomin tents. There was a good hundred yards between the treeline and the edge of the bluff that continued west for a quarter of a mile.

"We had the help of over seventy Gnomin miners," Zephyrn informed her, "both in planning and building."

The dark commander gave a quick nod. "I thought as much." She glanced over a cloaked shoulder to make sure that the columns behind were on the move and, seeing that they were, urged her horse forward once again. "Do you mean for us to camp along the line to the right?" the Roshan asked, directing the question to Traejan, though she did not look at him.

"It seems fitting in both plan and purpose," he said, keeping his eyes fixed ahead. "Unless you think..."

"No," the dark commander interrupted. "It will serve well. These five large tents already raised to our right," she said motioning with her chin, "those belong to Vikemen?"

"They do," Traejan agreed. "Ryen Glace, along with nineteen other men from the Vikes, have come to give their support."

The lips of the Roshan curled up at this news, making the elfin prince rankle with irritation.

"If you are not too tired from your journey," Traejan continued, his voice slightly louder than it had been, "I can show you around the camp and introduce you to the other leaders that are here."

The dark commander glanced at him, her lips still turned up. "I am sure I will manage, my captains as well." She gave him a nod and looked over her left shoulder. The dark-haired youth was by her side in a breath. She spoke softly to him but Traejan caught every word, as did the other elves. With elfin hearing, it would be impossible not to hear even whispers at such a distance - not that it was meant to be private. Traejan was the only one jolted by her words.

"Raise our tent there," she instructed, lifting her chin towards where the five large tents ended. "Close to that big yurt, but not too close."

Our tent?

Traejan found himself powerless not to stare at the black-eyed young man on the nervous roan.

She glanced at the blonde-haired man next. "Direct my column there," she commanded, pointing. "Your troops to the east of mine, and Gavan's next to yours."

The blonde youth named Rhys gave her a curt nod. "It will be done," he assured her.

"Please," Traejan said, lifting his chin, "take time to unpack and refresh yourselves. If you can…"

The Roshan held up a black-gloved hand, cutting off his next words, as she looked over her shoulder to mark the progress of her troops. The foremost riders had reached the top of the earthen ramp and were drawing to a halt.

"Set camp," she instructed her men. "Do not pen the horses, yet. Have them staked outside the same quarters as their riders, and have them quartered along the ridge. Foot soldiers should be to the north, with supply and support north and east of them."

Gavan and Rhys responded with one nod to their dark commander and then another to the elves before turning their horses towards the east side of Kriegslager and galloping off without another word. The raven-haired youth paused, as if waiting more instructions, but the Roshan jerked her head in the direction of the departing captains and he put his heel to his skittish roan and galloped after them.

Traejan was not sorry to see him go.

"Who oversees your troops?" the Roshan demanded once

they had departed. "Do you command the captains?"

Traejan dipped his head. "I do. Along with Dell and an elfin warrior from…"

"Take me to him," the Roshan commanded. "The sooner we all meet, the sooner we can organize. Time is the first enemy we must face, Elfin Prince."

The young prince froze and then gave her a nod before prodding Peg gently in the flanks. He had thought (hoped, at least) that once free of her troops, she might return to her former self. He knew she was undoubtedly the most lethal warrior living in the New World. She was serious but she was not without humor - often a begrudging one. He had seen her smile a hundred times, even if it was a mocking grin that bespoke a latent and dangerous temper. He had heard her laugh – throaty chuckles and girlish giggles.

More than the warrior he had known her to be, she was the woman who had melted into his arms just one summer past. The woman who loved him and swore to him that he was the first she had ever truly loved - and that he would be the last.

Traejan led the way, his mind and insides in a turmoil.

Ember gigged her Night Stallion and the attenuated party approached the new-made structures and the Roshan glanced at the elfin prince. "Your brother called this place Kriegslager?" she asked. The young prince nodded without looking at her as the horses brought them closer. "Do you know what that means?" she asked, arching an auburn brow at him.

"It means war camp," the prince replied, keeping his face forward.

The Roshan gave a short chuckle. "It does indeed," she agreed. "It does indeed."

The horses moved purposefully onward with their riders, trotting gracefully until they were pulled up to a halt some yards from the middle building and she cast a glance over her black-cloaked shoulder.

The two captains and the young man on the roan broke to the right just as the column leaders were crossing the space between the bluff and the encampment. Their troops followed in precise military parade. Gavan and Rhys signaled to the column leaders and the equestrian infantry changed their course a fraction to meet the captains where they waited.

"Traejan said your skill with a sword is unsurpassed," Zephyrn said to the Roshan as their horses continued on towards the wooden structures.

"Did he, now?" the Roshan asked, a mocking smile barely surfacing as she regarded the youngest prince.

"He did," Zephyrn affirmed, "and I have seen how skilled he is after training with you. With the threat of the Crommags, elves have been training in swordsmanship once again, myself included." He paused and gave her a beguiling smile. "Perhaps, when you have the time, you can show me a thing or two."

The Roshan stared blankly at the young elf for a moment, so astounded by his suggestive tone and glib demeanor that her own words fled. Her first instinct was to laugh in his face but, as he was a prince and one of her hosts, she had the wherewithal to simply bow her head.

"Certainly, my lord," she agreed, her sardonic smile tucked into the corner of one cheek.

Traejan felt his skin prickle in irritation, both at her and his brother. Zephyrn was being flippant to the point of embarrassment. Traejan knew that his brother's words carried a double meaning, one that the Roshan did not miss.

"Zephyrn," he said pointedly, moving forward to break the line of sight between the Roshan and his brother. "Perhaps you should ride ahead to Tuar Ceath," he suggested. "Let Xander know that we will be there for dinner."

"And miss her meeting Halloran?" Zephyrn replied with a nod towards the dark commander. "Not a chance. And, besides, Xander already expects you for dinner."

"Halloran?" the Roshan asked, looking askance at Traejan. "He is your commander?"

Traejan's lips finally breached a smile. "We have referred to all of our different leaders so far as captains - save for Dell who, as Major, manages them all. But, if there was a single commander, Halloran would be it."

"The grizzled commander," Zephyrn snorted.

The Roshan raised her brows but neither brother offered further comment so she followed Traejan as he guided Peg in front of the wooden structures. He stopped in front of the largest one in the middle and swung down from his saddle. It was across from this building the corals for the Elfin Cavalry had been erected. It was empty of horses, but there were supplies and feed, as well as a pair of elfin grooms.

Traejan handed Peg's reins to a waiting groom who took them without seeing the prince. The young elf meant no disrespect, he was simply trying not to recoil from the Night Stallion that now loomed over his head like a reaper.

The Roshan swung a leg over the back of the monster and dropped four feet to the ground, landing lightly on her feet although there was a soft chime of metal, perhaps only detectable to elfin ears.

She tossed the reins to the small elf. "Feed him some oats, unless you want him to eat *you*," she warned.

"Y..y..y..yes ma'am! I mean, my lady!"

Traejan avoided rolling his eyes, but only by shifting them away for a second. "Give them all oats," he instructed, "but keep them saddled."

The frightened groom nodded enthusiastically as he handed both sets of reins to the other wide-eyed elf before quickly moving to take charge of the other horses.

The young prince fixed his brown eyes next on Garamond. "Please check with the red troops to see if there is anything they require," he instructed. "Then find Master Glace. Tell him the captain of the red army has arrived." The elf nodded and rode away, leaving the Roshan with the young princes and their Praetorian. Traejan turned and led the way to the last building. "The structure on the east side," he told the Roshan, "we will use for supplies, including a storehouse of weaponry. The center one will serve as a mess hall…"

"For soldiers," Zephyrn interrupted, dipping his blonde head towards the Roshan's ear as if to share a confidential morsel, "not officers or those of royal blood."

"I am neither," the dark commander told the younger of the princes with a look that mingled amusement and disgust as she walked briskly. "I will eat with my men, wherever you deign to put us."

The young prince looked at her from under his pale blonde hair, his blue eyes flashing in the sun as they passed in front of the large building towards the smaller one to the west. "Do not take my words in disrespect, my lady," he said quickly. "I will wait on you myself, if you wish."

"That won't be necessary," Traejan answered as they reached a set of double doors to the smaller building that was, as of yet, unguarded. Dell and Dirk took a few long strides to put themselves ahead of the small group and pull open the doors. "This," Traejan said softly, standing aside for her at the opening, "is where the officers will meet to do most of our planning. We call it the white room," he said with a smile that was both amused and apologetic, "for lack of a better name. Or, sometimes, simply the cabin."

It was the closest she had been to the young prince since their parting almost a year ago and Traejan could feel the heat from her body as she walked by and her scent filled his nostrils. The breeze pushed her black cloak away from her lithe form and brushed the stray hairs from her face. The young prince found suddenly that he had to turn away as she passed in front of him and needed to restrain himself from grabbing her arm and demanding she tell him what was happening.

The Roshan entered the building and took the entire area in with a single sweep of her gem-like eyes. "The War Room," she surmised aloud, her voice so low that it was almost a purr. Her soft tone was one of long-awaited contentment. "This is where I will be."

The structure was made of birch logs, large and white, mortared with a pale mud clay. It had a plank floor topped with tables of white ash. A few maps were carefully placed on their tops, held down on the corners by smooth stones. The Roshan saw that each table held a map depicting a different region around the elfin kingdom. She hoped they had been wise enough to have a commander for each of them as well as planned defenses.

Barrels, only partly stocked with rolled maps, stood sentry to the tables. Three pairs of braziers, one on each side of the center walkway, were filled with wood but unlit at this time of day.

At the center of the structure was a table larger than the others by far, this one completely littered with maps and presided over by an elf of great size and age. He leaned across the table, knuckles planted on its surface over the span of a broad map, two younger elves at his right elbow. He looked up as the company approached and then, seeing who it was, dismissed the younger elves as he himself straightened and waited, polite and calm.

His hair was iron gray and clipped short, showcasing his long, pointed ears. His face was more square than narrow, which was odd for an elf, and creased with scars of both time and war. His gray brows arched high above eyes the color of steel and he lifted his chin as the small party approached, bowing deeply when they stood before him.

"My lords," he greeted in a voice so graveled that it bespoke centuries of tobacco use and a good deal of shouting, "welcome."

"General Halloran," Traejan replied with a dip of his sandy

locks. "I would like to present Captain L'chiross."

The Roshan approached the grizzled commander, trying to control her look of puzzlement, and stuck out a black-gloved hand before he could even begin to bow. "Please," she instructed, "call me Ember."

Surprised, the old elf grasped her small hand tightly in his own. "Certainly," he agreed with a smile while the red-haired warrior stared at him. His gray brows rose higher over his steely eyes. "Is something wrong?" he asked, his voice a low growl.

Ember smiled apologetically. "I'm sorry," she said quickly, not taking her eyes from his face. "I've never seen an elf..." she trailed off, expectant. She could sense Zephyrn by her side, smiling and unhelpful, as the commander's gray brows went up even further. "I mean," she continued, "never seen an elf with..." she motioned to her own jawline with a black-gloved finger.

"Oh!" the commander exclaimed, a smile breaking across his face. "The shadow!" His hand went up to rub his chin, a chin that showed the stubble of a salt and pepper beard. "Yes," he said, his tone thoughtful and touched with a feigned melancholy, "a gift from a human somewhere back in my bloodline."

"A human?" Ember asked, astonished before she could recover herself. "I am sorry, Commander." she apologized quickly, casting her eyes down. "I meant no disrespect. You just," and here she chuckled softly as she looked back up him, "caught me off guard. It does not happen often."

Halloran echoed her chuckle. "No apologies necessary," he consoled. "I shave it to fit in more with my people, but it has been a part of me so long that I forget it surprises others."

Ember dipped her head in understanding. "I run into the same thing from time to time - sometimes from my hair but more often from the fact that I am a woman."

"I can imagine," the commander agreed, jocund.

"Our differences aside," the Roshan continued, "let us speak on our common cause. What is your best strategy for winning a war, General?" she asked, again surprising him as she quickly changed tack.

The grizzled elf looked thoughtfully at the dark commander. He measured her eyes and found himself being measured in return. Another surprise. A large hand rose to stroke his stubbled jaw as he thought and when he spoke again she realized that, along with his gravelly voice, he also had an accent that was different from the other elves. It came rolling out from deep within his chest while he spoke slowly and enunciated carefully - as if every word was the beginning a long story.

"First," he said, "I ask myself if there is any way the war can be won without actually having a war. If the answer is no, I ask myself if there is any way the war can be won without fighting. If the answer is still no, I think of the fastest way to send my enemy to the Seventh Circle."

Ember bowed her head to him and then favored him with a smile. "You are both a wise and patient strategist indeed. I always skip those first two."

The commander favored her with a smile of his own. "Have you ever fought in a war, young lady?"

Ember almost laughed. She did not remember ever being called a young lady. "No, sir. Many battles, but no wars. Nothing this grand."

Iron gray brows drew together over steel eyes that had gone cold as Halloran frowned. "War is not grand. It is a horror. Sometimes you will think you are in the Seventh Circle yourself."

The dark commander dipped her head of blood-red hair in apology. "I beg your pardon. I meant, nothing on so grand a scale."

"Ah!" The elfin commander leaned back and nodded

approvingly. "I see. Of course! Well, wars are merely battles of a different sort. Some are large, some are small, sometimes many at once. But they are all important."

"Indeed," the dark commander intoned. "I have brought three hundred soldiers, including myself. How can I be of use?"

"You are the most skilled fighter in your group?"

"In this whole damn army!" a voice boomed. Ember turned to see the Vikeman, Ryen Glace, standing inside the doorway of the room, grinning broadly. Her impulse was to run and jump on him but she quashed it immediately, knowing she would lose the respect of the general if she acted like a child. Worse, like a girl. Instead she bowed to him as he entered the cabin.

"Master Glace," she greeted formally, bending at the waist. Now Ryen's laughter echoed off the wooden walls as he entered, followed by another Vikeman who had to duck low to clear the doorframe. Ember spied him as she rose from her exaggerated bow and her tawny eyes widened.

The Roshan had seen many Norsemen in her travels but none that were bigger than Ryen. Yet this man was both more broad in the shoulders and at least half a head taller. She forgot what she had been about to say as their eyes met and at the same instant a smile spread across his face.

My Gods! Ember thought as the two bordermen made their way closer. It took her breath away to look at him and she did not stop to wonder why. He was handsome to be sure, but it was his height that she marveled at.

He is so tall! And those eyes!

She could tell that she would barely come up to his chest. The thought wanted to chase a shiver down her spine but she braced herself against such a weakness. Ryen was speaking but she could not follow what he was actually saying.

Some bullshit, no doubt, her mind whispered amiably as she stared at the giant following her old friend. *In a second he will be standing next to me,* she thought breathlessly. She knew she was gawking and could not help herself.

Ryen was still blathering on in his normal jovial tone but it was not until he finally stood before her that she pulled her eyes from the colossal man at his elbow and held out her gloved hand.

Ryen glanced at her hand and with another resounding laugh, grasped it and pulled her into an embrace, squeezing her tight. He gave her a zestful kiss on the top of her head and then leaned down. "You owe me more later," he said into her ear, incorrigible as ever and making no attempt to keep his voice low. The Roshan pushed him away, clapping him hard on his arm.

"It is good to see you, old friend," she exclaimed with a grin before shifting her gaze back to the Vikeman that loomed over his shoulder. Ryen turned to Traejan and Zephyrn and dipped his rose-gold head.

"My lords," he greeted before turning to Halloran. "Commander."

They murmured greetings in return as the Roshan waited out the formalities with mounting impatience. Ryen finally turned to the blonde Norseman who had not taken his eyes off of the Roshan.

"Ember, this is Crag," he said. "Of all the Vikemen here, he is the most seasoned fighter. Other than myself, of course."

The giant Norseman stepped past Ryen and grasped the Roshan's gloved hand, making it disappear entirely. "Ember," he greeted warmly, his voice deep. "A fiery name for a fiery woman. Though not quite appropriate, as you seem more like the fire itself, rather than the remains."

The Roshan gave her red head a quick shake. "A man may pass his hand through fire unscathed, but to touch an ember will leave a scar forever." Ryen chuckled in agreement as the small warrior continued, looking way up into the face of the Norseman. "*Your* name is the one not appropriate," she remarked. "A crag is a cliff, whereas you look more like the entire mountain."

The Vikeman laughed heartily at that, most of the others joining in albeit in much softer tones. "You have me on that one," he told her, "but in my family, I am my mother's smallest son." The elves looked at the giant borderman in amazement and a wry smile touched the Roshan's lips.

The look on Traejan's face however, was far from amused. He had watched the quick reunion of Ember and Ryen with a sick sort of dismay and the short banter between her and Crag with a slight horror. It deepened as Ember continued to stare openly at the hulking Norseman as he turned to the grizzled commander and held out a hand the size of a bear's paw.

"Commander Halloran," he exclaimed, "I don't believe we have been formally introduced."

Halloran let his hand be swallowed by the massive fist of the Norseman as he gave it a firm shake. "Not yet," he agreed. "But you are well met."

"Ryen said you are an experienced fighter?" she asked and Crag gave a quick nod.

"In my borough, boys are fighting as soon as they are walking."

"No girls?" the Roshan asked, arching an auburn brow at the blonde warrior.

"None that look like you," he returned with a smile.

"Alright!" Ryen interrupted with a look of irritation that was only partly feigned. "Crag has more experience with Crommags than any of us – fighting, tracking, knowing their habits, etcetera."

"Excellent, that will be of great use to us when the time comes."

"Is that time not now?" Ember asked, cocking her head. "I would think that we should start planning as soon as possible."

"We should," Halloran agreed, his voice a soft growl, "but not without the other captains. And before we plan, we need to organize. Establish a chain of command along with proper titles and ascertain who is charge of what, where and who else." He looked at the two princes, flanked by their Praetorian. "Would you agree my lords?"

Traejan, who found nothing agreeable about the meeting, nodded nonetheless. Zephyrn did likewise.

The grizzled elf looked at the others and continued in his gruff voice. "We can speak more this evening, if time and company allows. Otherwise, we will be meeting here every morning from here on out. I know Captain L'chiross, even if not weary, would like to see to her troops and see them settled." The dark commander gave a quick nod of assent. "Gentlemen," he said to the Vikemen in a tone that left no doubt they were being dismissed. "My lords," he said, nodding to the elves. "My lady," he finished with a short bow to the Roshan. The Roshan dipped her head in response.

Zephyrn took a step towards her and Traejan stepped deftly between them. She looked up at him - for though he was not as tall as the Vikemen he was certainly taller than she was. A lock of red hair had come loose and lay stranded on her cheek and he felt himself torn with emotion.

"The other captains will be at dinner tonight," he told her. "You can meet them then." The Roshan gave him a nod but her expression gave him nothing. He almost said that he would return to escort her, then changed his mind. "I will send an escort for you," he said stiffly, then gave a short and equally stiff bow before turning on his heel and leaving the room, Dell a silent shadow at his side.

"That won't be necessary," Zephyrn informed her with a disarming smile as they and the Norsemen made their way to the exit. "I shall escort you myself." His own Praetorian trailed a few steps behind as they went through the door, a slight smile of his own edging his lips.

The Roshan was about to object when Commander Halloran called Crag back for a question. He excused himself and Ember, wanting to speak privately with Ryen, acquiesced quickly to the young prince simply to be rid of him.

"If you can find me at the appropriate time," she told the elf, "I would be honored." She gave him a short bow and he dipped his blonde head in acknowledgement to both her and Ryen as they left the white room behind, then turned on his heel and headed for the Gnomin camp to the northwest.

"Come with me," she told Ryen. "I want to get a look at the vale from above while my tent is being raised."

 10. OLD FRIENDS

The Vikeman and the Roshan rounded the corner between the white cabin and the large pavilion the Gnomin had built as a mess hall. A few steps took them away from prying eyes and Ryen picked her up for a more private embrace, holding her tight against him. Ember laughed breathlessly as he put her down, kissed both her cheeks and hugged her again with her feet on the ground.

"It is so good to see you!" he exclaimed. "Believe it or not, I was starting to worry! I expected you to make it here weeks ago, before me even."

"It is good to see you, too," she told him, grinning. "But an army, even a small one, moves much slower than just a few riders."

"It does. And better late than never."

Ember snorted. "I'm hardly late."

"Late for me. You will be a nice change of company. I have already tired of smelly Vikemen."

Ember gave him a crooked smile. "No elfin women have caught your eye?"

"Plenty," Ryen admitted. "But all in the kingdom proper are too reserved. And I haven't sunk, pun intended, to Gnomin women. Not yet anyway."

Ember laughed. "You haven't changed a bit!" She nudged his frame with her shoulder and started walking with him between the white cabin and the mess pavilion.

"I can't say the same for you," he admonished. "You look the same, as always, but you seem different."

As if to prove his point, at that moment Garamond and an elfin soldier rounded the edge of the pavilion and walked towards them on their way to the cabin. Ember paused at their approach and bowed low.

"My lords," she said, as they passed by.

"Captain," they acknowledged in turn, dipping their heads as they pressed on.

"Stop that bowing," Ryen scolded after they had passed. "It's unbecoming of you, plus you look ridiculous."

Ember laughed with the delight of a child. "You should have seen me earlier this morning," she confided as they continued on their way. "I got down on my knee before Prince Xander."

The Vikeman's lip curled up in obvious distaste. "I'm glad I wasn't there for that. Besides, I thought there was only one prince you…" Ryen's words stopped short. Faster than a whip Ember had whirled and was pressed against him, the point of a dagger against the skin of his neck.

"Unless you want your next words to come from a hole in your throat, my friend, you might want to swallow them."

The apple in Ryen's throat moved slowly under the tip of her blade as he did indeed swallow – not just the words he had been about to say, but his continual astonishment at her speed and sudden turn of temper. Then his face split into a huge grin. Within a breath Ember could not help but return a crooked smile of her own. Her dagger disappeared and they continued walking as if nothing had happened.

"Speaking of Gnomin women," she continued, "is Gatha among them?"

Ryen shook his head. "She had come with the initial party, but left almost immediately – so I was told." They reached the back of the pavilion and turned left, the cliffs and the valley to their right. "Do you love him?" Ryen asked, not ready to drop the subject but neither ready for her answer. "Or was it just a summer romance?"

Ember gritted her teeth. "How do you always know everything?" she asked, her brow furrowed.

"I have my ears and I have my eyes," he told her and then smiled at her look of irritation. "But, in this case, he told me."

That caught her by surprise. "He did?"

"He did," Ryen affirmed. "And he was very adamant about it, though I did not believe him."

Ember slowed their steps as they passed behind the pavilion, wanting more time alone with the Vikeman. "I don't want to talk about the elfin prince, or what happened between us. I have more pressing matters at hand."

"Does that mean I still have a chance?"

"A chance at what?"

"You, you numbskull."

The Roshan snorted. "What would you want me for? You have more women than I have bottles of wine, and go through them just as fast."

"Maybe," he acquiesced with a smirk as they walked closer to the edge of the bluffs, "but I'm not going to let you go without a fight."

Ember shook her head as she glanced up at him, giving him a wry smile. "Behave yourself," she scolded.

"We'll see," he answered with a sly grin.

Her tawny eyes swept across the prairies below that were carved into a bowl shape by the cliffs that curved around them. "This is good," she said appraisingly. "A large river runs to the east?" she asked, moving east herself again.

"It does," Ryen agreed, walking slowly by her side, watching her take everything in. "Your tents are hardly up yet," he noticed aloud. "Let's stop for a drink."

"I'll never turn that down," the Roshan said, grinning up at her friend. He looked down at her and, for once, his smile was wistful.

They crossed the road that sloped down into the valley. As they reached the yurts of the Norsemen, Ember paused to survey them. They were tall and wide, with entrances suitable for the size of the inhabitants. Ryen pointed to one and led the way, opening the flap for the Roshan who was able walk through without having to duck her head.

Heavy cloth covered the earthen floor and cots lined the canvas walls. Two braziers lay cold and unused at the back next to piles of furs. Small tables and large chairs had been unfolded in the center of the structure and weapons lay wherever they had been dropped. The whole place smelled like a pair of old and dirty boots.

Two Vikemen with hair the color of a darkening sunset were there sharing a jug of cider and Ryen introduced them as the brothers Haldor and Halvar. Haldor had a mighty beard that matched his wild orange hair while Halvar had a mustache that hung down on either side of his wide mouth in long braids bound with silver beads.

Along with Ryen, Ember pulled up an oversized camp chair and shared their cider and a good deal of vulgar banter with them. Within half of an hour they were all joined by Crag, who had to stoop to enter even the high flaps of the tent. He was slightly breathless, as if he had made the trip back from the white room in a hurry. A grin spread across his face, seeing her there.

Ryen drained the horn in his hand and stood up.

"Thank you, gents" he said, "but we should be getting along."

Ember drained her own horn as he pulled her to her feet.

"Are you sure?" Crag asked, closing the distance between them in only three strides and bringing himself up close to the

Roshan. Ember had to crane her neck back to see him, making her red braid swing between her shoulder blades. Ryen cocked his head to peer up at the other Norseman with a look of annoyance.

"I'm afraid he is right," Ember affirmed. "I should see how my own troops are progressing."

The giant Vikeman's mouth was slightly open and she could see the tip of his tongue run along the edge of teeth that were white and even. "Alright," he acquiesced, moving his huge form gracefully to the side. "Though you must promise me a moment or two at some point. I have heard much about you, but would like to get to know you myself."

The Roshan grinned, unable to tear her gaze away from his green eyes. "It seems that my reputation has preceded me, on many fronts. I will do what I can."

Ryen made a grunting sound and wrapped a hand around her shoulder, guiding her to the front of the yurt, keeping his body between her and the blonde Norseman. She managed to turn enough to take in the brothers with a sweep of her flashing eyes and gave them a grin as they saluted her and called out to come back at any time. Then she was half-propelled through the high entrance. She looked up at Ryen as soon as they were outside.

"I've never seen a Vikeman with that coloring, have you?"

The Norseman gave her a shrug though he kept his gaze fixed ahead as they moved past the Vikeman camp.

"His eyes, especially," she continued, her voice soft and distant. "I have seen many green eyes before, shades of olive, forest, and hazel. One woman, in Redtown, had eyes like emeralds. But his... I have a dagger in my collection, made of polished stone rather than metal. I can't recall the name of it..." she trailed off as she searched her memories.

"Jade," Ryen said, his voice flat.

"Yes," she agreed, "that's it! Jade."

"It's very common in his borough."

"The stone or the eye color?"

"The eye color," Ryen retorted, irritated.

The Roshan gave him a sharp poke in the ribs with a finger and he swatted her small hand away. They left the Vikeman encampment behind and were greeted by the sounds of shouts and busy hammers as they crossed the short distance to where most of the new tents had already been erected. Row upon row of burgundy canvas had been raised and secured with stakes and ropes, most of their flaps tied open. Firepits were being dug in front of each and wood was being stacked. Five tents were larger than the others, four of them denoting the tents of her captains. The first one, closest to the yurts and also the largest, was Ember's.

As the Roshan and the Vikeman approached, the young man with black hair and dark eyes walked out. His shoulders were broad and his crimson shirt did not hide the well-muscled body underneath. He spied the Roshan and moved quickly to meet her.

"Ryen," Ember said when the young man had reached them, "this is Ian. Ian, this is Ryen, a good friend of mine."

The young man smiled, showing a row of perfect teeth, as he offered Ryen his hand. Ryen shook it, though he looked at the youth with a good deal of suspicion.

"A *very* good friend," Ryen added. "And you are?"

"My steward and squire," the Roshan answered for him, throwing the Norseman a look of annoyance before she turned her face back to Ian. "How goes it?"

He switched his dark eyes to the Roshan, his handsome face lighting up. "Very well. The Gnomin are on the far side of the encampment, helping build the latrines as you instructed. Gavan and Rhys are setting up a perimeter and posts for guards. Troy is seeing to the cavalry horses and Richard is seeing to personal mounts."

"Ah!" the Roshan exclaimed. "That reminds me, send Richard for Coal once there is a tie for him."

"Already done," Ian said, turning away so she could see where a giant eyebolt had been driven into the ground next to her tent. Tethered to a smaller eyebolt was his own horse, the skittish roan he called Meghan. "Would you like me to get him myself?"

"Please, and thank you. I am sure that poor elf is ready to be rid of him." Ian acquiesced with a nod and turned to leave but stopped as she spoke. "You have done well," she said over her shoulder. The young man beamed at her, gave another nod to Ryen in farewell, and turned and left. The Roshan glanced at the Vikeman and, seeing the look of distaste on his face as his blue eyes followed the departing youth, she laughed. "Come on!" she said, smacking his chest with the back of a gloved hand and heading for the entrance of her newest domicile.

Ember pushed aside the flap and entered her tent. Ryen followed, having to duck to clear the entryway but able to stand once he was inside. She took in everything in a glance and nodded approvingly. Heavy rugs had been unrolled to cover the floor. There was a desk guarded by a pair of chairs. On the desk were some rolled parchments along with an uncorked bottle of wine, a clean cup, and a tented napkin. Ryen lifted the napkin to see a carefully arranged plate of nuts and cheese. He rolled his blue eyes and finished surveying the Roshan's current residence. Wooden crates lined the burgundy canvas walls and braziers stood in each corner - stacked with logs, ready to supply light and heat when it got dark. In the back were two cots with bedrolls, one on each side, with a square, flat-top trunk of polished wood between them. On top of the trunk was a basin and a pitcher of water.

"Two cots?" Ryen asked, a ginger brow arched high with sarcasm. "Not a double cot? Or a single set of bedfurs?"

The Roshan gave him a wry smile as she pulled off her gloves and threw them onto another trunk. "Not quite cold enough for that, yet."

Ryen's lips pulled down at the corners as she pulled off her cloak and tossed it over her gloves. His eyes traveled over the crates lined along the walls as she poured wine into the cup and sat in one of the chairs. She kicked the other one towards Ryen in an invitation to take a seat but his eyes were still on the wooden boxes stacked against the burgundy canvas.

"Weapons?" he asked, his face riddled with confusion. The Roshan gave him a look of exasperation and he sighed. "Wine," he realized aloud, making her laugh. He went to the box that was already open and moved the lid aside, peered in, and retrieved another cup. He poured himself a measure from the open bottle and sat in the chair facing the Roshan.

"Tell me about your men," she instructed, moving the napkin and selecting a piece of cheese. Ryen frowned.

"Tell me about yours," he retorted, rather sour. "There seem to be quite a few of them these days."

"Stop it," she said.

"Stop what?"

"Acting like a child."

"I can't help it. You bring it out of me."

This time it was the Roshan that made a sour face. "Well, you need to get it together," she told him. "We are preparing for a battle like none we have ever seen. Romantic affairs have no place here." Ryen grunted in what she hoped was an assent and took a drink from his cup.

"Tell me about Crag," Ember prodded, drawing a look from Ryen that made her laugh. "What?" she asked.

"You'll do well to stay away from him," he warned, pointing a finger at her.

"Why is that?"

"I don't like the way he looked at you, or the way you looked at him!"

The Roshan laughed. "You mean the way I *stared* at him?" she asked. "Circles, Ryen! He's almost as big as a Crommag! I'm sure he gets stared at everywhere he goes. And you better get used to men looking at me. I am one of very few women amongst hundreds of men – they would stare even if I was covered with warts."

"I get that," Ryen grumbled. "But the way he looked at you was different. I know that look, I've seen it before."

"I'm sure you have," the Roshan agreed, her cup paused before her lips, "every time you look in a mirror."

Ryen gave her a look of exasperation. "Very funny," he said, sarcastic. "But keep your distance. His people are well known to be rapists, and worse."

Ember's auburn brows went up as she sipped her wine. "What could be worse than rapists?" she asked, putting down her wine and wiping her mouth with the cuff of her dark sleeve.

"They are known to be incestuous as well. As a borough, they want to keep their bloodline pure. The crazy bastards believe they are the direct descendants of Odin himself. And they don't just rape their own kind, but Crommag women as well, if they can get their hands on one. The Gnomin are not the only race hunted for sport, you know."

The Roshan sighed. "I'll keep what distance I can," she told him.

Ryen relaxed a bit in his chair and then straightened as something occurred to him. "You said you were one of a few women here, not the only woman here. Did you mean the Gnomin women?"

The Roshan pursed her lips as if unsure or perhaps unwilling to answer. "No, I have a few women from Redtown – and before you can say anything I will give you the same advice, stay away from them."

"Mmhmm," the Norseman murmured in mild accord.

Ember shook her head in exasperation selected another

piece of cheese from the plate on the desk. Ryen looked up to the sound of hoofbeats outside the tent, followed by a good deal of snorting and stomping.

"It's just Ian," she said, "with Coal." She could hear the young man's soothing voice as he secured the Night Stallion and unsaddled the great beast.

"And just where did you find that boy?" Ryen asked. "A pillowhouse in Redtown?"

The Roshan smiled. "Not exactly, though he spent most of his life in one. How did you know?"

"I know the look," Ryen said, his voice and expression laced with disdain. "Did you save his life?"

"Just his hand."

"I'm sure he appreciates it just as much."

Ember laughed. "Well, you are correct, except that he is not a boy. He is as old as I am. Older perhaps."

Ryen's blue eyes narrowed in suspicion. "That can't be."

"It is. How long were you in Redtown?"

The Vikeman's broad shoulders went up in a shrug. "Not long. Why?"

"Did anything there strike you as peculiar?"

"Many things."

"Did you notice that the people there all seem to be roughly the same age?"

A look of surprise crossed Ryen's face, quickly replaced by one of understanding. "Not that exactly but, now that you mention it, yes. I noticed that every person I saw was very good looking, beautiful in fact, and some of them looked eerily similar. What struck me the most was that there were no children."

The Roshan nodded as she swirled the wine in her cup. "You are correct on all counts. Marco risks much by sending these men." Her eyes flicked up as the flap of the tent opened to allow Ian to pass through.

Ryen's expression fell as he regarded the young man with raven hair.

"Coal is settled," he informed the Roshan. "Can I get you anything?"

"Yes. Find Sedhi and Ellie. Let them know I will need something to wear tonight for my dinner with the elves. Nothing too fancy."

The handsome youth gave her a smile, showcasing his perfect teeth. "And?"

The Roshan sighed. "And probably not black," she said in mock defeat. Ian gave her another dazzling smile, sharing it with Ryen as well, as he left the tent. The Vikeman watched him go with a look of distaste that bordered on jealousy before his blue eyes darted back to the Roshan.

"Sedhi and Ellie?" Ryen asked suddenly, remembering two of the women he had met on his visit to Redtown. To say that they were beautiful would fall far short of the mark. "They are here?"

Ember could not help but grin at him, her face full of love and amusement. "We're two daggers in the same clutch, aren't we?"

Ryen returned both her grin and expression. "We certainly are, my dear. We certainly are."

 11. FORMALITIES

Traejan rode hard for Castle Song after leaving the white cabin, much harder than was needed. Dell kept pace and kept quiet, letting the prince work through his ire. Upon reaching the stables, the young elf slipped down from his horse the moment she slowed and stormed through the yard like a roll of thunder, leaving Dell to collect Peg's reins and turn them over to a startled groom with instructions for both of their mounts.

Dell entered the castle moments later, looking right and left for his charge. His dark eyes met those of a steward who looked meaningfully at the staircase that led to the south tower. The Praetorian heaved a sigh through pursed lips and puffed cheeks and headed for the stairs.

Five, ten, fifteen, twenty... Dell counted the steps as he wound his way up and around, around and up. Two hundred and eighty steps and he stood in front of the door to Traejan's bed chamber. There was no need to knock, the door had been thrown wide open and left that way. He could see the prince pacing furiously in front of his cold fireplace. The Captain of the Jägers entered and the young elf whirled on him, his fists clenched in fury and frustration.

"Could you believe that?" he demanded of his guard. "Could you?"

Dell's hands dropped to his sides as his heartbeat began to slow its rapid beat from the strenuous climb. "I'm not sure what you..." he began when the prince cut in quickly.

"Her!" he shouted. "Him! All of them!"

Dell, though they were twenty stories high and quite alone, decorously closed the heavy oak door. Ponderous, yet almost silent, it swung home with a muted *shwump* and the Praetorian raised his high, elfin brows at his charge. "All of them?" he queried.

"Yes!" the young prince confirmed heartily, as if Dell had agreed with him. "All of them!"

His guard absently fingered the hilt of the dagger on his hip and waited for an explanation. The wait was short.

"Zephyrn!" Traejan cried in amazement, holding up his hands as if beseeching Dell for an answer. "Acting like child! A child with a crush and a, a, a..." he trailed off and began pacing again, unable to find an appropriate word for his brother's inappropriate behavior. "Ryen!" the prince continued, shaking his sand-colored hair over his pointed ears. "At least he was no worse than I expected. But that brute of a Vikeman that he brought with him!" Traejan spat and cursed in Elfin.

"Crag?" Dell ventured.

The prince whirled around to face his guard, his expression bright with rage. "Yes! Crag!" he agreed. Then his face darkened and his hands curled into fists. "And how could she stare at him like that? That *garish beast*! I can't believe..."

Dell's dark eyes grew incrementally wider by the second as he listened to the prince rant and rave until he sucked in great breath of air and let it out in a roar.

"Traejan!"

Glass rattled in the high windows and cold ashes fell in the hearth. The young prince froze in his tracks and stared at his guard as if slapped. There had been no formal title, not even a sarcastic one. And never before had Dell shouted at him. Yet the Praetorian drew up his five-foot frame and faced the younger, taller elf with indignant authority.

"Get ahold of yourself!" he ordered, his voice dropping to a hiss. The Jäger tugged on his vest and took a deep breath of air through his nostrils, trying to get a hold of his own anger and compose himself. One deep breath was all it took but his next words were not easy for him to say. "I know," he started, then took another deep breath, as if preparing for a plunge, "I know that you love this woman. And I do not know the depth of that. But I do know that the elves of this world – our people, *your* people - are facing *annihilation*, and that the other races will suffer the same fate as well should we fail. I believe that matters of the heart should pale next to such a thing! Am I wrong?"

Traejan's face tightened into a mask of pain and anger and grief. He wanted to shout at Dell that he *was* wrong, that *yes*, love was more important than anything else in the world. He wanted to leave the castle and ride to where Ember was setting camp and settling the troops that had come to their aid. He wanted to shake her, he wanted to yell at her, he wanted to kiss her, to do anything that would elicit a response greater than the flat and emotionless look she had given him, the horribly distant tone she had used when speaking to him. He wanted, he wanted, he wanted...

It does not matter what you want, you fool. What matters is your duty.

The resolve that the Roshan always armored herself with began closing around his own body as well. Cold steel clamps on his mind and his heart and his soul. The iron fortitude that was a warrior's responsibility.

Shamefully, Traejan felt himself fight against it. Forcefully at first, his arms straining against unseen shackles, his legs pulling against invisible chains - but his strength was quick to fade. To fail as a warrior would be to fail himself, to fail his family and his people, and to fail her most of all.

The elfin prince hung his head and his sigh ended in a choking sob. For two seconds his body shook, warring with his emotion. His passion made one last mad attempt and his body wriggled as his heart commanded him to dash past Dell and go to her. Then the iron resolve became steel and he straightened as it encased him from head to heel.

His ragged breathing smoothed out and became even. His eyes were surprisingly dry and his mind clear. It took the young prince a moment to become accustomed to the feel of strength that surrounded him, but it took hold with a startling surety.

"No," he told Dell, in control of himself once again. "You are not wrong. I beg your pardon, Sir Dellion."

Dell's shoulders slumped. "There is no pardon needed, and certainly no need to beg. But your people need you. Believe it or not, *I* need you."

Traejan sighed again but this time it was free of grief and full of determination. He clapped Dell on the shoulder.

"I don't know if my people need me," the elfin prince admitted, "but you certainly do."

Dell sighed. "Then grab a quick lunch, meet with your captains, and dress for dinner." A hopeful smile broke across his countenance and his arched brows rose up over his dark eyes. "You are the only date I have."

He saw his smile mirrored on the face of the prince.

"What else is new?" Traejan chortled as he bowed to his guard.

Dell's smile faltered. The transformation had happened so fast that he could hardly believe it, and now he was abruptly hesitant to leave. "Are you sure you are alright?" he asked.

The young prince nodded. "I was foolishly unprepared," he admitted. "I am now."

The Praetorian looked him over doubtfully. "Alright," he acquiesced, his smile returning as he pulled the door open and headed down the staircase.

The smile on Traejan's face slipped away and he straightened slowly, drawing himself up. It truly felt as if he wore a suit of armor.

It was a bit constrictive, and warm. But there was strictly no room for hurt, which he liked. He rolled his shoulders back, as if adjusting a cloak for comfort, and remembered something that Ryen had once told him about Ember.

Her heart has no walls, the Vikeman had told the young prince. *That is why it does not hold fear. I am afraid however, that in the same manner, it does not hold love either.*

Traejan had been daunted by the statement at the time, but also had refused to believe it. Something about it, though, made sense to him now. The armor he now wore, the armor of a warrior, kept out the hurt. And the love was, now, something distant. Part of him battled against it, and the armor shimmered for a moment like a desert mirage, but the warrior won.

He grabbed a quick lunch, just as Dell advised, and then met with his captains. Dell was but a shadow as always, but the prince could feel his approval. As he dressed for dinner, Traejan could feel something else as well. It was a heat, coming from the invisible armor he had used to cloak himself. When he stood before his long mirror late that afternoon, after he had readied for dinner, he realized what it was.

It was anger.

Not raging or defiant, just present. Like a dangerous stranger, armed and watching from the shadows.

The day was deepening into twilight and shadows skulked along the walls and huddled in corners. The torches were yet to be lit but dusk was seeping into Castle Song. It crept like a mist between the stones and gathered in every recess, swelling up through the towers and oozing through each staircase and passage.

The prince smoothed down his vest and descended into the darkness.

❧

Castle Royce was anything but dark. Candles, torches, and electric flambeaux lit every corridor and courtyard as if it were midday. There was music and laughter and a feeling of normalcy that cheered every soul, at least every soul not wearing a sword. Word had been passing that forces from the Southlon had arrived to aid the elves. Whispers were exchanged about their commander.

Running the length of the great hall was the arcade, a long gallery with fluted columns and a steeply arched roof. Large curved beams of ivory stretched upward from the carved pillars, dividing the ceiling into triangular sections that were covered with a glittering mosaic of tiles in white and green. One long side had enormous doors that opened onto the great hall. The other had glass doors that had been thrown wide for the party so guests could walk out onto the flagstone courtyard and enjoy the evening air.

Parties of the elfin aristocracy stood in small groups both inside the arcade and outside on the patio as servants passed between them, offering drinks and savories on gleaming silver trays. Traejan moved gracefully through the throngs of those gathered and joined the royal court inside while Dell, who had been at his right arm as ever, melted away to join the other Praetorian guards. The protocol for court was quite different from that of the atheneum or the white room.

The queen was attended to by no less than half a dozen elfin women garbed in gauzy gowns of pearlescent gray. His father, the king, was backed by his two closest advisors and Xander was accompanied by his young wife, the lovely Maralan.

Those of royal blood were clothed in shades of ivory and cream, save for Traejan who wore a dove-gray vest over dark gray linen shirt and pants. Gray boots with brass buckles came to his knees and his longsword hung from hip.

"Mother," he greeted, giving the queen a light kiss on one porcelain cheek and then the other. "Father," he said next, giving the king a short bow. Xander, as his brother, did not require a formal greeting, but his wife, Maralan, certainly did. Traejan bowed to her as well. "Maralan," he said, "you look absolutely beautiful." The lovely Maralan blushed and gave a half, yet formal, curtsey to the young prince.

Traejan noted that Zeph was not present, but did not dwell upon it. He had undoubtedly stayed behind at the camp to escort the Roshan. A serving girl paused with a tray of drinks and Traejan plucked up a glass of cut crystal filled with summerwine. He was careful to select a glass with a silver stem, rather than gold. The gold-stemmed glasses contained honey, something of which he wanted no part.

His mother put her own, empty, gold-stemmed glass on the tray and selected another as she turned her light blue eyes upon her second son. Her gaze traveled down his body and her lips pursed slightly in distaste. "Traejan," she scolded lightly, "your clothes are so dark, especially for this time of year. And must you wear a sword to dinner?"

Traejan smiled at her. "Mother, there will be a great many men here wearing swords. It is best you get used to it." His mother gave him a faint look of displeasure, both at his suggestion and his facetious tone, and sipped her honeyed wine as a small line formed between his brows. "Speaking of which, how do you have the tables arranged for dinner?"

The queen brightened. "Oh! I have it arranged perfectly. Xander has given me the names of all the captains and they each have their own table, surrounded by the finest ladies of the court along with a stolid elf or two for good advisement and conversation."

Traejan drew up slightly and the hand holding his wine dropped in accordance with the corners of his mouth. "That will not do at all," he said, his eyes searching out his mother's attendants and beckoned to the only one he recognized.

Gelica paused momentarily and then hastened to the side of the prince.

"All of the captains need to be seated at the same table," he instructed. "It does not matter who is next to who, as long as they are together."

Gelica's blue eyes darted nervously to the queen, who was about to protest until the king himself gave her attendant a nod to continue, and to do it quickly. Gelica hurried away and the queen looked at her husband and son with equal disapproval.

"This is dinner, not a war meeting!" she scolded quietly, eyes the color of a spring sky darting to and fro. She smiled broadly as she did so to hide the discomfort she felt, and to assure those who might be watching that everything was perfectly fine.

Traejan, who normally would have cringed at displeasing his mother, found that his newfound armor kept him safe in this realm as well. "I am sure all will appreciate the lovely evening you have provided," he consoled, "but these men will be fighting and dying alongside one another within a matter of weeks. It is only just that they get to know one another."

"To what end?" the queen asked lightly. "By this time next year they will be consorting..."

"By this time next year?" Traejan cut in, his brown eyes wide under his raised brows and keeping his voice as hushed as he could. "Mother, let your keen eyes mark all of the men in here tonight," he commanded and then watched as her blue eyes traveled over the arcade that was quickly filling, especially now that the upper class was joining the aristocracy. "If half of them remain," Traejan continued, "it will be a miracle."

All eyes of the small royal party darted about the long room and the outdoor patio, disconcerted by the stinging words of the young prince, before they moved to the queen. She gave a dainty sniff, as if troubled by the onset of a summer cold, and then nodded graciously to her son.

"Very well," she acquiesced. "I know nothing of such matters as war, and I will defer to you in this case."

Traejan gave his mother a disarming smile. "I promise the only battle you will have to see tonight," he assured, "will be the ladies fighting to dance with Zephyrn."

His mother laughed, always delighted by the proposition of antics by her youngest son, and the sudden mood of solemnity was lifted.

"Speak of the devil," Xander remarked and all eyes followed his gaze to where Zephyrn was entering the other end of the arcade accompanied by the woman commander of the red troops and the tall and lean commander of the Vikemen.

Ryen Glace wore a long jerkin the color of a dried pumpkin over tan breeches. A short sword hung from his belt in an ornately decorated leather sheath. The Roshan wore a shirt of claret silk under a crimson vest. Rust colored pants that fit close to her slim form were tucked into brown riding boots that had been polished to a high shine. Her red hair was down and outshone her boots by far.

"Who is that woman Zephyrn is with?" the queen asked, watching curiously as the dashing young prince introduced the Roshan to those along the way.

"That," Xander said, "is the commander of the troops sent to us by the Crimson King."

"It is?" his mother asked, her eyes as blue and wide as a summer sky.

"Indeed," Xander affirmed, "the same warrior that trained Traejan last summer."

"That is the master fighter?" the queen asked, her delicate white hand fluttering to her chest. "A woman?" She looked to Traejan but spoke again before he could answer, looking back at the person in question as Zephyrn introduced her to an elfin lord and his wife. "Ah, yes! I seem to remember that being mentioned somewhere. I must have forgot. Well, she is not as brutish as I would expect, especially for a human."

"How very noble of you, Mother," Traejan said, a smile ghosting his lips.

"Thank you, son," she replied, her eyes on the trio as they made their way towards them, oblivious to her son's delicate sarcasm. "She is dressed like a man," the queen remarked. "But at least she had the decorum to come to dinner unarmed," she added, throwing a meaningful glance at Traejan.

The young prince laughed softly. "Trust me, Mother," he said, his sand-colored locks shaking with his mirth, "she is armed to the teeth. Zeph better watch where he puts his hands, unless he wants to be missing one, or both." Traejan laughed harder at his own remark, his hand coming up to cover his mouth as his mother's eyes shot daggers at him. "Excuse me," he apologized, "but I should go see if Gelica needs help rearranging our guests."

The royal party bobbed their heads in unison as he departed and then turned in the same unintended synchronicity to watch the approach of the youngest prince and the odd pair he was escorting. Zephyrn, like most of his family, was dressed in shades of white. His blue eyes shone from under his swath of pale blonde hair. He gave Xander and Maralan a nod of greeting before facing his parents.

"Mother, Father, I wish to present Ember L'chiross of the Midlon, and Ryen Glace of the Vikes." The Vikeman and the Roshan both bowed as Zephyrn turned to them, smiling broadly at Ember. "This is my father, King Rowland of Arcadia, and my mother, Elyse of Seleucia, Queen of the Elves."

The royal pair dipped their heads in polite recognition and, as they had both already seen Ryen a number of times, kept their attention fixed upon the young woman. "So very nice to meet you," the queen said, her voice light and cheery.

"And you as well," Ember agreed warmly. "I can see where

Zephyrn gets his fine features," she said, "if it is not too bold a thing to say."

The queen laughed, delighted. "Not at all," she assured the woman warrior. "And what a lovely…" she paused as her eyes traveled over the Roshan's body as she searched for the right compliment, "…outfit you have on."

Ember glanced down at herself before looking back up at the queen. "You think so?" she asked. "It's borrowed, actually," she admitted with a crooked smile. "Everything I own is black and even *I* knew that my own clothes would not be appropriate for a royal dinner."

"Black?" the queen asked. "Absolutely everything?"

"Absolutely everything," Ember affirmed, smiling at the queen's surprise as a servant presented a tray of libations to Zephyrn and his guests. "I find it hides any wine I might spill on myself."

She looked over the glasses, seeing that they were marked but unable to decipher the meanings of the stems. A glass with a silver stem was selected by Traejan as he rejoined the group.

"It also masks blood," he said, handing the glass to the Roshan without looking at her. He smiled at his mother, who was regarding him, aghast. "If she is wounded in a fight, it conceals a possible vulnerability to her enemy."

All eyes of the small party returned to the red commander, nearly as astounded as those of the queen.

Ember gave the group a jaunty grin. "I will do my best to avert either situation this evening," she promised. There were a few chuckles and giggles by those gathered near while the queen gathered her composure, taking a long drink of honeyed wine.

"The seating arrangements have been made," Traejan assured his mother softly before turning his attention to the Vikeman that loomed next to the Roshan. "I have Captain Espytin seated close to you," he informed, "he is one of the few captains you have not yet met, but he has quite a bit in common with you."

"Let's hope not," Ember murmured before taking a sip from her glass. Ryen put an elbow in her ribs and she was careful not to spill her wine or glare at the tall Norseman. The pair smiled sweetly at the royal party as a bell was rung to announce the dinner seating to begin.

Servants dressed in blue silks began to filter through the guests to escort them to the great hall, carrying their glasses for them on gleaming silver trays, showing them to their seats.

"I can show you to your table, and introduce him personally," Traejan offered, his soft brown eyes fixed on the Vikeman. "Captain Jennings, as well. He is one of the infantry captains."

"I can do it," Zephyrn offered, enthusiastic. "I know both Espytin and Captain Jennings - his daughter, at least," he added in a softer tone but with a rapacious grin.

Traejan, grinning as well, shook his head in mock exasperation and gave a departing nod to the trio. His gaze never lit upon the Roshan.

Ryen looked inquisitively at Ember as the prince turned and walked away. The air became littered with chatter as everyone present began to make their way, following the royal family of course, from the long gallery of the arcade and into the great hall.

Zephyrn offered Ember the crook of his arm and, after deliberating for only a second, the Roshan slipped her hand inside his elbow. The young prince smiled as her fingers closed over his arm and he flexed his biceps muscle.

"That's not even my sword arm," he confided to her, his voice soft.

The Roshan, despite all confidence she had in the realm of fighting, found herself blushing. She mentally cursed Zephyrn for putting her into such a quandary. She could hear Ryen's soft chuckle at her discomfort and cursed him silently as well.

They entered the great hall through high, arched openings from the arcade. It was an enormous room and oval-shaped, making it different from most great halls that were typically rectangular. The ceilings were high and the curved walls were the color of buttermilk. Marble pillars supported a balcony that ran along the entire circumference of the room. The lower walls were hung with silk tapestries woven to display scenes of stars, moons, and suns along with planets of blue and green. The walls above the balcony were covered with more glittering tiles set into beautiful patterns.

High above, in the center, hung a magnificent chandelier, glowing with light and sparkling with drops of cut glass. Four more smaller versions of the same fixture were suspended at equal distances from the center. Silk bunting in cream and emerald was draped in graceful arcs from the top of one pillar to the next.

There was a single, rectangular table at one end of the hall on a curved platform of white stone three steps high. The rest of the floor was made of perfect squares of polished marble of white and green, laid out in a checkerboard pattern. There were four round tables on each side and two in the middle.

It was to one of the center tables that Zephyrn led the Roshan and the Vikeman. The rest of the royalty continued towards the head table and, as the rest of the aristocracy and elfin elite filed in, Ember could feel their eyes and hear their hushed whispers. They were almost at the round table closest to the platform when a servant girl in green silk with a worried expression stopped Zephyrn to question him about the seating arrangement.

Ember took the opportunity to extract her hand from the arm of the young prince and move a step closer to Ryen.

"How are you doing?" the Vikeman asked from the corner of his mouth, keeping a smile on his face as he took a sip from his wineglass. He, too, felt the stares and heard the whispers, though they bothered him much less. The Roshan wished she had held onto her own glass, instead of letting some servant carry it for her, but she was lost and confused in such an environment.

"I feel like a specimen in a zoo," she said, keeping her voice low, also forcing a smile as they walked slowly towards a young elf in green silk who motioned to them, holding out a hand to indicate their places. Another passed by with her wineglass on the tray and she plucked it off expertly.

Ryen laughed. "Nonsense! Think more of yourself as a prized weapon on display."

Ember smiled. "Yes," she agreed before taking a sip of wine, "I like that better."

The servant girl was joined by Dirk, also to speak with Zephyrn. The prince appeared less than pleased.

"His older brother," the Vikeman remarked without looking at her but keeping his gaze on the young elf, "the one so recently in love, seems to have learned detachment at some point."

Ember smiled and nodded to a pair of elves as they passed by. "Well," she said from the corner of her mouth, "he didn't learn it from me."

Ryen smiled broadly as his eyes, icy blue and quite serious, looked askance at her. "Didn't he?" he asked.

The Roshan's smile disappeared, only to resurface as Zephyrn turned and motioned them towards their table. The pair continued without him and stopped where the young elf in green silk remained at the chairs where they were to sit. A number of others were already there, standing behind their own chairs, waiting for the royal family to take their seats.

Zephyrn returned to them, his smile looking a bit forced.

"I am sorry," he said, "but it seems that I must sit with the royal family."

"How very strange!" the Roshan exclaimed in mock surprise as the others nearby laughed lightly.

"I know!" the prince agreed emphatically, his blue eyes bright. "But I promise to return the first chance I get."

The Roshan began to bow, as did the others, but straightened in shock as the prince swept up her hand and kissed it. She looked around to see if anyone else had noticed but only saw the quick approach of another elf. He took up the Roshan's hand as the young prince departed and grasped it in greeting as the others straightened from their bows to the prince.

His hair, neither long nor short, was a dark blonde and his almond-shaped eyes were dark blue with a mischievous glint. Ember assumed from his blue and gray attire he must be part of the elfin military but something about him seemed to lend him a bit of flair. Possibly the sparkle in his eyes when so many others were somber. As to his age, she had no idea.

"I am Alven Espytin," he said, introducing himself. "You must be the commander of the red army."

Ember gave him a soft laugh as she shook his hand. "Is that what they are calling us?"

"Indeed," he replied, "though, since will all be the same army now, I suppose we should call you the red troops." He turned to Ryen and shook his hand as well. "And you must be the commander of the Vikemen."

"What gave you that idea?" Ryen asked, looking down at the elf who, though tall, was more than a foot shorter than the Norseman. Espytin laughed and then straightened abruptly by a musical call to attention. A trio of horns sounded to announce the arrival of the royal family at their table, then light applause cascaded through the hall as the king and queen took their seats.

"We can sit down ourselves, now," a gravelly voice assured firmly. Ember and Ryen turned as one to see Halloran, clean shaven and smartly dressed for dinner. "That is, if you have met everyone?"

Ember's sharp eyes traveled over the rest of the elves standing around the table. One that she had not yet been introduced to was tall and rangy, with graying hair at his temples, and another was quite young. Halloran followed her gaze and held out a hand first to the older elf.

"This is Nevin, a captain of our infantry," the grizzled commander announced as the tall elf gave her a bow. "And this is Alastair, captain of our archers." The younger elf bowed while Halloran cast his steely eyes about the room, a furrow between his dark gray brows. "Captain Jennings seems to be running late, which is odd for him." His face however, brightened almost immediately and he held out a hand towards the Roshan's chair, inviting her to sit down.

She took her seat, the general taking the one next to hers while Ryen sat himself on her other side. Captain Espytin sat himself next to the Vikeman as the others put themselves to Halloran's right.

"If I am not mistaken, you are young to be a captain," Ryen remarked to Espytin as he took his seat. "You must be very good at what you do."

Espytin laughed as he shook out a linen napkin and laid it across his lap. "I am," he agreed, "both young to be a captain and very good at what I do."

"And what is that?" Ember asked, mirroring his movements. "I mean, what or who are you the captain of?"

"Supply," Espytin informed her with a mischievous grin. "I am an elf who can get things."

The Roshan laughed, unable to help herself, as her eyes moved to Ryen. "Your elfin counterpart!" she proclaimed.

Ryen opened his mouth to speak but, before he could do so, another elf appeared behind the empty chair at their table. He was a bit older, Ember noted. She was learning quickly to see that it was in the eyes, and the fullness of their lips. This one licked his thinning lips, and his eyes were furtive, though she sensed it had nothing to do with his age.

"So sorry that I am late," he apologized. "I was looking for my daughter, Allyson. Unable to find her, I assumed she must already be here." His worried blue eyes traveled over the faces of the many people taking their seats but did not stop on anyone.

"This is Captain Jennings," Halloran declared, "our other infantry captain."

Ryen and Ember both bowed their heads in greeting. Jennings did the same, his eyes darting up immediately afterwards, searching the crowd. He took his seat, distracted.

"Are these all of the elfin captains?" Ember inquired of Halloran. The grizzled commander pursed his lips and nodded.

"For the most part," he rumbled in agreement. "The king's guards," he said, motioning with his head towards the royal table, "are in charge of the garrison – defending the castle if we need to fall back this far."

The Roshan paled. "Let's hope it does not come to that."

Halloran leaned to one side to give the servant filling his wineglass more room. "You noticed these castles were not built for defense, eh?"

"Everything but defense, it seems," Ember said softly, not wanting to offend anyone. "Though they are very beautiful."

She had, in fact, been speechless when she first set eyes upon the castles as she had ridden to dinner with Ryen, escorted by Zephyrn and his Praetorian, Dirk. The sun was setting and painted the graceful towers and delicate spires in shades of ripe summer fruits. To the Roshan, the triad of castles looked as naked and vulnerable as woodland babes, abandoned in the forest.

The largest of the three, Castle Royce, was the summation of beauty without reason. It was the only of the three castles with a wall, though it was low and unmanned. It had enormous gaps that had no gates. The entrance, through which they rode, had a raised portcullis that was entirely for decoration. The Roshan saw no chain and suspected that the sparkling grate was only half built and completely a façade.

Between the ornamental wall and the castle itself, technically the bailey, were rows upon rows of flowerbeds and cutting gardens. Delicate but fastidious knights cloaked in petals, guarding the gentle fortress in a myriad of subtle hues.

The elfin prince had smirked at her, interpreting her expression of shock for one of amazed admiration. The Vikeman knew better.

"Too bad the Crommags weren't attacking Redtown," he had said to her. She had only nodded in response.

"When we came to the New World," Halloran continued, "we did not expect to have war ever again." He sighed as he picked up his glass, took a drink, and then gave it a nod of approval. "We were naïve to think so, but we had hope."

He looked meaningfully at Ember, who was waiting while her own glass was refilled. When the server had finished pouring, the Roshan lifted her glass. "Maybe hope can be restored," she offered, her voice solemn.

The grizzled commander touched his glass to the rim of the Roshan's and they both drank.

"There is also Jaden," Espytin informed her, breaking the gravity that had settled over the table, "captain of our scouts."

"He should return sometime tonight," Jennings informed the group. "You will meet him on the morrow, the first time we will all be together to begin to plan in earnest."

With wineglasses refreshed, dainty bites were served on tiny plates, along with small bowls of soup.

"Might we establish titles tonight, Commander?" Ember asked with a spoon in her hand. "I worry about offending anyone."

Halloran wiped his mouth with a napkin, taking a moment to think. "First, there is no need to worry, I doubt anyone at this table would take offense. Second, I will need to run any of our decisions by Prince Xander and Prince Traejan for their approval."

"Of course," Ember agreed before helping herself to a spoonful of soup.

"Last," Halloran continued, "I think we should stick to what we already have, as much as possible."

"Soldiers," Ryen interposed, "led by captains."

"Correct," Jennings agreed. "Sir Dellion was appointed Major by Prince Traejan, as he is the liaison in charge between the infantry, scouts, archers, and the Praetorian."

"In charge of them all, along with daily strategy and overall battle plans," Espytin added with a nod towards the grizzled commander, "is General Halloran."

The general nodded and pushed his empty bowl to the side. It was whisked away immediately. "If you are comfortable with such arrangements," he said, looking at Ember and Ryen, "it only leaves you two and your troops."

The Roshan nodded as her own bowl was taken and replaced with a plate of roast capon and spring vegetables. "I have captains as well, though I would not classify myself as a major, and certainly not a general."

"How about commander?" Halloran asked.

The Roshan smiled. "That will suit me just fine, thank you."

All eyes went to Ryen next, making the big man laugh. "I need no such titles," he assured them, "especially since I have no captains. I will fight next to Commander L'chiross, and feel it best to designate small groups of the Vikemen to each infantry platoon, or have them fight together as a single unit. It will depend on what the situation demands, and the plans of General Halloran."

"Still," Espytin commented, "you are their leader.

Commander as well? It would keep it simpler for everyone." The young elf glanced at Halloran for confirmation and the general nodded in assent.

"Commander Glace!" the Roshan announced with a grin, looking at the Norseman. "Who would have ever thought?"

"Not me," Ryen informed the group, bringing a laugh to the entire table.

"A woman warrior," Jennings remarked, smiling at Ember as he tore a wing from his capon. "And a commander as well. I wish Allyson was here to meet you. I raised her myself and she has always been strong-minded. She would admire you greatly." His eyes rose up again to scan those seated at the tables. "Where the Circles could she be?" he muttered, clearly aggravated.

Dinner wound to an end after what seemed, to Ember, an eternity. One thing she had noticed, was the joviality of General Halloran as the last of the plates were finally cleared. She had drunk quite a bit more of the wine than she had intended and reached out with her dessert fork and tapped his wine glass with it as she regarded him with raised brows. It had a silver stem, as did hers and Ryen's.

"No honey for you?" she asked, bold.

The general gave her a broad smile. "No need. Another gift from my human ancestor," he confided. Then, leaning closer, "I was told that you have quite a collection of red wine with you."

Ember pressed her lips together but could not restrain a smile. "I do."

Many of the guests began to leave their tables to mingle with others as plates were cleared and trays of teas and smaller desserts began to circulate. Ember could see that many were making their way to the center tables to talk to the captains and commanders.

Ryen rose, then, offering thanks and good-byes to those seated. Instinctively, the Roshan did the same. All of the elves at their table politely rose with her. Partings were exchanged before Ryen turned and bowed to the royal table, Ember mimicking his movements.

She turned to Halloran before following the Vikeman from the hall. "May I call on you privately, sir? I have many questions I would like to ask about war in general – if you don't mind."

"Of course you may," he said smiling. He laid a hand on her arm as she bowed her head and she looked up, curious. "Bring a bottle of that red wine," the general suggested conspiratorially. "I am curious to see what the grapes of the Southlon taste like."

"I'll bring two," she assured and bowed again before she took her leave from the smiling commander, walking out with the tall Norseman.

Zephyrn caught them in the gallery.

"Leaving so soon?" he asked, stopping them. His blue eyes went to the Roshan. "They will be serving cordials later, and there will be dancing."

Ember froze, stricken by the very idea.

"I am afraid so," Ryen said quickly. "The red commander wishes to see that her troops are settled."

"Of course," Zephyrn agreed, bowing his blonde head. "But I would sincerely like for you to appraise my skills as a swordsman," he said, giving her a rakish grin. "I know that now is not the time, but tomorrow - tomorrow in the evening, perhaps?"

"Perhaps," the Roshan agreed. "Until then, please give your parents and your brothers our warmest regards."

"I certainly will. Until tomorrow then." The young prince flashed her a brilliant smile before he bowed and left.

Ember waited until he had reentered the great hall and was swallowed by the noise there before she heaved a sigh. "What is with him?" she asked Ryen, incredulous.

The Vikeman smiled. "I think he has taken a liking to you," he informed her as they walked towards the arches where their horses were waiting with a line of carriages. "Or, at least, is intrigued by you. Most people are."

The Roshan snorted, indicating that the future might hold a surprise or two for the young elfin prince.

"It appears we are the first to leave," she remarked, looking around as they crossed the gallery and went through the open glass doors and into the night. "Is it rude to do so this early, or impolite that we did not say our goodbyes to the royals?"

Ryen shook his head. "We could have, but it is not necessary. If everyone made a point to do so they would be plagued by every departing guest and it would take half the night."

"How do you know so many of these social graces?" she asked as they crossed the brightly lit but mostly empty courtyard.

"I have traveled extensively, you know that."

The Roshan snorted again. "And I haven't?"

The Vikeman laughed softly. "Of course you have. I have just traveled in different circles."

The Roshan nodded in understanding. "One thing is for sure," she announced to her friend as he escorted her towards the stables.

"What is that?" Ryen asked, his blue eyes glittering in the semi-darkness of the courtyard.

"You were right about all this bowing. I'm done with it already."

The Norseman laughed. "Good!"

12. PRELIMINARY PLANS

As Ryen and the Roshan were breaking their fast the next morning, Ian brought an elfin messenger into the tent. At first, Ember thought it was Dell. He bore a striking resemblance to Traejan's Praetorian; same build with dark hair and dark eyes. A second glance showed that he was much younger and the Roshan remembered that the Skye Elves were descended from two other races of elves – Arcadian and Seleucian.

"Good morning," the messenger greeted cheerfully. "I was sent to tell you that the first meeting will be held not in the white room, but at Castle Song. It seems that there are still maps and charts the general needs but have not yet made their way to the camp."

"Same time?" Ryen asked over the rim of his mug. The messenger nodded briskly. "We better get going then," the Vikeman stated, finishing his coffee in three long swallows.

Ember stood, brushing biscuit crumbs from her hands. "Thank you..." she paused and the elf smiled at her

"Dash," he told her. "I'm Dash."

The Roshan nodded as Ian wrapped her sword belt around her waist and buckled it. "Thank you, Dash. Please alert my captains."

"Word is being is being sent as we speak," he informed her.

"Then you are as quick as your name implies. Thank you." She turned her face to Ian. "Would you please saddle Coal?"

"He has a groom already taking care of it," Ian said,

indicating Dash with a tilt of his dark head as he cinched her belt.

Dash grinned and gave her a wink before he disappeared through the flap of the tent.

"I better hustle," Ryen said sourly, "the elves did not send a groom to care for my horse and I do not have a steward to dress me."

The Vikeman stuffed the rest of his biscuit in his mouth and stood as the Roshan gave him a gleeful smile and finished her coffee. Ian handed her a pair of daggers which she made disappear into her clothing.

"Who are you bringing today?" she asked Ryen as she tucked away her personal arsenal. Ian held out her cloak and she shook her head. They were on the border of the Northlon, possibly even within the borders, but it was high summer and the cool morning air was already beginning to warm.

"Kamut, Yasgir, Haldor and Halvar…and Crag," he finished with a sigh of resignation.

The Roshan favored him with another grin as she handed her empty mug to her steward. "Lucky me."

The Vikeman rolled his eyes and left her tent.

Ryen rode with his five Norsemen, the Roshan with her four captains, escorted by Prince Traejan and Sir Dellion. Traejan had already been acquainted with the Vikemen, but had yet to meet the Roshan's captains. Two of them he recognized from their arrival – Rhys, the handsome blonde and Gavan, the equally striking brunette.

The other two he recognized as well. They had ridden out with the Roshan yesterday upon their arrival, though she had sent them back before Traejan could get a good look at either one. One had auburn hair, a round boyish face that was spattered with freckles, and eyes the colors of amethysts. The other had hair that was white, tinged with silver, making the young prince think at first, and from a distance, that he must be old. But his heart-shaped face was unlined and his eyes, the silver-blue of a stormy sky, sparkled with youth. They had instruments slung across their backs that resembled bows, but mounted on a frame of sorts.

The grade that allowed passage from Morgan's Vale to the cliffs above flattened out and had, as of late, continued as a road that led from the vale towards Tuar Ceath proper. It cut between the supply building and the yurts of the Vikemen and then, moving northward, divided the Gnomin camp from where the corrals for the elfin horses were being built. Continuing on, the dirt lane gave way to beaten grass until it finally petered out into the Fosse Meadow – the grasslands between the valley in the south and Tuar Ceath in the north.

As the party passed the trio of structures, the Roshan jerked her head in the direction of the tents on the west side – the ones that were currently empty.

"Just when are you planning on filling those?" she asked Traejan, riding on his left side.

"The soldiers train every day at Castle Song," he informed her, keeping his gaze fixed ahead, "but return to their homes every night. I wanted them to spend as much time with their families as possible, and I am putting off actual mobilization for as long as I can." He expected a scathing reply but could see her nod from the corner of his vision.

"That was a wise choice," she replied.

The young prince was startled by her words and surprised again at his own reaction to her response. He found he did not like it. Her approval sent the emotional armor he wore into a dilemma. It was difficult to be angry when she praised him.

"We began moving foodstuffs and supplies once the Gnomin

had set up their camp," he continued hastily, "and even more so when the Norsemen arrived. Now that your army is here, we will finish moving all of the maps, charts and weapons as well."

The Roshan, thankfully, had nothing more to say and simply gave another nod, taking in the landscape with her eyes of green and brown and gold. The grasslands opened before them with the forest rising far to their right and the mountains even farther to their left, scratching the blue belly of the sky.

Within minutes there was a gentle grade that led up from Fosse Meadow into Tuar Ceath proper. The horses took the short and easy climb that led to the edges of the Great Lawn and the riders found themselves in sight of the elfin castles. Past acres of emerald green grass, three imperial buildings rose gracefully in the morning air, bathing in the mists from the many falls of water cascading down from the mountains.

They looked as beautiful and delicate and ephemeral as the rainbows that surrounded them.

The Roshan had already addressed her men about the castles, and to keep their opinions to themselves. Still, as they rode near and she could sense their incredulity, she discreetly held one hand out with her fingers splayed in silent command to keep their mouths closed.

Ryen had done no such preparation with his men.

"Mighty Odin!" Halvar exclaimed as they neared Castle Song. "That, for certain, is a palace for Freya herself!"

"You are a dolt, brother!" Haldor scolded with a grin, his dark orange hair shining bright in the morning sun. "Freya rides beside you!"

"Freya or not," Crag muttered, "it is a palace indeed, rather than a fortress."

"Which is why we set up camp where we have," Yasgir interjected. "The elves have wisely chosen a place for defense."

Trotting slightly ahead on his white palfrey, the young prince smiled at him from over his shoulder. "Thank you for the kind words, Yasgir, but we are quite aware of our folly. When the Skye Elves came to the New World, they expected nothing but peace."

"My apologies, Prince Traejan," Halvar said, "I meant no disrespect. But understand that we have never seen buildings such as these, and had heard of them only in tales."

"And even in the tales," Haldor added, "places such as these were not fit for mortal men, but for the gods themselves."

Traejan's smile broadened. "No offense was taken," he assured them, and none was. He had spent a bit of time with the brothers from the north and found that though they were as uncouth and vulgar as warriors could be, they had an innocence to them that was often child-like. "Besides," the young elf continued, "my castle is one of which I think even Odin himself might approve."

Within another two minutes the brothers, as well as the others, knew what he meant. The rolling grasses gave way to trampled earth and birdsong was replaced by the song of steel. The other two castles seemed to fade away as Castle Song rose before them, gleaming towers that speared the morning air.

The castle was built like a capital E. The largest and longest building was in the back, made of huge blocks of glimmering stone and topped with three towers. Two wings stretched out from either side, also made of stone. Between them, scores of elves in orderly formations sparred with swords. On the southern side of the castle, lines of archers were being drilled in speed and repetition.

The Roshan's tawny eyes moved over them all, taking in everything from the simplicity of the drills to the style of fighting they were being taught to the speed with which they moved.

The short, middle line of the E was a stout entryway that led to a squat turret at each corner of the castle. It was set with a pair of large doors of red oak. The dozen riders moved between the two outstretched wings, heading for the building on the left that housed the stables. As they entered the courtyard, however, they were met by half a dozen elfin stable hands. The prince and his Praetorian dismounted and began handing over the reins of their mounts to waiting grooms.

The Roshan slid from Coal's back and down into Crag's massive grasp. Her surprise at his immediate presence was matched by her consternation of his grip. His hands were so large that they encircled her entire ribcage. His pinky fingers were around her hips and his forefingers were just under her breasts, almost cupping them.

"Careful," he said, making sure she was steady on her feet before letting her go, "the ground is uneven." His voice was deep and vibrated through body.

"Thank you," she replied, hoping her voice was as firm as her stance as she turned her attention from the giant Vikeman to the waiting groom.

The Night Stallion, however, snarled and gave his dripping fangs a mighty snap. The young elfin groom let out a yelp and jumped back.

"Coal!" Ember scolded. She reached for his bridle but he jerked his massive head up and out of her reach. "What has gotten into you?" she demanded.

Ryen shouldered Crag out of the way and grabbed Coal by the noseband and retrieved his reins, handing them to the Roshan. Coal snorted, slightly calmer, but clearly still agitated. Ember looked around and, spying the stable hand in charge of Traejan's palfrey, motioned him over.

The young elf shot the prince an anxious look but Traejan gave him a nod to go and assist. The groom led Peg over to Coal and her presence calmed him further.

"Keep them together," the Roshan instructed, handing over his reins. "He won't be a problem if she is near." This time the beast went without a fuss.

"I don't know why you didn't bring Ian," Gavan remarked as the horses were being led away.

"I didn't think I'd need him," the Roshan said, turning to follow Dell and Traejan back around to the front of the castle.

Ryen followed her with Gavan and Rhys while the other Vikemen brought up the rear. "Does she take that boy with her everywhere?" he asked.

The handsome youth nodded as his golden eyes glanced at the Norseman. "Everywhere. But he is no more a boy than I am, or Rhys."

Ryen smiled. "Is it too much to hope that he is a girl?"

Gavan laughed. "No. I just meant that we are much older than we look."

"I don't know if that makes me feel better or worse," Ryen muttered.

"You know I can hear you both," Ember said.

Gavan blushed. "My apologies, Roshan. I did not mean to speak out of turn, or overstep my bounds."

The Roshan scowled over her shoulder at Ryen. "It is not your fault," she told her captain. "Commander Glace has a way of bringing that out of people."

Ryen flashed him a grin. "It's a gift."

The front of this castle had no portcullis, decorative or otherwise. Two enormous doors of red oak banded with polished brass were thrown wide, the opening large enough to allow three riders abreast. The party followed the prince and his Praetorian inside, pausing to look around. Ember smiled crookedly as she took everything in, knowing what Traejan had meant about Odin approving of the castle.

Upon entering, there were open doors on either side. Stone-walled corridors led to the short turrets where the Roshan could see masses of shining steel. The great room before her was high-ceilinged and mostly empty. The people there were not dressed for dinner or dancing, but war. Soldiers and stewards and messengers hurried about, most of them armed.

Haldor gave a low whistle as he entered the great room. "I see what you mean, Prince Traejan," he said. "This is my kind of palace!"

The young prince smiled at the Vikeman, though it slipped away as Zephyrn entered behind the group, sheathing a slim sword. He was dressed in a belted white tunic over cream trousers and leather boots that had been bleached the color of alabaster. Dirk followed close behind in the pearly gray garb of the Praetorian.

"Good morn!" he said to all in greeting, but moved purposefully towards the Roshan. "I have been practicing with the infantry, but I was hoping for some time with Commander L'chiross."

"We are headed upstairs to meet with General Halloran and the elfin captains," Traejan informed his brother.

Zephyrn smiled, not put out in the slightest. "Well, I am one of the archer captains, so I better join you."

"You should," Traejan forced himself to say politely before looking at the others. "This way," he instructed, leading them past the set of stairs that spiraled up the south tower and to a stairway that simply went up the side of one wall to the floor above.

Here, doors to smaller rooms opened onto one great room in the center where charts and lists were tacked to the walls and the many tables were covered with maps. Elfin soldiers moved between them, making marks and conversing quietly. The grizzled commander looked up from where he was bent over one of the tables, his large hands planted on either side of a diagram of Tuar Ceath. He stood up and brought his hands together in a single clap.

"Excellent!" he exclaimed. "And good morn! My Lord

Princes," he said, his voice deep and gravely, with a nod to Traejan and Zephyrn. "Commanders," he said to Ember and Ryen as they approached, "I believe you have already met our captains, save for Jaden here, who returned late last night."

"Captain," she greeted, shaking the hand of the small elf. He was one of the few Sylvan elves she had seen amongst the Skye Elves. He was not quite five feet tall, with a round, boyish face under his dark curls, and had ears that were more sharply pointed than those of the other elves. She knew the look well, since all of the Wildboys were Sylvan elves.

"Commanders," he greeted in return with a smile that was as youthful as the rest of his appearance.

"You remember, Nevin," the general said, motioning to the elf on his other side. He was good-looking, if a bit weathered. He had dark eyes and dark hair, with tendrils of a smoky gray creeping from his temples.

"Yes," Ember said warmly. "Though we did not get to speak much."

"A mischance that will soon be remedied, I am sure," he remarked with a genuine smile.

"Nevin," Halloran continued, "was a soldier in the Old World and is a veteran of two wars. He, along with Prince Traejan, have been training our swordsmen."

The Roshan stepped aside and turned slightly towards the four young men who had accompanied her to the castle. "This is Gavan and Rhys," she said, indicating the handsome man with brown hair and golden eyes along with his blonde counterpart. "They captain our mounted infantry." She turned to the young man with auburn hair and the white-haired youth next to him. "This is Patrek and Sloan," she said, "captains of our foot soldiers." She turned her eyes to the elves and introduced them, starting with General Halloran, and then turned to Ryen so he could introduce his leaders as well.

When all the names had been exchanged and murmured

and sufficient nods given, Halloran held an inviting hand out to the map he had been studying when the others had arrived. He was about to begin when Yasgir cleared his throat as politely as possible.

"Excuse me, General, but – before we begin – might I enquire about the weapons worn by Sloan and Patrek?" the black-haired Vikeman asked.

Zephyrn looked about at the others, a grin spreading across his face. "I was wondering the same, myself," he said.

The general's lips turned up in a smirk. "If memory serves," he offered in his graveled voice, "those are crossbows."

Patrek and Sloan both smiled. "They are," Patrek agreed. He looked questioningly at his Roshan, who gave him a nod, then unslung the bow from where it was strapped across his back. "It is much like a bow," he explained, laying it on the table. "But it is mounted on a tiller, or a stock, and - instead of an arrow – it has a bolt. Once the string is cocked, the bolt is released by depressing the trigger." Patrek turned the weapon over so they could see what he meant.

"It is heavier and a bit more awkward than a bow," Sloan told the group, "and it takes more time to reload. But the bolt is solid, and travels faster than an arrow, and can be shot from farther away. We think it will be a good weapon against the Crommags. I will be glad to show you, later, what it looks like in action."

"I would like that!" Zephyrn agreed, enthusiastic.

Sloan gave him a nod of assent before Patrek threw the crossbow back across his shoulders and Sloan did the same. Everyone turned their attention back to the general who cast his steely gray eyes down on the map in front of him.

"Here," he said, tapping the parchment, "is where our encampment is. The red army arrived through this forest here, the Elfin Greatwood. This is also where we expect the Crommags to make their camp."

"It makes sense," Crag said, his massive arms crossed over his great chest. "It offers them cover and concealment, as well as game and fresh water from this river here." He reached out and poked the map with a huge finger.

"Wouldn't they get here faster if they cut through the Echo Sea and came through the mountains?" Ember asked.

"Yes," the general agreed, "but our scouts have already tracked them to here," he said, indicating an area along the Slag River to the west. "It would be a waste of time for them to head north again. Besides, the Gnomin have rigged the passes to collapse upon them should any of them try to breach the Mountains of the Sun."

"What about here?" Ryen asked, pointing. "East of the Mountains of the Moon? Do we need worry about another force coming from that direction?"

Halloran glanced at Jennings. He obviously expected the elf to answer but he was looking across the room, not paying attention. "Captain Jennings?" he asked, his deep voice startling the captain from his reverie.

"I am sorry," he apologized. "What was the question?"

"It was in regard to the Crommags breaching the Mountains of the Moon," he said, scowling at the other elf.

"Oh!" Jennings exclaimed. "Those passes are much too small. They would have to come through single, possibly double, file – if they squeezed."

"What if they went farther north, going around the mountains?" Ember asked.

"No," Kamut said. It was the first time he had spoken all day, even on the ride into the elfin kingdom. His voice seemed to come from somewhere deep within his broad chest, like a rumble from the depths of a mountain. "My borough extends from the mountains all the way to the Ice Floe. They cannot come that way."

"That only leaves the sea," Ryen finished. "I think we are

fairly safe from that direction. The Crommags have never shown themselves to be sea-farers."

"They have never shown themselves to be migrators, either," Crag told him, "yet here they come."

"Walking down here is easy," Kamut interjected, "raising a navy is not."

Prince Traejan leaned over the map. "What we are supposing is based on what they have been doing, we are simply following their lead. However, we do have sentries posted along the sea and along the edge of the forests: here, here, and here," the young prince told them as he pointed out the spots on the map he was indicating. "Just in case. I believe it is the best allocation of our resources without spreading them too thin."

"Agreed," Halloran exclaimed softly, his gray eyes lifting from the table to seek out the red commander. "And now that your troops are here, the Gnomin will begin to set traps in the Greatwood." The general gave her a grin. "A sort of welcoming party, if you would."

The Roshan returned his grin. "Excellent. And do you intend on waging the battle at the edge of the forest? Try to keep them contained there?"

Halloran shook his head. "Their numbers are too great, ours are too few. We would be strung out across too much land, making a fighting line impossible to maintain. The slope you climbed yesterday when your troops arrived will be our major line of defense. The Gnomin have already hollowed out the areas under the cliffs, making them unscalable. Any attempt will just cause the cliffs to collapse upon them." He took two fingers and drew them down the sides of where the slope was indicated on the map. "Here, we will begin digging fortified trenches in an effort to funnel them up the hill, where we will have the advantage of the higher ground."

"It is a sound plan," the Roshan said, her eyes on the map.

"Could we take the excavated earth, and build berms along here, and here?"

"Certainly," the general agreed. "Are you thinking of placing your crossbowmen there?"

"Yes. They could cover our swordsmen until they need to draw their own swords, falling back to the slope itself if they are overrun."

Halloran nodded and then looked at Prince Traejan. "Those berms, they could serve you as well, eh?"

Traejan smiled. "They certainly could."

She waited to see if there would be more, then looked back at the general. "What is the best way you see of integrating our forces?"

The grizzled commander scowled, thoughtful. "By not integrating them at all," he stated. "They have been trained differently, and are under the command of different captains. I think it most advantageous for the different troops to fight in waves, letting the tired and injured fall back, while a fresh force presses ahead every time."

The smile the Roshan gave him was small, but full of admiration. "I will have to give some thought on how to organize our troops for such maneuvers, but I think it is an excellent course of action."

The general nodded. "We can discuss such details in depth, later on as each battle presents itself. Now that we have the broad-strokes of a plan, my next concern is to know what you are need of regarding supplies. Which, actually, will be taken care of by Captain Espytin.

The young elf flashed her a smile. "I am at your service."

"We need bolts for the crossbows," the Roshan said without hesitation. "We brought as many as we could carry, but will still run out quickly. They are simple to make, the Gnomin can turn them out by the hundreds, we just need the material. It can be steel, but could be untempered iron as well."

The blue-eyed supply captain shot a questioning glance at Prince Traejan, who gave a him a slight nod. "I believe we have a supply," Espytin answered, "but it would be good for you to check and make sure it will work for you. Prince Traejan," he said, shifting his gaze, "I would also like for you to approve, to make sure we are thinking along the same lines."

"Of course," Traejan agreed, looking to the general for dismissal.

Halloran gave him a nod. "By all means," he encouraged. "But I would like more information from the Vikemen about the area to the north. And I am sure Alistair would like to speak more with the bowmen?" He glanced at the young elf who nodded vigorously.

"Certainly," the Roshan agreed, motioning for Gavan and Rhys to remain behind as well before following Traejan and Captain Espytin from the room. They led the way back downstairs and into one of the turrets in the back of the castle.

"Do you think Prince Zephyrn will want one of these new weapons?" Espytin asked Traejan casually.

"Of course," the young prince answered. "But how long he will stick with it is questionable."

The supply captain grunted as if this response was no surprise. The Roshan followed them down a stone corridor and into a massive, curved room that was full of wooden crates. Espytin selected one at random and, producing a slim dagger, looked questioningly once again at the prince. Traejan gave him a nod to proceed.

"We are of the same mind, then," Espytin said as he pried the top off the crate, "but I wanted to make sure." He lifted the lid free and placed it on the ground, leaning it next to another stack. He reached inside and pulled out a handful of material that glimmered like metal but moved like cloth and held it up for the Roshan's inspection. It was a shirt made of fine links of steel.

"Chain mail," she whispered, incredulous. She looked at the dozens upon dozens of stacked crates before turning her eyes to the captain. "These are all chain mail?" He gave her a nod, his dark blue eyes undoubtedly serious, and she turned her gaze to the prince. "What did you hope to accomplish with this?"

"Nothing," he replied, his voice flat save for a glimmer of anger. "I know such finery would only weigh a soldier down, and do nothing at all against an axe or a sword of a three hundred-pound Crommag. But when the call for war came, every elf responded, and each wanted to help in any way they could. I turned none away."

"Good thing, too!" Espytin exclaimed with what felt like forced cheer, "for now we have a ready supply of steel for you, if it will serve?"

The Roshan nodded, though she did not look at him. Her eyes were still fixed on the prince. "And how have you been training your men?" she asked as if suddenly jabbed with suspicion.

"Close-quartered fighting to overpower the enemy, with short weapons."

The Roshan's face hardened for a moment in anger and disbelief, then broke with a crooked smile as she realized he was being acidly sarcastic. Traejan, however, did not like that smile. Not at all. He found it was another chink in the emotional armor with which he had cloaked himself. Espytin, weighted by the tension in the room, searched for something to say.

"If you have the need for more bolts," he told the Roshan, "we also have a supply of plate mail that can be melted down. We thought first we would see if the Vikemen could use it, though it would be..."

"Captain Espytin!" The three in the room turned to see a young elf standing in the doorway. He spied the prince and bowed quickly. "My Lord Prince," he greeted, his sharp blue eyes darting back to the supply captain in a silent plea.

"If you will excuse me?" Espytin asked but, before he could receive an answer, moved quickly into the corridor to speak with the elf.

Finally, the elfin prince and the Roshan Simorgh found themselves alone for the first time in a long time. Ember, once assured of Espytin's distraction, looked soberly at the young prince.

"You understand, of course..."

"Of course!" he said sharply, cutting her off.

Espytin slipped back into the room. "We need to go back upstairs. Immediately."

Without question, the prince and the Roshan swiftly followed him back down the corridor and back up the stairs. The room they had left so recently was full of rising voices, all of which died down at their entrance. All eyes went to the grizzled commander.

"The Crommags have reached the Greatwood," he announced.

Traejan looked as if he had been stabbed. "That cannot be!" he exclaimed. "They were not supposed to be there for weeks! Besides, our scouts would have alerted us if they had moved past the borders of the Echo Sea!" His eyes went to Jaden, the captain of the scouts, and his muscles went slack at the sight of the expression on the young elf who had gone as pale as curdled milk. "Unless the scouts were caught," the prince finished softly.

"We have not heard from Cotter and Grae," Jaden informed them, his voice cracking on the last. "But Blaine and Dutch have confirmed that the majority of Crommags are on the edge of the Greatwood."

Prince Traejan's eyes moved from Jaden to the small elves by his side. The were both Sylvan, like their captain. They were dirty and disheveled from an obviously long and hard ride. One looked as if his face was streaked with tears as well as sweat.

"Can you show me on the map where they are?" Traejan asked them gently.

They nodded in unison and Dutch, the less tear-stained one, stepped forward and placed a small finger on the map laid out before the general.

"They are moving in large groups," he told the prince, "and three of these large groups have crossed the bottom of the Echo Sea. The first one is encamped here, on the edge of the Elfin Greatwood. The next is behind them with maybe half a mile between. The third is back another half mile from the second."

"Do you know how many travel in each group?" Halloran asked pointedly.

The young elf swallowed. "About a thousand."

Most of those around the table nodded slowly, digesting the information.

"How is it that they are moving so quickly now?" Traejan asked. "Even without our last...report... they should still be weeks away from the Greatwood."

Dutch expelled a heavy breath. "They have left the women and children and most of their wagons behind at some point. It is just the men."

All eyes raised and traveled around the room, alighting briefly upon other eyes. It was not just three thousand Crommag refugees, but three thousand fighters that were almost upon them.

"Do they have the Gnomin captives with them?" Ryen asked.

Blaine nodded. "They are with the middle group."

"How fast are they moving?" Halloran asked.

Dutch moved his finger on the map from the edge of the Echo Sea to the place in the Greatwood where they expected the Crommags to make their stand. "They should be here in a week, maybe ten days."

The Roshan looked up and met Traejan's eyes with her own. "It's time to mobilize your men."

13. COURTING DANGER

"Knock, knock!" Ryen called out as he ducked into the Roshan's tent, smiling while his eyes adjusted from the bright sunlight outside to the comparative dimness inside.

"Hello!" Ember called back, craning her head around to see him. She was holding up her red braid while Ian fastened a clasp at the back of her neck.

Ryen's smile melted into an expression of distaste. There were two places downstream dedicated to washing and bathing and Ryen guessed Ian must have just gotten out of the river. Hoped. He was wearing just his boots and trousers, his black hair and golden skin still glistening with drops of moisture.

The young man was more heavily muscled than Ryen had suspected. His biceps and shoulders were round and hard as stone. His chest looked like plate armor and his abdomen rippled with muscle. He looked like a sculpture Ryen had once seen.

Ian stepped away from the Roshan and she let her braid fall back down.

"What do you think?" she asked, lifting her chin so Ryen could get a better look but the Vikeman was still busy scowling at her steward. "Ryen? Ryen!" she called.

The Norseman turned his attention back to her, then moved closer for a better look. A circlet of steel, four-fingers high, surrounded her neck. She turned her head one way and then the other, getting a feel for it.

"What do we have here?" the Vikeman asked. "Are you

planning on serving the Crommags your head on a platter?"

"Ha ha. It won't save me from a beheading, if one gets close enough, but it should prevent one from opening up my jugular."

"Getting slow in your old age?"

The Roshan gave him a dour look and then edged back to Ian, holding up her braid again. "Who pissed in your cider?" she asked the Norseman.

"No one," he said, again scowling at Ian who was lifting his arms to the back of her neck, his muscles flexing. The bastard did not have single ounce of fat on him. "Though, now that you mention it, I could use some."

"I'll come with you," Ember suggested as Ian removed the collar of steel from her neck. Ryen ducked back out of her tent and waited in the bright sunshine. A moment later, she pushed aside the flap of her tent and joined him outside. The late morning was warm and growing warmer, so she went without her vest but still wore her brace of daggers over a long-sleeved black shirt, black pants and black boots. A longsword hung from her hip and a pair of short swords crossed at the small of her back.

All around was a bustle of activity. The elfin soldiers were moving into their tents and the Gnomin and red troops alike were helping in any way they could. The air, so quiet just the day before, was now full of the sounds of voices, horses, and hammers.

"I was hoping Gatha would get here before the Crommags," he said as the Roshan adjusted her clutch of daggers. "Return to her duties and maybe relieve you of your steward and squire."

The Roshan gave him a crooked smile. "Ian serves me in ways Gatha cannot."

Ryen looked down at her, his reddish brows drawn close together. "What does that mean?"

The Roshan only grinned at him in response and turned

on her heel, almost colliding with a tall and comely youth with blonde hair and lively blue-green eyes. The Vikeman shifted his gaze away from scowling at her and his expression thawed straightaway.

"Jack!" Ryen exclaimed.

"Ryen Glace!" Jack greeted.

Ryen resisted the urge to hug the lad and instead took up his proffered hand and shook it vigorously.

"What are you doing here?" Ryen asked. "Are you a soldier?"

Jack laughed, tipping back his head. The sound captivated the Vikeman. "No," Jack told him. "I am part of the support crew. I was actually on my way back from seeing Captain Espytin."

"Are we short on any supplies?" the Roshan asked, concerned. They had only just arrived, she could not imagine they had run out of anything yet.

"No, no, no. Nothing like that. He was asking me about trade with the Southlon, Redtown in particular."

"It's strange he didn't mention it to me," Ryen said. "But you live there. I guess it makes sense."

"It does," Jack agreed. "What *was* strange was that he was talking with some other elves when I arrived about trade with the Crommags. Talking about if war was really necessary and if perhaps there was money to be made." Jack blinked his blue-green eyes at the Vikeman and the Roshan, who had both gone very still. "Isn't that strange?"

"Yes," Ryen murmured. "Very strange."

"Well," Jack continued cheerfully, "I need to get back before lunch to make sure everyone has what they need."

"Of course," Ember agreed.

"Good to see you, Jack," Ryen said, though he was much more subdued than only moments ago.

Jack, however, was undaunted. He gave them a sweeping bow and a dashing smile and headed for the eastern end of their camp.

The Roshan looked up at the Norseman. "Should we go back in my tent for a private word?" she asked.

Ryen glanced at her tent, his scowl returning. Ian had probably found a shirt by now but the Vikeman had no desire to watch him dote on Ember.

"Let's go to my tent," he said. "We were after cider, weren't we?"

"We were," she agreed. "Besides, you're right next door." They turned as one and headed for Ryen's yurt, only a short distance away.

Coal snorted at them as they passed by, and Ian's roan jerked her head and danced away to the side as far as her lead would allow.

Ryen's current domicile was four times as large as her own and he stood aside for her as they reached the entrance where both flaps had been tied open, holding out an arm in an invitation for her to enter.

"Welcome to my palace!" he announced theatrically.

"Ugh!" Ember grunted, waving a hand in front her face as she entered. "A palace in size maybe. Certainly not smell!"

"Hey!" Halvar admonished. He was sitting on his cot with his boots off, scratching the bottom of his foot through a dirty sock.

Haldor, relaxing in a camp chair and taking a large gulp from a horn of cider, lowered the vessel and belched loudly. "What do you mean?" he asked, wiping his dribbling beard with the back of his hand.

Ryen grinned at them, immediately preferring their company to that of the half-naked steward in the Roshan's tent. "She means get her a horn of cider!" he commanded.

"Skol!" Haldor shouted, pleased. "And me as well!"

Halvar pulled on his boots and levered himself off of the cot and then lumbered to a table against the side of the tent. "At least the Gnomin have treated us like kings, and supplied us with a king's ransom of this liquid gold!" he exclaimed, thumping on a wooden keg with one meaty hand as he looked for two clean horns. There were none, so he selected two that did not smell quite as ripe as the others.

The Roshan took a seat in one of the oversized chairs at their table, thanked Halvar, and took a sip from her horn, wrinkling her nose at the smell. Ryen did the same, blinking water from his eyes as well.

"So!" her friend exclaimed, lowering his horn and holding it away from his face. "Tell me what you are thinking."

"Of Espytin?"

"Of course."

The Roshan shrugged. "It is shocking to hear, certainly. I'll admit it caught me off guard. But not really that surprising if you think about it, now that I've had a minute to do so. He is a young elf, young enough I think to be born here, which means he has never seen war and can probably not comprehend the scope of it."

Ryen grunted and took another pull from his horn, grimacing at the smell. "I suppose," he agreed softly, "but to say such things openly..."

The Roshan gave him her crooked smile. "I am sure he is looking for money, not looking to spread dissent."

"You could be right."

"I could be wrong."

Ryen frowned at her. "I hate when you contradict yourself. But I doubt you are wrong. You hardly are."

"Hardly?"

"You want me to say never, but I'm not going to give you the satisfaction."

Ember's smile widened into a grin.

"What's that?" Halvar asked, sitting back down. "Who is not satisfied?"

"I'll give you satisfaction, my lady," Haldor said, joining them at the table and giving the Roshan a wink.

Ryen ignored them. "He still bears watching," he advised.

Ember's eyes glittered in the shadowy light of the tent. "Everyone does."

"What bears watching," Halvar said, "is me in a fight."

"Is that so?" the Roshan asked, switching her gaze to Halvar, ending her conversation with Ryen as he rose to refill their horns. The rank smell seemed to be going away. By the end of her second horn, she did not notice it at all. The brothers, by then, were giving her a lesson in history. And, in their cups, were courting the Roshan openly.

"The Vikings were the first to settle this world," Haldor told her earnestly. He had three fingers and a thumb curled around his drinking horn but his index finger pointed at the Roshan. "But they were no one without their queens. Come home with me after this elfin war, and I will make you a queen. I will cloak you in the richest furs and adorn your arms with golden rings!"

The Roshan threw back her head and laughed, her red braid swinging between her black-clad shoulders while Ryen watched, bemused.

"Bah!" Halvar spat. "Women do not want precious metals, they want precious gems!" He leaned forward over his massive thighs, fixing the Roshan with a bleary stare while the lengths of his braided mustache swung back and forth. "Return with me, and I will adorn you with jewels the colors of your eyes!"

"Fools!" Crag rumbled.

All heads turned to see the massive Norseman standing in the entry to the tent. The blonde giant was stripped to the waist, covered with sweat and dirt.

Ryen's shoulders sagged as he rolled his eyes. "For all the Circles!" he muttered. "Out of the frying pan and into the fire."

Crag turned his green eyes from the brothers to gaze at Ember, smiling. "Can't you see she wants none of these things?" he asked. He walked to the table they had gathered around and stopped before the red commander and his voice dropped until it was like a purr from a lion. "Come away with me, my lady, and I will cloak you in cold steel by warm fires, and shelter you from the storm."

Ember laughed softly, looking way up to see his face, and gave her head a small shake. "What storm?" she challenged.

Crag leaned down and laid a colossal hand over her own. "The one that rages inside of you," he whispered.

Ember went still and felt something within her body bloom like a spark to tinder. Her tongue became rooted and she found herself lost in his eyes of jade. His lips were slightly parted and she could see the tip of his tongue run along the bottom of his top row of teeth. A tremor went up her spine and she licked her lips and drew her hand away gently.

"I am sorry to disappoint you, gentlemen," she said, her usual smile resurfacing, "but I have already been seduced by the Southlon, and .... its heat."

The brothers threw up their hands in frustration and returned to their argument over what women wanted more, precious metals or precious stones.

"Been helping the Gnomin?" Ryen asked Crag, trying to draw the man's eyes away from Ember. The man did so, with an effort, but it was another voice that responded.

"He certainly has been!" Wilhelm exclaimed as he entered the tent. The Gnomin male, though he was large for his race, was comparatively tiny next to the man from the North. The miner looked up at the Norseman, glowing with pride. "He can do the work of three steam shovels!" Wil informed them. "In half the time!"

"It is ditch-digging, at its finest," Crag said modestly, wiping his face with a rag.

"You might feel better after a dunk in the river," Ryen advised. "The red troops have been doing so."

Crag smiled, though he kept his green-eyed gaze fixed upon the Roshan. "And miss sharing a cider with the dark commander?" he asked, pulling another chair up to the table and seating himself in it. The wooden framework of the camp chair groaned under his weight and the cloth sagged dangerously low.

Wilhelm was there a second later, handing Crag a drinking horn topped with foam. He clasped his hands in front of his chest as he peered at those already seated. "Can I offer to refill another horn while I am up?"

"Thank you, but I think we are all full," Ryen told him. "Would you care to join us, Wilhelm?"

"No, no, no," he replied quickly. "And please, call me Wil. I will return to the Greatwood to oversee the progress there. Thank you for your help today," he told Crag earnestly.

"Don't mention it," the giant Norseman replied without looking at the Gnomin. His gaze was fixed on the Roshan. "I'll be there tomorrow too."

Wilhelm bowed graciously and took his leave.

"The Gnomin leaving some welcoming gifts for the Crommags?" Halvar asked.

"They certainly are," Crag agreed, his eyes never leaving Ember. "Some as simple as pits full of sharpened stakes, others more complex – explosive charges rigged to trees."

"The Gnomin excel at such things," Ember said, meeting his gaze. "I'll wager that the explosives are not only meant to be lethal, but to fell the trees they are attached to as well, causing further mortal damage."

Crag nodded and took a mighty drink from his horn. There was a weighted pause where the tent was all but silent, then he raised his cup in her direction. "Tell me about yourself," he encouraged.

Haldor and Halvar took long drinks as well, and listened, abruptly attentive.

The Roshan smiled. "What do you want to know?"

"Who taught you how to fight?"

"Originally, another Roshan Simorgh – a fighting master – of course. The rest I learned on my own."

Ember was still mesmerized by his eyes, but she did not like the look that had come into them. It was a mix of condescension and disbelief. It was no matter, she knew, he would see for himself soon enough.

"Have you ever fought a Crommag?" he asked.

"More than I can count."

"Really?" Crag asked with obvious surprise. "And?"

The Roshan shrugged. "The bigger they are, the harder they fall."

The brothers had a hearty guffaw at that, Halvar losing what cider had been in his mouth into his clipped orange beard.

"That is what I am talking about!" Haldor shouted, still laughing. "You are truly a Viking at heart, if not in size! Ryen! You must steal her away at the end of this war and take her to the Vikes where she belongs!"

"What do you think I have been trying to do?" Ryen asked, the tip of his horn balanced on his thigh. "Though I love the cold no more than she does. I may just follow her back to the Southlon."

"Nonsense!" Crag exclaimed. "She just needs to be kept warm." The look in his eyes had been replaced with lust once again and the Roshan had to pull her own eyes away with an effort.

"Speaking of following me," she said, turning her gaze to Ryen, "you have been doing much of that lately."

"I enjoy your company," he said testily. "And someone needs to keep you from all these wolves."

"No luck with the women who came with me from Redtown?" the Roshan asked, chuckling into her cider as she raised it to her lips.

"No!" the Norseman replied with a scowl. "As I am sure you know!" The Roshan laughed harder, bringing looks of confusion from the others at the table as Ryen continued. "I went to pay a visit to Ellie and Sedhi, whom I had met when I was in Redtown last year." Ryen leaned forward, closer to Ember. "I found out," he whispered hoarsely, "they do not lay with men!"

The Roshan leaned forward, closer to Ryen. "You don't have to whisper," she told him. "It's not a secret."

"Well, it was to me! I'd never heard of such a thing! I am guessing that the other women, the female soldiers, are the same way. They hardly spare me glance when I am in your camp."

"What?" Haldor demanded in confusion, his eyes going back and forth between Ryen and the Roshan. "What are you talking about?"

"The few women that have come with me from Redtown," Ember explained to the others, "prefer women to men." The look of bewilderment on the faces of the brothers was so complete it was comical. She shook her head, laughing, before looking at Ryen. "I'm sorry, but you're going to have to explain it to them."

"Someone has to explain it to me first," Ryen said, disgruntled. He took a drink of cider and lowered the horn till the tip was resting again on his thigh. "You never told me much of your time down there," he said, changing the subject. "Did the Red King truly know something of your past?"

The Roshan's black-clad shoulders went up a shrug. "A piece of the puzzle, nothing more."

Crag's green eyes narrowed at her from across the table, a small and curious smile on his full lips.

"Excuse me, commanders?" All heads turned to see Dash standing in the opening of the tent. "General Halloran would like to see all captains and commanders in the white cabin in an hour."

"Thank you, Dash," Ryen said. The elf bowed and disappeared back out of the tent. Ryen finished the cider in his horn and put it on the table as he stood up. "I will tell Kamut," he said.

The Roshan drained her own cup, put it on the table, and followed him. "I better find my captains," she said. "Gentlemen," she announced, looking at the others as they rose to their feet, "I will see you soon."

"My lady," Haldor said.

Halvar belched.

The Roshan laughed and followed Ryen out of his bachelor's abode. Crag's eyes followed her hungrily.

There was no doubt that he had wanted the woman from the moment he first saw her, but it was not until now that he realized how badly he wanted her. It was like nothing he had ever experienced before in his life. It was more than just lust, though she evoked it inside him in a powerful way.

She was physically desirable enough, with her flashing eyes and flaming hair, but it went much deeper than that. The grace and poise she displayed coupled with her unflinching confidence were characteristics he had never seen before. Her flaming spirit and strength of will lit a fire inside him. She was a woman who could make a man a lord and make a lord a king. She had a power that he felt, if joined with his own, would be an unstoppable force. She would be a queen of legend, and bear sons that would write history for ages.

I want to possess her, he comprehended. *In every way possible.*

❦

An hour later, the Roshan and her four captains entered the white cabin with Ryen and his leading Vikemen right behind them.

"Commander L'chiross!" Zephyrn called from the middle of the room where the general, a few scouts, and most of the captains stood around a large, rectangular table. The young prince motioned for her to join him while exchanging a few short words with his Praetorian. Dirk left his place at the table and took up post by the door while the Roshan took his spot next to the prince.

As Dell stepped back from the table, Ryen joined Traejan - noting the acerbic look the prince was giving his younger brother.

"He's not the one you need to worry about," Ryen said softly. Traejan looked up sharply at the Vikeman who glanced meaningfully at Crag. The giant Norseman had broken apart from his own group to follow the Roshan. Traejan's eyes went to the huge form that loomed behind her and his brother while the other Vikemen gathered behind the elves, easily looking over their shoulders at the map that had been laid out upon the table.

It was a map of Tuar Ceath and the surrounding lands and Ember noted that it was the same map they had examined yesterday at Castle Song. It seemed the general was getting things down here quickly. Other maps were laid out on other tables, or rolled tightly and held together by string. A few were tacked to the walls - two of them showed closer images of the valley below and another one was newly made and depicted their camp.

The grizzled commander looked around the group, his iron gray brows pulled together in a fierce scowl.

"Where is Jennings?" he growled.

"He will be here soon," Espytin quickly informed the general, who was not appeased in the least.

"What in the Seventh Circle has gotten into him?" he demanded.

A few pairs of elfin eyes darted about, uneasy. Espytin squared his narrow shoulders and spoke up again, though he dropped his voice a bit. "His daughter, Allyson, has been missing for three days."

Halloran's face went slack. "Oh, my apologies. I had no idea." After a moment of indecision he lifted his square chin. "Well, let us proceed for now." He looked across the table at Jaden, his steely eyes expectant.

The Sylvan cleared his throat and leaned over the map so he could reach a spot in the markings that showed the Elfin Greatwood. "The first group of Crommags is here," he told the group, "and should be *here* by tomorrow night," he said moving his finger from one spot to another. "I think our assessment of them being here in a week to ten days will lean to the later estimate."

Zephyrn nodded. "They are moving awfully slow," he remarked.

"They aren't in open country anymore," the Roshan told him, studying the map. "They can't see for miles in all directions. And this is this first time they have moved through a forest. It is likely that most have never seen one."

Crag grunted. "You think they are nervous?"

"I think they are being cautious, and rightly so." Her eyes moved back to Jaden. "Anything else?"

The Sylvan smiled. "The second party has not yet entered

the Greatwood. It seems they are waiting for the third group to catch up but, in so doing, are now a good two miles behind the first party."

Ember found herself returning the elf's smile, she was unable not to. "Something tells me you have more."

His smile widened. "They don't travel at night." He looked to the small elf named Dutch for confirmation and the other Sylvan nodded.

"I don't think they can see very well in the dark," the scout informed the group. "Blaine and I can get quite close to their camp at night, so close to their guards that we can almost touch them."

Everyone around the table exchanged looks of surprise.

"I never knew that," Kamut said.

"Me neither," added Ryen, "but it is good to know."

All heads turned as Jennings entered the cabin. His blue shirt and gray trousers were dusty from a long ride.

"I am sorry," he apologized to the group, "I was...delayed."

"Quite alright," Halloran growled softly in an effort to be soothing. "Any word from Allyson?"

Jennings' blue eyes leapt to meet those of the general. "You know?" he asked, clearly startled. When Halloran nodded Jennings looked away, downcast. "Unfortunately, no."

"I am sure she is fine," Halloran told him. The captain looked at him doubtfully as the general continued brusquely, "Jaden will catch you up on what he has already told the others."

Traejan watched Ember as Jaden repeated his report softly to the infantry captain. She had her right elbow cupped in her left hand and was touching her thumbnail to her bottom lip while she studied the map. He knew she was intent upon something, and had a good idea of what it was. She looked up and saw Traejan watching her and smiled. The young prince looked away, his armor trembling dangerously until Crag put one of his massive hands on her shoulder and leaned down to whisper in her ear.

From a being so large, however, a whisper was near impossible. Especially in a room full of elves.

"What are you thinking?" the Norseman asked softly. His voice was so deep that Ember could feel it vibrate from her eardrum to her neck and felt the skin all over her body prickle with heat. His hand was incredibly heavy and she suddenly felt as if it was holding her to the earth. She shook off such feelings and glanced up to meet the eyes of the general, a small smile edging into her cheek.

"I am thinking about leading an attack on the first group," she shared. She was met with a wall of silence, quickly broken by Jennings.

"They are twenty miles away!" he exclaimed. Another silence followed, this time broken by Nevin.

"A hard ride there," the rugged elf muttered, "but doable. Getting back will be harder, especially if we have any wounded."

"And fatigued horses," Espytin added. "I am not sure it is a good idea."

"I agree with Captain Espytin," Jennings said firmly. "We are just getting our army here. They are outfitted with weapons already but I don't know how soon they can be mobilized…" he trailed off, looking at Nevin who was voicing possibilities and concerns softly to Alistair.

The mumbled voices became a gabble as Haldor and Halvar chimed in as well to voice worry to each other about the ability of their mounts to keep up with the elfin horses.

"Gentlemen!" Crag boomed, silencing every tongue and making every man and elf go still. "Let her finish," he advised in a much softer tone. He removed his hand from her shoulder and its absence left a chill on her skin.

"Thank you," Ember said amid murmured apologies. "I am

not talking about mobilizing the entire army. I am suggesting a small force making a quick strike in the dead of night - causing as much panic, confusion, and damage as possible – and then getting out just as quick."

"If it works," Alistair said, "we could do it repeatedly - harry them for the rest of their journey."

The grizzled commander rubbed his square chin that was, even at this hour, truly grizzled with the salt and pepper stubble of a beard. "When?" he asked, looking at the Roshan.

"Tomorrow night," she answered. "Once they have set up camp and we have confirmation from the scouts on their location. We can ride out at dusk to cover our own movements, rest the horses for as long as possible, and strike. The moon will not be out again tomorrow until almost dawn."

"How many men?"

"Twenty elves," she replied, "and twenty from the red troops, myself included."

"I'm going too," Ryen stated, firm.

"I as well!" Haldor stated, his voice just as firm and a bit louder.

"Me too!" Halvar exclaimed, louder than his brother.

"I'll go," Nevin offered and then the whole room was a cacophony of voices, all insisting on taking part.

"Quiet!" Halloran shouted. "Have you all taken complete leave of your senses? We are not sending all of our officers on some damned raid!" He looked around the table and his scowl deepened as his steely eyes fell upon the elves. "Do you see the captains of the red troops behaving in such a manner?" he asked.

The eyes of the Vikemen and elves alike went to the red captains where they stood closemouthed behind their commander.

A mark of their training, Traejan thought, looking at the

fine-looking men who stood straight and stoic, their hands on the hilts of their swords. *They know to be still, and not speak out of turn lest they raise her wrath.* He glanced at the Roshan who was smiling at him once again, as if reading his thoughts. The young prince quickly averted his gaze, his anger warring with the feeling that smile raised in him.

The general cleared his throat. "Very well," he announced, taking in his company with a sweep of his steely eyes. "Captain Jennings will select nineteen men. Commander L'chiross, who will be in charge on this mission, will select nineteen as well. In addition, Captain Jaden or one of his scouts will escort the raiding party." He turned his steely eyes to the red commander. "Do you intend to move in as a single unit?" he asked.

The Roshan shook her head. "Since we have not trained as one, it would be better if we moved in separately for the attack. Also, I think we would cause more confusion if we struck from different directions." Her tawny eyes glanced at the map and then back up at the general. "I would like to lead my troops in from the east and have the elves circle around and attack from the west."

The general gave a single quick nod. "A sound plan. Go over the details with Captain Jennings." The Roshan bowed and Halloran's steely gray eyes traveled over the others as his voice rose in a soft growl in his throat. "The rest of you are to see to the army getting settled here and prepared for battle within a fortnight."

14. AMBUSH

Ian paced nervously outside of the tent he shared with the Roshan. He had been doing so for the past half an hour. Sounds in the camp had alerted him to the first of the returning riders and he went outside to see Dash already there, waiting to take charge of Coal upon the Roshan's return. Though the young elf had become quite familiar with the Night Stallion and his mistress, his eyes darted around nervously.

"Something is wrong," he said straight away.

Ian felt a chill across his back, though the summer night was warm. His own horse was shifting about nervously, but that was nothing new. Meghan was naturally skittish. He took her long nose in his hand and stroked it to calm her as he looked this way and that, trying to see what had Dash spooked nearly as much as his mare.

There was muffled noise coming from the vale below, letting them know that more riders were returning. Moments later, horses came up over the edge of the slope carrying elfin riders. They turned west and disappeared. The evenings fires had burned low, daubing the tents with a ruddy glow and casting long shadows in the recesses.

"What is it?" Ian finally asked.

The elf just shook his head. "I don't know, but it's not good."

The Roshan's steward threw two logs onto the dwindling cookfire in front of the tent and put a kettle of water over it before rejoining Dash. Together, they listened to the noises carried to them on the breeze from along the bluff and, though the sounds were very near muted, they made their own camp eerily silent. After what seemed like a very long time, though Ian knew it was really only a few long minutes, riders from the red troops that had been sent on the raid came riding back.

The young man knew at once that Dash was right, something was terribly wrong. It had been a well-planned raid and the Roshan had been confident of a successful mission. Ian had never known her to be mistaken, but one look at the riders told a different story. They were bloodied, burned, haggard, and too few.

And the Roshan was not among them.

Moments later, the three Vikemen that had gone on the raid came galloping into the camp on khusars that were lathered and snorting from a hard ride. Logs were thrown on the fires and the shadows were driven back as the air was filled with curses from the Norsemen.

The dark-haired young man and the dark-haired elfin messenger waited anxiously, but of the Roshan there was still no sign. Ian was ready to abandon his post and go question the Vikemen when Gavan came riding into the camp. His barrel-chested bay was snorting, stomping, and chomping at the bit.

Ian hailed him and the young man turned, the bay dancing wildly beneath him. His golden eyes took on a reddish hue in the light cast from the camp fires and they had a glassy look from adrenaline. His soft brown hair was matted with blood and he had a nasty cut on his cheek. His clothes as well were blood spattered and torn.

"Gavan!" Ian exclaimed, shocked. "What happened?"

Gavan waited until the horse had turned enough so that he could see the Roshan's steward. "It was an ambush," he said.

"An ambush?" Ian echoed in disbelief, "but that would mean..." he trailed off, more anxious than ever. "Where is the Roshan?" he asked.

Gavan shook his head to indicate he did not know. "She

stayed behind to make sure everyone got out, everyone that was still alive anyway." He looked around quickly, taking stock. "I have to go. We are supposed to meet at the support tent before we report to the cabin. Gretchen and Tom will be treating the wounded and I need to get a handle on our losses." Without waiting for a reply, Gavan spurred his horse and headed east.

Ian shifted his dark eyes to the elf by his side who licked his lips nervously. Together, they peered into the night in the direction the raiding party had taken down into the valley. Despite the growing noise amongst the tents, Ian could hear his own heart thudding in his chest. Just when he was again ready to leave his post and go find Ryen, four riderless horses came charging up the hill out of the dark. The Roshan was right behind them on her Night Stallion, leading two more. She slid off the back of the great beast before it had come to a complete stop, landing on her feet.

The fires had grown, banishing the darkness, and both men could see the Roshan quite clearly. Her face was smeared with blood and her vest was soaked, as well as her sleeves up to the elbows. Neither the shadows nor her black clothes could hide the fact she was covered in gore. She let the reins of her stallion drop and when Dash moved to get them she grabbed his arm with a bloody glove.

"Never mind him for now!" she said forcefully, making an obvious effort not to shout. She pushed the reins of the two horses she held into one of his long-fingered hands. "Take care of these and round up the others."

Dash nodded wordlessly and hurried to do her bidding. Like Ian, he had never seen so much blood - nor the terrorizing fury in the Roshan's eyes. She strode past them both, her fury building even more, and stormed into her tent, nearly ripping the flap from the rest of the canvas.

"All the Circles of the damned!" she shouted, yanking off her gloves and throwing them across the small room. She looked around, wishing she had something heavier to throw. Ian was by her side in an instant, gently touching her. The Roshan looked at him, shocked for a moment, before waving him away. "It's not my blood," she assured him, scowling. When he hesitated, she waved him away again. "Pour me a cup of wine," she ordered, casting her eyes about the tent as if looking for something or someone.

Ian, glad to have task, filled a goblet with steady hands and brought it to her. The Roshan raised it to her lips and took three large swallows as he unbuckled her sword belt and pulled it free. It, too, was covered with gore. He tossed it aside to be cleaned and began to undo the fastenings on the brace she wore that was usually full of daggers. She let him, calmed a little by the wine and his gentle touch. He would only have to clean the brace - all the daggers were gone. He was peeling off her vest when Ryen shouldered his way into the tent.

"Are you alright?" he demanded, walking right up to the Roshan so he could get a good look at her. She nodded, silent, though both men could see the rage that still burned within her. Ryen looked her up and down and nodded as well. "Good. The general wants all captains in the white cabin for a report and," the Vikeman paused to blow a burst of air through puffed cheeks, "a head count."

The Roshan took another gulp of wine and handed the goblet to Ian. "Bring the rest of that bottle to the cabin, along with two more cups," she instructed before following Ryen out of the tent. Ian watched them go, wishing he could have first cleaned her face. "Have you sent for Gavan?" she asked Ryen once they were outside. The summer air was beginning to cool.

"He's already there."

As they passed the Vikemen encampment they were met by Crag and his green eyes grew wide when he saw the Roshan. "Are you alright?" he asked, falling in step with them as they passed the supply structure.

"I'm fine," she replied, not looking at him as they strode

rapidly past the mess pavilion. Ryen pulled open the door to the cabin and she entered first, her eyes scanning those gathered around the main table and ascertaining immediately that she was the last one to arrive. Almost.

"Commander L'chiross," Halloran greeted in his graveled voice as the two Vikemen followed her inside. "Are you alright?"

"Yes!" she replied testily. "Why does everyone keep asking me that?"

"Perhaps because you look like you have either been mortally wounded, or bathed in blood," he reprimanded, gruff. "And I have asked the same of every captain that has returned tonight."

The Roshan sighed and dipped her head. "Of course you have. I am sorry. I am just...upset."

"Reasonably so," he said, his voice softening. The Roshan approached the table, marking those that stood around it. It was easy to distinguish who had fought tonight by those that were bloodied and those that were clean. Traejan was among those that had not gone on the raid and, though angry, his face was impassive. He had wanted to pace the room like a caged tiger the past two hours, but had made himself be still.

Major Dellion and Captain Espytin were equally unmarked though unfazed at staying behind. But it was Espytin who had a sly look that Ember did not like. Crag, as well, stood out in sharp contrast to Ryen who was besotted with blood and ashes.

"Where is Jennings?" Ember asked, her eyes still moving across those that were gathered.

"As of yet," Dell informed her, "he has not returned. But he is a very resourceful soldier and we hope that he will show before long." The Roshan was still looking at him, measuring his words, when Halloran spoke.

"Haldor and Halvar?" he asked, looking at Ryen.

"Halvar has some bad burns," he informed the general.

"Haldor is seeing to him."

"Will he be alright?" Halloran asked and the Vikeman gave him a quick nod of assent. The commander grunted, thoughtful for a moment, and then continued, looking at the Roshan. "Everyone, of course, has been talking about the raid. But, as your team was the first in, I want to hear your account first. Then Commander Glace since he was with the other team. Then I want a casualty account from Captain Gavan and Major Dellion."

Prince Zephyrn and his Praetorian were also absent, but not missed. Traejan had assured his brother that he would miss nothing if he skipped the debriefing and that everyone would be waiting around all night for nothing but reports. Zephyrn, who despised boredom and supposed the Roshan would be too tired to give him a sword lesson much less anything else, decided to stay at Castle Royce.

Traejan watched Ember's hands curl into fists as she fought to control her anger. She could feel blood drying in the creases of her palms and on the backs of her fingers. Crommag blood. It only made her angrier and her fists tightened.

"They were waiting for us," she said, her voice low but even.

"You are sure?" Halloran demanded. He looked around at the other grim and bloodied faces and all nodded their assent. "They were not just quick to respond?" This time there was a mutual shaking of heads. He turned his gaze back to the commander and waited for her to continue.

"Dutch led my party between the posted Crommag guards. I led the way into the eastern end of the encampment along with Haldor and Halvar, followed by Gavan and his men." Halloran's dark gray eyes flicked to Dutch who met the commander's gaze.

"They were quiet," he affirmed. "And not just for humans," he added with a humorless smile. The small Sylvan was blood-spattered and disheveled. "But what I failed to notice, until it was too late, was how quiet the Crommags were. No snoring, no muttering, no movement. I realized, at the final second, that it was as if the entire camp was holding its breath."

Halloran's strong jaw clenched and he turned his steely eyes back to the red commander.

"And it was too dark," she added. "We had planned on lighting their tents with any wood still burning from their cookfires, but there were none. I would have signaled a halt, but the only one with eyes who could have seen it was Dutch." She looked at Ryen and the Norseman nodded.

"It was the same on our side. But once we were all in," he said, "they lit fires. Not normal camp fires, but pans of oil that lit up the night as if it were day. The Crommags were all up, armed, and ready. They fell in on us from every side."

Halloran's jaw clenched even tighter. "It is fortunate that as many of you escaped as you did," he finally offered.

"We owe this night, and the lives of those who returned, to Commander Glace," Jaden informed the general. "If not for him, we might have all perished in that camp." All eyes turned to Ryen who shook his head and looked away. His ginger beard was singed along the right side of his face.

Halloran's eyes went to Gavan next. "I lost eight out of twenty men," he reported, his voice as tight as the expression on his handsome face.

"Twelve of our twenty," Dell reported, his countenance set. "Thirteen if Captain Jennings does not return."

"Did anyone see him fall?" the general queried. Everyone shook their heads. No. The grizzled commander sighed and rubbed his stubbled chin. "Circles," he muttered. "I, too, can only hope he was able to get away." He looked to the Vikeman commander. "You saved the night?" he asked, the surprise but a murmur in his tone.

Ryen shrugged. "I was only trying to take away the advantage they had sprung on us."

"He ran through the camp like a wild man," Jaden told

those around the table, "kicking the pans of oil up onto the Crommags, right in their faces. They were engulfed in the flames as they ran about, burning themselves and blinding others. He turned their advantage into a weapon, surprising and debilitating them while in turn running at them headlong, swinging his sword."

"Brilliant," Crag whispered.

The grizzled commander as well favored the Norseman with smile. "Indeed," he agreed.

"Tents and small carts were beginning to catch fire," the Roshan continued, "and it was mayhem. We can, at least, label that part of the mission a success. Even still, they had us ringed in. We had to fight our way out."

The general spoke softly, his gray eyes loosening their hold on the Vikeman. "Can anyone offer more details of the raid?" Grim faces moved slowly from side to side as the grizzled commander cast his steely gaze across them. "Very well," he announced, "we shall all meet again here after breakfast. Commander L'chiross and Commander Glace, please remain. Everyone else is dismissed. Get your wounds seen to and get some rest."

Those that were bloodied were relieved to go, the others who had not fought followed almost reluctantly.

As Captain Jaden passed her, Ember touched his hand, making him turn. "You fought well tonight," she said. The young elf gave her a glimpse of a smile, then left with the others.

Though formally dismissed as group, Crag and Prince Traejan remained - along with Dell.

As the others left, Ian entered followed by a Gnomin woman holding a steaming pot with a pair of towels over her arm. The steward stopped as he saw everyone staring. The Roshan beckoned him towards her and turned her eyes back to the grizzled commander.

Ryen turned his blue eyes to Crag as Ian put cups on the table between Ember and the general.

"Please check on Halvar," he said, politely dismissing the giant Northman. Crag looked at the others, obviously not wanting to leave, but he had already been effectively dismissed by them as well.

"General?" Ember asked, pointing to an empty cup.

"By all means!" Halloran said. "Thank you."

"Don't forget me," Ryen intoned, turning his attention back to the group as Crag left, casting one last glance over a massive shoulder, his gaze trained on the Roshan.

Ian filled a cup for Ryen and his dark eyes looked up at Traejan. "My Lord Prince?" he asked.

I am not your lord nor your prince, the young elf thought acidly, but said nothing. He simply shook his head, as did Dell when the youth looked at him.

Ian put the bottle down and motioned to the Gnomin woman as Ryen, the Roshan, and Halloran pulled chairs up next to the table. They sat themselves as he took one of the towels and dipped it in the pot before wringing it out.

Traejan remained standing with Dell by his side. Ember leaned back in her chair and Ian tried to gently wipe some of the blood from her face. Ember took the towel from him with a look of annoyance.

"Thank you, Ian, that will be all. I'll clean up when I get back." The handsome young man looked for a moment as if he might argue, but then dipped his head of raven black hair and left with the Gnomin woman. Traejan watched him go as the Roshan scrubbed her face with the wet towel.

That should be me, his mind wanted to bellow. *I should be the one taking care of her.* His armor, however, kept out such clamoring. Passively, he turned his brown eyes back to the Roshan.

"Are you thinking what I am thinking?" she asked the

general, cleaning her hands next on the bloodied towel before tossing it aside.

"That, despite casualties, the mission was a success?" he asked, taking a sip of wine.

The Roshan's lips curled down in a sneer. "A success!" she scoffed before picking up her own cup.

"You said so yourself," the general informed her. "You accomplished what you set out to do - killing as many Crommags as you could, causing mayhem and confusion."

"At a higher price than I wanted to pay," the Roshan replied, scowling.

"Every life is important," the general conceded, "but we will lose more than some. We will lose many, possibly most of our soldiers before this vile thing is done. But we did not lose you, nor any of our captains. Though the plan was simple, it was no mere raid. This is war, Commander L'chiross. There will be casualties."

"Of course," the Roshan agreed cursorily, "but that was not what I was thinking." She leaned forward in her seat until her forearms rested on her thighs and when she spoke her voice was but a harsh whisper. "They were waiting for us, General. They knew we were coming."

Halloran's iron gray brows drew together over his steely gray eyes. "What are you thinking, Commander?" he asked. "A spy?" His brows went up at his own query and he looked around at those gathered at and near the table. "Here? Among us?"

The Roshan sat back in her chair and her gimlet eyes also darted over those present. "Not among us, no. But a spy, yes."

"No," Traejan whispered, mortified. The Roshan spared him a gentle glance but he would not meet her gaze.

"If it were so," Dell said softly, "it would have to be an officer. Which is difficult to believe."

"No," Ryen said, "not difficult to believe, just something

you don't *want* to believe. I don't want to believe it either, but I agree with her. There has to be a spy. They *knew* we were coming."

"Not necessarily from a spy," Halloran countered. "They could have scouts that saw you coming."

This time it was Ryen that leaned forward. "When they attacked us, I charged west, instinctively trying to get to her," he said, jerking his chin towards Ember. "When I broke through their line, there wasn't a single Crommag for a hundred yards. It made breaking through the next line easier, for they had their backs to my party." The Vikeman narrowed his icy blue eyes at Halloran. "Do you see what I am saying, General? There was no one in the middle. They were massed at the east and west sides of their camp."

"They did not just know we were coming," the Roshan said, her voice flat. "They knew *where*."

The room was silent as each person contemplated the possibilities, those at the table with cups in their hands, their wine momentarily forgotten. Then all eyes went to the door as it opened and they all widened as they realized who it was. Captain Jennings entered, closing the door behind him. Those seated rose to their feet as he strode quickly towards them and bowed low.

"Forgive my tardiness," he said, straightening his tall form, "but I was unavoidably detained."

"Better late than never, old friend," Halloran said, clasping the other elf's hand in his own. "What happened?"

"I became separated from our party," he told everyone, "but I was able to slip away in the confusion. I was pursued by a number of Crommags, forcing me in the wrong direction. By the time I made my way to the north side of the woods, everyone had gone, including the horses. I returned on foot."

The general smiled and clapped him on the back. "Well, you made good time for an elf your age! And we are happy to have you back, and safe." The grizzled commander looked happily at the others. "Unless anyone else has something more to add, I think we can call it a night."

There were nods of assent and Ryen and the Roshan drained their cups, leaving them on the table. Everyone left together, Jennings and Halloran heading west towards the elfin camp. Traejan and Dell turned right, headed for their horses to take them to Castle Song. Ryen and the Roshan followed them on the way back to their own tents. They lagged behind and spoke softly, but the elfin ears of the prince and his Praetorian still caught most of their words.

"What are the chances there is a spy in our camp?" Ryen asked. The Roshan shook her head.

"Impossibly slim. But I don't know what else it could be. Sometimes the most obvious answer is the correct one."

"We will know soon enough," Ryen said. "Hopefully before it costs us more dearly than it did tonight." Traejan and Dell glanced back as they followed a path to the left and Ryen and Ember gave them a small wave as they continued towards their tents. "Do you think we will have slowed them down?" Ryen asked.

The Roshan shook her head again. "Not enough to make a difference. They will still be here within ten days." Ryen gave her half a smile and put a hand on her shoulder as they passed the supply room and ambled into the light of the dying fires of their own camp.

"We'll be ready for them," he assured her. She turned her face up to him and smiled back but he knew the look. She didn't believe him.

 15. SMALL REINFORCEMENTS II

Traejan found himself on the front of two wars. The enemy outside and the one from within. One threatened his land and his people, the other threatened his sanity. He cursed his emotional armor and cursed his impatience even more. Why hadn't he let her finish her sentence the one time they had been alone together? What was it she assumed he understood? If he had remembered his training, just the seemingly small and insignificant part where she had taught him to be still, he would not be tormented as he was now.

He finished dressing and buckled on his sword belt, looking around his bedchamber as he considered the war that was coming.

Ember and Ryen believed there was a spy among them.

Their reasons were convincing, but the young prince could not even begin to conceive who among them would betray his people. Surely not an elf.

A Vikeman then? A bargain struck with the Crommags to protect their own lands? If that was the case, could it be the Gnomin for the same reason – to protect their people? Traejan discarded both ideas as folly. Both races hated the Crommags so deeply and, besides, there had not been any Gnomin present at any of the war meetings. Or had they? There was often one or two about, helping in one way or another.

No, Traejan thought. *There is no way.*

But it had to be someone.

Maybe it's the Roshan, his mind whispered. *She has already betrayed you, has she not?*

"No," he said aloud to the empty room, feeling his emotional armor close around him, shutting off the voice. "They have to be wrong," he murmured, thinking of Ember and Ryen as he fitted his quiver and knives over his back. "One raid gone awry does not mean we have a spy."

He ran his thumbs under the leather straps that held his small arsenal in place, smoothing them. A glance at the mirror before he left showed that he was becoming gaunt again and the prince made a mental note to eat a hearty breakfast.

There is just no way we can have a spy, the elf thought as he left his room and descended the stairs of the south tower. *No way at all. They are mistaken. They must be.*

Kriegslager was now a hive of activity. Traejan had standing orders for his soldiers to drill between breakfast and lunch and the summer air was full of swordsong as he rode into camp. He and Dell dismounted at the corral built for the elfin horses, though theirs would be kept separate and ready to ride at a moment's notice. Two more corrals had been built on the east side for each cavalry from Redtown. The fresh-split logs and rails laced the air with the smell of sap and sawdust.

Also on the east side and close to the edge of the Elysian Forest, between the tents of the red troops and the tents of the Gnomin, Zephyrn and his archers practiced with the crossbowmen. Yasgir was the lone Vikeman in the group, easily discernible by his flowing black hair and hooked nose. Though stocky for a Vikeman, he loomed over the slight form of Sloan as the white-haired captain instructed him on how to load and shoot the mechanized weapon.

The white cabin was full of soldiers coming and going. Traejan ran a hand through his sandy hair as he surveyed the room. The Roshan was by herself, leaning over a side table close to the door with her hands planted on the map before her. None of the Vikemen were present as of yet.

As his eyes finished their journey across the room, they fell upon Halloran. The general was looking right at him and, when their eyes met, he motioned for the prince to join him. Traejan crossed the room with Dell at his elbow.

They exchanged formal greetings as they met and then the general, obviously tense, took a few inconspicuous steps closer to the wall of birch logs. Traejan and Dell moved with him.

"Am I to assume correctly," Halloran asked softly, "that neither of you have spoken about the discussion that occurred in here last night?"

"Not even with each other," Traejan confirmed.

Much of the tension visibly drained out of the general. "Good," he said, his voice still low but firm. "It is something we should keep to ourselves for the time being, for obvious reasons."

Both elves nodded in agreement. Talk of an infiltrator would only alert the infiltrator – if there really was one.

"I should have advised you as such last night," he offered in his graveled voice, "but my head was spinning, to say the least."

"Of course," Dell said.

"We were no different," Traejan admitted with a trace of a smile.

The general pursed his lips and nodded. "Very well. We will speak of it more, privately. Until then, keep your eyes and ears open."

The prince and his Praetorian nodded their assent and returned their attention to the room. Dell noted Captain Espytin immediately. The young elf was flanked by two soldiers that leaned in towards the captain, deep in discussion. Espytin, however, was not speaking and instead was completely still, staring at Dell and the prince.

"Where is Jennings?" Traejan asked his guard as he noticed the absence of the infantry captain.

Dell looked around, surprised until he remembered the manifest for the day. "He is down in the Greatwood," he informed the prince, "checking on the work done there by the Gnomin."

Traejan nodded absently, his soft brown eyes inexorably drawn to where the Roshan stood, clothed in black and dressed ready for the war to begin at any second.

Ember leaned over the map table, blessedly alone for a moment with her thoughts, intent upon the areas the general had assured would be occupied by the Crommags. The map she was studying had been made by Wilhelm and it showed the traps the Gnomin had laid for the enemy. She was trying to decide if more should be set closer to the river when she heard Ryen clear his throat in an obvious manner.

"Excuse me, Commander?"

Ember barely gave the Vikeman a thought, much less a glance. He knew she was in a foul mood from the previous night and should have well known to leave her be. She spared a brief glimpse from over her shoulder. He stood in the entrance to the cabin, half in and half out. Her eyes returned to the map, definitely seeing a spot by the river that could use another pitfall.

"Commander?" he asked again, louder this time. Ember sighed and marked the place she was looking at with a finger.

"What is it?" she called over her shoulder.

"Your reinforcements have arrived."

Ember turned around, frowning. "My *what*?" Her scowl softened until it had melted away.

Ryen stood aside as what appeared to be five boys entered the cabin. They were bone thin, half naked, and covered with dirt. Each wore ragged shorts or horribly tattered breeches, as well as feathers and paint – which could have just been dried mud. Most had a knife of sorts attached to a belt, others had spears made of sharpened sticks that had been hardened by fire. A few had beads or knots tied in their hair.

They were undoubtedly elves, with almond-shaped eyes under high, arched brows though they were markedly different from most of those in the camp. Predominantly by their smaller stature and ears that were distinctively more pointed. Soiled and unkempt set them apart as well, but those were not inherited traits.

The tallest, who was almost the same height as the Roshan and obviously the leader of the small group, looked to be no more than fourteen. He grasped a real spear that was short, but tipped with forged iron. His dusty curls were squirrel-brown and ragged from knife cuts. Ember suppressed a smile as best she could and went to him, taking his hand and squeezing it.

"Aiden," she sighed. "What are you doing here?"

Aiden flushed with pleasure at his hand in her own. He would have preferred an embrace, but he knew he would lose all credibility (though he did not know the word) from those that were watching, which he knew was everyone in in the room. "We have come to fight with you," he announced proudly, "me and my men."

The Roshan's body went rigid but her eyes flicked up to Ryen.

"There are twenty more waiting outside," he informed.

Her eyes went back to Aiden who was beaming with pride. "Simon stayed behind on the Mountain with the little 'uns. Otherwise, I have the best of my tribe with me." He took a deep breath and his narrow chest expanded. "We have come to fight with you," he said again, standing tall – as tall as he could.

But for a rustle of paper and the scrape of a boot, the entire cabin had gone silent and the Roshan knew that every eye was on them. She dropped Aiden's hand and straightened, her expression hard.

"No."

Aiden's smile faltered and he cocked his head. "I am sorry, my lady, I don't understand what…"

"No," the Roshan repeated. "You will not fight in this war. Nor your men."

The Wildboy looked at her, taken aback. "I know we are not as big as the Vikemen," he said glancing at Ryen before shifting his brown eyes back to Ember, "but we are good fighters. And I see there are other true elves among you," he said, looking meaningfully at Jaden, the only Sylvan elf in the room.

"You are good fighters," she agreed, her voice still stern, "and warriors in your own right. But this is not your war."

Aiden frowned. "It is so!" he argued. "We have fought more Crommags than any of the pointy-eared men, and long before they fell from the sky!"

"Even so, this is not raiding or marauding for fun on a summer's eve."

"What was last night?" Aiden challenged, stepping closer to the Dark Lady. If she was surprised by his knowledge of the Crommag raid, she did not show it.

The Roshan stood her ground and jerked her head towards the door. "Get back to the Mountain before the Crommags get here."

The Wildboy's expression melted into one of hurt and disappointment before it hardened into anger. "Back to the Mountain? Who are you, to command me?" he challenged.

"Who do you think would have commanded you, should you have been allowed to stay and fight?" the Roshan asked.

"Allowed?" Aiden sputtered in fury, searching for more words, but finding none. He stomped a bare foot in consternation but still he could find no words to express his emotion. "Arrrrr!" he finally shouted at Ember before he turned on his heel and stalked furiously from the white cabin, shaking with rage. He was followed by the four Wildboys that had accompanied him inside, their eyes like moons in their dirty faces.

The second before the door swung shut, Traejan turned and followed them out.

The Roshan's piercing eyes found Ryen. "How did they get here?" she demanded.

"They crossed the Northlon," the Vikeman informed her, "and circled around behind the Mountains of the Moon. They had felled a sapling and were crossing over the rapids when one of Jaden's scouts found them and brought them in."

The Roshan's eyes, still blazing, looked at the door as it swung shut.

"Aiden!" Traejan called as he left the cabin.

The leader of the Wildboys, who had almost reached his waiting band of ragamuffins, swung around to stand before him. He was still shaking with anger, but it diminished as he was greeted by the young prince.

Aiden dipped his head in recognition. "Prince of the elf-men," he greeted. "I am sorry that I am not in good spirits to speak with you."

"I understand," Traejan told him, the ghost of a smile on the edge of his lips. "She makes me feel the same way as well."

"But she did not try to send you away!" Aiden argued, vehement.

Traejan moved closer until he was standing above the elf who was decades old, but looked a boy, and sighed. "You know, she only does that because she loves you." It was a statement, not a question.

The Wildboy's fury finally broke and tears shimmered in his eyes. "If she did, she would let me die defending her!"

Traejan smiled gently. "I don't think that is how love works.

In fact, I think it is quite the opposite."

Aiden took a number of deep breaths and finally regained most of his composure, and a bit of his previous spark. He gave the elfin prince a glimmer of a smile though his brows were still pressed tight together. "Are you taking care of her, like I asked of you?"

It was Traejan's turn to frown. "No. She won't let me."

Aiden's smile became genuine and he shook his head of dusty curls. "In that way, we are alike." His smile fell and he fixed the prince with his dark eyes. "I almost forgot," he said, "we received a bit of news when we crossed part of the Vikes. Tell Ryen that the Roskilde Borough found eight dead men in the spring thaw. They did not know if it was the work of Crommags, but I thought I should pass it along."

"Thank you," the elfin prince told him, "I will. You know," he added, "just because you do not fight, does not mean you are not welcome to stay in Tuar Ceath."

The Wildboy grinned at him. "And sleep in a bed, with pillows, and protected by a roof?"

Traejan could not hold back a smile. "If you wish."

Aiden rocked back on his heels, laughing. "Next you will want me wearin' shoes and eating with…" not know any name for cutlery, the Wildboy pantomimed cutting food with a knife and fork. He laughed even harder, this time joined by his band of grimy soldiers. They all repeated his pantomime and laughed uproariously.

It warmed Traejan's heart to see them behave in such a manner, and he was more than a touch envious of Aiden who returned so easily to his own light-hearted nature in the wake of what could have been, to anyone else, a crushing disappointment.

"Besides," Aiden told the young prince, his brown eyes twinkling with mischief, "who says I won't be fighting?"

The smiled slipped from Traejan's face. "Aiden…" he began

but the Wildboy laughed.

"Not to worry, Traejan, prince of the men with pointy ears! My men know their business, and I know mine!" The leader of the filthy pack scooped up Traejan's hand and gave it a quick shake as he threw him a wink. "I will see you again," he promised, "but first I must find where Ryen sleeps, and hide a snake in his bed!"

Traejan paled, even as he smiled at the prospect, while Aiden raised his spear and led his merry men east, toward the Vikeman's yurts. The prince had time to see one of the Wildboys hand Aiden a sack that looked half full of something, or somethings, alive and writhing.

The young prince turned to see Zephyrn and Dirk approaching on foot just as the door to the cabin flew open and the Roshan stormed out. Traejan could immediately sense the mood she was in and took a subtle step backwards, becoming perfectly still. She cast her gem-like eyes about, searching. Spotting the dust cloud that trailed behind the departing Sprites, she turned on her heel to follow before Zephyrn hailed her.

"Commander L'chiross!" he called, stopping her in her tracks. "Commander!"

Ember turned slowly and Traejan could see the patience she was forcing upon herself. He knew the look and knew the danger it bespoke, but Zephyrn did not. Moving slowly, he took another step backwards, melting into the shadow of the cabin.

"Prince Zephyrn," she greeted stiffly. "Dirk," she acknowledged as she glanced at the Praetorian.

"I knew I would find you here!" Zephyrn exclaimed. The Roshan's face remained expressionless but Traejan smiled.

Where else would she be at this time? Traejan thought with amused sarcasm. *Picking daisies?*

"With the raid done and the Crommags still days away," Zephyrn said cheerily, "I thought you might have time to give me a lesson in swordsmanship." When she did not respond he gave her his most winning smile. "Xander has commanded me, or condemned me rather, to stay on the cliff, with the archers." The young prince took her silence to mean she was considering the idea, and he pulled his sword from the scabbard on his hip.

Traejan bit his lip, waiting. He knew her silence meant she was seething, but making herself be still. He found he enjoyed seeing *her* have to fight for control and for once he was delighted at Zephyrn's persistence.

The youngest prince motioned with his chin towards east. "There is more room by the tents," he suggested. "I have tent there, myself. And, if not a lesson," he entreated with a beguiling smile, "some advice, at least."

Without a word and with the speed of a snake, the Roshan leapt forward and kicked the bottom of Zephyrn's hand, sending his sword straight into the air.

The young prince snatched back his hand and held it to his chest. All eyes lifted as the sword continued up, and then came down. The Roshan caught it smartly and held it out, hilt first, towards the stunned elf who took it back, slowly and with much caution.

"My advice," she told him, her words icy cold and swift, "is to stay with the archers."

Then she turned on her heel and left, heading west.

Zephyrn, cradling his hand and his blues eyes full of disbelief, was struck speechless. Then he spotted Traejan in the shadows of the cabin.

"Was that really necessary?" he asked.

"Probably," Traejan said, his smile widening.

Zephyrn gave his hand a shake, trying to return the feeling to his injured fingers. Then he smiled as the shock passed, then chuckled nervously. "She's fast," he declared.

"And dangerous," Traejan added. "Don't toy with her. You're lucky all you have is a bruised pinky."

"Did she ever hurt you?" Zephyrn asked.

His question was asked merely from curiosity, but Traejan stiffened as if stabbed.

"Many times," he answered. "But physical pain is…"

"Is what?" Zephyrn prodded when his brother trailed off and did not attempt to finish his sentence.

"Is nothing," Traejan said. He turned and left, deciding to check on his infantry and their drills.

Zephyrn rubbed the edge of his hand and gave Dirk a look of feigned irritation as they continued on their way, not to the cabin now but to the mess hall.

"And just where were you while I was being attacked?" he asked his guardsman.

Dirk gave him a partial smile. "I didn't want to interrupt your…lesson."

Zephyrn grunted and bumped his Praetorian with his shoulder.

"I'll give *you* a lesson," he promised.

Dirk's smile widened into a grin. "You do all the time, my Lord Prince. You do all the time."

16. THE BATTLE BEGINS

The air about Kriegslager was hectic but hushed, the tension high as the midsummer sun began its descent in the western sky. The elfin scouts had been tracking the progress of the Crommags and the first of the beasts were expected to arrive in the forestlands that bordered Morgan's Vale the following afternoon.

The Wildboys had not been seen since the day of their arrival and querulous departure, not even by the scouts. Traejan hoped they had heeded the Roshan's command to return to their mountain. Ryen hoped he would get his hands on Aiden to give him a sound beating. The Vikeman had been awakened that night by a tree snake slithering up his leg. Two days later, he found another in his trunk while looking for a clean pair of socks. Both times he felt his heart stop for as long as it took him to gasp before it started back up again with a terrifying ferocity.

There had been some bitter arguments over the past few days as the preliminary battle plans were laid out. The Roshan already had tactics in mind on the day she had arrived with her troops. Strategies that involved her mounted infantry, three columns wide, and leading the first assault.

"No," the general had told her - as flat as she had told the Wildboys they could not fight at all.

"Excuse me?" she had responded, her auburn brows high over her eyes of brown and green and gold.

"You have come to help us," Halloran gruffly reminded her,

leaning back and crossing his arms over his stout chest, "and for that we are eternally grateful. But you are here to aid in this war, not fight it for us. Prince Traejan's infantry will lead the first assault, and keep the field for as long as they are able."

The Roshan's eyes went to the young prince who stood tall and unsmiling, yet obdurately smug, enveloped inside his suit of emotional armor. He was not so smug when he had almost the same argument later that night with his father and older brother.

"No," King Rowland said.

"Excuse me?" Traejan asked, his sand-colored brows high over his soft brown eyes. "But I am the captain of the infantry. I have been training these men for almost a year - I need to be with them on the field!"

"No," his father repeated. "You, and your brothers, will remain on the high side of the cliff, with myself and your grandfather. Your captains will be briefed on the plans, and lead the assault."

Traejan, flabbergasted, looked at Xander. It was the eldest prince, this time, that looked undeniably self-satisfied and Traejan knew that the crown prince had a hand, or least some choice words, that led to this decision.

"Even the general won't be on the field of battle, Traejan," Xander said, his tone much like a mother consoling a child who did not get the toy he wanted.

"The general did not train these men!" Traejan retorted, his voice rising to near a shout. "I did!"

"And you need to stay alive to command them," Xander told his brother.

"Trust me," Traejan said, "our men are the best fighters this New World has seen. Yet, should the enemy prevail, I will be the last one standing among them."

Xander's nose gave a snort of skepticism that might have sent another man into a rage. Traejan however, felt a strange stillness settle over his body even as his muscles went taut.

He smiled savagely at his brother. "If you doubt my fighting ability, we can go outside and I would be glad to show you."

Xander scowled deeply, provoked for the first time Traejan could remember. "Are you threatening me?" he demanded.

"Boys!" the king bellowed, though the both of them had seen well over a hundred summers. "Stop this!" He fixed his dark eyes upon Xander first. "You need to drop that condescending tone with your brother, you are only goading him and I am quite sure you know it." The king's gaze found the younger elf, smirking at the reprimand given his brother, and he continued as he stepped closer to his son. "And you will do as you are commanded!"

Traejan's smile fled from his face and he knew the argument was over. Bristling, he bowed to his father and left the room.

He returned to Castle Song, his hands balled into fists, wondering why the emotional armor he wore kept him completely protected from his mother, mostly protected against the Roshan, and not at all against his brother.

Because he knows where the weak points are, he realized with more than a touch of disgust, *and exploits them.*

Leaving through the gallery, he almost ran headlong into his grandfather.

"Whoa!" the Battle King exclaimed, catching Traejan in hands that were still quite strong. He caught sight of his grandson's eyes and his expression of surprise melted into one of sympathy. "They are not going to let you fight?" he asked. "Is that it?"

"You knew?"

The Battle King shook his head, his white hair falling past the shoulders of his white robes. "No, but it is not hard to guess, looking at you. Do not take it personally, it is not uncommon for kings or their children to be kept from the fray."

"Is that how you won your battles?" Traejan asked his

grandfather, struggling to stay respectful and falling short. "By staying with the rear guard?"

"I won my battles," his grandfather said, leaning close, "by choosing them wisely. And I did not make those choices based on what I thought I could win, but what I believed in."

Traejan got the feeling he was alluding to the unspoken battle with his brother, rather than the one about to be waged on the plains to the south. He bowed to his grandfather, regaining his composure, despite how irked he still felt. He knew good advice when he heard it, even if he did not like it.

In the end, it was the Roshan who had come out on top, talking the general into letting her lead the second wave of the first attack. Traejan tried the same ploy with his father and brother but was still sentenced to watch the battle from atop his horse and at a very safe distance on the higher ground. He was disgusted beyond words.

C8&0

The Roshan stood on that higher ground now, looking out over the low meadows to where they disappeared into the vast forest the Skye Elves had named the Elfin Greatwood. She could hear someone approaching her from behind and knew immediately from the heavy step that it was Crag, but did not turn her head to look at him until he stood next to her.

His hair was wet and a clean shirt of blue linen clung to his damp skin. She had to look way up to see his face as it looked in the same direction hers had been, across the low meadows of the vale and into the trees on the far side.

"No pits to be dug in the Greatwood today?" she asked. The giant Norseman had been working tirelessly with the Gnomin for over a week, unlike most of the other men from the Vikes, who preferred drinking cider while exchanging stories that were either outlandish or lewd, or oftentimes both.

Crag smiled, his eyes still fixed south. "Work's all done," he said, "though I am sure Wilhelm is intent upon taking me home with him as the 'living steam shovel,' whatever that is."

Ember smiled, thinking of the mining leader, and her gaze lowered slowly until she found herself eye-level with his elbow. Above it rose a massive arm, his bicep as round and hard as stone, and she found herself suddenly wanting to touch it.

"Jennings is with him now," Crag continued, pulling her out of her reverie, "going over the details of the traps they have laid."

"Is that so?" the Roshan asked, abruptly attentive. Crag nodded and she turned her tawny eyes back to the forest as if she could see them through the trees. Unable to do so, she changed the subject. "I heard you offered to personally guard King Rowland," Ember ventured. "Very noble of you."

"Hah!" Crag scoffed. "There was nothing noble about it, I assure you."

The Roshan grinned. "Well," she stated, "I will send someone from my army as well, to stand guard with you. I cannot allow you to make the only show for the elfin people. I would be disgraced!" she teased.

He finally moved his eyes to her and smiled. "To be honest, I care nothing for the elfin people." The Roshan looked at him and her expression was so abashed that it made him laugh. "Do not look so shocked, my lady. I am a man of the north and, not unlike Haldor and Halvar, I seek honor and acclaim and riches." He turned his body to face her and laid a hand upon her upper arm, swallowing half of it inside his palm. "But I would forsake all of those to whisk you away with me and return to the lands of frost and snow, spending the rest of my days lost in your gaze and your touch."

The Roshan stared at him, mesmerized by the color of his eyes, the sheer strength that emanated from his very being, and the honesty she could hear in his voice.

He would, she thought in amazement. *He really would.*

His fingers tightened ever so slightly around her arm and he pulled it gently. Had she not been steady on her feet she would have stumbled forward into his arms. But she was stronger than she appeared.

Crag's lips parted slightly and she could see his tongue at the edge of his teeth. As always, the sight of it sent a near imperceptible shiver up her spine. "This is not our war," he whispered.

"Our?" the Roshan challenged, but her voice, too, came out in a whisper.

"I know you have felt alone most of your life," he said softly as her gem-like eyes grew wide, and then wider as he continued, "lost, without a family and without a people. Searching for purpose." Had he tugged on her arm now, just the slightest bit, she would have undoubtedly fallen forward. At that moment he could have knocked her over with a feather. "I too," he confided, "have felt isolated and alone all of my life." He released her arm and caressed it tenderly before raising his hand to her face and stroking her cheek in the same manner. "Let us go away, this very night, and together we can find our place in this world."

The Roshan went still, very still, and let her eyes close. She let herself take in everything about him – his touch, his great size, his smell. Her eyes opened only a second later.

"I am sorry, Master Vikeman," she apologized, "but, my war or not, I have already promised myself to the elfin people, and the lands that they protect."

Crag gave her a smile that was both disarming and seductive. "Well," he conceded, "as long as you have not pledged yourself to any one particular person, perhaps you will let me come to your tent tonight, and try to persuade you further."

The Roshan paused long enough to consider what it might

feel like to have those considerable hands upon her body, and then gave him a rakish grin.

"My apologies, again, but I would hate to miss the meal and festivities the Gnomin have planned for us tonight in the mess."

Crag paused for a moment as if weighing an argument, then returned her grin. "Very well, my lady, but my offer will stand for as long as I do."

❦

Down the slope, across the meadows and deep within the Greatwood, Dell stood gazing at the rubicund rays of the setting sun as they came slanting in through the trees. He had seen many a sun set while in that forest, shafts of sunlight caressing the trunks of the soldier pines, moving slowly between their green and gray limbs. It was always the most powerful yet the most peaceful time of the day for the Captain of the Jägers and he savored it every chance he could. Something about the quality of the light as it deepened from gold into rose changed the colors of the forest, making them sharper somehow in brilliant gilded clarity before fading away altogether.

Dell had gone deep into the forest this evening, almost to the river, circumventing where the Gnomin had laid their pitfalls, tripwires, traps and explosives. Wilhelm was back there now with Jennings, going over the locations of the carefully hidden treasures that were in store for the Crommags upon their arrival.

He could hear their voices, but let them become lost in the sound of the river as he let himself be mesmerized by the light as it outlined each leaf on every bush and each needle on every tree, every fiber of bark upon each trunk.

Jaden's last report had been a thousand Crommags would be in this very wood by tomorrow's eve. They would be evenly matched, for a time. The elves had close to eleven hundred fighting men, and almost one hundred humans, plus the three hundred of the red troops and the odd number of Vikemen. They might actually hold the field for quite some time.

But at least two thousand, possibly more, Crommags were following to take up the slack when any of their brethren were wounded or killed. The elves would have no one to replenish or replace their fallen soldiers. Their fight would be long, but most likely go down to the last man. Dell did not harbor any illusions on the outcome. Faith he had in his people and his leaders. Hope, it seemed, had not come to the New World.

The sun had almost set and the light was almost gone, the colors of the forest fading with the deepening twilight. Dell was about to turn and follow the river back to the low meadows when movement in the distance between the trees caught his eye. The Praetorian took a step closer to the nearest pine and froze with his hand on the hilt of his sword.

A lone figure was approaching from the direction of the river. Had Dell's eyesight been any less keen he might have mistaken him for a Seleucian elf. The Jäger, however, marked him as a human male, but not one he recognized from Kriegslager. The figure was tall and slender - garbed in soft blue breeches with a sea-green vest over a shirt of blue linen. His hair, as white as seafoam, seemed to glow with its own inner light in the growing darkness.

It only took the lone figure a few more steps before Dell *did* recognize him. The dark-haired elf stepped immediately away from the tree so as not to startle the young man as he got near. Even so, his movement caught the man's eyes, eyes that were the same blue-green as the lagoon where he was born, and he paused. Then, spotting Dell, a smile broke across his handsome face and he hastened to where the Captain of the Jägers waited. The Jäger noted that there was a scar, no more than year old, on that handsome face.

"Prince Tristan," Dell greeted formally, bowing low.

The Atlantean prince dipped his white-blonde head at the

Jäger. "Good evening," he returned. "And you are?"

"Dellion, of the Praetorian Guard."

The smile on Tristan's face broadened. "Which explains how you know who I am." He paused for a moment, his smile slipping away before he continued. "Are you ready for them?"

Dell did not have to ask who he meant. He took a deep breath and nodded slowly. "As ready as we can be," he told the prince, meeting his blue-green eyes with his own. Tristan, however, did not buy the forced confidence of the Praetorian.

"The Roshan Simorgh," he asked, "she is with you? Commanding the troops of the Red King?"

"She is," Dell agreed.

"I would speak with her," Tristan ventured.

"I don't think that should pose a problem," Dell said. "Would you care to accompany me back to our camp, or should I send a messenger?"

⚬⚬⚬

The very next evening, the elfin cavalry stood in formation on the east side of the slope that led into Kriegslager, looking down upon the Elfin Greatwood. The cavalry of the red troops stood on the west side. Between them were eight Vikemen on khusars, two Gnomin on donkeys, and the red commander upon her massive Night Stallion. They had been alerted two hours before by the elfin scouts that the Crommags had nearly reached their expected destination.

Both regiments had prepared for battle, should it come this night, mounted their horses, and formed their columns in preparation to charge down the slope if the situation demanded such. Then they waited.

The two Gnomin were Otto, who had returned along with Gatha and ten more Gnomin, and Wilhelm. The team leader was there to inform the general of the traps as they were sprung. He had tried to explain the different sounds different explosives made but, after staring at Halloran's steely and unchanging gaze for ten minutes, the Gnomin simply offered to be present. The general was glad to accept.

There were scattered, if soft, conversations for over an hour among the troops. Then, as word came that the Crommags were near, mouths fell silent. Reins were grasped tightly in anticipation and readiness. Hands rested on the pommels of swords.

The horses were well trained and, other than an occasional stomp or snort, were still. The exception being the skittish horse under the red commander's squire. Meghan was too high strung to be still for long, but under Ian's gentle hand and soft words she was able to limit herself to prancing in place where she waited impatiently behind Coal.

Traejan glanced at him, unconcerned, as the raven-haired young man soothed his mount. The young prince, however, did wonder absently for the hundredth time what the handsome youth was doing there. He was obviously not a soldier and was still armed with nothing but a long knife sheathed at his belt. His eyes, black as the Night Stallion before him, never wavered from the Roshan.

The elfin prince could see them clearly and watch them openly from where he, astride Peg, stood well behind on the higher end of the slope. His brown eyes found their way to Ryen, astride his large gray khusar between the Roshan and the Vikeman named Crag. Traejan knew that Ryen had placed himself there strategically, as he often did – not just to be at Ember's side, but to keep the other Norseman at a distance. Traejan was glad of it. The giant northman was always trying to stand close to the Roshan, and also touch her at every opportunity.

No matter, the young prince thought, brushing his irritations off of his emotional armor as if they were gnats. *I have a war before me.*

Indeed, he did. Not a second after Traejan had turned his attention back toward the valley, sounds could be heard coming from the west. The sporadic stillness amongst the waiting troops became frozen silence. Even the skittish mount under the Roshan's fetching steward seemed momentarily rooted to the ground.

Dell, by the side of the prince, was picturing the quality of light that was surely in the forest at this time. The shafts of sunlight waving and shifting through the trees as they made their descent towards the forest floor where they would rest and dwindle until they faded away completely. He wondered if he would ever see that lazy waltz again and then forced his thoughts from his mind, much as the young prince had done.

Minutes later, movement could be discerned in the Elfin Greatwood.

They were coming.

From west to east they moved through the trees like a slow and swelling wave. They were deep enough into the forest that no bodies could be seen, but they did nothing to hide their approach. There were the unmistakable sounds of men, large and heavy, as they moved through the woods. Twigs and branches snapped and cracked like logs in a fire. Wooden wheels squeaked and carts creaked as they were dragged or pushed along.

"There," Wilhelm said pointing. "Do you see the pine that is taller than all the others?"

Halloran's steely eyes traveled west along the line of the treetops until he saw what the Gnomin meant. In a relatively even treeline, a lone point protruded obstinately at least two feet above his brethren. The general acquiesced with a sharp nod.

"That is where the first trap is laid, but it will not be tripped until they go past it. We rigged it with a delayed charge, the same we use in the mines that give the miners time to get out. This way, as more Crommags come, more will go."

Halloran nodded sagely. "It is called expanding the kill zone," he said gruffly. "Well done."

Wilhelm looked a bit nervous at the phrase the general had used, but the smile on Otto's face was wide with satisfaction. He liked the term. He was the youngest of six boys and only he and one other were still alive due to the Crommags raiding the Gnomin Vale every year for sport.

Like a field of corn moving with a summer's breeze, the Elfin Greatwood shifted and rustled with the invasion of the Crommag army. Troops upon troops along the curved bluff waited with bated breath, as the forefront of the invading host moved gradually eastward. Most of those waiting atop their horses knew the point where the Gnomin traps and explosives had been laid.

Slowly but surely, the movements in the forest billowed, moving steadily closer. The tension built until Ian's mount was not the only horse shifting nervously. With the noise that accompanied the march of over a thousand enormous feet, the watchers on the slope could easily mark the progress of the Crommags. Eyes went back and forth between the undulating limbs of the trees and brush to where the lone pine stood taller than the others. They watched as the army closed in to no more than a hundred yards, then fifty, then twenty-five. Then, nothing.

From the ripple of movement in the forest and the sounds that had accompanied it, it was clear that the army had stopped at least twenty yards from where the first trap had been laid. The spectators waited, watching to see if the Crommags would start moving again en masse, but they did not.

A murmur ran through the elfin army while subtle glances were exchanged among the red troops. General Halloran looked down at the Gnomin from where he sat astride a great blue-gray destrier.

"We would hear the explosions from up here, would we not?" he asked, his gravelly voice deep and slightly mocking.

"We most certainly would!" Otto exclaimed, perturbed. Not at the general, but at the turn of events.

"Is it possible they spotted the traps?" Kamut asked.

"No!" Wilhelm answered, vehement. "A Sylvan elf would have trouble seeing those wires! I had to point each one out to Captain Jennings last evening, otherwise he would have tripped them himself!"

"Perhaps Dutch was right," Espytin offered, "and they cannot see very well in the dark. Dusk is settling over the lands, and more so in the forest. It is possible that they simply stopped for the night."

Ryen and the Roshan exchanged ominous looks that Traejan did not miss. Nor did the general.

"Keep an entire company here until full dark," he told Nevin, "but reduce it to a double watch should nothing happen by then. Notify me if there is any enemy movement. I want all the captains in the white cabin immediately. The Gnomin will be serving supper in the mess hall to everyone else."

"Yes, sir," Nevin answered, gigging his horse and calling orders as the general moved his great blue-gray steed away from the slope and back towards camp. Ryen and the Roshan dismissed their men with orders to be ready for an attack at any time before they followed him.

Otto and Wilhelm trailed behind on their donkeys, arguing over possibilities.

For Ryen and the Roshan, there was only one possibility. Ember hoped that it was now clear to the general as well.

From the top of a boulder, a nightingale sang, his own worries lost in the notes of his song.

The next morning promised to dawn clear and bright and the Roshan could tell that it would be a perfect day. Warm, but not hot, with a sweet breeze that would blow intermittently throughout the day. A lazy day, a beautiful day, a day of hope. Ember could hardly believe it was a day for war.

When the Roshan imagined war, it was not on a day like today. Her mind's eye saw winter, bitterly cold. Frozen mud and flurries of snow. Men with ragged clothes and missing boots and skin red and raw from the cold. Gaunt faces from living for months on rationed food. Frozen hearts and a desperate will to triumph and be free.

Ember looked down into the vale from astride her Night Stallion and felt the predawn breeze caressing her cheek. The light was just starting to bud in the east, turning the indigo sky into the color of a sleepy sea. It would be moments before the horizon blushed like a rose and only minutes later the entire valley would be flooded with the growing warmth and light of the summer sun as it graced the New World and its people. It seemed ridiculous that a battle would be fought on such a day.

But the battle was coming, she could feel it. She could smell the oncoming death, like the heavy premonition of sex in the room of a whore. Coal had seen enough of death to know the same and kept perfectly still. He did not snort, stomp, or shake his mane. Patient as his mistress, he waited.

To the right of the Roshan rode Ryen, accompanied by the Vikemen brothers, Haldor and Halvar. To her left was Gavan, mounted on his chestnut bay and leading a double column of mounted infantry that stretched back from the top of the grade down the newly trampled road. At the rear of the column, on his prancing red mare, was the Roshan's black-haired steward.

On the west side of the slope the ground rose slightly for a dozen yards before it banked down on the north towards the supply building. On the knoll, mounted on their horses, were General Halloran along with every male in the royal family and their guards.

At the bottom of the slope were rank upon rank of the elfin infantry. They were lined along the base of the cliffs across the length of the low meadows and all the way to the three-foot-high berm of earth running east to west that bisected the meadow.

The general sat astride his blue-gray charger at the top of the knoll with Traejan to his right and Dell on the far side of the prince. Behind them were Prince Xander, King Rowland, and the Battle King himself atop their horses, watching from behind a ring of mounted Praetorian guards.

Two riders were mounted between the Praetorian guards and General Halloran. On the largest khusar Traejan had ever seen, was Crag – armed with a four-foot long broadsword and a war hammer the size of a Gnomin. Next to him was a soldier from the red troops named Shane. The Roshan promised that he was the largest and fiercest fighter that she had in her army.

One look at the man was enough to confirm at least half of her claim. Though he was nowhere near as large as Crag, he easily dwarfed all of the elves in height and girth. He was barrel-chested, broad shouldered, and blonde. He had a shield slung across his back and a mighty sword that was already unsheathed and lying in wait across his lap. His eyes were sky-blue and restless. Though his body was as large and still as a statue, those eyes were always moving.

As the dawn crept into the broad meadowlands of Morgan's Vale, those on the cliff could see unnatural markings on the flat portion of the valley floor. There were two lines running lengthwise across the prairie from east to west, dividing it into thirds. The first line was a raised berm of earth, deposited by the Gnomin who had excavated hollows under the cliffs to make them impossible to scale. The second line was harder to distinguish from the cliffs and even more difficult from the ground. It appeared to be a strange ripple in the earth.

As the eastern sky turned pink and the sun began to spread a thin arc over the trees, the Crommags emerged from the forest. All along the bluff, bodies stiffened and hands tightened on the hilts of their weapons.

The Crommags did not come out marching, or stomping and bellowing as many expected. They came forward as if it were the most natural thing in the world for a thousand heavily armed barbarians to be out and assembled at the rise of the sun.

They emerged as one massive unit, the forefront stretching out over two hundred yards wide and at least fifty Crommags deep, with more lined deep into the forest. They were massive, eight-foot tall monsters covered with thick fat and powerful muscle. The front line of the army held long spears and were backed by hundreds armed with swords, maces, hammers and cudgels – all made with forged steel.

Leading them was a beast among brutes. A mountain of a man, Ayala stood over most of them, hefting a broadsword as tall as a man in one hand and a spiked mace in the other. His beady eyes scoured the cliffs, his eyesight improving as the sun slowly rose, taking in the fearful elves and their paltry allies. His eyes, dark and close-set, fell upon what he was searching for and a wide smile broke across his gruesome face. He held his sword high and shouted something unintelligible to elfin ears.

His army answered in the same guttural shout, holding their weapons high. Their eyes, too, were adjusting to the slowly growing light and now they could make out the figures of the elves, all but invisible moments earlier. Dressed in their blue and gray uniforms they were hardly more than wraiths, clinging to the morning shadows beneath the cliffs. It was all they needed to see.

They roared, echoing their leader, and charged forth. Ayala did not rush with them, but did instead as Noga had advised and climbed up onto a flat rock where he could watch the first assault. The Great Men poured out of the forest, moving around and past him like the waters of a flood.

The wild charge was a sight to behold and the ground shook with their passing. Ayala gnashed his fangs in anticipation as they ate up the distance, knowing the elves must be filled with terror. He could not believe they chose the base of the cliffs to make a stand. His spearmen would skewer most, and pin the rest against the wall of earth behind them like bugs.

Yon clambered up onto the rock to stand with Ayala, a great banded horn grasped in one of his mighty hands.

Together they watched the mad charge of Great Men across the prairie, their numbers great and their strength monumental. Both of their chests swelled with pride. The front line of charging Crommags, wielding their spears, were halfway to the strange ripple in the ground that cleaved the meadow by a third when they disappeared.

It was so sudden that neither Ayala, nor Yon, could understand what had happened. More, it was so fast that the line of warriors behind the spearmen could not stop their momentum. The pair atop the rock leaned forward, squinting, and could see that their men had fallen into a long and concealed ditch.

The Gnomin, on such short notice, could only make the channel three feet wide and only six feet deep. Not far enough down to cause any Crommag to fall to its death, but it was deep enough for them to fall and break legs, and be trampled to death by their oncoming brethren. Even from their place so far back, Yon and Ayala could hear their guttural screams.

Indeed, the following wave of Great Men crushed the skulls of their comrades with their passing, although many of them became entangled and they fell as well. Still, the Crommags charged recklessly, trampling their dead and wounded in a rush to reach the elves – hating them now more than ever.

"My gods!" Zephyrn exclaimed, watching the horror below. "They are hideous, and so big!"

"And so many," Dirk muttered, watching as the beasts poured from the forest in seemingly endless numbers.

The monsters were fifty yards from the second line – the soft ridge of earth that marked the last third of the field - when the elves drew their swords. The Crommags let out a great roar in response and continued their heedless charge. They closed the distance quickly with their strong and powerful legs, focused on the forms that waited in orderly ranks against the bluff.

The crest of dirt that marred the meadow, only three feet high and nothing to the eight-foot tall Crommags as they charged, was thirty yards away when Patrek and his crossbowmen rose up behind it. The crimson troops, wearing brown cloaks and triangular shields upon their backs, rose to their knees and unloaded hundreds of bolts into the oncoming rush. Sloan and his crossbowmen stood up behind them and shot another volley of quarrels while the first team reloaded.

The first line of rushing Crommags dropped, then the second. But more came crashing over their fallen bodies, closing the distance to twenty yards. Patrek's men loosed more bolts, followed by another razing from Sloan and his men. More and more Crommags dropped and more and more rushed in to take their place. When they closed the distance to ten yards, the crossbowmen dropped back down to the ground, crouching behind the berm. The beasts gave a mighty roar, intent upon smashing this new enemy into pulp where they cowered like lambs.

Forgotten were the elves, though Ayala could see them from his vantage point. He shouted at his men but his warning was drowned out by the din of their stampede.

Traejan's infantry elite had advanced steadily until the Crommags were almost upon Patrek and Sloan's men. When the crimson troops dropped, the elves broke into a run. Using the shields of the crossbowmen like a ramp, they ran up their backs and leapt high over their bodies. Down they came, driving their swords deep into Crommag flesh where their thick necks met their wide shoulders. As the monsters crashed to their knees the elves pulled their swords free and cut their throats.

The Roshan looked approvingly upon the battle from her vantage point atop her Night Stallion. She resisted the urge to turn her head and smile upon the young prince who had trained the elves below. The sun cleared the horizon, warming her face and turning her hair into the fiery red for which she had been named.

The next wave of beasts surged forward, just as another wave of elfin infantry dropped from over the backs of the crossbowmen. The scene repeated itself again and again until the entire infantry elite stood on the south side of the line, fighting.

Now we shall see, she thought. *How well did you train them, Traejan? Did you honor at least two of your gods and do them justice?*

It appeared he had. Where the monsters of the north had size and numbers, the elves were skilled fighters, often taking two or more Crommag lives for every elfin soldier that fell. But still, fall they did.

Ayala watched from atop the rock, thinking almost the same thoughts.

Now we shall see, he thought as the armies finally engaged in brutal battle. *Now that you have played your tricks tiny men, now you will see the power of the Great Men.*

The rising sun hit him full in the face and he shot it a look of irritation. The Great Men needed the sun, for they needed to be able to see in order to fight. But what they had not anticipated was that so far south from their icy homes, the sun could get almost unbearably hot.

Many men had dropped during the long journey to the elfin lands simply from heat exhaustion. It was something the Crommags had never before experienced and had no idea how to handle. The best they could do was to drag them into the shade and leave them with a skin of water, hoping they would be able to continue when the next group came along.

Ayala would have to watch carefully for the signs, and be ready to recall his men. At his command, Yon would sound the horn to signal retreat.

The elves were fast in their attacks, but not every strike was lethal. It often took many blows to take down one of the monsters, and even after being hacked at with an elfin sword, they would not always go down. On the other hand, the Crommags were slow, but when they landed a strike it was sure to cost the elf his life. The field was a harsh discordance of sound, full of the clash of metal, grunts of pain, and screams of agony. The song of war filled the air of the vale as blood soaked its ground.

Two hours passed and the elves began to tire. Ryen's blue eyes glanced at the sun, halfway to its zenith, and then went to the Roshan. He had never seen her so heavily armed, though he had fought many battles with her before. Along with her usual arsenal of long sword, short swords, and her brace of daggers, she wore a number of throwing knives strapped to her arms and thighs. He knew she was itching to use all of them. Watching the elfin ranks begin to buckle, he knew she would have her chance soon and the Vikeman drew his own sword.

The general, atop his warhorse on the bluff, saw the same and signaled for the next maneuver. All along the top of the cliff, elfin archers fitted arrows to their bows and loosed them, raining them down into the masses of Crommags. Hundreds fell, though because of their thick hides, only a fraction of those died. Still, the confusion it caused stalled their attack and the elfin infantry began to split apart at the center, breaking away to the left and right.

The archers on the cliff rained down another volley and by the time the Crommags realized there was a widening gap in the elfin defense, the Seventh Circle was riding towards it.

Coal charged down the slope, leading Gavan's cavalry and

flanked by the Vikemen – forming a wedge. Ember's boots left the stirrups and she pulled her feet up and underneath her as she draped the reins over the horn of her saddle. Only yards before crashing into the exposed line of Crommags, the Night Stallion came to a skidding halt with his legs locked and braced. His massive hooves dug long furrows into the ground as he came to a shuddering stop, lowering his head. As he did, the Roshan slid down his neck and hit the ground running with the fury of hell.

The Vikemen also vaulted from their horses, preferring to fight with their feet on the ground. For the Roshan it was a necessity. Trying to fight while leaning down over her massive stallion limited her reach and put Coal at risk. A Nordic war cry was bellowed and echoed by every Norseman, including Ryen.

Ember led the charge, rushing forward as her sword cut a path through the line of beasts in her way. Crommags began to fall in every direction around her as the two columns split behind the small wedge she had formed with the Norsemen.

Fanning out to the left and right, the mounted red troops took up the battle, letting the elfin infantry fall back, dragging their wounded comrades. Behind them all, on his dancing mare, was Ian. Coal, followed by the khusars, galloped towards him, coming to a stop almost next to his mare who shied away with a whinny.

Traejan's eyes flicked to him for a second, thinking Ian's purpose might be to look after the horses, but the dark-eyed youth ignored them, focusing only on the red-haired warrior engaged in the fight. His mount danced beneath him, her eyes rolling in their sockets, but he took no notice. With his thighs gripping the horse and the reins tight in one fist, he was intent upon only one entity.

That entity was moving with unbelievable speed, her sword flashing gold in the bright sun as it cut throats and severed limbs. At times it was too fast to track, even with elfin eyes, and the only evidence was the carnage in her wake.

"Holy Christ," Zephyrn muttered, watching from above.

Halloran grunted in agreement while Traejan, despite his armor, felt his heart swell in his chest as he watched her fight. He simply could not help it.

Ryen fought diligently, if not as quickly, at the Roshan's right side - knowing well enough to give her plenty of space. Halvar learned the same when he got too close, and got a kick in the backside to send him farther left towards his brother. Ember took the Crommags down two, sometimes three at a time. Ryen, trying to match her, found himself on four occasions almost overwhelmed. Each time, however, at least one of his attackers collapsed - the grip of one of the Roshan's throwing knives protruding from its throat.

Ayala, watching from his rock, frowned at this new assault. He watched it for the better part of an hour, until he saw his men were falling back, and they were slowing. He looked up angrily at the sun, sweat pouring down his own face, and motioned for Yon to signal retreat.

The Great Man from the Snow Leopard tribe raised the enormous horn to his lips and blew. The sound it made was low and deep and reverberated across the plains. The Crommags heard the sound and, with immense relief, began to fall back. The mounted troops, however, were having none of it.

Gavan shouted at his men and rallied them to give chase, harrying and cutting down the Crommags until the beasts were forced to turn and fight or run for their lives. The battle became a rout.

The cavalry chased them as far as the trench full of Crommag bodies, then wheeled their mounts and headed back to the cliffs to escort the crossbowmen as they retreated up the slope. From atop the bluff came a victory cheer from everyone that stood watching – elf, human, and Gnomin alike.

Even Xander, though he remained aloof, was impressed by the outcome. His eyes sought out Traejan as the barely controlled elation of the Praetorian guards died down. "Your men did well today," he told his younger brother who, also aloof, dipped his head at the recognition. "I will escort the king and grandfather back to Castle Royce. Send word immediately if there is any movement of the enemy."

"Of course," Traejan acquiesced. He looked at his father and grandfather as they turned their mounts for home and both of them were regarding him with undisguised pride. The young prince smiled and turned to Halloran.

"They did more than well today," the general told him before turning to Jennings. "See to the wounded and post a watch."

"Should I summon the captains to the white cabin?" Jennings asked.

Halloran scowled as he considered the request. "No," he answered. "But we should all sit at the same table in the mess, where we can rest, eat, and plan all at once. I expect they will attack again once the heat of the day begins to fade. We should be together and prepared when that happens."

Jennings gave him a quick nod and then spurred his horse. The general gave the prince a quick dip of his head and followed the captain at a smart trot, Zephyrn and the others following close behind.

Traejan was left alone on the bluff with Dell to survey the scene below.

The Crommags were melting back into the woods, snarling and spitting as they went. The elfin wounded and dead were being put on horses to be taken back to the camp. Among them were also wounded and dead soldiers from the red army, but they were few. Very few – but even those few were precious.

Sloan watched with his silvery blue eyes from under his silvery white hair as one of his bowmen, now lifeless, was lifted and put into the back of a horse-drawn wagon. A hand came down on his shoulder and his face snapped to the side to see the Roshan, looking at him with concern.

"Are you alright?" she asked.

Sloan nodded. "I was not injured."

"That's not what I meant." She looked at the body, now being joined by the limp forms of elves, and then back at Sloan. His heart-shaped face turned back to the dead.

"This morning, they were all fierce, fighting men. Full of pride and promise and purpose. Now..." he trailed off, sounding fearful and sad.

"Now their purpose has been fulfilled," the Roshan said gently. "It is only their bodies that are left, their souls have moved on."

The white-haired youth turned his silvery eyes to her. "Do I have a soul?" he asked, his voice as soft as a child's and ripe with fear - fear of what her answer might be. She knew it was a topic often discussed by many of the residents of Redtown. Usually in hushed tones.

"Yes," the Roshan answered, her own voice firm. "You do."

"What will happen to the bodies?" he asked.

"The elves bury their dead, giving them back to the earth."

"Does everyone do that?" Sloan asked.

"No, the Vikemen burn their warriors with their weapons in great funeral pyres, sending their souls to feast with their gods."

A small smile finally found its way onto Sloan's youthful face. "I like that," he said.

"Good," the Roshan said. "Now get your men to the mess and get something to eat."

From atop the knoll, Traejan watched Ember speak with her white-haired captain and climb onto the back of her massive stallion to follow the last of the troops up the hill. South of them, the plains were littered, in some places heaped, with dead Crommags. It was a sickening scene, but he flushed with pride.

His men *had* done well that day.

But I should have been with them, he thought, sour. *Fighting with them. Fighting with her.*

His eyes scanned the low meadows of the vale one last time and then he gigged Peg, urging her into a trot towards the mess. He and Dell left their mounts with a pair of grooms at the elfin corral and walked the short distance to the mess pavilion.

When he entered, still clouded by the disappointment of his absence from the battle, he was greeted by cheers from his men as they all stood for him, filling the room with their shouting. The red troops and Vikemen were on their feet as well, holding high their steins of cider.

The young prince smiled and raised a hand at them as he spoke softly over his shoulder to his Praetorian. "Why do they cheer for me?" he asked Dell. "I did not fight."

The normally taciturn elf smiled. "You taught them how," he said. "Because of your training and leadership, they are alive, and our kingdom is safe."

"For now," Traejan muttered, spotting a large table in the back center of the mess hall where Halloran was taking a seat amongst most of the captains.

"Now is all we ever have," Dell told the young prince with a paternal smile and nods of acknowledgment to the soldiers that they passed. "Stop being a martyr. This victory belongs to you as much as them."

"As you say," Traejan remarked softly.

The mess hall was huge, the largest by far of the three structures built by the Gnomin, with many long wooden tables and benches. The tables had already been set with pitchers of both water and cider and the Gnomin were setting down plates laden with potatoes and sausages in front of the soldiers.

Only the seriously wounded had gone to the medical tent to be treated for their injuries. All else had come straight to the mess. Those who had fought were dirty and scraped and bloodied, but all in good spirits.

At the back table, Ember sat between Ryen and Gavan. Her steward stood behind her, unfastening a piece of steel that circled her throat. She had a nasty cut on the corner of her jaw but just as disturbing to the prince was the way Ian drew his fingers gently over the back of her neck after he had removed the metal guard. Traejan looked away as the steward withdrew and sat himself at a nearby table, his dark eyes fixed on the Roshan.

The young prince and his Praetorian found chairs at the table and the captains greeted him warmly. He forced a smile as a Gnomin male wearing a heavy canvas apron clunked down steins in front of them. A Gnomin female was right on his heels with steaming plates of food.

"It's a bit early to be celebrating," he said stiffly as he looked around at the great mugs of cider, "don't you think?"

"Come on, Traejan," Zephyrn said, "It's cider, not mead. The elves won't be altered by it."

"It won't affect my men either," the Roshan assured him. "Even still, they are only having water."

Ryen looked askance at Haldor who quickly put down his stein, wiped his mouth with the back of a fist, and belched into it.

"She said it was alright!" he exclaimed in his defense, bringing chortles of laughter from those around the table.

"I actually think we will be fine for the rest of the day, and night," the Roshan remarked. "I do not expect them to attack again until tomorrow. Still, we should always be prepared."

"We are," Halloran said, his voice gruff but pleased. "And we can mobilize before the enemy makes it halfway across the plain."

"What makes you think they won't attack again today?" Crag asked Ember. The Roshan, her mouth full of food at the moment, simply shrugged.

"How many men did we lose today?" Traejan asked, looking

at Nevin.

"Three score," the older elf answered before looking to Gavan. The captain of the Roshan's cavalry bore bloody marks from the battle, but they were small and he was no less striking.

"Eight," the handsome captain informed them between bites of food. His golden eyes gleamed from a face streaked with dirt and sweat. "Plus two horses."

Traejan pushed his plate away, discouraged.

Halloran finished chewing, a frown creasing his iron brows as he looked at the elfin prince. "Comparatively, this morning was a success. I estimate we took out a third of their army, maybe more."

"A third of what has arrived so far," Espytin said softly.

Halloran tipped his head to the side and shrugged. "We will take each day as it comes," the general said, and put a forkful of food in his mouth.

"I would like to talk about tomorrow before it gets here," the Roshan said, wiping her mouth with a napkin. Halloran motioned for her to continue while he kept eating. "How far back is the next company of Crommags?" she asked, looking at Jaden.

The Sylvan elf put down his stein of cider. "Two days, at their current pace," he answered assertively.

The Roshan nodded. "We need to take out as many of them as we can, before more get here. It is the only way I can see that will give us an advantage."

"What are you thinking?" Espytin asked.

"I'm thinking of a cavalry assault," she advised. "And not on the battlefield. Gavan's horses are well trained for hard forest riding. He can take his cavalry in for a mounted assault on their camp."

Halloran chewed thoughtfully, his steely eyes distant as he

considered the possibilities. "If they are beaten, and scattered," he mused softly, "when their reinforcements arrive, it will be both difficult and discouraging for them. Yes!" the general agreed with sudden surety. His eyes sought out the Roshan and he gave her a smile. "If you are right and no attack comes today, bring a bottle of that red wine you have to the cabin at sundown – we will need the maps to plan accurately." His eyes moved across the others seated at the table. "The rest of you, eat what you can, get cleaned up, and have your wounds dressed. See to your men."

"Yes, sir," was the chorus around the table and, as the general stood, the rest of those seated rose respectfully as he left. A few sat back down to finish eating but most were ready to move on and get washed-up. Traejan was one of latter, though he had not eaten a bite of his food, but found his sleeve caught by Gavan.

"My Lord Prince," he said, motioning to the untouched plate, "if you are not going to..." he trailed off and Traejan forced a smile.

"Go ahead," he encouraged. "I am sure you are famished after today."

Gavan grinned his thanks and sat back down, moving the plate in front of his own seat. Halvar was doing the same with his brother's meal until he was caught by Haldor and promptly shoved away. Ryen moved the rest of his food in front of the hungry Vikeman to avert a squabble.

The Roshan wiped her mouth with a napkin and stood, only to find herself face to chest with Crag. She tipped her head back to look at him.

"Would you like some help cleaning up?" he asked with a wicked smile. "The day is just but half done."

"Thank you," she said, smiling crookedly, "but Ian will see to my needs."

The young man in question was already by her side, his

dark eyes glaring at the Vikeman as if he could bore holes into him.

"Lucky Ian," Crag murmured, touching her affectionately on the cheek.

Traejan turned away, spotted Dell, and motioned for him to follow. The Roshan drew her gaze from the Vikeman's green-eyed stare and laid a hand on Gavan's shoulder.

"Be where I can find you if I need you," she advised.

Gavan swallowed his food. "I'm going straight to the river, then straight to my tent. Unless you want me in the cabin, planning for tomorrow."

"No," the Roshan responded. "Halloran said we can fix the details at sundown. Check the horses after you have cleaned up, then stay in your tent and get as much rest as you can. Tomorrow will be a big day for you and your men."

She glanced at Crag who was still looming at her shoulder, and paused as if she meant speak to him. Then she turned and left, moving between noisy tables and benches, Ian a silent shadow at her right elbow.

17. UNPLEASANT SURPRISES

Outside of their tent, Ian put a kettle of water over their outdoor cookfire as the sun began to descend towards the trees that cupped the western edge of Morgan's Vale. Inside, he helped the Roshan undress.

"Today went well, didn't it?" he asked with a shy smile as he unlaced the vambraces that covered her wrists.

"Yes," she replied. "It did."

His dark eyes glanced up her face. "Then why are you so anxious?" he asked, pulling off the right vambrace and then the left.

She gave him half a smile and rubbed her wrists as he unbuckled her sword belt and pulled it from her hips. "You can tell I am anxious?"

A small line formed between his dark brows. "Of course I can."

He laid the sword aside and unfastened the laces of her brace that was, once again, empty. Her expression became as serious as her voice. "Today has gone well, so far. But today is not over."

Ian undid the straps on her arms that had held her throwing knives, then unbuckled the carriage that secured her short swords. Everything he threw onto a pile to be cleaned. "Your boots?" he asked.

"I can get my own boots off," the Roshan answered, walking to a side table and picking up a bottle of uncorked wine. "Just find me a clean set of clothes, and see if that water is warm yet. Please," she added, filling a golden goblet with the heavy red liquid.

"You really don't think there will be another attack today?" he asked.

The Roshan shook her head as she sat herself in a chair. Ian watched her for a moment but, when she offered nothing more, moved quickly to do her bidding.

Ember took a sip of wine, hardly tasting it.

Yes, she thought, *today was a success. Today showed us much. Tonight will show us more.*

She thought about Crag and the way he looked at her, the way he touched her and the response it always triggered in her. She wondered what he would do if she asked him to fight by her side.

She wondered what it would be like to have his massive body on top of her own, if he would crush her.

"Only one way to find out," she said, laughing.

"What was that?" Ian asked, coming back into the tent with hot water.

"I said I need more wine," she told him, and laughed again.

In the Elfin Greatwood, Ayala was brooding in his own tent, sweating profusely. The hides that covered his yurt had begun to stink weeks ago. Though the goat skins had been cured, tiny fibers of flesh clung to them - flesh that remained frozen and thus unnoticeable in the Bitterlands but had decayed and rotted in the heat of the Northlon summer. All the yurts stank.

"Where is that water?" he demanded of Yon. The Great Man was about to shrug but thought better at the last second and stood instead.

"I will find out," he assured his leader, glad to be out of the stifling tent. At least, in the woods, there was a breeze.

Ayala, thirsty like he had never been before, had sent for water half an hour ago. He had no idea what could be taking so long, they had camped purposely close to the river. They had also camped at a safe distance from the traps the elves and their friends had left for them.

The Crommags had stopped carrying their own water months ago when they started following the river, lightening their load considerably. The only drink they carried with them now was their grog, transported in barrels on two-wheeled handcarts, but as of yet Ayala had not allowed them to be tapped. He, as well as his men, needed water after a day of fighting in the heat – not grog. More would suffer the heat sickness if they did not have water.

We should not need much, he thought morosely as he licked his dry lips. *There are just more than half of us now.*

The elves and their allies had shown a surprising amount of wiliness and determination. And skill. Ayala saw today they were small fighters, but good ones. He knew something else as well, he had to keep up the spirit of his men now, just as much as he had on the long march to the elfin kingdom. The Great Men had suffered terrible losses today, but they needed to stay proud and confident. They needed to be eager to fight. Ayala knew he had to keep that in them.

But first, he needed some water. He did not bring them all this way just to die of thirst in sight of his goal.

Yon ducked his head back into the tent then, his beady eyes somewhat larger than normal.

"What?" Ayala demanded. "Where is my water?"

"Uh..." the other Crommag responded.

"Uh?" Ayala repeated loudly, rising to his feet.

Yon's small eyes shifted nervously and he backed clumsily out of the tent with Ayala following. "Uh, I mean, the men are saying the river is cursed."

Ayala froze. The Great Men were exceedingly superstitious and took curses seriously. How else could one explain winters that lasted years, the sudden loss of animals, crops, and loved ones?

His dark eyes moved across the clearing in which they had camped. The leaders of the other tribes were sitting or standing and talking in front of their hide-covered shelters. The Great Men did not stop when they saw him, but they slowed their movements and their voices dropped and Ayala knew they were listening. He wanted to question Yon privately but changed tack immediately.

"Water!?!" he shouted at Yon. "Do not bring these men water! These are fighting men!" He fixed his eyes on Higa and pointed his massive hand at where the kegs of grog were stacked nearby. "Open those barrels! These are Great Men! Great fighters! We soaked the ground in elfin blood today!"

There were guttural cheers from every Crommag that was close enough to hear, but Ayala's words quickly spread through the camp and proud shouts of excitement were heard throughout the woods.

"We lost men today," Ayala growled, "but we, as Great Men of the Bitterlands, know that the weak always die first."

There were murmurs of assent and knowing nods as the Crommags repeated the words of their leader. This, they knew to be true. Centuries of living in the most unforgiving of environments taught them that the weak were always the first to go, sometimes within moments of their first breath.

"YOU," Ayala thundered, "ARE THE STRONG!"

The roar from his warriors, Great Men from many clans, shook the trees of the forest so hard that pine needles rained from above. Higa drove the sharpened tip of a horn into the edge of a barrel top and pried off the lid. The Crommags began to grab drinking vessels made from horns and skulls and lined up at the kegs, cheering and clapping each other on their broad backs.

Ayala, secure and proud, licked his dry lips and motioned for Yon to get them both some grog. The Crommag from the Snow Leopard tribe pushed his way to the front and dipped a pair of skulls in the strong fermented ale and joined his leader, handing one skull to him. The mountain of a man took a long drink, soaking his tongue and slaking the thirst in his throat. He wiped his lips with the back of a hair-covered arm and stepped closer to Yon.

"Tell me about the river," Ayala said, watching warriors that had gone from glum and suspicious to proud and smiling in just moments.

I did that, he thought as he remembered something that Noga had told him years ago.

Words can be as powerful as spears, the runty Crommag had told his brother. *And feelings such as doubt and discouragement are dangerous enemies.*

They had just begun making plans to unite the tribes and move them south. Ayala had thought then that he got his brother's meaning but now he knew firsthand. He would not forget.

Yon nodded as he took a large gulp of grog, his eyes also on the men as they smashed their drinking vessels together in celebration. "The waterway is wide, and full of rocks," he said, lowering the half-empty skull, "but low and calm. Until someone nears it. Then it rears up like an animal and snatches the man from the banks and washes him away."

Ayala looked at him in disbelief but Yon was not joking. Far from it.

"Did anyone try from a place farther downstream?"

"Yes," Yon told him, frowning over the heads of the Great Men as he stared in the direction of the river. "They tried different places, and with two or three trying at once. Each time the river rises, and only in the place where a Great Man stands, and swallows him whole. We lost six before no man would venture near the water."

"Bijah!" Ayala cursed. Six men. Just trying to get water. "The elves must have their own gods, as wily as the little bastards that praise them." Disgusted, he wanted to spit but knew better than to waste what little he had. At least it felt as if the heat had passed its peak. "Get me a runner."

Yon cast his eyes about and signaled to a young Crommag named Yip who was tall and still lean, relatively. The youth came quickly to where the leaders stood.

"I want you to take a message to Pel, whose group is following ours." The young Crommag nodded and waited. Since the Great Men had no method for writing or reading, all messages were delivered by word of mouth. "Tell him to bring water with them, the ways here are too slippery." The youth nodded again and Ayala took a gulp of grog. "And tell him to hurry."

"To hurry?" the young Crommag asked, clearly surprised. He wanted to glance at Yon for confirmation but was afraid to take his eyes off of the Great Leader.

Ayala grinned, showcasing a terrifying set of fangs. "If he wants to kill any elves - for they may all be dead when he gets here!"

The youth grinned, showing his own fangs, though they were much less frightening. He dipped his head and turned and ran.

Yon looked at the Great Leader with admiration. It was cunning, how he had handled the message.

"We will not fight again today," Ayala said. "Let these men feast and rest. Tomorrow will come soon enough."

And the day after will bring more men, he thought with satisfaction. If Noga's estimation of their numbers were even close to correct, there was no way the elves would be able to hold out forever, no matter how wily they might be or what allies they may have.

Yon's great form bent slightly in acknowledgement as Ayala took a long drink from the skull in his massive hand. Then he turned and reentered his stinking tent. He had more brooding to do while he waited for his brother to return. Once Noga came back from his daily undertaking, they could decide better what to do about the water. And how to throw another hyena bone at the elves.

The Great Man took another huge gulp from the skull and grunted in anticipation.

⚜

On the bluff, the general air in Kriegslager was one of victory. Soldiers recounted the day, excitedly telling each other of individual fights and showing off minor injuries. Men and elves had been posted twenty feet apart, all along the cliff, and were visited frequently by those not on duty. Many stayed to help watch for a while. Everyone wanted to know if there had been any enemy movement. Rested and refreshed with an unexpected victory under their belts, they were eager to fight again.

The fight, however, did not come again that day – just as the Roshan had predicted. By sundown, she and General Halloran had already gone over the broad strokes of a cavalry assault by Gavan's men into the Crommag camp and were now awaiting a bottle of Redtown red wine that she had sent for earlier.

All of the captains had been briefed on the planned attack. Some then returned to other duties but most were still in the white cabin. Gavan was assembling his men in the mess hall to go over the details of the mounted assault and get something to eat before they called an early night.

Traejan was in a corner of the white cabin, going through lists. Captain Espytin had asked Zephyrn for the list that showed bow types and how many had been moved to the camp. Of course Zephyrn had something much more pressing than paperwork to see to, so he had asked Traejan to get it for him. Traejan had agreed, knowing he should be present in the cabin while all the others were, and wanted something to keep his hands and mind busy.

All lists concerning logistics were rolled into scrolls and stored in two barrels. They were horribly disorganized. It seemed that anything that wasn't a map was considered unimportant and was consequently rolled and stuffed into the wooden containers. It was no wonder that Espytin had asked Zephyrn for the help, the young captain had his hands full coordinating with Patrek's men to get them restocked on bolts and checking with all troops to replace any lost or damaged weapons.

Traejan stood quietly in the din and clamor of the cabin, the building busier and more full of soldiers than he had ever seen it. Messengers came and went while the captains took reports and spoke with each other. Huge copper braziers on iron stands burned brightly, their smoke rising through holes in the ceiling. Even Dell was absorbed with Jaden, taking reports from the Jägers' scouts.

The young prince worked quietly, absorbed in the tedious monotony of his task. He would pull a scroll from the barrel, unroll it, scan it to see if it was what he wanted, then roll it back up and put it back. Unroll, check, reroll. Unroll, check, reroll. Unroll, check, reroll. He was almost halfway through the first barrel when he could feel someone looking at him.

Traejan looked up and glanced about the busy room. His eyes fell on Ryen, who stood between the boisterous Vikemen brothers and Kamut. Ryen, however, was silent, his eyes fixed on the elfin prince with a curious stare. Traejan looked around the room again and this time his eyes fell on Ember.

She stood with Crag, leaning over a map table. Her hands were on the table for support, but she was not looking at the map. She was looking at Crag as he spoke to her, his hand laid gingerly over hers.

Traejan flicked his eyes back to Ryen, but the Vikeman only raised his eyebrows at him. The young prince turned back to his work but he was unable to focus on what he was looking at. All he could see was Ember looking into the other man's eyes, and his giant mitt all but swallowing her slim-fingered hand.

It's not important, Traejan told himself. Crag had done nothing to conceal his obvious interest in the Roshan and, though it disgusted the elfin prince, he did not think much about it. He was just glad that Zephyrn had given up his vain quest to get a private lesson from the Weapons Master.

If it's not important, he wondered, *then why does Ryen seem so concerned?*

He glanced back up to see Ember smiling at the massive Norseman, then laughing softly at something he said. The young prince clenched his jaw and felt his armor close up around him as he returned to his task.

After going through a few more scrolls without seeing what was writ upon them, Traejan gave up and headed for the door. He almost crashed into Zeph as he was coming through it. His brother's hair was tousled from the wind and his cheeks were ruddy from the ride, or something else.

"Did you find it?" Zephyrn asked, his blue eyes bright.

"It isn't there," Traejan told him. "You'll have to do a physical inventory."

Zephyrn groaned. "Can you..." he started, but his brother had already turned away, his hand on the door. The younger elf cursed and looked about to find a squire to help him. Traejan opened the door to the cabin to find Ian coming in with two bottles in one hand and three cups of beaten copper in the other.

"Would you like some help?" Traejan asked.

"I would! Thank you." Ian smiled and the prince suddenly wanted to smash him in his perfect face. Instead, he held the door open for the Roshan's steward and followed him to the back of the cabin where the general was dismissing a messenger.

Despite the commotion in the room, neither Ryen nor the Roshan missed Ian's entrance and effectively left their other conversations behind to congregate in the back with Halloran as Ian opened the bottles and poured the wine.

"I would think," Ryen remarked as he accepted a copper vessel and handed it to the general, "that the heat down there would sour the wine."

"Not unless you leave it out in the sun after it has been uncorked," Halloran informed the Vikeman in his rough voice as he sat himself at the back table. "But hot temperatures are actually very beneficial to produce a fine wine."

The Roshan looked at him, impressed, before turning her gem-like eyes to Ryen. "It's true," she agreed. "The heat stresses the grapes and makes their flavors more intense." She sat herself in a camp chair next to the general and took a drink from her cup.

Ryen took a sip and tipped his head to the side as he savored it for a moment, and then nodded appreciatively. "Whatever it is, they are doing it right. The Southlon wine really is better than most."

"Probably because they grow it for the taste rather for the effect," Ember told him.

"You mentioned the same about the cider," Ryen said, his brows slightly drawn. "Are they some breed of elves?"

"No," Halloran mused aloud in his deep gravelly voice. "But they are some breed of something," he said, the lids low over his steely eyes as he looked at Ian.

"What do you two...Gatha!"

The Roshan's auburn brows went up and she followed the Norseman's gaze to the entrance of the cabin where Gatha had just entered and was making her way to the back where the three were enjoying the Redtown wine. The Gnomin woman smiled at Traejan as she passed him and put down a plate of cheese and crackers on the small table between the Roshan and the general. Her gaze went to Ryen and her expression hardened into scorn.

The Vikeman did not miss the change.

"The elf gets the smile and I get sour grapes?" he asked.

Gatha looked at the Roshan and made a few quick motions with one hand. Ember laughed.

"Yes," she told the Gnomin.

"Yes?" Ryen asked. "Yes, what?"

"She wants to know if you are still," the Roshan paused as she searched for the right word, "a scoundrel."

"I am not a scoundrel," Ryen said defensively, turning his blue eyes to the small woman. "And I'm helping take care of her," he said, pointing at Ember with his wine cup. "Why aren't you?"

The mute Gnomin motioned at Ian before she tossed her head of coarse blonde curls, leaving Ember to translate.

"She said Ian is doing fine, and she is needed elsewhere."

Ryen grunted and Gatha finally favored him with a grin as she turned and left. Ian gave the group a charming smile and followed her, passing the other captains that stood around the map tables as they took reports from their runners.

Espytin took three lists from one and looked them over before he dismissed the elf that had brought them. "The men are in good spirits," he remarked to Jennings as he rolled the papers together. The older elf forced a smile.

"Let them enjoy it while they can," he said. "It is only going to get uglier." He paused and Espytin thought he might say more, but Jennings only shook his head and left the supply captain to ponder his brief but ominous words.

Dash passed him as he entered the tent, his bright eyes

moving quickly until they spotted Halloran sitting with Ryen and the Roshan. The young elf moved swiftly to his side but seeing Traejan there, paused, unsure of who to address. He decided quickly and addressed them both.

"The Battle King is on his way," the small elf announced softly. "He wishes to see and speak with you."

"Is that so?" Halloran exclaimed. He looked around at those in the cabin and stood up to address them. "Attention!" he called out smartly. "The Battle King is on his way here. Ready yourselves, and act accordingly."

The elves became suddenly somber, smoothing down their clothes and lifting their chins while their human counterparts followed suit. The Vikemen looked at each other, unsure.

Crag took a few giant steps towards the general and leaned down to speak as privately as possible.

"Does he have the witch with him?" the Norseman asked in soft tones.

The general frowned, his gray brows pulling together. "I am not sure I know what you mean."

Traejan, however, could not keep the smile from his face. "Karamine," he said. "I believe he means Karamine."

Halloran's scowl fell away, as did the color in his cheeks. "I don't think 'witch' is an appropriate word…" he said, trailing off as he looked about at the others for support.

Traejan laughed softly. "Actually, I think she would be tickled at it."

"Still," Crag said stiffly, "my religion prohibits me from associating with witches. I will take my leave, with apologies, and hope I have not offended anyone."

Kamut nodded in agreement. "I as well," he said.

Ryen rolled his blue eyes and waved them away. "Go!" he commanded. "Be ready an hour before sunrise!"

Crag and Kamut both bowed and strode quickly from the

cabin. Haldor and Halvar, discernibly unsure of what to do, bowed as well and followed the other Norsemen from the room.

"Superstitious goats," Ryen muttered as they left.

"The Battle King?" Ember asked Halloran, though her eyes looked askance at Traejan.

"Yes," the general affirmed. "Acqtraejale Royce. He is the father of King Rowland, veteran of more battles than you or even I could imagine."

The Roshan gave him a crooked smile. "That is not saying much, for me. My imagination has always been a limited thing, a slave to calculation, prediction, and possible outcomes."

Halloran's gray brows went up in surprise. "Do you mean to say..." he started when the door swung open and the Battle King himself entered and everyone that was not already standing rose swiftly.

He wore sweeping white robes that were matched by his long white hair. In contrast, the woman by his side had skin and hair as dark as ebony, though her layered robes were bright shades of blue. Her hair was a mass of long and tiny braids, every one of them adorned with three beads each, also in shades of blue.

The two of them made their way through the room slowly, elves and men alike bowing to them as they passed. The pair paused occasionally to speak with one of the captains and the Roshan stared at them, unable to help herself. They both brought on an overwhelming sense of déjà vu but, since the memories were not connected, it took her a few moments to recall them.

The Shama, Ember thought suddenly, feeling her insides go slack. *She looks like the woman I sought out in that small fishing village on the Sabado Sea, so many years ago. The woman who sent my father to his rest.*

Once she was sure it was not the same woman, she moved

her gaze to the Battle King. The resemblance to Traejan was unmistakable. The same eyes, the same facial structure. She speculated the young prince looked more like his grandfather than either of his parents. There was something else, though, something familiar. Then it hit her. Being an elf, his build was more slight, but he bore a striking resemble to a certain stone mason - a sculptor to be exact – that she had once met.

Ember fought to break the strange spell she felt was being cast on her when the pair reached those waiting in the back and Traejan quickly stepped forward to bow to them and make the introductions. They bowed in return, smiling at the prince, but as they straightened the Battle King's eyes fell upon the Roshan and his expression fell.

"It's you!" he exclaimed.

All eyes went to the former king, none more surprised than the Roshan herself.

"Excuse me?" she asked, but Acqtraejale had already composed himself and was smiling apologetically.

"I am so sorry," he said quickly, "I am clearly mistaken." He laughed nervously and looked at his grandson. "This is obviously the commander of the red troops," he said. "Is it not?"

"It is," Traejan agreed. "And my Roshan, who instructed me last summer, Ember L'chiross." He looked at her as she dipped her dark red head of hair respectfully and the young prince continued, "please allow me to introduce the Lady Karamine, and Acqtraejale Royce, former king and father to Rowland, King of the Elves." They gave her a nod as the prince turned and introduced Ryen.

"My, you're a tall one!" Karamine said, eyeing the Vikeman with a dazzling smile. Ryen, always ready to flirt with a beautiful woman, had to bite his tongue. He knew that it was not the proper time nor the appropriate company. All he could do was grin in return, hoping his expression was as depraved as he felt.

The Battle King, however, gave him a knowing smile before he turned and exchanged greetings with Halloran. "I believe today was a success," he announced to the general.

"It was," Halloran agreed. "The elves fought valiantly, and the help of the red troops and their leadership was invaluable, the Vikemen as well."

Ember's eyes caught quick movement at the front of the building and she turned her face to see Dash, along with Bryce from her own troops, quickly making their way towards her from across the room.

"Please excuse me," she said abruptly, sketching a short bow before turning away. She only made it a few steps, silence in her wake as the group she left behind watched curiously. Her gaze flicked over those left in the cabin. Zephyrn, with Dirk standing close, was engaged in conversation with Dell and two Jägers. Two messengers lingered by a table close to the door, talking quietly while waiting instructions. Espytin had followed Jennings out at some point.

Then Bryce was before her. He had washed up since the battle and his face was clean, though she could see the wound on his chin that he had gotten during the ambush. He was dressed in the normal attire for the red troops of burgundy riding leathers, and his soft brown eyes were blazing.

"I am sorry to disturb you," he apologized, his fine-looking face drawn and intense, "but our horses were set loose."

The Roshan's hand clenched around the hilt of her sword, though she was not surprised. "Did you see who did it?" she asked, her voice tight. She could sense the others drifting closer to find out what was going on.

Bryce shook his head, a slight flush creeping up over his sharply angled jawline. "No. I was on watch with Dalton when we heard a cry go up and saw flames on a tent nearby. We ran to help and returned quite swiftly, but the gate had already been thrown wide and the horses spooked into running."

"Was anyone hurt?" the Roshan asked.

Bryce quickly shook his head. "No. I am so sorry..." he began but the Roshan cut him off with a wave of a hand.

"You did the right thing," she said, keeping him fixed in her stare. "You were posted at the west corral?"

Bryce nodded. "Yes. First Cavalry."

The Roshan's eyes narrowed and her lips pressed together into a thin line. "Gavan's horses," she stated. Bryce gave her another sharp nod. "Have you told him?"

"I sent a runner."

"And the horses? Did anyone go after them?"

"Only the ones we could see. I did not want to send anyone out into the woods without checking with you first. I thought it could be a distraction, like the fire, or a trap."

"Good thinking. Get those horses calmed down and get me a count of how many are missing. I'll meet you at the west corral when I am done here," she told him. He bowed and turned to leave but the Roshan stopped him. "What about Second Cavalry? Or the elfin horses?"

Bryce shook his head. "I checked on them while Dash rode to the elfin camp to check on their horses. Nothing."

The Roshan looked at the small elf who was quick to concur. "Nothing out of the ordinary at our corrals," Dash assured her, "but we doubled the watch with instructions not to leave unless by order."

"I did the same for us," Bryce added.

The Roshan looked at them a moment longer and then dismissed them with a wave of her hand before turning to the group that had congregated behind her.

"Just Gavan's horses?" Ryen asked. She nodded and the Vikeman looked at Halloran. "Do you have any more doubts, general?"

Halloran stared at a nearby table, a deep crease between his iron brows. "I never doubted," he said, gruff, "only hoped." His steely eyes raised to find those of the Roshan. "You will take care of this?" he asked. "You think you can?"

The Roshan nodded solemnly. "I can. I will."

"I am sorry," the Battle King said. "I wanted to congratulate everyone, but I feel like we have intruded. Please forgive us, we will be on our way." He held out an arm for Karamine but the general turned his scowl towards them.

"Nonsense!" he declared. "You, more than anyone, know that some of the nastiest battles are not fought with steel and sword. I will be glad to fill you in on our discussion."

"Later," Acqtra told him. "I can see this is not the time." He looked next to Ember and Ryen. "It was a pleasure to meet you both, I am sorry it was not under better circumstances."

The Roshan and the Vikeman both smiled and bowed.

"Maybe, when this is over, we can meet again," Ryen suggested, smiling at the dark elf.

"I would like that," Karamine murmured softly. The Battle King grunted as they both turned their attention next to the Roshan.

"My lady," Ember said, extending a slim-fingered hand. The already quiet group became completely still, save for their eyes, which moved from the Roshan's hand to the face of the black elf.

Karamine smiled, her white teeth contrasting sharply with her black skin. "You are indeed a bold woman," she said as she reached out a delicate hand and gently wrapped her dark fingers around those of the Roshan. "Many fear my touch, and most who would brave it, only do so in private."

"I harbor no secrets," Ember assured her - though, in truth, she was more than anxious about what the woman might say.

"Indeed you do not," Karamine agreed, still holding her hand. "But you are surrounded by choices, and you are torn."

Karamine could feel the warrior's pain, and the will she was imposing on herself to look neither at the prince nor the Vikeman next to her. They were foremost in her mind, along with a young man with black hair, full lips and dark eyes. As well, she could see another in the mind of the Roshan, a man with green eyes and so large that he would tower over even the tall Northman by her side.

The Roshan nodded slowly. "I am. But does your sight... does it tell you..." she trailed off, unsure, before lifting her chin and pressing on. "Is there any advice you might give me?"

The black elf took a deep breath, expanding her narrow chest, and let it out. "Yes," she announced softly. "Do not look behind you." In her mind flickered an image of Traejan, and then one of Ryen. The Roshan's eyes widened as the seer continued, "Search your feelings for the truth and you will do the right thing." Her hand tightened on the Roshan's. "You have made it this far without second-guessing yourself. I suggest you do not start now."

The dark warrior and the dark lady faced each other for moment, the air pregnant with silence, and then the elfin woman stepped away, releasing the Roshan. Ember bowed her head respectfully and Ryen cleared his throat, breaking the silence.

"If you were to take up my hand, my lady," he offered with a grin, "I would not be so quick to let it go."

"Then don't wait too long," she advised with a rakish grin of her own. "I would hate to see you shortened by a Crommag's sword."

The small group chuckled as one, the air somewhat lightened.

"Your Majesty," the Roshan called softly, addressing the Battle King as he made to leave. Acqtraejale turned back, his white eyebrows raised inquisitively and she was struck once again by his resemblance to Traejan.

"Yes?"

"When you first spied me, you thought you knew me? Or that I reminded you of someone?"

The Battle King chuckled. "Not someone," he corrected, "something. Made so perfectly that it seemed to be alive, save for the white chill of the stone it had been carved from." He gave her a smile but she had gone as pale and still as the marble from which he was certain he had once seen her likeness, long ago.

# 18. MORNING RAID

That night Ember went to sleep thinking about Crag, so it was no surprise that she dreamt about him. It was not the first time.

This time, however, she dreamed she was standing on the cliffs behind Kriegslager, looking down into Morgan's Vale. She was on the edge and the wind blew through her hair and whipped her cloak out behind her. She could see all of the land laid out before her, a now empty battlefield.

Crag stood a few feet away from her, facing the wind as well. He was so big that it filled her with trepidation, something no man had ever done before. And, though his mouth was closed, she knew he was running his tongue along his teeth the way he did when he looked at her.

What she could hardly believe was the way he spoke to her. He had been alarmingly blatant about expressing his feelings, and it seemed to surprise him as much as it did the Roshan.

Still, she worried, *it is too soon.*

Don't wait! Don't wait! the nightingale called from some oneric tree.

I need to know more about him!

There was a tug at her sleeve and she looked down to see Gatha. Ember waited for her to sign with her hands or point and grunt, as she was apt to do, but Gatha opened her mouth to speak instead.

"He is the one," Gatha told her, giving the Roshan a jolt. "You knew from the very first. If you have truly cared for the others in your life, you must act now. To delay will only cause more pain. Be done with it."

Ember could only nod. For the first time she was the one rendered speechless.

It was her voice - Gatha's voice that did it. So beautiful, so light. It reached into her and touched her soul. It was the voice of the nightingale.

The Roshan awoke to the feel of Ian's gentle fingers pushing her hair away from her face. She opened her eyes to see him looking at her from the light of a candle, his black eyes framed by thick lashes.

"It is time," he whispered.

She nodded and rose, stretching her neck and then her arms. Ian handed her a damp towel and she used it to scrub her face. She ate a biscuit and drank a mug of coffee in the dim light of their tent as he helped her get ready. No braziers were to be lit that morning. Though the tents of Kriegslager were well back from the edge of the bluff, the Crommags were to be given no sign that the troops were stirring so long before dawn.

"I want to go with you," Ian whispered as he fastened the brace around her ribcage.

"I know," Ember whispered back. "But I already told you of our need for silence, which means no horses. Especially Meghan."

"I can go on foot," he offered, wrapping her belt around her waist. "I have a sword in my trunk I can bring. I can fight if I have to." The Roshan gave him a smile in the darkness.

"I'd be too worried about you. Besides, I need you to be ready for when I get back. It's going to be a long day for me. For all of us."

Agitated, Ian pulled hard enough on the Roshan's belt to make her huff, then cinched it tightly, ignoring her expression. He didn't like it. Not any of it. But he trusted her. He handed over her pair of short swords and then her longsword, watching as she sheathed each one. How she moved so easily or silently with all that metal was beyond him.

The red commander slipped from her tent, just a shadow among shadows. Outside, waiting, were fifty more shadows. Sloan and his men. Sloan himself wore a hooded cloak to hide his hair lest it shine in the light of the setting moon. The Roshan turned left and her men followed, moving soundlessly. They headed past the Vikemen yurts where all was quiet and still. The Northmen, like the horses, had not been invited on this particular soiree. As loud as they were, even when they strained for silence, the Roshan did not even want them awake in their tents at this moment.

Past the yurts was the once beaten track that had now become a road leading to the slope down into the low meadows of Morgan's Vale. There, waited Nevin with a hundred elves. The graying but ruggedly handsome elf gave a nod to the leader of the red troops and, wordlessly, the two parties fell in on each side and followed the pair as they turned and descended the grade.

The moon had almost set, but still gave them a little light as they moved down to the Vale with no more sound than the westerly breeze. The bodies of the fallen elfin soldiers and those of the red troops had been removed, but the Crommag dead littered the prairie. Their weapons, many still held fast in the grip of the dead, glimmered in the light of the departing moon.

The Roshan caught Nevin's eye as they passed the bodies, and motioned to the cold steel and lifeless hands. He nodded, getting her meaning immediately. The weapons should be recovered by the elves, before they could be reclaimed by the enemy.

The war party passed the berm of earth deposited by the Gnomin after they had carved out the cliffs to make them unscalable, and the remains from the concealed ditch they had hastily dug. A few moments later, on feet as quick and quiet as cats, they passed the ditch as well. A trench that was now full of thick and heavy bodies. Stealthily, the small war party climbed over the carcasses and pressed on.

Another minute brought them close to the edge of the forest where Nevin held up a fist, calling them to a halt. He and the Roshan dropped down into a crouch, their troops doing the same. The Jäger's eyes scoured the tree line, the Roshan doing the same by his side.

"I see three guards," she whispered, leaning close to him.

Nevin shook his graying locks. "Five," he whispered back, raising a gloved hand to point to one guard that was far to the north, and another that had slumped to the ground, asleep. The Roshan smiled.

"Alright, five. I'll take care of them."

"All of them?" Nevin asked with one brow raised high over an almond-shaped eye.

"If you don't mind waiting," the Roshan said with feigned annoyance.

Both of Nevin's brows raised this time and he held out a gloved hand in invitation. "After you, my lady."

In an effort to preserve the silence, the Roshan held back a snort. Silently, she crept forward. At the edge of the wood she came to an abrupt halt, then advanced again until she disappeared from even the sight of the elfin Jäger.

Nevin counted seventy seconds before he saw the northernmost sentry crumple into a heap. Forty seconds later, the next one fell. Twenty seconds before the next one toppled over, but a good thirty seconds until number four went down, falling forward on his face. The last one remained motionless, leaving Nevin to wonder if she had left that one alone or killed him in his sleep. He guessed, correctly, that she simply killed him where he lay.

She was back by his side within only a few more heartbeats.

The whole task had taken less than five minutes.

"You know," he whispered to her, "this war would be a whole lot easier if you could just do that to all of them."

The Roshan grinned at the elf. "I would if I could," she assured him quietly. She pointed towards the woods and he saw that she still held her dagger, a long one, dripping with blood. "Did you see where I stopped?" she asked. He nodded and she continued. "They have their own trench dug there, studded with stakes."

The elf's face became serious. "They were expecting an attack by mounted troops," he said softly, his voice heavy as he looked in the direction of the woods. His eyes flickered slightly as they sought out hers. "Or do you think it is just a coincidence?"

"Do you?" the Roshan countered.

Nevin frowned. "I have no way to know. But, at least they have made our job easier." He rose up slightly and motioned to the north, and then to the south. His troops split in half, running in a crouch towards the woods. "Use the trench!" he whispered as they passed.

One line of elves ran north, lining up along the ditch, while another line ran south, doing the same. Then the Roshan motioned to her own men who followed in almost the same manner.

It was an hour before dawn.

The elves got to the ditch and spread out along its entire line and knelt down on the ground, removing casks from their backs. Sloan's men took up post behind them, one man for each pair of elves, and unslung their crossbows. The Roshan and the Jäger moved closer, keeping watch.

Sunrise was still almost an hour away, but the eastern sky was beginning to lighten. The moon had set. The elves uncorked the casks and began pouring their contents into the ditch along the woods.

At first it just soaked into the ground and Nevin was afraid that there would not be enough. Then the oil began to gather on top of the soil, and then pool, and then run together.

The Roshan's eyes flashed in the changing light, moving everywhere as she absently cleaned her dagger with the edge of her cloak.

In the forest, they could hear the sounds of the Crommags stirring.

The elves emptied the wooden casks and then placed them carefully in the trench, adding more fuel. Four elves with flints looked expectantly at Nevin, waiting. The infantry captain looked at the warrior clad in black but she shook her head and held up a hand.

Nevin was anxious that the oil would soak into the ground and be all but useless but he held himself, watching the dark lady. The Roshan glanced at the ditch that was now a small river of oil and worried the same, but waited. She knew that to induce fear or distress when it was already set would feed it, possibly producing panic.

Only a moment later they heard a shout of alarm as the dead body of a sentry was found, and then another. Crommags began to rush to the tree line. Ember gave Nevin a quick nod and he signaled the elves with flints. Hardly a breath passed before it was sucked from their lungs in a great rush of heat.

The elves, along with their captain and the Roshan, took a few quick steps backwards as flames shot up in a wall of fire that was neck high. Sloan and his men stood their ground and, when the first of the Crommags reached the scene, they released fifty bolts of steel through the flames.

Nevin calmly signaled for a retreat and his elves began to back further away from the burning trench while the red troops reloaded their crossbows and also began to back away. The Roshan, however, held a hand in the air, holding them fast.

Squinting through the smoke and flames, she waited until

there were enough Crommags again gathered in disorganized confusion before signaling for another volley, and then retreat.

The crossbowmen fired another fifty quarrels, slung their bows on their backs, and followed the elves. They moved in a quick trot, as they had been instructed, ready to turn and fight at any moment.

But no fight came.

The Crommag camp was clearly in pandemonium.

The troops, both men and elfin, made their way steadily across the plains as the sound of Crommag screams and curses fell away behind them. To the east, the sky brightened, shearing the blue sky with streams of rose and gold.

They made it to the slope and began to climb, the weight of their task lightened by the feeling of accomplishment, and the cheers of those that waited on the bluff.

The regular troops had assembled as commanded, ready for battle an hour before dawn, only to see the success of the morning war party that only few had known about. They held their swords high and cheered the soldiers as they returned. Elves and crossbowmen were clapped on the back and congratulated as they passed, returning to their normal ranks.

There was one, however, waiting atop the cliff that was not so pleased. Nevin and the Roshan bowed before Prince Traejan who had dismounted and left the knoll and the troops behind, his eyes blazing blue in the morning light. The Jäger and the red commander motioned for their own troops to continue.

"And just what in the Seventh Circle was this?" the prince demanded, keeping his voice as low as he could while the oncoming soldiers took the hill and split right and left for their respective camps.

"A sortie," Nevin said, his voice also low yet much calmer than that of the prince.

"A sortie?" Traejan asked heatedly. "A sortie that did what? Light a few bonfires? Put a hundred elfin lives at risk?"

"A hundred elves returned," the Roshan said, struggling to keep her own voice down as she narrowed her eyes at the prince. "As well as fifty Southlonders, who also risked their lives."

"My Lord Prince," Nevin said, dipping his head, "I am truly sorry if this has displeased you in any way. General Halloran approved of the raid..."

"But I sincerely doubt this was the general's idea," the elfin prince interjected. "Am I wrong?"

"No," the Roshan answered. "But your anger is severely misplaced." She turned her searing gaze to Nevin who appeared to have aged a decade in just the last minute. "You are a good captain," she told him. "You made this raid a success and, by doing so, have saved many lives."

Nevin bowed to her. "I think the success of this mission is your doing, but I will take any acclaim you give me." He rose and turned his eyes to Traejan. "My Lord Prince?" he asked, waiting for dismissal.

"Very well," the young prince acquiesced. "Go. Rest and await the general's next orders."

Nevin bowed stiffly and left.

"Have you taken complete leave of your senses?" she hissed.

"What was this raid really about?" Traejan demanded as quietly as he could.

"It was a probe," she answered, calming herself. "To see the lay of the battlefield, the lay of the woods. To see when they awake and how many guards they post... but mostly to see if they had prepared for a mounted assault."

"And had they?" he asked softly.

"Yes. And, as a bonus, we have delayed their morning attack."

"They will still attack," Traejan argued.

The Roshan heaved a great sigh, becoming increasingly

agitated. "But not now. Not within the cool of the day, when they are most powerful. Can you not see how the heat of the sun wears them down?"

Traejan looked away, casting his angry gaze over the meadows that were beginning to gleam in the morning sun, and knew her words to be true. It had been something he had noted, but ignored because of other things occupying his mind.

The Roshan's shoulders sagged. She glanced over her shoulder. The troops were well away from them now but she took a step towards him and leaned close, speaking softly. "Don't let your personal feelings…"

"Feelings!" Traejan hissed, taking a step back, moving away from her. "I feel nothing! Nothing save for anger at this underhanded insubordination! The only thing that concerns me is this war!" He looked her up and down, his expression full of anger and disgust, then turned on his heel and walked away.

The Roshan felt as if she had been run through. Pierced somewhere she had never been wounded before. Her throat constricted painfully. She stood there for what felt like long moments but was most likely only a matter of seconds, before she felt massive hands come down over her shoulders.

"Do not look so longingly after him." Crag whispered in her ear, leaning far down to do so.

The Roshan straightened her form and turned slightly so she could look up at him. "Do I look longingly at him?" she asked.

Crag's voice was a purr in her ear. "Only when you think no one is watching."

The Roshan turned fully so that she could look upon him and his hands, reluctantly, fell away.

"How is it that you see so much?" she asked, truly curious.

"Because I look into you," he said. "Instead of just at you, like the others do." His green eyes raised and he jerked his chin in the direction Traejan had taken, before they fell again upon her face.

"And what would happen if I were to look into you?" the Roshan asked softly.

Crag smiled, showing his perfect, even teeth. "Maybe you could find a home," he said, even softer, reaching out to run a giant hand down her black-clad arm.

Ember turned her head to where she could see Traejan entering Kriegslager, moving confidently among his troops, not looking back.

"Maybe," she agreed.

And maybe this will be easier than I believed, she thought, letting Crag lead her to the top of the cliff.

⊰⊱

Traejan wanted to return to his tent. He wanted to pace, to shout, to pull out his damn hair. Instead, he felt his armor tighten about his body and soul, then he signaled for Peg. Dell, already mounted and waiting, put his heel to his own horse and brought her over to the prince. Traejan pulled himself gracefully up into the saddle and turned the white palfrey towards the eastern side of the bluff.

"Did you know?" he asked Dell, urging Peg forward.

"Only just this morning," the Praetorian answered, riding next to the prince. "I guess the general was still hoping that it could be anything but a spy. I was told that while he and the Roshan were finishing their wine last night, he asked if there was any way that the gate on the corral could have come unlatched and the horses gotten loose on their own – maybe ran because they were spooked by the fire."

Traejan made a face as they neared the raised knoll. "The cause of the fire seemed legitimate. A piece of wood from a cookfire got kicked close to the tent and it caught. Still, it could have been kicked, or placed there on purpose."

Dell nodded in agreement. "The red commander offered to lead a party to confirm her suspicions. I take it she was right?"

"Of course she was," Trajan said, angry. "And I take it that everyone else had gone to bed? That Nevin was the only one still there and they thought it prudent not to wake any of the other captains about a mission that carried such little risk?"

Dell suppressed a grin. "From what I have gathered, that is exactly what happened."

"What remarkable timing," the young prince remarked, his tone like acid. "Which was, also, no accident. Damn her!" he cursed.

Dell's grin broke free but, thankfully, they had reached the knoll and he turned his horse away and then edged her backwards to take his place next to the prince. Traejan greeted his father and grandfather, then his brothers. Shane greeted him warmly from atop his mighty warhorse. As he was turning Peg, he noticed the giant Vikeman, watching him from atop his khusar. The Norseman shifted his jade-green eyes away, but the young prince did not miss the look of contempt that had been in them.

The general rode up then, accompanied by two messengers on swift horses. He bowed to the kings and then took his place close to the younger elfin princes, surrounded by their Praetorian guards. Together, they looked down onto the plains of Morgan's Vale, now flooded with morning light.

Within seconds, the contempt Traejan had seen in the eyes of the giant Northman, he began to feel for himself.

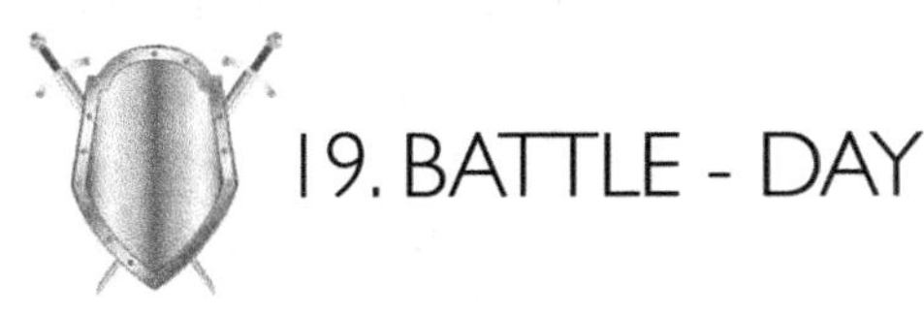

19. BATTLE - DAY TWO

The fires along the edge of the Elfin Greatwood were finally beginning to die down. They had burned hot from the oil, and long – fueled by the wooden casks left by the elves and the wooden stakes that had been driven into the trenches by the Crommags.

The elfin troops that day were to be led by Drustin and the elfin cavalry. They had already descended the grade and were spread out, picking their way slowly across the field of war. They stopped fifty yards before the ditch full of dead Crommags.

Behind them was the second cavalry of the red army, led by Rhys – his golden hair shining in the light of the rising sun. Behind the red cavalry, on foot, was the Roshan. She was flanked by six Vikemen, three on each side, none of which Traejan recognized save for Ryen. Dash and a tall groom from the red troops lingered near them, holding Coal as well as the Vikemen's khusars. Behind *them*, Traejan could see Ian on his dancing red mare.

She looks so small from here, Traejan thought, looking at the dark form of the Roshan. *So vulnerable.*

A chill spread across his back as a feeling of dread settled over his shoulders like falling ash.

What if something happens to her in this battle? he thought, unexpectedly apprehensive. *What if she is killed?* He felt panic rising in his chest and he did his best to quash it.

Stop it! he told himself. *She's going to be fine. She just looks small because of the distance and because she is next to those massive Northmen. She is the same size she always was, and the same fighter. Gods only know how many battles she has survived, she will certainly survive this one.*

Still...how much sleep has she had? She was up at dawn yesterday and fought for hours on end. Up late last night with the general and up even earlier today for that raid.

The young prince tried to drive the doubt from his thoughts but all he could think of was how exhausted she must already be. And all he could see was the look in her eyes when he hissed at her that he felt nothing. She looked as if he had slapped her.

If I lose her today, the last thing she would have seen of me was the way I looked at her, right before I walked away.

Traejan felt as if an iron fist was squeezing his heart and Peg shifted nervously beneath him, sensing his anxiety.

For all the Circles, get a hold of yourself! he commanded inwardly. *She is going to be fine.* He felt a stab of doubt again but forced himself to become still and it faded. *She will see this battle through and many others.*

He searched for the emotional armor he had been wearing since her arrival, even tried cloaking himself in anger, but it had deserted him.

You're going to lose her, his mind whispered, and something of the tone had a taste of premonition. He tried to swallow and found that his mouth had gone completely dry.

No, I am not. I will not.

But, when this day is done, I am going to go talk to her. She needs to know how I feel. At the very least, I need to tell her I love her. I still love her. I never stopped loving her. After that...

His eyes, as well as the eyes of every other soul on the knoll, caught movement at the edge of the forest. The Crommags began to emerge, seeping from the Elfin Greatwood like pus from an infected wound. One of them, a mountain of a beast, climbed atop a rock and shouted. The other beasts responded and, though they were far, the sound carried on the breeze and it was unmistakable. It was laughter.

Ayala had waited until a good number of Great Men had lined up, getting a good look at their enemy. Then he pointed with his sword at the elfin cavalry where they waited on their horses beyond the trench of the dead.

"Look!" he shouted. "The elves brought us dinner!" The Crommags boomed laughter. "Drag those beasts back after battle, and tonight we shall truly feast!"

The Great Men roared their agreement and began to advance.

Drustin held his up his hand silent and waiting. As soon as the beasts were within fifty yards, he dropped his hand.

The elves let up a cry and charged forward, the hooves of their horses eating up the distance to the ditch full of bodies before vaulting over it. The Crommags ran to meet them and the sound made when the armies collided was like an avalanche of rock hitting the valley floor.

Atop their horses, the elves were more than a match for the Crommags and cut through them like butchers. But the elves were no match in strength and size of the monsters. Like the previous day, if an elf failed to land a lethal blow, it often resulted in the Crommag pulling the elf from his mount and tearing him apart.

Drustin's men fought valiantly for more than two hours. Then his three lines of horsemen became two lines and, in a few places, was only one rider deep. Before the lines could buckle altogether, General Halloran signaled his trumpeter. The elf put his horn to his lips and blew, the sound echoing onto the plains below even as it was repeated by other trumpets along the face of the bluff.

Drustin's cavalry disengaged from the enemy and split, half riding west and half riding east as the mounted red troops came charging across the fields and the battle resumed anew. The new soldiers, untired and eager, began to drive the flagging Crommags back towards the Elfin Greatwood.

The fresh wave of fighters was discouraging to the Great Men, who gnashed their fangs in frustration. Clashing the hilts of their weapons upon their shields, they shouted curses even as they resigned themselves to the new foe and began to push back with renewed vigor.

Just as the huge monsters started gaining momentum, the lines of horsemen pulled apart in the middle like a river going around a rock. The Crommags near the divide stopped in confusion, unsure of which way to turn when they found themselves facing a charge of roaring Vikemen and the flashing sword of the black-clad warrior with hair like flame.

The Crommags cry of anger was thunderous. Many recognized the warrior from the day before and knew she had slain many Great Men. Ayala, as well, recognized the small but lethal warrior. Last night, as he had sat with Noga drinking grog, his brother had called her "the angel of death." Their language, however, had no word for "angel." It translated better into "the spirit of death." Ayala was forced to agree.

The leader of the Great Men watched her now, cutting down his men as if they were blades of spring grass. Ayala gnashed his fangs and pointed at her with his sword. "Kill her!" he bellowed.

Many Crommags heard the command but could not see who their leader intended, and they lowered their swords as they looked around, searching. The moment of hesitation was their last as they were destroyed instantly by Rhys and his cavalry. The Great Men close to the Roshan, however, snarled in anger and pressed forward, trying to reach her as she swung her instrument of death.

Traejan, atop the bluff, watched her as well, feeling smug.

See? What in the world were you worried about? Look at her – she is unstoppable. He watched as the wedge formed by the Roshan and the Vikemen drove the Crommags back, closer and closer to the tree line. Traejan smiled as he watched her fight, amazed as always at her uncanny speed. *She is so fast!* he marveled, his chest swelling. Seconds later, his smile faltered and his heart hitched. *Too fast.*

She is going too fast.

As Ember drove the head of her wedge of fighters closer to the trees, the young prince watched in growing dismay, for he could see from his high vantage what she could not.   The wedge behind her was growing thinner, from an arrowhead to a spear point. The Norsemen were fighting hard, and well, but they could not keep up with her as she dropped Crommags left and right.

Then it worsened as the great beasts began driving at the sides of the thinning spearpoint of Vikemen with everything they had, trying to cut her off from the rest of the army. The tip of the spear thinned into a line, and Ryen, finally realizing what was happening, shouted out a warning that she did not hear. She drove on with a fury, unaware or uncaring that behind her the line had broken.

The Roshan reached the tree line and finally turned, her back to an enormous soldier pine, and faced a ring of Crommags as the battle raged behind them.

She was cut off.

Uncaring, she swung her sword in a tight circle on her right, then on her left. It whickered though the air like an invitation.

Traejan thought they would converge on her at once and take her down like a flood of dark, seething water, but they did not. They rushed at her one at a time, as if they each wanted to be the one to single handedly bring down the fiery demon that had plagued them the previous day and still fought on relentlessly. When she cut them down swiftly they began to rush her two at a time, and then three.

Still, her sword whickered through the air as if it had a life of its own, dropping the beasts as soon as they charged. She was faster by far, often stepping nimbly aside to let them drive their swords through each other at the last second. But the ring was getting tighter and the Crommags faster. Traejan could see that Ember was finally starting to wear down, the exhaustion catching up with her as he had feared it would. The tide he had seen through his elfin eyes was rising up to consume her.

Ryen was shouting wildly at the Vikemen and fighting doggedly as he tried to break through to her, but the Crommags on that particular part of the field had become united in facing a single foe and the Northmen could not cut through. Then, as the Roshan was driven back almost into the trees, the heel of her boot caught on a protruding root and she went down.

The young prince barely stifled a scream as the Crommags, tasting victory, surged forward as she rolled away, and the Seventh Circle broke free.

There was a mighty yell from many throats as the Crommags were consumed in a hail of rocks and sticks. Then a gaggle of what appeared to be half-naked children dropped from the trees in a wild rush of thin, flailing, dirty limbs. Wielding knives and spears, they landed on and among the converging monsters.

"Aiden!" Traejan cried out, his voice breaking.

The attack momentarily shocked the Crommags, giving Ember a second, the only second she needed, to leap to her feet and start cutting her way free. While she did, Aiden and the Wildboys clung like barnacles to the backs of the beasts, stabbing at the monstrous creatures. Some found their mark and a few Great Men fell, but most simply reached behind their necks to grab the crazy pests and fling them away.

The boys only rose up and charged the Crommags.

The sight, Traejan supposed, would have at any other time looked ridiculous. The boys came no higher than the belts of the Great Men and the reach of the giants was so great that it seemed the tiny annoyances would be smashed to bits. But the lithe boys simply darted right under those massive hands, stabbing wildly as they came.

The elfin prince watched, transfixed.

"Get her, Aiden," he breathed. "Get her out of there."

As if he could hear him, Aiden did indeed cut down the last Crommag between Ember and Ryen, hamstringing the lumbering giant with a swing of his knife. The boys swarmed in a half circle around the Roshan as they began to cut their way back to the main body of the army.

They might have been small, and crudely armed, but the Wildboys fought as fiercely as any human or elf ever had, maybe more.

Ten of them had spears and wielded them with a surprising amount of speed and strength. They would smash a Crommag in the face with the butt of a spear and then whip it around and run him through. They surrounded the Roshan and slowly began to make their way out of the enemy's ranks.

From his perch at the base of the knoll, Traejan watched helplessly as events collided.

Simultaneously, the remnants of the Vikemen that had formed the wedge behind Ember broke through the line of Crommags, reuniting her with the main force. At the same time, a smaller Crommag in the thick of the fighting, struck down Aiden with the swing of his sword.

Ember screamed in fury and cut the neck of the Crommag so deep it nearly severed its head from its body. She swept Aiden up as he fell, unconscious, now looking for escape. A sheet of blood covered the Wildboy's face. Ryen was there.

"Get him to my tent!" she ordered, handing over the thin and limp form to the Vikeman, "I'll follow with the rest of them!"

Ryen nodded and turned on his heel, easily carrying Aiden's bleeding body through the wedge of Vikemen as he beat a hasty retreat.

"Follow him!" the Roshan shouted at the Wildboys that were still busy cutting the legs out from under the Crommags.

The crazed band of Sprites abandoned their task and followed Ryen as he fled north through the battle, cutting a swath of death and blood in front of him as he went. The boys trailed him as fast as their thin legs would allow and the Roshan followed, killing every Crommag that got near.

They made their way through the remaining Vikemen and the mounted red troops, their ears filled with the clash of metal and the scream of horses. Once past, they ran through the trampled grass to the trench heaped with dead Crommags. The Roshan vaulted over it to find Ian, pulling his red mare around in a tight circle.

"Are you hurt?" he demanded.

"No," she informed him, looking around.

Dash had released Coal and the Night Stallion was galloping towards her. Ryen had snagged a khusar and was already at the top of the hill, spurring it towards her tent. The Wildboys were crawling over the corpses, loudly voicing their disgust.

"Tell Dash to take them to the mess and get them cleaned up and fed. Then get to our tent as fast as you can."

Coal came to a skidding stop and she grabbed the riding harness and pulled herself up and into the saddle. She turned him and then put her boots to his flanks - hard. The Night Stallion took off, racing across the meadow. He made it to the earthen grade and ran up it with ease. She leaned down, clinging to his neck, urging him on.

She slid off his back as soon they reached her tent and left him, untethered, outside.

Inside, Aiden was laid out on her cot with Gatha leaning down over him, washing the wound on his head. There was blood running down his face, soaking his hair. Ryen stood to the side, idly tapping the hilt of his sword as he watched.

"Is he alright?" Ember asked, pulling off her gloves as she went to the cot and knelt by Aiden's head. His eyelids fluttered open at the sound of her voice and he smiled.

"Hello, Dark Lady," he whispered.

"Hello, brave warrior."

"I told you we could fight Crommags."

"I already knew. Because I know you have no fear," she told him, making his smile brighten his dirty face. "But this is what I feared would happen."

"Not me. True elves do not fear death."

"You are not going to die," Ember told him firmly. She sought out his small hand with her own and gave it a squeeze.

"When I saw you last," Aiden said, "you had the mark of death upon you." He looked away and his high, feathery brows drew together as he thought. "Not that you knew you were going to die, but that you were ready to." He shifted his gaze to meet her eyes. "And I knew that if you were going to die, then I would as well, fighting by your side."

"Well," she stated, blinking tears from her eyes, "I am not dying, so neither are you."

"At least I got to see you one more time," he said softly. "And I got to go down fighting."

She glanced at Gatha but the Gnomin woman was too busy to meet her gaze, or was avoiding it.

The Roshan placed her free hand on Aiden's soft curls, staying clear of the gash the Crommag had carved into his head.

"You are NOT going to die," Ember said emphatically.

"I will if you send me away again," he whispered, his smile slipping away.

"I won't," she assured him. "Not ever. You can be my personal guard. You and your men."

Aiden smiled again and closed his eyes. Gatha held a pad of white fabric to the wound, making the Wildboy wince in pain.

She motioned for the Roshan to hold it in place and traded it for a long strip of cloth which she began to wind around his head. When she got to the end she tucked the strip up under the bandage she had made.

The Roshan ran her hand lightly over his curls and he opened his eyes again. To Ember, they were the color of the forest at dusk. They glanced about, touched with awe.

"I never knew I had so much blood in me," he said.

"Head wounds bleed a lot," she informed him. "Even shallow ones."

Aiden seemed to ponder this and then his eyes closed slowly, as if he were falling asleep. A moment later they fluttered open. "Can I have some mead?" he asked softly, making the Roshan smile.

"Gatha will bring you some soup."

"And some mead?"

The Roshan grinned and leaned forward to place a soft kiss on his forehead. Aiden closed his eyes, smiling. "Get some rest," she advised as she rose to her feet. "I think he's going to be okay," she told the Vikeman who, though pleased, did not return her smile.

"You moved your furniture around," he remarked.

The Roshan looked about her tent and saw that the desk had been put to the side and the cots were now very close, though one was on its side. She realized it was that way because the cots had actually been pushed together but someone, Ryen undoubtedly, had kicked it aside as he brought in the injured Wildboy.

"Oh," the Roshan said, nodding as she remembered. "Ian was supposed to move things around for me. It doesn't look like he had time to finish."

Ryen gave her a dark look and strode from the tent. The Roshan watched him go and turned to Gatha. She had learned signing by watching the Gnomin woman, but had never done it herself.

Will he really die? she fumbled.

Gatha gave her a smirk of exasperation, one the Roshan knew quite well, and signed back.

Only if dirt can kill.

The Roshan grinned and left the tent.

Ryen was there, holding the reins of his khusar as well as those of Coal. "Feel like seeing how the war is progressing?" he asked with exaggerated gallantry. "Or rejoining the battle, perhaps?"

The Roshan cast her eyes to the sky and saw that the sun had just crossed its zenith. "If they wear out today like they did yesterday, there might not be much to go back to. Let's see how it is progressing."

Ryen gave a nod as he swung himself into the saddle of his khusar. "I know just where to go."

The Roshan did as well, but climbed atop Coal and let the Vikeman lead the way at an easy gallop to the knoll where the elfin royalty watched the battle down below. After an arrival accompanied by bows and nods where she was careful not to meet Traejan's eyes with her own, she edged her giant horse up next to Halloran and looked down on the plains below.

The carnage was sickening but she could tell in a single glance that her troops were holding well.

"It won't be much longer now," the general affirmed, his deep voice rolling from his throat. "They have been growing weary with the heat, even before you left the battle."

Together, they watched the fight below where neither side fought with ferocity but neither seemed to gain nor lose ground. Though the sun had passed its apex in the sky, the temperature continued to rise.

Finally, a great horn sounded from below. A Crommag horn.

The beasts took a few last swings, covering their departure

as they gnashed their fangs at the enemy and melted back into the forest.

On the battleground, no sound came to order a pursuit. Swords lowered while voices and fists were raised in shouts of victory. Atop the knoll on the bluff, shoulders sagged in relief.

The general turned his gaze towards the Roshan only to find himself staring at her black-clad shoulder. He raised his gray eyes to her face, suddenly aware of the size of the beast that she rode.

"I believe you are right," he said. "They are quite overcome by the heat."

"If they are limited by how long they can fight in the day, and limited by the light," Xander said from behind them, "it gives us more of an advantage than we had ever thought."

"There may be hope for us yet," Zephyrn said cheerfully.

"It is only the second day of battle, my sons," King Rowland said from the top of the knoll, his voice grave.

"But," the Battle King added, no less serious, "there should always be hope."

Ember and Ryen exchanged glances that were less optimistic and the general cleared his throat.

"I think we should assemble the troops in the mess," he said. "We can speak to them individually or as a whole."

The Roshan gave him a curt nod as she turned her massive horse, carefully keeping her gaze away from the royalty. "Whichever you see fit, of course." She was about to gig Coal when she heard Traejan speak up from behind her.

"How is Aiden?" he asked.

The Roshan tuned her face to answer, but she did not look at him. "He will live," she said, then put her heels to her horse, driving him away while the general gave orders to his messengers to have the captains set a watch.

Atop his sturdy khusar from where he guarded the king of

the elves, the jade-green eyes of the Northman followed her.

20. STRANGER IN THE NIGHT

Many came back wounded that day, but few, very few, were wounded grievously. There had been losses, but they were not as heavy as they could have been. The air was once again victorious.

General Halloran gave a rousing speech in the mess as the men feasted on sausages and a breaded pork dish the Gnomin called schnitzel. When he finished, steins of cold beer and cider were raised in cheering shouts before they were upended into the mouths of the soldiers.

Traejan, the pledge he had made to himself still as fresh as the fear of losing her, watched the Roshan intently. She moved among her own men, Ian a muscled shadow at her side. She had a personal word or two for every one of them, but Traejan noticed that her movements were strange - as was her expression. The way she moved among them and talked softly with each soldier seemed familiar, but so out of context that he could not place it – not at first.

Then the prince remembered a time when he had caught a fever. Nothing truly threatening, but he could recall his mother visiting him frequently, checking on him. This looked so similar and the concern of the Roshan so striking that it took him back to a time when he had sat before her fire and she had bandaged his wounded hands.

I'm about as tender as an old boot she had remarked when he had brought up how gentle she could be. It was the first night that his eyes had ever bent the blue and he had known without a doubt that he loved her.

Then why are you here now? he asked himself. *Standing silently at the side of the room while she talks to her troops?*

He had to talk to her. He was determined he would tell her that he loved her before another day went by. If something happened to either of them, she needed to know that much.

It's not going to happen anytime soon, the young prince realized. *I cannot take her from what she is doing now. And I should talk to my own men as well.*

Traejan straightened his form, forced a smile, and began to move between the tables, speaking first with the elves that had fought that day. Within seconds he found his smile was not forced. He listed to them recount the battle, each one having a different story simply because each story was told from a different point of view. Some were terrifying, some hilarious, some exceptionally poignant.

After an hour of moving amongst his men, the young prince found himself next to Ryen, the Vikeman staring down at him curiously with his bright blue eyes.

"It is amazing," the elf admitted, "every man has such a different idea of what happened. Two men, fighting right beside one another, see it so differently. To hear what they saw, or felt, you might doubt it was the same war."

The side of the Vikeman's face twisted up in a smirk. "Every man fights his own battle," he said. His eyes left the elf to travel along the men at the tables before they came to rest on the Roshan and the giant Norseman by her side. The smile fell from the young elf's countenance.

"Where's Ian?" Traejan asked, something he never thought he would say.

"She sent him for wine," Ryen answered, his eyes on the Roshan. "But, if looks could kill, he would be standing over Crag's dead body right now."

Traejan felt his blood run cold as he watched the blonde

Vikeman put a hand on Ember's shoulder as she leaned down to better hear a soldier recounting his day. Then she straightened and leaned back, laughing, and Crag's large hand dropped to her hip. The young prince stiffened, then turned unbelieving eyes to Ryen only to see the muscles clench in the face of the Norseman.

Then the Roshan turned to the Vikeman by her side, speaking only to him with a smirk on her face that bordered on a leer. Traejan could not make out her words due to the din within the mess hall. Even Crag had to lean down to hear her and, when he did, she put her small hand around his neck and pulled his ear to her lips. When he rose again his green eyes were bright and his only response to the Roshan was a regal dip of his blonde head before he turned and departed without another glance in any direction.

Traejan was about to voice his concern to Ryen when the Roshan turned and spotted them. She excused herself to the soldiers at the table and made her way through the tables and chairs to where the Vikeman and the elfin prince stood watching, waiting.

The Roshan took Ryen by the elbow and smiled at him and, though she turned her face slightly to Traejan, she did not look at him. "Please excuse us," she said softly from over her shoulder, "but I must speak to Commander Glace."

Traejan dipped his head respectfully, and was about to inquire if he could speak with her later, but Ember was already leading the Vikeman away. His elfin ears could not miss her first words.

"I hear you are man who can get things," she said, her voice mocking and light.

Ryen chuckled in response. "Now where did you hear that?" he asked, letting her lead him toward the doors.

After that, their voices were lost in the sound of the men eating and talking and cheering within the mess. Traejan watched them go, and watched as a line formed between the brows of the Vikeman. The pair paused near the doors of the mess and the tension seemed to build, the sound seeming to rise and engulf them, before Ryen finally gave her a nod, and turned away.

The Roshan left through the double doors and Traejan's brown eyes followed Ryen across the room to where Captain Espytin stood laughing with a group of young elves. The Vikeman leaned down to speak into his ear while the elfin captain held still, listening intently. Then the young elf straightened and gave the Vikeman a broad grin before giving him a sweeping and exaggerated bow.

Though a deal had obviously been made, Ryen looked less than pleased and turned to leave the mess. Espytin, meanwhile, was making departing remarks to his company and meaning to follow, when Traejan intercepted him.

"My Lord Prince!" Espytin exclaimed, as Traejan loomed before him, blocking his way. "How can I be of service?"

"You can tell me what the Vikeman asked of you."

Espytin's eyes darted to the closing door before looking back at the prince. "Uh, my lord, he had some requests for the red commander."

"What were they?" Traejan asked outright.

"Well, sir, it seems she has asked for a bath, a tub, actually, to be brought to her tent. And... some silks."

"Silks?" Traejan asked.

Espytin, who was becoming increasingly uncomfortable, simply sighed and leaned closer to the elfin prince.

"There has been a number of soldiers, Your Highness, asking to send gifts to the red commander," he said softly, "but these I think she requested personally."

Traejan drew back in surprise, fixing the captain in his stare. "Gifts? What kind of gifts?"

"Her steward has come to me a number of times, asking

for weapons or such," Espytin said. Traejan shook his head and motioned for him to continue. "Haldor asked for a golden goblet, for her wine. Paid me in gold coin." The young prince narrowed his eyes at Espytin, making him shift from one foot to another. "The Vikeman, Crag, asked me to procure golden rings for her – not for the fingers, like elfin women wear, but the kind that the Viking women wear on their arms. I am still looking for that one, since he asked for one in the shape a of a dragon."

"There are no dragons," Traejan whispered, echoing something he heard Ember once say.

"My Lord Prince?" Espytin said, his voice soft. "If I have done something wrong, or if you do not want me to deliver these things…"

"No," Traejan said sharply. "By all means, assist in any way that you are able. You are the supply captain, after all."

Espytin bowed deeply yet the young prince could tell the supply captain was not sure of what to make of the situation. He left the mess quickly, wanting to fulfill the Vikeman's request and then find himself a glass of honeyed wine.

The young prince remained for the better part of an hour, talking with soldiers, mostly those of whom had fought the Crommags. When he left the mess, Dell followed silently.

The sun was just kissing the westernmost trees of the Elfin Greatwood. Traejan walked toward the bluff where he proceeded to check with his men and take reports from those keeping watch. He worked his way along the lines behind the tents until he found himself on the most western edge of Kriegslager, close to his own tent. He looked out over the beaten plains and at the red-tinged sky. It made the fields below red as well.

The noise carried on the breeze from the Elfin Greatwood was muted, but clearly celebratory as well. The Crommags were obviously done for the day. He was not.

Stop stalling!

The young prince eyed his bodyguard, standing respectfully to the side, his right thumb absently circling the pommel of his sword. Traejan admired his calm demeanor and reflected on his own situation.

I thought, this morning, that I might lose her. Forever. And I decided, at that moment, that I would not let another day go by that I did not tell her how I felt. Not one single day. If I do, I will only suffer again tomorrow.

"I need to speak with the general about tomorrow's assault," Traejan informed Dell. "I am going to clean up, but I will be back in a few minutes. Will you please let him know?"

Dell bowed deeply and then hastened to deliver the message.

The elfin prince turned and began to take long strides back across the camp.

His steps took him back past the white cabin, the mess pavilion, and the supply building. The area was busy now as men and elves were returning to their tents, grooms and stable boys were feeding the horses and rubbing them down. Gnomin hurried everywhere to help. As he passed the yurts of the Vikemen he could not help but notice that Ryen stood alone by the side of his own yurt, arms over his chest, scowling at the night air.

The young prince pressed on and, only a few footsteps later, he stood before the Roshan's tent. Ian sat before a kettle on the cookfire, uncharacteristically intense, his expression as dark as his eyes. On the closest bush, a nightingale was hopping from branch to branch, singing as if it had gone mad.

A pair of Wildboys guarded the canvas doorway of the commander of the red troops. One, his body as straight as the spear he held, had white linen wrapped around the wound on his head. The elfin prince smiled in spite of himself.

"Hello, Aiden."

The Sprite smiled in response. "Good evening, prince of the man-elves."

"I am glad to see that you are on the mend."

"Just a scratch," he assured the man-elf with a smile that the prince returned with a chuckle.

"I wish to speak with the Dark Lady," Traejan informed him. The expression on the Wildboy fell, becoming quite serious.

"I am sorry, my Lord Prince," Aiden stated formally, "but you may not enter here. Not tonight."

Traejan raised his brows. "No one? Not even me?"

Aiden swallowed. "Especially not you," he said, his voice low. "Not tonight. She has... a meeting." Aiden emphasized the last word, latching on to it eagerly, the way a wolf would latch on to the bone of a deer. "Yes," he said, agreeing with himself, "a war meeting. A private one. No one is to enter, by strict orders of the lady."

Traejan's raised brows drew together in a scowl and he looked askance at Ian. The youth, who had been listening to them with a similar frown, turned away.

Traejan backed away slowly. "Very well," he acquiesced. "If you could be so kind to tell her that I was here, and that I wish to speak with her tonight..."

"Of course!" Aiden said quickly. "I will. I promise."

The young prince got the feeling that the Wildboy was very eager for him to leave. Though he was reluctant to do so, Traejan dipped his head and walked away just as he began to consider all of the events of the afternoon.

The Roshan's requests from the supply sergeant via Ryen had been strange yes, but not that crazy. She had to be dying for a decent bath. But Traejan knew she would go the whole war with nothing but a basin of water and towel and be just fine. *And silks?*

And what meeting? When did she ever have a meeting where Ryen or Ian was not hovering by her side? Yet, tonight, *both* of them were outside their own tents with almost identical expressions of sullen anger.

But it was Aiden that really made Traejan begin to wonder what was happening. *Especially not you* he had told the young prince. *Why especially not me?*

Traejan looked about hurriedly. He had walked into the Gnomin part of Kriegslager. Cookfires and tents lit bright from inside were plentiful as was the inviting aroma of cooking food. Gnomin men and women smiled and bowed as they walked by and he forced himself to do the same as he turned and began to make his way back to the red camp.

Maybe she is meeting with Halloran, his mind suggested. *It seems unlikely, though if there truly is a spy, which it seems there must be, and they wanted to speak privately, her tent would be the place.*

He was rounding the copse of trees that divided the red camp from the Gnomin camp when he was overcome with a sense of danger, warning him.

The feeling swarmed over his neck and back like biting ants.

His first instinct was to rush to Ember but all his training, all *her* training warned against it. Quickly he stepped back into the shadows – his eyes searching the night. The tension grew in him by the second but he forced his eyes closed, the better to see.

Ember was still in her tent. He could hear her breathing, slow and even. Whatever threat lurked in the night, it had not reached her yet. But he opened his eyes and saw with a jolt that her guard was nowhere to be seen.

Aiden would not abandon his post. Not ever. The only reason he would not be there would be if he were dead.

Or, Traejan thought, *if she sent him away.*

The young prince looked to his left and saw a nightingale watching him from the branch of a bush, silent.

Growing more unsettled with each second that passed,

Traejan turned his eyes back to the Roshan's tent.

There were no signs of a struggle, and the Wildboys would have been dragged away fighting to their last breath before leaving her. Unless she ordered them to go. Even Ian was gone. The dark-eyed steward had left his kettle of water simmering over a diminishing fire. But why?

The thought had barely risen in his mind before the answer walked into the light of the dying cookfire. Crag strode directly to the front of Ember's tent before pausing to adjust the vest he wore over the tunic on his broad chest. In his mind's eye, Traejan could see Ember as she pulled his ear to her lips to whisper something private, and the look in the eyes of the massive Northman as he had straightened and left.

Crag pushed open the flap to her tent and the young prince could only see a bit of what was inside, but it was enough. Braziers had been lit and he could see quite clearly that in place of cots, bedfurs had been laid out, covered with pillows and silks. The Roshan sat in the center of them, with her back turned to the tent's opening. A satin coverlet was pulled up only over her hip and her hair, brushed and shining, draped her naked shoulders like silken blood.

The Vikeman paused, suddenly aware he was not alone. His eyes searched out the shadows and fell upon Traejan. He paused for a second, startled, and then grinned. His leer was so knowing and so obvious in its intent that the young elf felt his stomach turn. Crag held his gaze a moment longer then turned and shouldered his way into the tent, closing the flap behind him.

☧

Ayala was in high spirits. The Great Men had suffered many losses again that day, but Noga had come with a barrel full of water. It was not much, but enough to slake their thirsts before they opened another keg of grog. Huge cookfires were lit as elfin horses that had been dragged from the battle ground were gutted and roasted. Ayla could not remember tasting anything so rich and exquisite.

The Great Men cheered each other and feasted while recounting tales of the lesser men they killed, the horses they took down with their heavy maces, and the elves they had torn to pieces.

Ayala was relishing a haunch of horse that had been charred to a crisp on the outside while still bloody on the inside, when Yip - one of his swiftest runners - ran into the circle of the leaders. The leader of the Great Men rose, his massive body throwing shadows against the trunks of the trees, the horse haunch lowering slowly as he still chewed, his demeanor now guarded, waiting.

The young runner bowed his head quickly and then gave Ayala a grin that showed his young fangs. "Great Ayala," he addressed, "Pel has arrived with the next group."

Ayala's eyes widened in surprise. He had sent Yip just yesterday to hasten the next group along, he had no idea they would make it this fast.

The runner continued, excited. "They brought more fresh water and..."

"Fresh fighters!" boomed the voice of Pel as he stepped into the firelight, followed by his closest men. A great cheer went up and Ayala moved to clap the great Ice Walker on his back. Pel looked at the leader of the Great Men and grinned. "I was led to believe you were going to kill all the elves without me!"

Ayala laughed and signaled for grog and meat to be brought to Pel. "We saved you a few!" he assured him. "Join us and be welcome! We have lost most of our weak, feel free to make use of their shelters. Just do not go east beyond our lines, traps have been set."

Pel dipped his head to show that he understood and then

cast his dark eyes about the encampment. "Is your brother Noga here?" he asked as he accepted a horn of grog from a member of the tribe.

Ayala shook his large, narrow head. "No. He is off on another plot to glean more information. His sources have been quite useful so far. Like the traps," he added, pointing into the darkened forest with his haunch of meat. "Please have your men join us after they have settled. This flesh is more tender, and much richer and more plentiful than goat. Have them come and fill their bellies!"

Pel nodded and drank deeply. He had pressed his men to hurry despite the heat and exhaustion and was now glad that he had. With such an air to arrive in, he felt as if the Great Men must have already won.

Ayala drank deeply as well, grog dripping from the corners of his mouth. They had lost many men, but so had the elves. And now, he had more men than before. The elves had only less. The leader of the Great Men opened his mighty fangs wide and tore off an enormous chunk of horse meat and chewed it with great pleasure.

21. UNCOVERED

Crag had never seen her with her hair down and unbound. It flowed across her slim shoulders like a river of blood.

The shock of her femininity was almost overpowering. He had thought her beautiful before because she was so strong, so powerful, especially for so slight a creature. Her face was pretty in her own way, but he was mostly attracted to her fighting spirit, and an overpowering will that she could bring to bear as she saw fit. He had never known the like.

Now she was laid before him, like an offering, a sacrifice. She was smaller without the arsenal of weapons she normally wore, and more powerful than ever.

She twisted her body slowly. Then she moved languidly to face him, her hair pouring off her bare shoulders. The firelight of the braziers made her hair alive and her eyes sparkle like cut amber. He felt breathless.

The floor had been padded with hides and laid with furs and silks. Close by was a wooden bathtub, steam rising from the water inside.

"I'm glad you came," she said softly.

"I didn't think this would happen until the war was done," he told her. She smiled seductively.

"I couldn't wait that long."

He unbuckled his sword belt and laid it on the nearest chair, never taking his eyes off her. He pulled off his heavy leather jerkin and unlaced the ties to the clean linen shirt underneath. He came to her, mesmerized, and knelt at the edge of her bedfurs. Even kneeling he was as tall as a man standing. Ember smiled at him again and he traced a finger along her silk covered thigh.

She's mine, he thought, feeling victorious. *She's mine.* He leaned closer to her, putting a hand into her shimmering hair.

"It's you," she whispered, entwining her fingers into his short blonde locks, pulling him down. "I knew the moment I first saw you, and I was crazy to doubt myself. I never should have waited this long."

Outside, Traejan staggered away from her tent, the weight of betrayal crushing him with anger and confusion. His breath came in short gasps and he lurched back into the copse of trees, weaving his way among bushes like a drunkard. He was blind and deaf to anything and everything.

I can't believe it, I can't believe it, were the only words that echoed in his head. He tried to turn around to head for the western part of the camp, but suddenly everything looked unfamiliar to him.

He thought nothing could feel as terrible as the ambivalence she had treated him with since her arrival, but this was worse. Much worse.

This had nothing to do with propriety, or keeping a military professionalism while they were fighting a war. This meant that last summer was nothing to her. Less than nothing. She did not love him.

Even worse, when he thought nothing could be worse than her not wanting him, she wanted someone else.

Overwhelmed with pain, he could hardly keep himself upright. He stumbled forward, trying to keep his feet, and came out of the trees at the far end of the western camp, almost to where the horses of the red troops' First Cavalry was penned.

I can't believe it, repeated again and again in his mind.

He turned around and headed in the opposite direction, mildly thinking that he did not want to go back to his tent. He wanted to go back to Castle Song. His sense of loss was so sickening he could hardly comprehend anything else. He swayed on his feet, thinking he was about to be sick.

He looked around, blinking like a drunkard, trying to determine which way was west. *I can't believe it, I can't believe it. How could I be so wrong?*

Then faintly, so faint he almost missed it, something inside whispered back, *don't believe it. You were not wrong, not until now.*

He stopped and pulled himself upright. He listened for that small voice to return, but it did not. He did what he could to recall what it said, and more importantly, what it meant. He tried to hold himself still but his body swayed like a sapling in a strong wind. He turned back towards the direction he had come and took a deep breath. The weight of betrayal was on his shoulders like an iron shroud. He shrugged it off and took another deep breath. Blood. He could smell it. Blood and betrayal. The feeling of being crushed was upon him again. Ember seemed to be the only person that could bring that feeling upon him.

Think with your head, not with your feelings.

She wouldn't.

She couldn't.

Not any more than you could or would.

Traejan felt as if he had been slapped. He felt as if he should have slapped himself long ago. He got his bearings and he ran.

The elfin prince darted through the trees as he angled west and came out of the woods. Back through the red camp he dashed, dodging campfires and groups of men.

Fool! he thought, cursing himself.

How could he not know it? How could he let this happen? He ran till it seemed he must have run the whole length of the camp. Where was her tent? Did he pass it? How could he have come so far and not known it? To the Seventh Circle with her! How could he not see?

He stopped short and looked quickly around. He had not passed it – it was still a few tents away. His blind wanderings had taken him to the easternmost part of the camp and he had lost his bearings. Now he saw her tent, only a few campfires away. He ran, hoping he was not too late. The scent of blood was so strong he thought his nostrils must be full of it.

He reached the Roshan's tent, still unguarded, and burst in to see Crag laying over her, shirtless, his broad back obscuring the woman underneath. The Vikeman was perfectly still for a moment and then rose up gradually before turning and crashing to the floor of the tent, Ember's dagger buried to the hilt in his neck.

Ember stood slowly, warily, as she gathered the silken coverlet around her body.

Crag clawed at the dagger in his neck and she kicked his hand away, but the huge man was not going to die so easily. He rolled back onto his front and began to rise to his knees.

"How?" he gurgled, blood streaming down over his broad chest. "How?"

"How did I know?" the Roshan asked, her eyes intense in the light of the braziers. "How could I not?"

The giant man from the north, despite the gouts of blood that were pumping out the side of his neck, still had a surprising amount of strength and staggered on his knees, reaching for his sword belt on the chair. The Roshan produced another dagger from seemingly nowhere and it flew through the air, embedding itself to the hilt in Crag's throat. It drove him back slightly and he rocked on his knees, then he lurched for the Roshan.

Traejan, though shocked beyond words, did not hesitate. His own sword was free of its scabbard and flashed in the light of the braziers, relieving the monstrous Northman of his head. It rolled across the hides that been laid over the rugs on the floor and came to a stop, its jade-colored eyes staring up endlessly at the roof of the tent. The giant body fell over, the hilts of the Roshan's daggers protruding from the stump atop its shoulders.

The young prince turned to face the Roshan only to find she was already in front of him, her arms going around his waist as she pressed her head against his chest. He let his sword fall to the ground and put his arms around her, holding her tight as he buried his face in her hair.

All breath, blood, and life seemed to leave him at once. He had prepared for this moment for so long, had hoped for it for so long, but he had suddenly gone numb. There were things he had wanted to say, even to hurt her, as she had made him hurt by keeping him away and in the dark, feeling cold and alone.

Then everything melted away. His hurt, his anger, his uncertainty, his armor. He was not sad to see it go.

He kissed her hair, her eyes, her face. He pressed his forehead to hers and all of the lost time between them vanished like it had never been.

"Traejan," she whispered, clinging to him.

There was only that quick moment for them before Aiden and his second-in command, Landis, came into the tent and they stared at the body on the ground. Their eyes were like eggs.

"Gods of the Forest!" Aiden exclaimed. "He is *huge*!"

"Was huge," Landis corrected.

"Shorter now, for sure," Aiden agreed, "but still, so big!" His gaze lifted and found Ember's. "You were right to send me away, my lady. I never would have let that brute inside with you, not to mean offense."

"None taken," she told the Wildboy as Ian entered and took in the scene with a sweep of his dark eyes.

Traejan was afraid Ember would move away from him with the others coming into the tent but she held onto him tightly, making his heart swell so much that he thought it might burst inside his chest.

Aiden looked at the sword on the ground and then looked up at the elfin prince. "This was your doing?" he asked, motioning to the severed head. Traejan nodded and the leader of the Wildboys grinned at him. "Well done!" he exclaimed. "Maybe you are part elf after all!"

Traejan's shoulders shook as he chuckled soundlessly, resting his forehead on the crown of Ember's head, feeling her tremble as well with silent laughter. Even Ian grinned as he brought the Roshan a cloak. Instead of draping it over her shoulders, however, he handed it to Traejan. The young prince gave him a look of thanks as he took the dark cloak and wrapped it around her. She dropped the sheet of silk she had been using to cover herself and turned away from him - but kept close enough to stay in his arms.

"Circles," Ian muttered. "So much blood." He looked at Aiden. "Do you have enough men to drag that thing out of here?"

The Wildboy straightened, his thin chest expanding. "I could drag him out myself..." he began to announce proudly before the Roshan cut him off.

"Not with a head wound!" she interjected.

Aiden looked defiant for a moment and then relented. "Very well. I will assemble a few of my men to drag this beast out of here." He paused and then looked at Ember. "Where to?" he asked.

"To the front..." she began when Ryen ducked into the tent and straightened, surveying the scene. His searing gaze swept the room, anger burning in his blue eyes for everyone present.

"What in the Seventh Circle happened here?" he demanded.

"Isn't it obvious?" the Roshan asked. "Prince Traejan has

killed the spy,"

"The spy?" Ryen asked. He stared down at the decapitated Northman in disbelief. "Crag?" He looked back at the Roshan, clearly confused. "I thought for sure..."

"Jennings?" the Roshan asked. "Or Espytin?" She sighed, still clasped within Traejan's arms. "I did as well. But the night before the first battle I mentioned the ditch that the Gnomin had dug, to Jennings. And I took a moment with Espytin to request extra bolts while I disclosed my plan for a crossbow attack from behind the berm. Neither of those tidbits of information made it to the Crommags."

"Why did you suspect them in the first place?" Traejan asked.

The Roshan's shoulders drew up in a shrug. "They were the most likely candidates. Espytin was young and voiced his feelings that not only could the war be avoided, but money could be made from it. Jennings was not himself, distracted by the sudden yet prolonged disappearance of his daughter."

"Oh, yes," Traejan exclaimed softly. "Allyson! Only yesterday one of her friends confided she had run off with a sailor from Bayard."

The Roshan nodded slowly. "I had heard as much myself, but not before I considered the possibility that she had been taken hostage."

"And this bastard?" Ryen asked as he motioned to the body on the floor. "What made you suspect him?"

"Many things," Ember said. "But, mostly, it was his teeth." She leaned back and let her weight rest against Traejan.

"His teeth?" Aiden asked, his eyes, along with all eyes in the tent, going to the slightly exposed mouth of the dead Vikeman. "They look like normal man-teeth to me!"

The Roshan nodded. "He did have nice teeth – very nice. But it was the way he would always run his tongue along the edge of them, feeling them." The Roshan narrowed her eyes with memory before she continued. "Many years ago, I got hit in the face with the hilt of a dagger."

"Battle or barfight?" Ryen asked with a crooked smile.

"What's the difference?" the Roshan asked. Ryen huffed and she continued. "I thought I had broken a tooth, it felt so jagged and rough. It turned out to be merely a small chip, but my tongue would not leave it alone. It poked and prodded at it constantly. Even when the tip of it became raw from persistently seeking it out, my tongue still worried at it like a mongrel dog gnawing at a bone."

"What did you do?" Traejan asked.

"I went to a Sea Gypsy and he rubbed it smooth with an oyster shell. After that, it felt odd for few days but I got used to it."

Ian, who had put down hides to cover the rugs in the tent, knowing what she had planned, handed her a cup of wine. "And you saw him touching his teeth with his tongue?" he asked.

The Roshan nodded. "Repeatedly. I suspect this brute had a whole set of teeth, a whole set of *fangs*, that he had filed down. And his tongue was not yet used to the new feel and would not leave them alone."

Traejan's body stiffened and his eyes, along with the eyes of the Vikeman and the Wildboys, went to the head on the floor, staring in disbelief. "You think he was a *Crommag*?" he asked.

The Roshan nodded. "At least partially." She turned her face to Ryen. "You are the one who put the possibility into my head from the beginning, when you said that Vikemen in that borough were known to hunt and rape Crommag women. He's not as big as a Crommag," she said, jerking her chin towards the body, "but he was really big, even for a Vikeman."

"He had been there at all of our crucial meetings," Traejan admitted thoughtfully. "And he had worked with the Gnomin on all the pits and traps. He must have marked them somehow."

"He was giving them information this whole time," the Roshan said. "Which is how they knew about the raid we tried last week, and were waiting for us."

"And the horses that were set loose," Traejan remarked. "Only Gavan's horses, after you and Halloran had announced that he would be leading the assault." The young prince looked down at her, still in his arms. "You never intended to send in Gavan's infantry for a mounted attack, did you?"

The Roshan shook her head, her red hair gleaming in the light. "No. He had just fought. It was just a ruse to get one more assurance for Halloran that there truly was a spy. Rhys was next in line to fight and I did not want to risk him losing any mounts."

"And those bodies," Ryen said softly, piecing it together as well as he turned to Aiden. "You said that the Roskilde Borough found eight bodies in the spring thaw." He huffed softly. "The envoy. I guess they did send more than just one man."

The Wildboy nodded. "The tribe leader told me they sent six. One of the other bodies was that of a young man from their tribe that had been missing all winter. The other was a human. They supposed it was a Northlonder, but could not be sure."

"For the love of the Seven," Ian whispered, looking at the pieces of the spy that were still soaking the hides with blood. "Let's get it out of here."

Ryen looked at Aiden. "You two get the head," he instructed. "Ian and I can drag out the rest."

Aiden and Landis tossed their spears aside and began to roll the head up in the hide while Ian and Ryen did the same with the body.

"Take it all to the cabin," Ember told them, "just not inside. Ask Halloran what he wants to do with it. I'm going to clean up."

There were only nods and grunts as the remains of the

Crommag spy were dragged from her tent. When they were gone she turned to face Traejan.

"I would love for you to hold me," she said, "but the only thing I want more right now is a bath. I have never felt so dirty in my life, not even after any battle."

Traejan smiled and walked with her over to the steaming water. He took off the cloak he had wrapped around her and held her hand as she climbed into the tub. She ducked her head under the water and came back up, sputtering out a sigh of relief. He knelt by the tub and dabbed at her face with a towel.

"Soap?" she asked. The young prince spied a pat of soap and handed it to her as something else occurred to him.

"Three Gods," he whispered, "My father."

"Was never in danger."

"Because you put Shane there. What did you tell him?"

"I told him not to let the big bastard get close to any of the royals, and to kill him if he tried."

"What did he say?"

"Nothing. My men don't question my orders."

"You didn't tell anyone you suspected Crag?" he asked as she scrubbed herself all over with the soap.

She shook her head, water droplets running from her hair. It was so dark when it was wet, like blood seen by moonlight. "That kind of knowledge is hard to keep to one's self, even without speaking. He was very aware of everyone's eyes, actions, and words. He would have known in an instant that his secret was out."

"And you shared your plans for tonight with no one?"

"Just Ian." She rubbed her hands up and down her arms, washing the soap off, and dipped her head back into the water one more time before she stood up.

"And just what is Ian here for?" Traejan asked, handing her a towel. His eyes went over her body, so scarred yet so perfect to his eyes.

The Roshan scrubbed her face dry with the towel and squeezed the water out of her hair as she stepped out of the tub. Traejan reached out and took her hand in case she might slip and she gave him a wicked smile.

"Let's hope you never have to find out," she told him.

Traejan frowned as she rubbed the towel over her neck and shoulders. "Just what does that mean?" he asked.

Ember forced a look of patience as she wrapped the towel around her body. "It's a long story..." she started when Ian himself ducked back into the tent.

"General Halloran would like to see you both," he said, "as soon as possible."

The Roshan nodded. "Just get me pants and a shirt," she instructed, going to a trunk by her cot and pulling out a pair of smallclothes. She dropped her towel and stepped into them, unmindful or uncaring that Ian saw her undressed. It obviously did not disturb Ian in the slightest, leading Traejan to believe that it was something she probably did often.

Why must she always keep me guessing about such things? he wondered, annoyed as he watched her take a pair of black pants from Ian and step into them. She pulled them up quickly and then took an ash-colored blouse from him and pulled it on over her head. She pulled on a pair of socks and her boots while Ian retrieved Traejan's sword and wiped it clean before handing it over to the elfin prince. By then, the Roshan was on her feet and motioning for her own sword belt.

"Will you need anything else tonight?" he asked as he buckled it around her waist.

"I hope not," she answered, "but have my things ready, just in case." He dipped his head in acknowledgement and she looked at Traejan, who gave her a nod as well. He was more ready than he had ever been. She gave him a slip of a smile and ducked out of her tent with him following close behind.

A few quick strides and he was next to her, both of them looking curiously about. The camp was always busy and there was always a presence of the Gnomin people, usually cooking or bringing food, or giving medical attention where it was needed. Tonight however, they all seemed to be out and about without purpose, which was utterly unlike them. They gathered in small groups, talking in hushed voices, anxiously tapping the tips of their fingers together.

Traejan and Ember exchanged a quick glance before they reached the cabin and went inside. They were confronted immediately by Dell, the Praetorian nearly beside himself with worry and wrath.

"Where in all the Circles have you been tonight?" he demanded, looking at Traejan. "I was looking for you everywhere!"

"Well," Traejan returned, discomfited, "obviously not everywhere, or you would have found me."

The captain of the Jägers looked for a moment like he might explode and Traejan had to suppress a smile, knowing it would only make his Praetorian angrier. He was saved from having to explain further by the general noting their entrance.

"My Lord Prince!" he called, beckoning with one hand. "Commander L'chiross!"

Traejan and Ember went to him with Dell, still simmering, following close behind. They saw that the other captains were already there, as well as Wilhelm and Otto, along with two other Gnomin that they recognized but did not know by name.

"Thank you for joining us," the general said, his voice as graveled as ever. "I know you have already had quite the evening." His gray eyes lifted as he saw Ryen enter the tent and motioned for the Vikeman to join them.

The Roshan smiled at the grizzled elf. "Thank you for not asking if I am alright," she said.

The general smirked, his chin cloaked in shadow. "I know

better by now, as well as the fact that if you are standing on your own two feet, you are just fine." There was a soft chuckle from the group and Halloran turned to Jaden as Ryen reached their group. "Captain, I believe your scouts have some news for us?"

Jaden dipped his head. "They do," he agreed, though he did not seem even remotely as jovial as Halloran. "The second party of Crommags has arrived," he stated. "Their supplies are refreshed, and their numbers even greater than before."

A silence settled over the group as his words sank in. Even though the elves had been triumphant in battle, if it came only to numbers, they were losing the war.

"Do not be discouraged," Halloran scolded, gruff. "We are still the better fighters by far, and we still have a chance to prevail!"

Everyone else nodded in agreement, albeit half-heartedly, and Otto took a step closer to Jaden.

"This second group," he asked, "they have Gnomin prisoners with them?"

The Sylvan glanced at the general who gave him a quick nod that gave him permission to answer.

"Yes," Jaden said. "They have a group of Gnomin prisoners."

Wilhelm and Otto rocked back on the heels of their work boots and exchanged glances, visibly pleased. Wilhelm's hands came together as if he were clasping an invisible ball, his fingertips patting restlessly against one another.

"Have they set up camp?" he asked Jaden. "Do your scouts know where they are keeping the prisoners?"

Jaden gave him a bit of a smile. "They do," he affirmed.

All four of the Gnomin exchanged looks of excitement and hope.

"Can you show us where?" Otto asked.

Jaden looked again to the general for permission but the

grizzled elf frowned. "Are you thinking of an extraction? A nighttime raid?" he asked Otto, mentally calculating the men and risk it would take.

The Gnomin laughed. "That is exactly what I am thinking. But, not to worry, general. We will not need military help."

Halloran's forehead wrinkled. "Is that so? And just how do you plan on entering a war camp of over a thousand Crommags and rescuing your people on your own?"

"We are miners," Otto reminded him with a look that was both knowing and wily. "How do you think?"

The general grinned and shook his head. "I should have known," he admitted. "Are you planning on starting here and digging straight down?"

Otto gave him a genial frown. "With all due respect, general, don't be ridiculous."

The Gnomin cast his eyes about and spotted the main table with the maps that centered on Morgan's Vale. He went to it, motioning for the others to follow. He studied it for a minute and then posed a few questions to Wilhelm in Gnomin. They conversed for a few moments, thumping spots on the map while the others waited. Finally, they paused and looked up at Halloran.

"Will you fight in the same parameters tomorrow that you have these past two days?" Wilhelm asked.

The general frowned. The spy had been caught but it still gave him a feeling of uneasiness to be forthright. Yet he had no reason to distrust the Gnomin. "We are not expanding the width of our lines, if that is what you are asking."

The miners exchanged a few more words in Gnomin and then Otto stepped closer to the table and put a stubby finger on the map. All eyes went down to the tip of his finger where it rested on the west end of Morgan's Vale. It was well west of where the fighting had been done so far, and on the far side of the ditch they had dug that was now full of dead Crommags.

"We will go in here," he said. "The shorter the tunnel, the quicker we can get them out." His blue eyes went to Jaden. "Where have they put our miners?" he asked.

The eyes of the Sylvan went to the table, studying the points on the map. "Here," he said, indicating a spot west of the battle fields but east of where the Gnomin intended to start their excavation.

All four Gnomin dipped and bobbed in excitement, the tips of their fingers tapping away while the two that the Roshan did not know produced metal measuring tools with hinges and strings and chatted away as they poked and turned their instruments upon the map. Finally, Otto looked up, a grin splitting his face.

"Excellent!" he proclaimed.

The general waited for something more but when the Gnomin did nothing but grin he raised his steely brows. "So?" he asked. "When do you start?"

"Tonight," Otto announced, firm. "We will begin under the cover of darkness and, by the time the sun comes up, our entrance will be hidden from Crommag eyes. We will continue to work, even as you fight tomorrow." His eyes went to the general and his hands came together, his fingertips nervously tapping together. "We will leave behind as many as we can to cook and aid with injured soldiers..."

"But this takes precedence," the general finished for him, his voice gruff but understanding. "We will do what is necessary in your absence. In the meantime, what can we do for you?" he asked.

Otto's eyes lit up and his body relaxed, visibly relieved. "Shovels," he said immediately. "As many as you can spare. And wood, to brace the tunnel. We should have enough rope, but a little more won't hurt."

The general turned his steely gaze to Espytin. "You can do this, no?"

"Absolutely, sir," Espytin agreed with a grin.

"Then make it happen," Halloran ordered. "Is there any other aid we can offer?" he asked Otto.

The Gnomin shook his head, almost too overcome to speak. "No, what you give is already so much, we are so grateful to you already..."

"To us?" Halloran asked, nonplussed. "But you have helped us build this whole village - you have fed our men and tended to their medical needs. All you ask for in return is shovels and wood? I feel it is poor trade..." he said, trailing off as he lost the words to explain.

Otto placed himself squarely before the general and, though he only came as high as the grizzled elf's chest, he looked him straight in the eye. "You have given us more than a few tools," he said. "You have given us hope, and pride, fighting monsters that we never had the courage to fight ourselves. And, more, you have given us the chance to rescue loved ones we thought we had lost."

The general grumbled quietly, not expecting such a show of appreciation. "Then may the Gods speed and bless your journey so you may return to us quickly. I like that pretzel bread almost as much as I like that cider!"

The four Gnomin laughed and clapped each other on the back and shook hands with Halloran as they departed. Espytin left with them to make sure they would get everything they needed.

Once they had gone, Halloran fixed his eyes upon Nevin and Jennings. "You two are next in line for tomorrow's attack," he stated firmly. "Are you ready?"

"Yes, sir," the pair replied in unison.

"If you are still set on ground infantry," the Roshan interjected, "I can offer one hundred crossbowmen, who are also excellent swordsmen."

Jennings stiffened at the offer but Nevin gave her a broad

smile. "We will gladly take them all," he answered.

"Patrek and his men will be waiting for you on the grade, half an hour before dawn. They will be yours to command."

"How will you be divided?" Ryen asked.

Jennings frowned as he thought. "Traditional military platoons, forty elves to each. Ten platoons." He looked to Nevin. "Ten across the board?" he asked. "Or five platoons, double deep?"

The elfin Jäger rubbed a graying temple with a pair of fingers. His blue eyes flicked up to find the Roshan. "One hundred men, you said?" She nodded to affirm and Nevin pursed his lips as he looked back down at the map. "Ten across the board," he advised, "if the red troops do not mind spreading out, covering our asses."

"They won't mind at all," the Roshan assured him. She looked around the room to see if there was anything or anyone else she needed to address before she left. She dipped her head at the elfin captains and made her way to the general to bid goodnight, Traejan did the same, following her with Dell in his shadow.

"And for my men?" Ryen asked. "Would you like them dispersed throughout your platoons or send them out as a single unit?"

Jennings and Nevin exchanged glances but it was Nevin that spoke. "Can we send them out as a single unit?" he asked. "I think they might inflict more damage that way, and raise more spirits in doing so. Either way, we will be able to get a better gauge on whether to keep them fighting in the same manner or space them apart where they would be most beneficial."

"Any way you see fit," Ryen answered, almost testily. He was clearly ready to be done for the day. "I will send an envoy of ten Vikemen to spearhead your assault, helping in any way you deem most advantageous." Both of the elfin captains bowed and the Vikeman did the same, hastily, before leaving the building.

The Roshan and the elfin prince had just departed as well and were descending the few steps from the cabin to the ground.

"Don't you think we should talk?" Traejan was asking the Roshan.

Ryen glanced at him as he joined them, his expression somber, before he turned his blue eyes to the Roshan. "I would like to speak with you as well."

Ember frowned at the both of them but her tone was both patient and quiet. "I have had a long day," she explained, "and I have hardly slept in the past fifty hours. I've spilled more blood in that time than I've drunk wine in my lifetime."

"I find that hard to believe," Ryen murmured, petulant.

The Roshan ignored his comment, though her scowl deepened, and she continued. "I am going to bed so I can get up in a few hours and do it all again." Her dark eyes flicked from one to the other in disgust. "If you two want to talk, talk to each other."

The Vikeman and the prince watched her stalk away in anger, and then looked at each other.

Ryen was the first to sigh, and finally gave the prince a playful bump with his shoulder. "Come on," he said encouragingly. "I'll buy you a cider."

Traejan gave him an equal, yet mild, shove on the shoulder. "The Gnomin don't charge us for the cider," he told Ryen with a slight smile.

"I know," Ryen told him.

Traejan laughed. "Besides, I should be buying one for you."

"Really?" Ryen asked, his ginger brows raised questioningly over his glacier blue eyes. "Why is that?"

"Because," Traejan tried to explain. He became increasingly uncomfortable under the Vikeman's gaze and finally sighed and plowed forward. "I think it's obvious that Ember wants to be with me."

Ryen laughed and looked at the elf with an expression of amusement. "What in all Seven Circles makes you think that?" he asked.

"Because," Traejan answered, feeling lame and exposed.

Ryen raised his brows again as they reached the mess, waiting for Traejan's answer.

"Because," he said once again, his mind still searching for an explanation when Ryen cut him off with a look of exasperation and sympathy.

"Because she lets you put a cloak over her shoulders?" he asked. "Because sometimes she tells you how she feels? Because she lets you see her when she is vulnerable, and you think you are the one who can protect her?"

Traejan's jaw clenched and he looked away. "How long were you with her, Ryen?" the prince asked, his arms crossed over his chest as he looked over the men coming and going from their tents. "If you don't mind my asking, that is."

The Vikeman gave his head a small shake as his eyes, too, followed the movements of men and supplies. "I don't mind at all. I was with her for a little over a year and a half, almost two."

Now Traejan's face did turn to look at him, his brown eyes wide with shock, dismay, and envy – and flecked with blue within their depths. Ryen glanced at him, smiled, and continued as he looked over at the bustle within the Gnomin camp. "Ember and I have fought many battles together, elfin prince, and traveled to many lands."

"For what purpose were these travels?" Traejan asked, regaining his composure. "Your sense of adventure?"

The Vikeman gave his head another small shake. "No, it was for her. She has been looking for her family, or any trace of them, for a very long time."

"And?" Traejan prodded. "What did you find?"

Ryen turn his icy blue eyes to the elf. "Nothing. Oddly enough, her first and only clues, began to surface here, at home."

22. RESCUE

As the elves prepared for another day of battle, the Gnomin prepared to dig. Workers began hauling wood and buckets down into Morgan's Vale as soon as it was full dark while the team leaders made quick plans in hushed voices.

"Three-foot-high tunnel," Wilhelm recommended.

"Means we will need a shaft nine feet deep," Otto said, "with six feet of earth over the tunnel itself."

"Eighteen workers should be enough," Wil said. "Nine miners and nine builders." The Gnomin always included builders with miners as they were needed to make wooden braces along the way to keep the mine secure.

Jaden, the captain of the elfin scouts, walked the plains with the Gnomin leaders as they muttered and conversed under the slight light of a slivered moon as it rose in the east. They came to an abrupt halt and turned to the Sylvan elf.

"Can you show us where they are keeping the prisoners?" Otto asked him.

Jaden faced the darkened Greatwood, his eyesight easily crossing the wide space of the prairie and delving deep between the trees to pick out the differences in the tents that had been raised there. He raised a small hand and pointed.

"There," he said, "do you see? It is a lighter colored tent, both lower and longer than the others." They did not have the keen eyesight of the Sylvan elf and it took some moments. He waited until both Otto and Wilhelm saw what he had described and then gave him a quick nod.

"Yes," Otto confirmed.

"I do," Wilhelm agreed.

"That is where they are keeping them," Jaden told them.

"How many guards inside?" Otto asked.

"How many guards outside?" Wilhelm inquired.

"Two outside," Jaden informed them, "but they do not seem very attentive. As far as I can tell, there are no inner guards at all. None have come or gone from inside the tent since they made camp."

The team leaders looked at each other in astonishment. "To leave prisoners unguarded," Otto voiced, "seems dangerous, does it not?"

The Sylvan shrugged his narrow shoulders. "Not if they do not seem to be much of a threat."

"They are most likely weakened," Otto mused aloud. "The First Circle only knows how they have been treated or what they have been eating this past year."

"They could be sick," Wilhelm said, looking sick himself. "Some could be injured."

"We need to be prepared to carry them out if we have to," Otto said.

"Should I get stretchers?" Wilhelm asked.

Otto tucked his bearded chin towards his chest as he thought. "Get some sling cots," he suggested. "As many as you can roll and fit in a back-sack. We can sleep in them, and then use them as stretchers if need be."

"Sleep?" Jaden asked, surprised. "How long will you be down there?"

Wilhelm grinned. "This is not a task we will complete before dawn," he told the elf. "We are good, but not that good. At least, not when limited with the number of workers and the need for secrecy." He gave Jaden a wink and hurried away.

Meanwhile, Otto corralled their troop of miners with the

shovels. He sighted from where he stood to the tent that held the Gnomin prisoners, then took two steps to the left. "Here," he announced, pointing straight down. "Dig the shaft here. Nine feet down then turn south and continue with a tunnel three feet high. Keep the southern heading. Use hammers and chisels until there is enough room for shovels. Take in buckets. We need a team taking out buckets of soil while others keep digging. Meanwhile, I want a small team of builders in there."

A stocky Gnomin named Heinz stepped forward. "I am in charge of the builders," he confirmed.

"Heinz," Otto exclaimed. "Good! You will be in charge of making the tunnel secure, both the sides and the roof. Shore up the tunnel sections with boards two feet long by two feet wide in joists that will reach from the tunnel floors to the ceiling. Fit flatboard in the ceiling, and support it with joists that are two feet by four feet."

Heinz nodded as he intermittently licked a pencil stub and scribbled away on a pad of paper, carefully repeating the numbers he had been given. His eyes raised and looked across the ground they were going to need to cover and glanced at the pile of wood they had laid by. There was not nearly enough. He shook his head at Otto.

"We do not have enough wood for such a tunnel," he told him.

Otto frowned. "That should be more than enough," he said, looking at the stacks of cut beams they had brought down to the meadow. "Hammer nails at an angle into the joists to support the flatwood. Add cross beams every four feet into lengths that will fit between your support joists."

The builder was shaking his head vigorously. "It is not as simple as that. You have not dug here. You were not here when we erected the structures," he reminded Otto, motioning towards the top of the bluff with a stubby hand. "In our mountains, such as at the Coil, the earth is more densely packed. It is rocky and is filled with sticky materials such as clay and hard materials such as ore. Here, the earth is grainy, the soil loose and dry. We need more wood, more closely placed, possibly butted against one another and secured. Otherwise, the sides and roof will simply spill through the beams – a slow but sure cave-in."

Otto's scowl deepened. It was true – he, like most Gnomin, only had experience digging mines into mountains. They blasted and dug, the tunnel supported mostly by the mountain itself with a few braces made of wooden beams every five yards put in just to be safe. Even then, a collapse was always possible.

A cave-in was a horrible thing. Miners swallowed by the earth, suffocating while those nearby clawed desperately at dirt and rock, trying to free their comrades from their tomb. His shoulders dropped and he turned his gaze up at the darkened cliff. "More support," he said absently, his eyes studying the silhouettes of the structures in the moonlight before turning back to Heinz. "Start digging," he instructed. "Use whatever we need to make it safe. I will get more wood."

The builder gave him a firm nod and began motioning for the miners to get digging while Otto picked four workers to accompany him back to the base of the slope where their donkeys were tethered.

Jaden and his scouts kept watch as the slivered moon rose in the star-chipped night sky. All had been silent in the Crommag camp for some time. Two hours passed and then three. The Gnomin had finished the shaft and were working on the tunnel, taking out buckets of dirt and taking in wood that had been cut in varying sizes. As the night passed, the pile of earth grew and the pile of wood diminished. Before it was completely gone, Otto and the four others returned along with Wilhelm.

Otto and the other four miners were dragging bundles of wood tied with rope. Wilhelm had a huge canvas sack on his back. All deposited their loads with a look of relief. Jaden's eyes widened in surprise.

"Was that all the wood you could find?" he asked Otto, keeping his voice low.

The team leader shook his head. "There is much more at the base of the grade. I did not want to bring the donkeys this close. They can be noisy beasts, especially at the most inopportune moments." He turned and jogged away with the others at his side to retrieve more wood.

Jaden motioned for three of his scouts to keep watch and for two to accompany him as he followed the Gnomin. He held back a whistle as they reached the donkeys. Otto and his beasts of burden had brought down a startling amount of lumber. Each donkey was dragging a large bundle made of stacks of thin but large squares of wood. The rest of the load was comprised of beams and boards that had already been measured and cut and tied in neat bundles that hung from short ropes that crossed each donkey's back.

"Where did you get so much, so fast?" the Sylvan scout asked the team leader, his arched brows raised high.

"The supply building," Otto answered, doling out bundles to the other scouts and Gnomin.

"Captain Espytin had all this laid by?" Jaden asked, astounded.

The miner chuckled softly as he handed the elf one bundle and then stacked another bundle on top. "No. The supply building itself. With Captain Espytin's approval, of course. His men, along with every Gnomin I could find, helped."

Otto loaded his own arms with two bundles and, with the others, hurried back to the work site. It took them two more trips to retrieve all the wood, dragging most of it behind them like the donkeys had done.

Jaden's men passed a waterskin and returned to keep watch.

Still, the earth came out and the lumber went in.

The captain of the scouts watched the silver splinter of the moon as it descended towards the Elfin Greatwood. One elf glanced at him, and then another. Jaden nodded and headed for the freshly dug hole in the battlefield where even Otto and Wilhelm were carrying buckets of dirt from the excavation. They set their buckets down, still full, their faces expectant.

"It is two hours before dawn," Jaden informed them. "You have an hour, maybe less, before the Crommags wake and begin to take the field."

The Gnomin nodded in unison, as if they had been expecting this news for some time, and then disappeared back down the hole.

The work continued for the next twenty minutes as it had the whole night and then the next twenty minutes were spent getting the remaining wood below ground, save for one last but large square of thin lumber. Then Wilhelm was climbing out.

He passed down the sack of cots he had brought to Otto, who passed it to the Gnomin behind him. Then Wilhelm passed down four other large sacks that had been laid by, one at a time. Jaden saw they were filled with food. Then the miner held his hand out to Otto to help him from the hole but the team leader shook his head. It took Wilhelm a moment to realize that the other Gnomin meant to stay.

"But, Otto," he said softly, "there is already a team leader for this expedition."

The Gnomin were not in practice of sending more than one leader unless absolutely necessary, should there be a mishap, calamity, or outright disaster. Just like with an army – if soldiers were few, captains were even fewer. Losing a worker was bad and losing a leader was dreadful. Losing two was worse, and prevented whenever possible.

Otto's expression, however, was set.

"My brother is in that camp," he told Wilhelm. "I hope."

Wil frowned. "Then go get him," he said. "Him and all the others." He stuck out his hand again and this time Otto took it and gave it a firm shake. Then he disappeared down the hole.

Wilhelm let out a deep breath and grabbed the large piece of flat wood and dragged it over the opening of the mineshaft. Then he took the four buckets of dirt that he and Otto had left there and dumped them on top, spreading it out evenly. He tore up clumps of grass and threw them on top of the dirt.

It was a poor job of camouflage and any scrutiny would show that something out of the ordinary had been going on it that part of the meadow, but it would do. The fighting had not come near the site of the excavation and any Crommag that noticed was most likely to assume it was another trap and avoid it.

The Gnomin team leader gave it one last look and then turned, exhausted but hurrying back to the slope as the sky in the east was just beginning to brighten. Jaden and his scouts fell in around him to escort him back to Kriegslager. The Sylvan elf had many questions and a good dose of fear about what the Gnomin miners were doing.

"How can they breathe down there?" Jaden asked Wilhelm as they made their way back to where the donkeys waited. "What will they do with the rest of the dirt?"

The team leader grinned, knowing the small elf had probably never been below ground, certainly not deep and certainly not for any real length of time.

"Heinz will drill airholes every ten feet with a crank auger. They will sleep close to the entrance, and take their breaks there. It has more air circulation than you think. It is also where they will take the earth, building a slope up the side of the hole that will be easier to go up, as opposed to a rope, when they climb out of the shaft."

Jaden gave him a look of admiration even as he gave his head small shake. His scouts untied the donkeys and helped Wil lead them up the slope. Jennings and Nevin were already assembling their companies at the top, with a dozen Vikemen and one hundred crossbowmen from the red troops.

The captain of the scouts bid Wilhelm goodbye and had his men escort him, and his donkeys, back to the Gnomin camp. Then the Sylvan elf, after quiet greetings and good wishes to the other captains as they made ready for battle, went off to find Dell to give him his report on the past night. Jaden and his men had been assigned to watch over the Gnomin, but also to watch for the next group of incoming Crommags.

His last team of scouts reported that the beasts were on their way, but moving slowly. It appeared they had been left to haul wagons, animals and supplies, so that the other groups could move faster. Still, they were expected any day.

The small elf ran his fingers back and forth through his short curls, scrubbed his hands vigorously over his face, and went off to find Sir Dellion and make his report as the sky brightened in the east.

On the western edge of Morgan's Vale, six feet under the ground, Otto and the other eighteen miners each ate a chunk of bread, an apple, and promptly fell asleep. There was no need for anyone to stay awake to rouse the others. After an hour of sleep, there was a great rumble followed by a muffled clash and muted shouts and screams. Above ground, the battle had begun.

The Gnomin returned to their work, slowly but steadily moving south towards the forest. The trips back and forth through the tunnel became increasingly longer as they took their buckets of dirt back to the shaft and then returned back down the channel to where the others dug on. All the while, the team of builders dragged bundles of wood down the earthen corridor and shored up the sides and roof.

Two hours into the morning dig, the miners began to notice a change in the soil along with a number of roots snaking down through it. They were nearing the forest. Otto called a break and he and Heinz stood at the end of the channel that had been carved below the meadow so they could converse. There was a good five feet of tunnel at its tip that had not yet been reinforced with wood and the two Gnomin ran their hands over the earthen wall.

"It is becoming more damp," Heinz observed.

"And the roots grow thicker and denser," Otto said.

Heinz nodded. "They will make the tunnel more secure, and we will not have to put in as much support, but they will make the going slower."

Otto nodded and was about to ask the builder how far apart they could now put in the wooden braces, when he heard something. The Gnomin cocked his head listening. "Do you hear that?" he asked.

Heinz also cocked his head. There was indeed a sound that was not coming from the battlefield. A scratching sound. One that was close. The heads of both team leaders turned, following the scratching as it grew nearer, their eyes coming to rest on the earthen wall to their left. Together, they watched in growing horror as the dirt began to crumble and fall.

"Komm zurück!" Heinz shouted.

All of the Gnomin close by turned tail and ran. Heinz and Otto, however, simply scurried back far enough to where boards held up the sides of the passageway. Clutching each other in terror of a cave-in, they watched as only a portion of the earthen wall collapsed, dirt pouring into their tunnel before it stopped completely - leaving behind a hole in the wall.

Their bodies sagged in relief.

"It must have just been a pocket of..." Heinz began when a head poked through the hole and looked around. The team leaders clutched each other again in fright before they realized it was the face of a Gnomin.

More dirt fell into the small cavern as he pushed it away from his body and the team leaders joined him, pulling away the earth to allow enough space for his body. The Gnomin grinned at them from ear to ear as they pulled him through. He wanted to say something witty, something about how much time they had saved him, but all he found he could do was hide his face in his hands as his thin body was wracked with sobs. Otto wrapped strong arms around him and patted his back. The team leader closed his eyes in compassion as he felt the Gnomin's shoulder blades through his threadbare shirt.

"Otto," the Gnomin moaned as he wept into his shirt. "Oh Otto!"

The team leader pulled back gently in surprise, his wizened face drawn. "I'm sorry," Otto said softly, "do I know you?"

The rescued miner looked at him, his eyes large and leaking tears. "Otto," he said, blinking, "don't you recognize me?"

Otto ignored his sunken face and peered at his hazel eyes and his dark blonde beard, one that would be considered quite dusky amongst the Gnomin. "Karl?" he whispered.

A fresh batch of tears leaked from the miner's eyes as he gave his brother a barely perceptible nod. Otto pulled him close again, crushing his thin body against his own, his own eyes now spilling tears down his cheeks.

The others, tentatively creeping back to see how bad the damage was, saw him and ran for blankets and food.

23. AYALA'S RAGE

The leader of the Great Men stared down at the severed head of his brother. It had been left close to the Crommag camp and discovered at first light by one of the sentries and brought to him, wrapped in blood-soaked cloth.

He could hear low murmurs and the scrape of weapons outside. He knew the Great Men should be moving out of the forest at this time, making good use of the light before the heat slinked into the day, but Ayala's feet were rooted to the dirt floor of his tent. Noga's strange green eyes, the color of frozen moss, stared blindly at him.

Reverently, the mountain of a man dropped to the ground on his knees and knelt before what was left to him of his brother.

Noga, who Ayala had saved from their father on the day of his birth. Noga, who had saved Ayala from an ice bear when the runt was only twelve. Noga, so crafty and cunning, who had planned a better future for a people that always treated him with repugnance and distrust.

The leader of the Great Men, squatting down on his hams, reached out with an enormous hand and closed his brother's eyes.

"All those plans," he promised, "I will see through." He took a few breaths through his clenched fangs and then Ayala rose to his feet, an anger that he had never known pulsing through his veins. He could feel his heart pumping harder than ever, and a pulse throbbing in his neck and at his temples. More than his brother's death, it was from the look in his brother's dead eyes. His last expression had been one of surprise, one that Ayala had hardly ever seen.

And what could surprise a Great Man as crafty as Noga? Among his own people he was a runt, but among the puny elves he must have seemed a god. What could surprise a man of that stature and cunning? Even Ayala knew there was only one thing – a woman. And he had more than just a good idea of which one. Noga had spoken of her every time he had come to deliver news of the enemy.

Noga had called her the Spirit of Death and Ayala had seen her many times but thought of her as the *cagna in neru*. The bitch in black. Noga would speak of her as if Ayala gave a shit about some human woman, and he always did so with a bit of a stupid smile on his face. His older brother could not understand why, until now.

She did this, the leader of the Great Men thought, looking aghast at what used to be his brother and best friend. *She enchanted him somehow. Deceived him. Led him into a trap. Killed him.*

He felt a hollowness inside his body that he had never felt before. A sense of loss that was surrounded by his pulsating wrath. The Great Man rose to his feet like a mountain being slowly thrust towards the sky by the shifting of tectonic plates. The fury within him spread and grew like a raging fire.

With his chest heaving from his building passion, Ayala cast one more glance at the head upon the floor of his tent, then picked up his sword and his mace and went outside into the clearing. His men were there, waiting to hear what he would say, what he would order them to do.

The leader straightened, a mountain of a man that drew himself up into well over eight feet of bristling muscle and ferocity as his scowl swept over the waiting warriors, then spoke loud enough that even those in the forest who could not see him, could hear him.

"The elves are running out of tricks!" he shouted. "And they are running out of elves!" There was a conglomeration of guttural laughs and a few cheers. "We are greater - in size and strength and numbers!" The congregational assent grew louder, spreading throughout the forest. "And today," Ayala thundered, *"I fight with you!"*

The Great Men held their weapons high above their heads and roared their approval, the sound shaking the trees and echoing throughout the Elfin Greatwood. Ayla moved his beady eyes to Mig, one of the young runners standing close to him.

"Boil the head and bring me the skull," he instructed, his voice a low growl. Mig nodded and went inside the tent to retrieve what was left of the runty Crommag that had been Ayla's brother and best friend. Then the leader of the Great Men turned and headed for the plains of battle and the Great Men of the Bitterlands followed.

I am going to take down that cagna if it is the last thing I do, he thought, baring his fangs. *But I will try to make it the first thing.*

Ayala stomped through the clearing and past the trees that bordered the low meadows, accompanied by over twelve hundred Great Men from five different tribes, their passage shaking the ground. They poured from the forest and into the early morning dawn - the news that Ayala would fight today still traveling throughout the army, raising their excitement. The leader of the Great Men hefted his sword in one hand and his mace in the other as the rising sun cast its rays upon his face and he grinned. Today he would fight for his brother.

The elves were already gathered on the far side of the plains, small shadows of blue and gray.

Farther back than normal, Ayala thought. *They are afraid to fight this day, as they should be.* He scanned their lines with his beady eyes but did not see the small warrior with hair like flame.

The leader of the Great Men threw back his shoulders and

screamed in fury, spittle flying unheeded from his lips. Over a thousand Crommags echoed his cry, bellowing at the elves as they clashed their weapons and gnashed their fangs before they followed their leader as he began to advance.

On the north side of Morgan's Vale waited Nevin and four hundred elves. They were supported by one hundred men from the crimson troops and ten Vikemen.

Ayala sneered at them. *They are so small, and so few. This will be done easily before the heat of the day sets in.* He stepped over the dead bodies of fallen Crommags, their bodies beginning to bloat and rot in the summer heat. On his left was Pel, hefting a giant war hammer and on his right was Yon, a sword the size of an elfin man held loosely in one massive hand.

They were great men among Great Men, but they were not Noga. They were not his brother.

Yon and Pel were flanked by Higa and Dolf, both wielding giant cudgels. They had grown close to Noga over the past year, close enough to appreciate that he was a Great Man in his own right. They been good advisors and had already shown themselves to be fierce warriors. They, too, were outraged by Noga's death and eager to soak the ground with elfin blood.

The line of Crommags, stretching out two hundred enormous bodies wide and hundreds more deep, reached the trench of corpses and passed it, many stepping over the mounds of bodies but many more simply stepping on them. Ayala kicked a severed hand out his way, his fury building into a frenzy.

They reached the berm of earth and the Crommags that had been present at the first battle, looked cautiously about and, not spying any of the men who shot the small spears that killed, stepped over it. Almost every one of them stepped over the berm and through the earth - onto rows of sharpened stakes the Gnomin had buried there. The wooden stakes went straight through their bare feet and the Great Men screamed in pain as they fell to the ground, alive but hobbled.

Ayala's great legs had taken him right over the hidden trench and he shouted at his uninjured men to keep moving.

Idiots! he shouted mentally. *For all of you to be alive and my brother dead! What a waste!*

The elves waited in the shadow of the cliff as the sun rose in the east and the Great Men expended their energy crossing the corpse-littered plains. Ayala knew quite well it had been their little design for the morning, to tire them out as much as possible, because they themselves were too small to fight. He knew the hidden stakes had been their little trick, their desperation at gaining any advantage because they were so weak.

Noga, he thought, *this had been our plan, but it had been your idea. An idea of a better life for people that never liked or trusted you. You should be here. You should share in the glory. You should finally be looked at by our people as the most cunning of the Great Men. You should be at my side!*

The leader of the Great Men threw out his chest and roared in anger and, as his roar was echoed by over a thousand mammoth Crommags, he began to run. His people followed and the ground shook as they ran towards the waiting elves who stepped out to meet them.

Behind the front line, one row of archers fired a torrent of arrows into the oncoming enemy, while another row shot a second volley into the air at a higher angle, dropping the feathered missiles into the deeper ranks of Crommags.

Ryen and the Roshan observed from atop the bluff on the backs of their horses, separate but not far from where the general watched with the king and his sons and their throng of Praetorian guards. They watched as the multitude of Crommags crashed into the elfin army. Despite Jennings' plans of slowing and weakening them, the elfin lines buckled when hit, and almost broke.

Jennings and Nevin, the only ones on horse, rode along the rear, shouting orders and encouragement.

"He should have put Patrek up front," the Roshan muttered.

"He's too proud," Ryen said of Jennings, keeping his voice low.

He won't be so proud tonight if this keeps up, Ember thought, not wanting to voice her opinion within elfin earshot of the royalty, only ten yards away. "Patrek and his men are useless in the rear," she said, watching the Crommags begin to cut through the elves as if they were made of paper.

"Unless he means to save them in case of retreat," Ryen advised.

The Roshan gave her blood-colored head of hair a small shake. "You had it right before, he is too proud for such a thing."

Ryen glanced at her, surprised. "You think he would let all his men die before he would call a retreat?" he asked softly.

"Let's hope not," she answered. "I'm certainly not going to do that to mine." Beneath her, Coal snorted and churned the earth with an enormous hoof. "If the Crommags break the line, I'm going down."

Concerned that she was still exhausted, Ryen had talked her into observing from the bluff with the argument that she should get a bird's eye view of the enemy and their movements. The Roshan had relented because there *was* something she wanted to see and Ember knew she could still join the battle in the time it would take Coal to charge down the slope.

The Roshan was not the only one apprehensive about the brutal happenings in the vale. From his spot atop the knoll, mounted on Peg, Traejan looked anxiously at Halloran.

"Sir?" he asked.

The general grunted in response, his steely eyes fixed on the battle.

"They look overwhelmed down there. A cavalry attack..."

"Would be too soon," Halloran answered, gruff. "They may look overwhelmed, but they are not."

"Traejan," Xander reprimanded, his voice low. "General Halloran knows what he is doing."

"With all due respect, Prince Xander," Halloran said without turning around, "Prince Traejan is one of my commanders, and has my leave to speak openly."

"I am glad you say so, sir," Traejan said, ignoring his impulse to throw Xander a dirty look, "because that is half of our army down there."

"And they are in good hands. Trust your men and trust your captains, they know their business."

Even as he spoke, the elves were beginning to recover. With the ten Vikemen at the center of the front line serving as an anchor, they began to slowly push the Crommags back. The entire group watched as Nevin pulled his mount to a stop next to Patrek, conversed briefly with the red captain and then put his heels to his horse, riding him hard only to stop just as hard every ten yards to speak with those in the rear guard.

Ryen and Ember watched intently as the crossbowmen began to divide into small groups and then gathered at the places where Nevin was stopping. Finally, the elf rode back down the line, his graying hair flying behind him while shouting commands the observers could not hear from atop the bluff. His impulsive plan, however, quickly became obvious to those on the cliif.

Every ten yards, the platoons of elves that were only four ranks deep, began to split apart. On the ground, it appeared as if their lines were breaking. From above, the Roshan could see they were simply opening corridors in the ranks. The Crommags, seeing the breaks and sensing a quick victory, rushed recklessly past the elves that stepped nimbly to the side only to find teams of Patrek's men.

As soon as the crossbowmen had unleashed a swarm of deadly bolts, the elves closed their ranks and cut down the remaining Crommags, some so stunned that they just stood there, stupefied and staring for one second too long.

Nevin rode hard for Jennings' troops on the west flank to employ the same tactic.

Ayala and his guardsmen were busy in the center of the battle, fighting Kamut and the Vikemen from Copen Borough. The Norsemen were almost of a size with the Crommags, wielding weapons just as large but able to move much faster. The Crommag leader had been surprised to see the Northmen, but it only enraged him further. He yelled to his Great Men, encouraging them to take down the men that had been their enemies for as long as anyone could remember.

Jennings' troops were now repeating the same sequence. The elfin ranks would break apart in a neat line only to close up after the enemy rushed headlong into the space. Then the line would collapse, cutting the perplexed Crommags off from the rest of their army. Many faced an onslaught of bolts while those that turned saw only elfin swords. And, each time, the elves pressed forward.

The going was slow, gaining only a foot or two of the battlefield at a time, and many elves gave their lives in the process. Confusion eventually began to ensue in the Crommag ranks as they began realizing that others were disappearing entirely in groups of five to twenty.

Two hours passed, the sun rising and warming the plains of Morgan's Vale that now reeked with the smell of blood and the stench of death.

The bewilderment of the Crommags was complete as they began to stumble over a number of their brethren, most alive but shouting curses, only to find themselves screaming and shouting as well. The elves had pushed them back to the berm where many lay crippled as they tried to bind their bleeding feet. Many more, who had been fighting all morning, stumbled back onto the sharpened stakes and found themselves equally hobbled or worse.

The elves fell upon them, driving their swords deep into Crommag chests and throats. Ayala realized their predicament and shouted at his men to avoid the pitfall but, given their current momentum, most assumed he was advising a cautionary retreat. Even Higa and Dolf were jumping over the berm, higher now with bodies. Pel the Ice Walker, with his long legs simply stepped over it, as well as over the wounded and dead alike.

The leader of the Great Men cursed them as he swung his mace, crushing the skull of an elfin soldier in an explosion of blood and bone and then drove his sword into the shoulder of the nearest Vikeman before he followed the other Great Men.

The elves did not follow them this day, and were too exhausted to cheer. Ayala sneered at them as he and his warriors backed slowly away. The day was getting warm, but not too hot to fight, and both sides knew it.

The elves withdrew as well, keeping a wary eye on their enemy. If a soldier came upon a fallen elf, he was hauled back with the others. Both sides had suffered heavy losses, but for the elves it felt tragic. And it was. It seemed there was one dead or wounded for every live elf, yet looking across the bloody grounds they could see that there were still so many Crommags. Many and more.

Ayala's sneer widened. He could smell their fear, taste it on the warming air. The Crommags had been drifting slowly back to the forest, instinctively seeking the shade of the trees, but Ayala stopped and pointed his sword at the elves. The others gradually came to a stop, staring across the beaten prairie.

"Look at them!" their leader shouted. "Look how afraid they are! How few!" Despite his thirst, Ayala spat.

There were guttural shouts from the ranks of Great Men, some laughing at the weakness of the elves. They watched as the elves slowly moved back toward the shadow of the cliff and others taunted and spat. Their excitement grew and grew, like hyenas seeing injured prey, and the tension quickly built like a dam about to burst.

Nevin and Jennings rode like the Seventh Circle behind the line of retreating elves in an effort to prepare them for the inevitable. They had made it back only a hundred yards.

"KILL THEM!" Ayala shouted without any more elaboration. His Great Men echoed his cry as they ran back across the bloodied ground, howling like wild animals.

Atop the bluff, Halloran's head snapped to the left. "Now!" he shouted at the trumpeter. "Call the cavalry now!"

The blow of horns came from all along the cliff and, waiting at the top of the slope with two hundred mounted elfin soldiers, Drustin bellowed for them to charge. The horses pounded down the grade, carrying elves with drawn swords screaming out *Tuar Ceath!* – the cry of their new homeland.

Ryen watched, feeling hollow. The Crommags were moving fast, especially for creatures that had been fighting all morning. They came after the retreating line of elves that was backpedaling painfully slow, dragging their wounded and dead. At least half of the Vikemen were injured as well, though none were being lugged along the ground. Nevin and Jennings rode up and down the backs of the ranks, shouting like devils.

"Are they going to make it?" Ryen asked, his voice low.

The Roshan smiled. "Who exactly do you mean?" she asked, her piercing gaze moving over the battlefield and all that was happening at once.

The cavalry was coming fast, but they had a lot of ground to cover. The elves were now going as quickly as they could, which was nowhere near quick enough, resolutely leaving no one behind. Every one of the Crommags vaulted over the berm of earth and bodies and stakes, none of them falling or falling prey to the traps this time.

When they were a hundred yards from the recoiling enemy,

they let out screams of triumph, tasting victory. The cavalry had just reached the base of the slope – but were still almost a quarter of a mile away. Simultaneously, the last line of elfin warriors hauled their wounded and dead past a line of a hundred crossbowmen.

"Now!" Jennings commanded.

Patrek and his men released a hundred bolts at the oncoming Crommags and each found its mark, dropping a body in its tracks. They reloaded without the order to do so and fired another onslaught as more of the monsters charged at them. There was no time for third. Each man slung his bow on his back and ran hard, angling east.

The enraged Crommags gave chase and followed them east, intent on pinning the infuriating soldiers in red against the curved wall of the cliff and killing them to a man. But before even the first bowman was reached, the Crommags were rundown from behind by Drustin's cavalry. The red troops had stalled the advance just long enough for the mounted elfin infantry to take the field.

The monsters did not see them coming, and those that did have time to turn and see them bearing down, did not have the time to raise a weapon. The elfin soldiers cut hundreds of them to ribbons before the others could even comprehend what was happening.

The crossbowmen wheeled back to the west, behind the new battle that had ensued, and headed for the earthen ramp and back up to the slope. The support unit from the red army was there, along with more horses, helping the wounded and battle-weary return up the hill. Patrek and his men stopped to help as well.

Ayala was caught in the midst of the fighting and the midst of the confusion. Without a vantage point such as he had on the rock, he could not see exactly what was happening, but he knew it was not good. "Back to the forest!" he shouted, though very few could hear him over the clamor of the battle and the screams of the dying. His narrow head shifted left and right and finally found Yon. "Blow the horn!" he yelled.

Yon was as dumbfounded as his leader at the turn of events but snatched the horn from the cord on his massive trunk and blew for all he was worth. The Crommags heard the sound and wasted no time beating a hasty retreat. Unfortunately for many of them, they had become turned around in the confusion and blundered into the elfin cavalry.

Drustin and his men struck down any that were not fast enough to get away, and chased down every straggler.

Atop the bluff, Traejan smiled at Halloran. "My apologies, General," he said, bowing his head of thick golden hair.

"No apologies necessary, my Lord Prince," he replied with a smile. "I have seen a few more battles, that is all."

The young prince huffed. "I am guessing it was more than just a few. Regardless, I will keep my opinions to myself next time, at least for a few minutes longer."

The general's smile widened and Xander edged his horse next to his brother's.

"You will send me a report this evening of our losses?" he asked Traejan. The smiles fled from both the young prince and the general.

"Of course," Traejan answered softly.

Xander held his brother with his gaze for a moment and then turned it to the general. "And you will notify us if there are any further movements by the enemy?"

"Of course," Halloran answered gruffly, openly taken aback.

Xander nodded with satisfaction and turned his horse, leading his father and their Praetorian back to the city. Zephyrn, seeing the Roshan approaching on her massive horse with Ryen on his khusar, waited.

The pair reached the small group and they bowed their heads in respect as their horses stopped before them.

"Well done today, General," the Roshan said.

The general dipped his head in acknowledgement. "Your men did well likewise. Perhaps more so. I do not think you lost a single one."

"They were hardly in danger," she said dismissively. "The elves, however..." she trailed off and gave her head a small shake.

"I'd say we lost close to half of the infantry that fought today," he said. "A bit less."

Traejan closed his eyes and felt the muscles in his jaw clench at this remark, delivered by Halloran as if guessing tomorrow's weather.

"And the Crommags?" the general asked in his graveled voice, looking at Ryen.

"Took the field this morning with over a thousand," he answered. "Left with a little over half."

"So," the general mused aloud, "we are about even in losses. They lose more, but they have more to lose."

"So many have died," Zephyrn said softly and all eyes went to the youngest prince atop his horse. The flamboyant elf had sobered considerably in the past three days, bearing witness to every battle. "So many more will." His bright blue eyes traveled over the group of steadfast commanders and came to rest on the Roshan. "Who wins in a war such as this?"

She met his gaze with her own. "The last one standing," she answered. "Sometimes it is no one at all." The face of the young prince went pale and she turned her eyes back to Halloran. "Did you discern their leader?"

The general tucked his chin, already covered with gray stubble, towards his chest for a moment as he thought and then lifted it. "I believe I have. The one who led the charge today, both times. Did you see him?"

"I did."

"He's a big bastard," Ryen remarked. The Roshan smiled and the general grunted in agreement.

"He watched the battle for the past two days from atop a rock near the woodline," Halloran said, "and ordered the retreat each time like he did today. I am not sure why he decided to the lead the fight today."

"Perhaps the spy you returned had been someone close to him," the Vikeman suggested.

"Perhaps he was waiting for the reinforcements," Zephyrn offered.

"Or perhaps he was just waiting to see how we fought," Traejan said, slightly impatient. "I doubt the why is important. What I do sense, is that you two," he said, looking from the general to the Roshan, "think *he* is important other than the simple fact that he is their leader. What is it?"

It was Ryen, however, who answered, his glacier blue eyes looking out over the plains below. He knew now why it had been easy to persuade Ember to watch the battle from above. "Because," he said, looking none too pleased, "if an army is only strongly united because of a strong leader, killing him could collapse the army in a single stroke."

The Roshan gigged Coal, turning him so she could better see the battered meadow below. There was no sign of the Crommags, at least none of the living. Hundreds upon hundreds of their corpses were strewn and piled across the field of battle. Already there were carrion birds circling in the sky overhead. She glanced at the general before turning her gaze to where the last of the elves – the living, the wounded and the dead – were still being moved up the slope.

"The elves had proven their valor," she said. "My men are at your disposal, but I would like to lead the defense, should there be another attack today, or lead the first assault in the morning."

The general was silent for a moment as he considered. "I

think that is a fine idea," he acquiesced. "Will you lead with ground infantry?"

The Roshan smiled, though her face was turned away and he could not see it. Traejan, however, could hear it in her voice. "I will. And I will find that big bastard, and I will kill him."

24. IAN

The next day dawned as the others had – clear and bright. A summer day perfect for weddings, picnics, and festivals. Certainly not a day for war. Not a day for men to scream in pain or to gasp their last breath upon the earth, their severed limbs lying just beyond their reach.

Already down in the Vale with her troops, the sharp eyes of the Roshan swept across the field of battle – once, twice, and then a third time. She saw him at once, but wanted to make sure. He was bigger than the others, and was being regarded with great respect as he was shouting commands.

The head of the snake, Ember thought as Coal shifted his prodigious bulk beneath her. *If I cut you off, let's hope the rest of the body will wither and die.* She was quick to take in every aspect of her enemy – the way he walked, the way he moved and held his weapons, the people that surrounded him. Everything was processed as she planned her own battle.

Ayala had already spotted her, as she was atop a massive beast and the only figure in all black, yet his thoughts were almost identical to those of the Roshan. *The cagna in neru!* he thought hatefully with growing ire. *I will kill her today, and her army will fall. I will end this war before the next group even arrives. It is up to me, and today is all I need.*

The Roshan slid down from the back of her Night Stallion, her black boots raising puffs of dust as she passed the reins to Dash. The elfin groom already held the leads of two khusars but took Coal's easily. She pulled free her long sword as she advanced with Ryen and the Vikemen brothers to her right. Past them were one hundred infantry soldiers led by the intrepid Gavan. To her left was the black-haired Yasgir and two Vikemen that Traejan had only just met. Past them were one hundred more infantrymen commanded by Rhys, his golden hair shining in the light of the rising sun.

The slope was guarded by Sloan and his company of crossbowmen, along with twenty Wildboys armed with spears. In front of them, but behind the infantry, was Ian on his skittish mount. The red mare jerked her head and danced sideways under the steward, his dark eyes intent upon the Roshan.

The sun commenced its slow climb over the Vale as the two forces moved deliberately toward one another and growls rose from throats as if they were wild dogs.

The armies closed the open distance on the battlefield but today their movements were careful and wary and tense as they advanced. It was like a preadolescent dance, full of apprehension, indecision, and jerky awkward movements.

The multitude of beasts moved closer and closer until they were only a few yards apart from the elves and their allies when a single battle cry was loosed. It was all that it took. The forces facing one another surged forwards, weapons raised to cut down any enemy in their path.

Traejan watched from his place upon the bluff as the waltz of death ensued, a formal but efficient dance as the infantry from Redtown began to slice into the Crommag army. Led by the blue-eyed Rhys and his golden-eyed counterpart Gavan, the soldiers cut down the monsters with fluid efficiency. They were fast, and even though one would occasionally not be fast enough, the young prince did not see any of them become mortally wounded. Each time one was injured, he fell back to the rear. The orders from the Roshan had been perfectly clear: no one was to fight to the death. Any injury at all and the soldier was to retreat. If she saw otherwise, there would be a Circle to pay.

The elfin prince tried to watch the battle objectively as it wore on, to mark how the red troops differed from his own and to see if there was still something to be done to improve his own fighters. But his eyes were constantly drawn to Ember.

The Roshan and the leader of the Crommags both fought where they had entered the battle, steadily pushing forward. It was a long and grisly dance that took place that morning, as the two warriors slowly and knowingly made their way towards one another.

There was no shouting of victory as they struck down their enemies, there was just the distance as they closed it, foot by foot.

An hour of battle went by, then another. The group of injured soldiers who had fallen back to where Sloan guarded the slope to the cliff was steadily growing. Traejan's heart began beating a little faster as he saw the lines start to thin out and he forced himself to be still.

His eyes sought out Ember, unflagging as she fought on. When he switched his gaze back to the slope, a hundred infantrymen from the red troops, led by Patrek, were descending the grade. Four columns wide and twenty-five deep, they reached the bottom where they stood in solemn ranks with their hands on the hilts of their swords.

A cry from Rhys went up and Patrek immediately directed half of the men to the right and half to the left. The columns peeled away from each other and rushed headlong into the battle, spreading out and replenishing the line as they went.

There was a roar of anger from the Crommags as they saw what was happening but they fought doggedly, if recklessly, on. Then the young prince found his heart speeding up once again and this time he was powerless to stop it. The commander of the Crommags and the commander of the red troops finally found themselves face to face.

Ryen battled his way closer, calling out to the redoubtable Haldor and Halvar. Together, the three fought off every nearby

Crommag, making room for the pair about to dance. They confronted each other like a mongoose facing down a cobra.

The Roshan, who was bloodied almost to her shoulders, grinned as she held out her arms and bowed deeply. Ayala, at first thrilled that she was finally before him, realized that she was mocking him and let out a bellow of anger as he rushed towards the cagna with his sword held high above his head.

By the time he realized he had been baited he was going too fast to stop. Rushing forward, his stomach and chest left open and vulnerable, he saw the cagna's blade come slicing towards his midsection. He twisted away, looking like the world's largest, most ungainly, and ugliest ballerina.

Then he caught his balance and turned around, snarling.

This time he planted his feet firmly before he swung his sword over his head, meaning to cleave her in two, but she danced away and he was cutting nothing but the air. Before he could swing again, her sword was coming at his own head and he barely got his own weapon up in time to block it. Then her blade was coming again, this time for his leg, and had he not been holding his mace on that side she would have crippled him.

Ayala shouted in surprise as he lurched back and struck at her, but she blocked his blade, turning it easily, and then used the momentum to swing her own sword back up at his face and then back down at his legs. The warrior was small, but fast. She parried every blow and struck quickly in return, outmatching his own assaults two to one. Within a minute he realized she was driving him back.

He roared at the small warrior and pushed forward, using his immense size to bear down on her. Once again, she simply slipped away and he found her swinging at him from the other side, her sword whistling towards his chin. He blocked with his mace and brought it down in an effort to crush her skull but she turned, her sword extended as she spun, and it cut straight through the burlap of his rough-spun shirt and enough of his skin to draw a thin line of blood.

Ayala's great fangs came together in a snap and he lunged for the cagna as he swung his own sword, meaning to take off her head, but again she stepped nimbly away. This time, however, she was not quite as fast and a chip of light flew from where the tip of his sword grazed the metal collar on her neck.

Had she not been wearing it, he would have opened her throat, and she knew it. The cagna bared her small teeth in a grin and swung at him in what appeared a haphazard fashion. Ayala stepped back, but not far. He could see that her reach would fall well short of his body.

At the last second, however, she turned her blade and brought it down on the hand that held his mace. The Great Man screamed in pain as his mace, along with two of his fingers, fell to the ground.

The Roshan moved in quickly, intent on finishing him off, but such a wound was insignificant for a beast of his size. What was left of his bleeding hand darted out, surprising her as it grabbed the guard of her sword and wrenched it free of her grasp. The Crommag bared his own teeth, a macabre set of interlocking fangs, in a grin only to see one dagger and then another flying at him in quick succession.

He jerked away in time to avoid one but the other found its mark and plunged into his chest just under his shoulder. Ayala bellowed in rage and pain as he tore it free and threw it away from him only to find the small warrior coming at him again, wielding a shorter sword this time.

His injuries were bleeding freely but still meaningless to him and he bared his fangs again in a snarl. The nuisance in black might still be armed but her reach was even shorter than before. And she was getting tired. Ayala grasped the hilt of his sword with both hands and swung it with all his strength, knowing the metal collar would not save her now. The Roshan, however, fell to the ground before his sword could reach her, rolling towards the enormous Crommag rather than away from him. She came up on one knee, the swing of his blade passing right above her head, and drove her short sword into his leg.

Ayala hollered in pain as the wide blade went deep into the muscle of his thigh. He swung his own weapon, bringing it down in a deadly arc, and the Roshan, this time, was too close to avoid it. She was turning away as she rose up, intending to come back down on his other leg, when his sword caught the top of her ribcage and ripped through cloth and flesh, tearing her open. She went down screaming curses.

"Ember!" Ryen shouted, seeing her fall. Ayala saw his chance and lunged at her with his sword but his injured leg gave out and he pitched forward, his bleeding shoulder slamming hard into the earth.

From atop the bluff Traejan almost shouted her name as well, biting his tongue as Peg danced sideways, feeling his angst.

"Haldor!" Ryen shouted. "Halvar!" The brothers dispatched the Crommags they were fighting and turned as Ryen ran towards the fallen Roshan and scooped her up like a sack of grain. They covered his retreat as best they could, yet he still had to fight his way free.

One handed, the Vikeman ran through the first Crommag that stepped in his way, and then the second, the Roshan cradled in the crook of his left arm.

"How bad is it?" he asked, looking down at her as he sidestepped a cudgel coming straight for his head. The Roshan had her eyes closed tightly and did not answer, but he could see her grind her teeth in pain and could feel her blood soaking through his own clothes. Under the dirt and sweat and blood, her face was as pale as milk.

Traejan watched in terror as the Vikeman tried unsuccessfully to break from the battle. There was one, however, charging towards him.

Ian, his dark eyes ever vigilant, had spurred his wild mare

towards the raging battle as soon as he saw the Roshan fall. The slim red horse charged, streaking past swords and cudgels with blinding speed. Leaping over the earthen berm and dodging corpses, she raced headlong into the fray, her neck stretched forward with the Roshan's steward clinging to her back. Ryen reached the center of the red army's ranks just as Ian did, pulling up his wild mare in a plume of dust.

"Give her to me!" he shouted, holding out his arms. Ryen paused for only a second, keeping her small form pressed close against his chest, then he let out a great breath of air and passed her to Ian who pulled her up into his lap. The young man put one strong arm around her as he spun his frenzied mount and rode hard for the slope.

The Vikeman glanced back at the battle and then ran, following Ian and his precious cargo as he yelled for his own horse. Landis was boosting Aiden to the stirrup of Coal's saddle as Ian rode by them in a blur. The leader of the Wildboys wiggled to the front of the saddle and leaned down to speak to Coal as Dash rode towards Ryen with his khusar. Within seconds, reins were being pressed into his hands and the Norseman was swinging one of his great legs over the back of the beast before riding it up the hill as fast as it would take him. Aiden joined him, hanging on to Coal's thick neck for dear life with his stick-thin arms.

Traejan had watched the entire incident with growing horror, almost screaming when he saw Ember go down. He saw Ryen pull her out and get her to safety, turning her over to her steward on his wild horse. The young prince decided he had watched enough. He gigged Peg and edged her out of the protective circle of the Praetorian guards.

"Traejan!" Xander barked. "Where are you going?" he demanded. The young prince whirled on his older brother and Xander recoiled, seeing his brother's eyes so blue they looked lit from within.

"To where I can be of some use!" he answered, making no

effort to disguise his anger. He glanced at the general who gave him a curt nod to get going.

Traejan wheeled Peg around and put his heels to her flanks. The palfrey leapt forward and took off at a run for the east end of the camp. The elfin tents went by in a blur before they passed the white cabin, the mess pavilion, and what was left of the supply building. Traejan began pulling up as they passed the yurts of the Vikeman and he reached the Roshan's tent in time to see Ryen and Aiden shooing out a pair of Wildboys. The elfin prince slipped down off his horse and was at the entrance to the tent in a single fluid motion, only to be stopped forcefully by the Vikeman.

Traejan looked up in surprise. Ryen not only had his large hand on the elf's chest, but also a great deal of Traejan's vest grasped in it. The Vikeman, a foot higher than the six-foot tall prince, looked down at him with his lips pressed together in a line and shook his head in warning.

Traejan's look of surprise hardened as he jerked Ryen's hand from his shirt and pushed past him into the tent. His eyes adjusted immediately to the lack of brightness within and saw that Ian had already lain the Roshan down on her cot. He had just removed the collar from her neck and was tossing it aside before throwing open a leather bundle full of small tools. The Vikeman ducked into the tent and stood tall next to the young prince.

"Aiden!" Ian called, spying the Wildboy hanging back by the entrance but who was at his side in an instant. "Fill this with water from the kettle in front of the tent," the dark-haired squire instructed, handing him a small metal pan. The Sprite raced away with the pot and as Traejan got his first good look at his Roshan he realized that Ryen had been trying to protect him by keeping him out.

Her face was a mask of pain and her right side was soaked, the black cloth shiny with blood. She tried to roll on her left side but Ian pushed her back and she choked down a scream as he did so, arching her back with her teeth clenched together.

Seeing her that way, Traejan doubted himself for a moment, and then pushed past the Vikeman and knelt by her head. He picked up her hand and her eyes popped open in surprise and then narrowed as she saw him there.

"Get out," she said. "Now." Traejan shook his head in refusal and her brows furrowed, not in anger, but in concern for him. "Please. Go." Again the elf shook his head and this time her frown *was* edged with anger. "Don't watch," she hissed.

But the elf was helpless not to, and stared as Ian snatched the long knife that was sheathed at his belt and used it to slice right through the brace that held her daggers. As it fell away he used it again to make a cut in her shirt - from the bottom at her waist all the way to under her arm. Then he grabbed the sides of the fabric and ripped them apart even farther, baring the wound.

The young prince froze at the sight of it. Worse than all the blood was the sight of her torn flesh under her parted skin, the gleam of bone here and there where her ribs were exposed. The elf felt himself go cold all over even as he broke out in a sweat.

Ian pulled the Roshan's remaining short sword free of the sheath and stood long enough to pass it Ryen. "Into the brazier," he instructed as he grabbed a half-gone bottle of wine from the top of a crate.

The Vikemen turned to the brazier that had been lit that morning but now had burned down to glowing embers. With a set expression he pushed the blade into the red coals. Ian pulled the cork free from the green bottle as he knelt back down and the Roshan took it from him, upending it into her mouth. Ian, with forced patience, let her get in a few good swallows before he pulled it back and poured the rest of it onto her open wound.

The Roshan shouted curses through her clenched teeth as her steward pulled a threaded needle from the leather bundle and proceeded to sew her up. Traejan finally moved his gaze to her face to see that her eyes were closed and her lips moving. He leaned closer, thinking she might be praying, but could discern after a moment that she was counting, in Gnomin.

After what seemed like an eternity but, if Traejan's Gnomin was any good, was really only just over one hundred seconds, Ian finished his stitching. He turned, looking for and finding, Aiden. He relieved the Wildboy, who stood watching with a pair of eyes like saucers, of the pot of steaming water and poured half of it over the wound before motioning to Ryen. The Roshan, having borne the pain of the scalding water, was groaning with her eyes scrunched shut. She opened them and began to take deep breaths.

Ryen pulled the short sword from the embers, its blade now as red as the coals, and handed it carefully to Ian. The Roshan looked upwards, away from the blade and nodded quickly. Traejan closed his eyes and pressed his forehead to hers as Ian pressed the hot metal against the lower half of the wound. The Roshan screamed through her teeth and squeezed the elf's hand as Ian turned the blade over to cauterize the upper half.

Traejan felt she might break his fingers and he focused on the feel of it, trying to ignore the smell of her burning flesh. Her face was bathed in sweat and her hair was plastered to her head like a cap of blackened blood.

Finally, Ian pulled the blade away and the Roshan shouted curses at the ceiling of the tent before searching him out with her eyes.

"Get me another bottle of wine!" she barked as he stood up and moved away. She closed her eyes, her air coming in short gasps, panting heavily. She lay like that for some time, until her breathing finally evened out. As soon as she could draw a decent breath, she turned her face to Traejan and her expression softened. "You should not be here," she whispered. The young prince gave her a ghost of a smile.

"You are wrong. There is no place else I should be."

The Roshan smiled crookedly in return. "Help me sit up," she told him.

Traejan pulled back slightly. "I don't know..."

Ember sighed. "Prop me up then, at least." The elf looked up as Ian passed him a firm pillow covered in scarlet brocade. He snaked an arm behind Ember and pulled her up as gently as he could. Even so, she groaned through clenched teeth as he wedged the pillow under her shoulders. Ian handed her a cup of wine which she took gratefully, swallowing half of it at once.

"By all the Gods!" Aiden exclaimed now that the worst was obviously over. "I'd never seen anything like that in my life!"

"And hopefully," Ryen remarked, "you never will again."

"Why the blade?" the Wildboy asked Ian. "You had already stitched her up neat as a pair of trousers. Wouldn't that have been enough?"

Ian suppressed a smile as he retrieved a small pile of linens from a wooden trunk. "It would," he agreed, "if you could get her to sit still in bed for two weeks." Aiden nodded in understanding, smiling as well. "Get some more hot water," Ian told him and the Sprite grabbed the pot and hurried back out of the tent.

"Get out of here," the Roshan told the young prince. "Let Ian clean me up. I don't like you seeing me like this," she added.

"Why?" Traejan asked, smiling as he pushed a damp lock of hair from her face. "This is how you will probably look when you have our first child."

The Roshan stared at him, stunned for a moment before she burst out laughing. "Ow!' shouted immediately, trying to stem the sudden mirth that was bubbling out of her. "Don't make me laugh, it hurts." She opened her eyes and shook her head gently. "The things that go through your mind," she remarked smiling. Her left hand came up slowly and touched his face. "I've missed you so much."

Traejan chuckled softly, feeling his love for her burn

through him with such ferocity that his eyes prickled with the heat. "I've missed you, too," he whispered.

Ryen stood frozen as he watched their exchange and let it sink into his heart. Then he stepped forward and gently laid a hand on the toe of the Roshan's boot. "I'll come see you later," he said softly.

"Not if I come see you first," the Roshan answered. The corners of Ryen's lips twitched and he turned and left without a word or a glance for anyone else. Aiden was returning with the water, followed by Cam, one of Gavan's soldiers.

"Commander?" he called, standing at the entrance to the tent.

The Roshan tried to sit all the way up at the sound of his voice but the pain in her side stopped her short. Grimacing, she leaned back down.

"Come in!" she ordered. Cam strode into the tent and stopped before her cot. Ian and Aiden paused, waiting for whatever news the soldier had brought.

"Commander," he repeated, softer this time, "the Crommags have retreated into the forest. It appears the fighting for today is done."

"Our losses?" she asked, breathless.

Cam took a deep breath and forced a look of optimism. "Remarkably low," he said. The Roshan narrowed her eyes at him, making him shift where he stood.

"Who?" she demanded.

Cam swallowed roughly, but met her gaze with his own. "Kellan. Tig. Casey." He named seven more and then stood silent.

"Thank you, Cam," the Roshan said. "Have Gavan come see me, but not for another hour." Cam bowed and turned, leaving quickly. He had seen a lot of horror over the past few weeks, but none were worse than seeing the Roshan torn apart and put back together.

Once he was gone, Ember sank back down against the small pillow, biting her lip to stifle a harsh sob. Traejan put a hand on her head as Ian looked at Aiden and jerked his chin towards the flap of the tent, encouraging a quiet departure. The Wildboy went, casting a glance back over his thin shoulder at the Roshan as she grappled with grief. He was surprised to find Ryen standing motionless outside, staring hard into nothing. Aiden took a deep breath and let it out as he stood next to the giant man.

"You know she did not cry when she was cut by that Crommag," the Wildboy observed aloud, "or when she was sewn up or burned. But at the loss of her men, she could hardly contain it."

Ryen's hard expression deepened into a frown. "That is because she cares for them more than she cares for herself. Just like she cares for that elf more than she cares for me."

"That's not true," Aiden scolded, quickly and in a raised voice, his youthful face twisted in a scowl. Ryen looked at him, startled.

"What do you mean?"

"He is not an elf!" the Wildboy told the Vikeman, irate. Ryen rolled his eyes and found himself unable to restrain a chuckle. He sighed heavily, shaking his head.

"Come on!" he exclaimed, laying a large hand upon the small and dirty shoulder of the Sprite. "Let's find some of that Gnomin cider." Aiden brightened immediately. He was ready to follow when, recalling his duties, he turned to the other Wildboys that lingered near the Roshan's tent.

"You are on guard!" he reminded them. "Announce any visitors to the Dark Lady before letting them enter!" The band of dirty miscreants stood up straighter, chins high, holding their spears tight in their grubby hands. Aiden nodded satisfactorily and then turned to accompany the Vikeman to the mess.

"Did you know?" Ryen asked the Wildboy, jerking his head

back towards the Roshan's tent. "About them?"

"Aye," Aiden agreed. "Didn't you?"

"The elf told me," the Vikeman admitted with a sour look. "But I did not want to believe him."

"Ah!" Aiden exclaimed, grinning. He attempted to elbow Ryen in the ribs and succeeded in jabbing his hipbone. "She is too much for the likes of us. You have to know that!"

"Maybe," Ryen agreed, petulant. "But, again, I did not want to believe it." His sour look deconstructed into a smirk as he looked at the Sprite by his side, marching along and swinging his arms like a child. "How old are you, Aiden?"

Aiden laughed. "What does it matter?" he asked. "What is age? A number of summers? Winters? We count it by laughs and scrapes - what you would call adventures. I must have had a hundred, does that make me a hundred? And again, what does it matter? All I know is that until you've had enough adventures, you are not done in this world."

Ryen looked at him approvingly. "I thought you measured life in mead and mischief," he remarked.

Aiden looked up at him, grinning. "That too," he agreed.

Ryen laughed and elbowed the Sprite, sending him stumbling away and cackling like a crow.

Inside the Roshan's tent, Ember released Traejan's hand. "Go now," she instructed. "Be at the mess for supper. Tell my men that I am alright."

"I will," he assured her. "Then I have something I must attend to, but afterwards I will return here. And I am never leaving your side again."

"Well," the Roshan said, giving him a crooked smile, "you are lucky that I will not be able to move too fast for a few days."

Traejan smiled and leaned forward, pressing his lips softly against her own. It was the first time their lips had met in almost a year and it was like touching a lit torch to a pool of oil.

The ardor flashed through them both, scorching and searching. He could feel her body rising up to find his and it took all the concern he had for her to break the kiss.

The young prince stared at the Roshan, astonished for a moment, and then cupped her face in his hand. "You need to rest," he told her. Ember laughed softly, both at his weakness and her own, as he stood. The elf glanced at Ian who was smiling to himself as he dropped a towel into a basin of hot water and picked up a pair of scissors.

"You did a good job," Traejan told him, making the handsome youth smile wider. "But," he said, looking back at the Roshan, "I think Gatha would have done equally as well."

Ember's face contorted in pain and it took him a second to realize it was because she was trying not to laugh.

"Can you imagine," she gasped, "Gatha riding into the battle to save me," (gasp), "on her donkey?" The Roshan's body trembled and tears leaked from the corners of her shut eyes.

Traejan laughed. "I guess not, I'm sorry. Stop laughing." Ember did so, but with effort. He dipped back down to kiss her damp forehead. "I will be back later," he promised, "but not until well after dark." The Roshan nodded as Ian began to cut away what remained of her shirt. The elfin prince gave her one last look and left, taking her smile with him.

He ducked out of the tent, hearing her berate Ian to get her more wine before he did anything else.

25. THE LONG NIGHT

Traejan found Dell waiting patiently for him outside in the hot, noonday sun. With his guardsman in tow, he made straight for the mess, knowing that those who had battled would be starving, and those that had not would be there wanting details. He found out that what most everyone really wanted was news of the Roshan.

The young prince moved between the tables of soldiers, congratulating them on a good fight, encouraging them for the next one, and reassuring them that the red commander was just fine. He told each one he met that it would take more than an army of Crommags to take her down. Everyone he told this laughed, and agreed.

After an hour and a half Traejan felt that he had talked to almost every man there, and that he himself was starving. He sent for a bowl of stew and found a table that had been deserted. "Hungry?" he asked Dell as he eased down into a wooden chair. The Praetorian shook his head in the negative. "Get something anyway," the prince advised. "It's going to be a long night."

Dell nodded and, with a look of resignation, took his advice and went to find himself something to eat. A Gnomin woman put down a steaming bowl of stew in front of Traejan and a mug of cider, bowed nervously, then hurried away. Ryen appeared in the place where she had just stood, looming over the table before kicking a chair back so he could sit in it.

Traejan began eating, keeping a wary eye on the Vikeman.

He knew that after what he had witnessed in the Roshan's tent, he could have no further argument about the Roshan, or her feelings for him.

The Norseman sat himself across the table from the elfin prince, idly shaking a handful of shelled nuts. "How is your stew?" he finally asked.

"As good as it gets," the young prince replied, though he felt Ember's was better by far. He gave Ryen a questioning look, his eyes searching his face. Ryen leaned forward to share a secret.

"I spit in it."

Traejan stopped chewing, but only for a second. "The whole pot, or just mine?"

"Just yours." Ryen smiled and leaned back, tossing a few nuts into his mouth and crunching them with enthusiasm.

Traejan cocked his head back slightly, watching him. His fork found a huge chunk of meat and he plunked it into his mouth and he chewed heartily, his eyes never leaving those of the Vikeman.

Ryen burst out laughing. "You truly are her," he said still laughing. "And she is you. Through and through."

Traejan thought it was the best compliment he had ever been given, but he leaned forward over the table and pointed his fork at the seven-foot Vikeman. "Does this mean you will stop trying to pursue her, and stop filling me with doubt?" he asked him.

Ryen's face screwed up as if he had been told something both foul and ridiculous. "Certainly not!" he exclaimed before his expression softened into one of good humor. "But I may back off a little. At least until I have a chance to talk with her privately."

The young prince rolled his eyes, shook his head, and took another bite of stew. *Why isn't anything ever easy?* he wondered, though he was not disheartened. He felt more in control than he had for an entire year.

But not entirely in control, he thought, agitated. *Something else that will be remedied before this day is done.*

Dell returned but remained standing as he tore off bits of a soft pretzel and popped them into his mouth. His dark eyes moved restlessly about the mess hall as he chewed. It was hot inside, both from the gleaming summer day and the heat of bodies. Traejan finished the last few bites of the stew and pushed the bowl away as he stood, wiping his mouth with a napkin.

"If you will excuse me, Ryen?" he asked. "I have business with my family that I must attend to this evening."

"Ah!" the Vikeman exclaimed with a broad grin. "Going to give the Royal Family the big news?"

"Something like that," Traejan acquiesced as he tugged his vest down and adjusted his sword belt. "Something almost exactly like that."

"Need some company?" Ryen offered, chuckling before he tossed another few nuts into his mouth and began crunching on them.

"That's what Dell is for," the young prince informed the Vikeman, throwing his guardsman a look of wicked good cheer.

The Praetorian exhaled deeply before giving his neck a sharp crack to the side. He took one more bite from his pretzel and left the rest on the table before he squared his shoulders, inhaled deeply, and gave Traejan a nod. He knew the afternoon was not going to be pleasant, but he was ready. Both elves gave the Vikeman a nod as they departed while he smiled and snacked, crunching happily away.

Traejan turned back to him as he was leaving. "You will check in on Ember, this evening, won't you?" he asked.

Ryen's grin widened and he gave the prince a sure nod. "You bet I will."

His whole attitude made Traejan want to stay back, to question him, to make sure he could trust him, but he truly did have matters at home that needed to be addressed immediately.

The young prince and his guard left the mess, found their horses, and rode across the rolling lawns of Fosse Meadow towards Castle Royce as the sun began to gaze longingly upon the horizon, a ball of fire suspended above the western curve of the Elfin Greatwood.

Traejan stopped in front of his parent's castle, where he and his brothers had grown to manhood together; the royal stronghold of the elfin people since they had come to the New World. He regarded it fondly for a moment, full of nostalgia and memories until the images blurred and ran like rain on a windowpane. He slipped off the back of Peg and tossed her reins to Dell.

The sun shone on his hair, turning it a burnished gold. His right hand rested on the hilt of his sword and he realized he was about to fight his first battle in this war. He took a deep breath and blew it out through pursed lips, then he crossed the stone bridge, nodding to everyone who stopped to bow, which was everyone.

He crossed the bailey garden and passed through the great hall to the atheneum where he knew his father would be at this time. The doors were closed but the guards on either side opened them without a word. He expected to find his father with his aides and advisors and their Praetorian, but it was only the king and his brother, the crown prince.

Rowland smiled broadly, pleased to see him. Xander, much less so.

"Father, brother," Traejan greeted each in turn.

"How is the red commander?" the king asked.

"Recovering," Traejan told him.

"Any movement by the enemy?" Xander asked.

"No."

"Then what brings you here?" Xander asked. His father

threw him a dark look as Traejan lifted his chin.

"I mean to fight tomorrow," he announced.

Xander gave him an impatient sigh and a look of exasperation. "We've been over this..." he began when he was interrupted.

"Very well," the king said. Both princes turned to him, neither more surprised than the other. "If that is what you wish."

"No!" Xander exclaimed, "I mean," he quickly corrected, "I thought it was your wish that..."

"It was!" King Rowland thundered, cutting him off again. "It still is! But, look at him - he is going to do it, regardless. I won't have him doing it against the wishes of his father and the order of his king!"

A silence fell as if a door had been shut against a storm.

Traejan drew himself up, breathing deeply with emotion, and then went to his father. He intended to bow but the king embraced him, and held him tight. "Thank you, father," he whispered hoarsely. He could feel tears burning in his eyes and a hot lump had formed in his throat, making it painful to swallow.

"Thank *you*, son. You have done your people a service that you will never know, and now you are prepared to make the ultimate sacrifice for them."

Traejan, however, was not doing it for his people, not any more. From here on out, his reasons were purely selfish. He declined to say so, however, since his father's voice had gone as hoarse as his own. The king released his son from his embrace but still held him at arm's length and leveled his dark eyes at him. "Go see your mother before you leave," he commanded.

"I will," Traejan promised. "Grandfather, too."

The king nodded his approval and gave his son's shoulders a squeeze before letting him go and stepping back.

Traejan bowed low and turned to leave. Xander glared at him, saying nothing, and for that Traejan was unquestionably grateful. He left the atheneum and went to seek out his mother.

He found her outside her chambers, on the terrace with her ladies in waiting as the sun was finally beginning its descent. They were enjoying the late afternoon with chilled glasses of honeyed magnolia wine as the light began to change into something almost magical. To see them one would find it hard to believe a war was raging on during the daylight only two miles away.

The young prince paused in the shadows, watching them laugh and whisper while they ate delicate summer fruits, and tried to gauge the mix of emotions the sight stirred within him. Part of him wanted to be angry, to feel that they were being heartless at the sacrifices elves and men alike were making on their behalf. But more, he wished that it could be this way for them forever, that they would never know the horror of what he had seen.

"Good afternoon, ladies," the elfin prince greeted, stepping out onto the flagstone patio. "Or evening," he amended as the paper lanterns strung above the terrace were lit. "Mother," he added, bowing his golden blonde head.

"Traejan!" the queen exclaimed, delighted, as she rose to her feet. The ladies rose to their feet as well, murmuring greetings as the queen went to him and took his hands while he gave her a gentle kiss on each of her porcelain cheeks. "To what do I owe this rare honor?" she asked.

Traejan kept the smile on his face by sheer will. "I am going to be fighting tomorrow," he told her. The queen made no such effort to keep an agreeable expression. She dropped his hands and walked inside, leaving Traejan to follow and silence in their wake.

"What are you saying?" she asked, turning to him once they were inside. "Do *not* tell me you are here to say goodbye." Traejan fought a real smile.

"Trust me, mother. I am sure I will last for more than one battle."

"Is this about that woman?" she demanded. His expression froze. For half a second he was torn between lying and playing dumb but he answered her as simply as she had asked him.

"Yes."

His mother drew herself up. "Do you love her?"

"Yes."

The queen took a moment to process the information, her lips pressed tight into a thin line. "How so?"

"How so?" Traejan repeated with a gentle smile. "I'm not sure I understand what you mean."

"You most certainly do," his mother insisted. "You love this woman, fine. But to what degree? Is this some silly crush? Is it worth risking your life?"

The young prince straightened, his face now serious - finally understanding what his mother was implying. "I love her like I will love no others," he told her. "I want to be with her, I want to protect her, even if she does not need me to do so. I know without a doubt that I would sacrifice everything I have to be with her, even if it was for just a short amount of time."

"How much time?" the queen asked, her tone flat.

"An embrace, a kiss, but even if it were only to touch her hand, or have one last look into her eyes."

The queen's face became hard and her blue eyes filled with tears. "Then it seems you have found love, my son. It would kill me to lose you, but it would be worse to see you lose yourself." She reached out her arms and pulled him close, holding him tight and breathing deep against his shouder. "I love you, son," she whispered. "Fight for her if you must, but get back to me."

Traejan hugged his mother and pressed his lips against her white-blonde hair. "I will," he promised.

"There is something else I want you to do for me as well,"

she ordered as she took a step back.

"What is it?" Traejan asked.

The queen put a slim-fingered hand on his chest. "I want you to make peace with your brother." Traejan's demeanor transformed immediately and she did not miss it. "I see you know what I mean. I will not have discord within my own family. It is up to you to fix it."

"Why me?" Traejan asked, feeling like he was twenty years old again, or ten, it didn't matter. "Xander is older, shouldn't he be the one to make amends?"

"Xander is older," the queen agreed. "He is wiser, he is the politician. But you are stronger." Traejan sank, feeling his heart warmed by his mother's words but inwardly balking at what she was asking of him. "Repair the rift," she told her second son. She saw the hesitation in him, the anger he carried for his brother, and she smiled. "After all, if you are willing to die for this woman, a woman you might want me to welcome into my home one day, how hard can it be to make amends with your own kin?"

Traejan looked at his mother, his teeth clenched tight though they showed in a crescent of a smile and he shook his head. "It seems as though Xander is not the only politician around this castle, is he?"

The queen returned his smile, though hers was not forced. "Perhaps not."

Traejan kissed her cheeks again and took his leave to find Dell waiting in the hallway. "Get the horses," he instructed. "I have to speak to Xander, then I will meet you outside."

Dell bowed quickly and left as the Battle King was coming down the hallway. Traejan waited for him and tried to disguise his anger with a smile but his grandfather saw through it straightaway.

"What is it?" he asked, concerned. "Xander?"

"Yes," Traejan said. "Mother wants to me to make amends.

It only just makes me angrier!" The Battle King stifled a laugh and Traejan walked away, stopping in front of a window to stare out at the dusky garden. "Why does he hate me? He has no reason to do so and he was never like this before! I do not understand!"

"Really?" Acqtraejale answered, genuinely surprised. "Hate is a strong word for his animosity, but is the reason not obvious?"

Traejan spun around. "What do you mean? Is *what* not obvious?"

The Battle King shook his head, his long white tresses undulating behind him. "As a king," he told his grandson, "your principal occupation and absolute purpose is to protect your people."

The young prince shrugged, unmoved, and the Battle King laughed softly. "Don't you see, Traejan? You have taken that from him."

The elfin prince leaned back, confused. He had nothing to do with Xander, he had made sure of that from the beginning. He had never wanted anything to do with politics. He certainly had never taken anything from him.

Acqtraejale sighed, approached his grandson, and laid a hand on his shoulder. "You are the one fighting for our people. You are the one protecting our people. You are the one who is not afraid to ride into battle against an enemy that outmatches us in size or number. Xander, who has trained all his life to be a good king, can feel nothing but overshadowed and ineffectual when compared to you. Are you truly surprised that he acts the way he does?"

Traejan gave his grandfather a shamefaced smile, slightly chagrined. "Not when you put it that way. I thought he was just being an asshole."

Acqtraejale smiled. "He is," he agreed amiably. "But not without reason. Try to give him the benefit of the doubt."

Traejan sighed. "I already am."

"Good! Then go get it done!"

The elfin prince bowed to his grandfather and left for Xander's chambers. He found him sitting in his parlor, staring into an empty fireplace, a forgotten glass of wine near his hand. He was, thankfully, alone.

"What is it?" Xander asked, rising to his feet. "The Crommags?"

Traejan shook his head. "I just wanted to speak with you before I left."

"About what?" Xander asked guardedly.

Traejan smiled gently. "I just wanted to tell you that I love you. That I think you are going to be a great king someday, and I know it is because you have already dedicated your life to it." As angry as he had been earlier, Traejan found the words easy to say. Probably because they were all true. What did surprise him was to see tears shining in Xander's dark eyes.

"Thank you, Traejan," he whispered. He blinked back the tears and embraced his younger brother. "It means a lot to me to hear you say that." He pulled away, still clasping Traejan's shoulders, and a frown was creasing his dark brows. "You're not telling me that because you think..."

"I'm not going to die tomorrow!" Traejan insisted. "Why does everyone think that?" Xander laughed softly and Traejan gave him a smirk. "I'm just saying that I know that what you are doing is not easy, Three Gods know I could not do it. And Zephyrn...."

Both brothers laughed at the unspoken suggestion of Zephyrn running the kingdom before Traejan caught movement from the corner of his vision, making him turn.

Dell stood in the doorway and his expression alone was enough to chill Traejan's blood. Mustering his self-control, he turned back to his brother, forcing a smile. "I need to get back," he said. "I am glad we were able to talk tonight, even if for a moment."

"So am I," Xander said. "I am proud of you, of what you have done, of what you are doing."

Traejan smiled and embraced his brother again, holding him tight before letting him go. Then he turned and walked as calmly as he could to the doorway and kept going, letting Dell fall in next to him.

"The Gnomin have returned," the Praetorian reported, making the prince stop in his tracks.

"With the prisoners?" Traejan asked.

"Most of them," Dell affirmed.

After a moment of silent thought the young prince resumed walking and his guard kept step with him. "Are they with Halloran now?" he asked.

"Yes."

"In the white cabin?"

"Yes."

"Has...everyone else been notified?" Traejan asked.

"Yes. Jaden was already there," Dell added. "It seems he has received news from his scouts."

Traejan frowned but he did not slow. News from the scouts would unlikely be good. An already long day was going to turn into an equally long night. "Our horses?" he asked.

"Are waiting outside."

The Praetorian followed the brisk steps of the prince through the castle and out into the gloam of twilight. They mounted their horses and rode back to Kriegslager, pushing their horses without driving them into a full gallop.

The night sky loomed above a horizon of lavender and violet, stars just starting to wake and wink as the pair left their horses at the elfin corral and headed for the war room. Traejan, as always, was full of questions. As they entered the cabin, some of them were answered without having to be asked.

The Roshan was there, pale in her blacks but standing on her own and wearing a sword on her hip.

Ryen and Kamut stood behind her and she was flanked on either side by Gavan and Rhys. The other captains were there, even Zephyrn, gathered around the large map table. Halloran brightened when he saw Traejan and motioned for him to join the group.

"My Lord Prince," he greeted, "thank you for joining us." He turned to the captain of the scouts. "Jaden?" he prompted.

The Sylvan elf faced the others, his expression pained. "The next group of Crommags is arriving even as we speak. Another thousand or so, bringing with them fresh supplies."

A silence pervaded the group as the news sank in. It was unwelcome news, but inevitable.

The general harrumphed and shook his gray head. "The worse of it is that they bring a supply of fresh soldiers."

Every pair of eyes in the cabin left the captain of the scouts to touch briefly upon each other. For many, reality was just beginning to set in.

They had fought so courageously and lost so many, but the Crommags were to be replenished as if never touched. It was disheartening to the lowest degree.

Jaden shifted his weight and Halloran's steely eyes fixed on him.

"Or is it worse than that?" the general queried.

Jaden gave him a hangdog expression, as if the situation were his fault and he was shamed by it. "They are followed by another party of equal size, or more," the scout captain said softly, delivering this last bit of news in a hoarse whisper as if to speak the news aloud would make it real.

Everyone around the table exchanged expressions that varied between shock and horror. Each looked as if they had been struck, save for the general who merely looked as if he had swallowed something unpleasant.

"We are almost down to a third, from when we began," he announced with a scowl, "and they are now almost double."

The heavy silence descended again upon the room, broken finally by the red commander.

"We cannot win this war," she said gently, looking at the others one by one. "At least not at this time, not with what we have."

"We will not give up," Nevin told her, firm.

"Can you retreat?" she asked. "Live to fight another day?"

The aging Jäger bristled at the suggestion, but he was wise enough to know it would be the only way to save the elfin people. The small army they had was not going to do it, no matter how well they were trained or how hard they fought or what allies they had. There were simply not enough of them. Everyone there knew it.

"I say no," Jennings announced, unflinching. "I would rather die fighting than see those beasts in our city."

"You might very well get that chance," Halloran told him. He waited to see if anyone else had an opinion they wanted to voice and then his eyes went to Traejan. "My Lord Prince," he said, "it is your decision."

The young elf swallowed as the choice was passed to him. He realized for the first time that he was truly the one in charge of the army. He was ultimately responsible for the lives of the soldiers, and for all of those they fought to protect. It was not a decision he ever thought he would have to make.

The warrior in him sided with Nevin and Jennings. He would rather go down fighting than to see the enemy inside Tuar Ceath. He knew he was not the only one, and that even those who felt differently would still stand by his decision and fight by his side.

But he was no fool.

It would be valiant for the soldiers to die fighting, but who would be next when all the soldiers were dead?

"Is there a way," he asked Halloran, feeling as if he had been punched in the chest, "to evacuate the city?"

Every elfin eye was filled with dismay at this question, though each one had been wondering the same.

The general pursed his lips as he thought. "We can take the Crook – the pass between the Mountain of the Sun and the Mountain of the Moon, but it will put us where we can run into more Crommags. We could go north, towards the Vikes, but it will be a hard trek, especially for the woman, the children, and the elderly."

"There might be another way," the Roshan ventured. All eyes moved to her and Traejan could see that she was forcing herself to breathe in a normal manner, but it pained her. "By boats and rafts, on the river."

"It would be less taxing," Nevin agreed, "but possibly just as dangerous as trekking through the mountains."

"Aye," Jennings agreed. "There are rapids to the south."

"Possibly not dangerous, though. I cannot say for sure, but I will find out as soon as we are done here."

There was a heavy silence, broken by the general. "Then, by all means," he announced, "let us be done here." His steely eyes went to Traejan. "That is," he continued "if that is what you command."

Traejan thought of how hard they had fought, of how much fight they had left in them. Then he thought of all of the Crommags that were still pouring into the Greatwood, unbloodied and bloodthirsty.

"It is."

Halloran wasted no time as he turned immediately to Zephyrn. "My Lord Prince, I would like you and Captain Espytin to work on the evacuation." The elfin prince and the supply captain gave him a nod of assent. "All of you other captains, start planning our defenses. I want to hold the field for as long as we are able before we have to fall back to the city."

There were more nods and then the entire party broke apart into smaller groups. Traejan went straight to Ember as Gavan and Rhys moved away from her to speak with the elfin captains.

"Don't ask her how she is," Ryen advised as the elf stopped in front of her. The prince gave him a reproachful look and a bit of a smile.

"I know better," he told the Vikeman.

"I need to get to a riverbank," she told Traejan. "Upstream from our camp."

"Can you ride?" he asked.

The Roshan gave him a curt nod.

"I'll get Coal," Ryen said, leaving quickly.

Espytin looked at Zephyrn and jerked his chin towards Wilhelm and Heinz. They approached the pair with disarming smiles.

"I don't suppose you know how to make boats?" Prince Zephyrn asked.

"No," Heinz answered with a smile of his own, "but that doesn't mean we cannot figure it out."

"If you already have one built," Wil said, "we can discern the dimensions and make as many reproductions as you need. If you have a boat builder that can answer questions for us, that would be even better."

"I can get you both," Espytin said.

Zephyrn chuckled softly and looked at Wilhelm in admiration. "The Gnomin are never so happy as when they are busy, your hands full of one task or many," he remarked.

The Gnomin team leader shook his head and corrected the young prince.

"Productive," he said, "not busy. There is a big difference. Anyone can be busy. We like to get things done."

The Roshan and the prince turned to follow Ryen, though moving much slower, throwing parting glances at Kamut and the grizzled commander.

"I know I'm not supposed to ask," Traejan said once they had left the others behind, "but…."

"It hurts like the Seventh Circle," the Roshan informed him. "But I'll live. I've been hurt worse."

She moved awkwardly and Traejan could hear her labored breathing. He wanted badly to put an arm around her and help but he knew, injured or not, she might still kill him if he tried. Especially in front of the others.

The grizzled commander, his strong jaw already salt and peppered with stubble, watched them go and sighed before he turned to the Vikeman.

The shaved sides of Kamut's head were also stubbled and his long braid was matted with sweat and blood. There was a slash between his eyes and under his vest there was a bruise spreading from his shoulder to his chest from the club of some Crommag whose body was now growing cold on the battlefield.

"I cannot thank you enough for your help and the service you have done to the elfin people," the general told the Norseman. "But if your men would like to evacuate with the others, I will be glad to offer you passage."

Halloran was tall for an elf, and broad-shouldered as well, but the Vikeman looked both able and ready to crush him.

"I will pretend you didn't say that," Kamut rumbled.

A slow smile made its way across Halloran's face. "Then I will do the same."

Traejan and Ember left the cabin, the door guarded by Dell and Dirk, though Dell fell in silently behind them. Outside it was finally full dark, save for a waxing moon rising against a bed of stars. Ryen was already returning on the back of the Roshan's Night Stallion and reined him to a halt in front of the cabin.

"He let you ride him?" she asked, astounded as the Vikeman threw a leg over the great beast and slid down. Despite his large frame, he still dropped a good two feet before his boots hit the ground.

"I think he knows something is going on with you," Ryen remarked, flipping the reins over the horn of the saddle. "I think he actually might be worried." From a nearby bramblebush, a nightingale called loudly and Ryen gave the Roshan a smirk. "And he's not the only one."

Ember clucked her tongue at Coal and, as the massive beast sank to his knees, she returned the Vikeman's leering grin. "You actually look good on him – very fitting. You should see into getting a Night Stallion of your own."

Ryen chuckled. "Let me know if you come across another. I certainly do not plan on fighting a Night Mare to get one."

The Roshan, wincing, climbed cautiously into the saddle, followed unexpectedly by the elfin prince. Her contorted face transformed instantly into a scowl.

"I don't need…" she started.

"I'm not asking," Traejan finished, putting his arms around her. He clucked his tongue at Coal and the Night Stallion carefully rose back up. The Roshan shook her head, a small smile tucked into the corner of her mouth.

"The south bend?" Dell asked. Traejan nodded in the affirmative and the Praetorian turned and jogged away to retrieve his own horse.

"We can talk when I get back," the Roshan told Ryen, taking up the reins. The Vikeman nodded as she put her heels to her horse, grimacing with the effort. Then she and the elfin prince rode off as he told her softly the direction she should take.

From his branch on the bramblebush, the nightingale tittered and the Vikeman scowled at it.

"Well?" he demanded. "Aren't you going to follow her?"

The bird flew off without another note.

The elfin prince and the Roshan rode slowly though the camp, angling northeast towards the Gnomin camp but, before they reached the Gnomin tents, Traejan pointed at a path that cut through the forest behind the tents of the miners.

"There," he said.

Ember guided the Night Stallion into the woods, grunting softly as the great beast went up a small inline, forcing her to lean forward.

Traejan pressed his face against Ember's red hair, made black by the darkness. And though his hands wanted to be everywhere on her body, he kept his arms low, wary of the ghastly wound in her side.

"I know," the Roshan said softly as she leaned back against his body. "I feel the same way."

"Will you come stay with me tonight?" Traejan asked. "I'm not asking that...that you...I know you are..."

The Roshan chortled softly at his distress. "I know that is not what you meant, but no," she answered, her shoulders dropping. "I must stay with my men and you must stay with yours."

Traejan nodded, understanding. The woods were quiet, even more so as they went along and left the sounds of the camp behind. The pair was silent as they rode, simply absorbing the feel of each other.

After two short minutes the young prince felt Ember stiffen, suddenly aware that they were being followed. "It's just Dell," Traejan assured softly.

The Roshan nodded. "His horse is as quiet as he is."

The Praetorian followed silently as they trekked through the forest until it opened up onto the river where it curved around a giant toss of boulders and continued on its way to the sea. The light of the silvery moon reflected off the water and illuminated the entire strand.

The bend of the waterway had an expansive shallow with a long sandy beach. The river was wide and moved slowly here. The Roshan's glittering eyes moved across it quickly, appraising it.

"Excellent," she said. "This will be perfect." She clucked her tongue at Coal and he carefully sank to his knees. Traejan was off in a blink, taking Ember's elbow to help her down. Her face was taut with pain but she refrained from making a sound as she climbed from the Night Stallion's back. She smiled at the elfin prince, grateful. "Stay here," she instructed.

Traejan gave a her a quizzical look but obeyed, taking Coal's reins before she turned and walked towards the water. Coal gave a snort and rose back up. The Roshan went to where the river lapped at the sand and knelt at the edge. She waited for a few moments, hearing Dell dismount behind her and join his charge, and then she tentatively stuck her hand into the water.

The river was shockingly cold, fresh snowmelt making its way south. It was very different from the Ravensbrook near where she lived, which traveled through volcanic mountains and over sulfuric hot springs before continuing on its way through the woods of the Southlon.

The Roshan held her fingers in the icy waters, waiting. The prince and his Praetorian watched.

Only moments later, all of them caught movement to the right, their heads turning south in unison. A man was walking out of the water, dressed in a turquoise tunic over sea-green trousers tucked into boots that were brown, and dry. His eyes were the color of a lagoon at sunrise and his hair was a blonde so pale that it would shame any Seleucian elf.

"Roshan," he greeted warmly, dipping down to retrieve her hand and pull her to her feet.

"My Lord Prince," she responded formally.

"I am not your prince," he returned.

You got that right, Traejan thought with a touch of irritation.

"Please," Greenwater continued, "call me Tristan."

Ember grinned. "And I am not your Roshan, please call me Ember."

The Prince of Tides dipped his white-blonde head in acquiescence as Traejan, his lips turned down at the corners, gave Dell a sidelong glance. *Can you believe this?* the look said. Dell smiled and turned his attention back to the pair at the river's edge.

Tristan's smile melted into an expression of concern. "You are hurt." It was a statement, not a question, and almost angry at the realization.

The Roshan tipped her head to the side, her shoulders moving in the smallest of shrugs. "I was wounded in battle. That is not why I am here."

Tristan's look of concern hardened. "Where?"

"Morgan's Vale," she said dismissively with a crooked smile.

The Prince of Tides frowned. "You know that is not what I meant," he said, stern.

Ember froze as if she meant to argue rather than answer, then she sighed and raised her right hand and gently touched her side.

"Come into the water," Tristan commanded. The Roshan paused, then unbuckled her sword belt and tossed it down onto the sand before walking into the river. Tristan walked with her until the water swirled around her thighs. "Show me," he said.

Ember reached down, grabbed the bottom of her black shirt above her hip and pulled it up to the top of her ribcage. The water prince winced at the sight of it. The seam of flesh that ran from her hip up her side was an angry red, swollen and blistered from where it had been cauterized.

Tristan put a hand on her opposite hip to hold her steady and then scooped up a handful of water and poured it over her injured side. The Roshan gasped. It felt as if her skin and the flesh underneath were burning and freezing at the same time. The Prince of Tides repeated his movements over and over, cleansing the wound.

Finally, he released the Roshan and stepped back. Ember looked down, craning her neck to see. The skin was smooth, mostly, and pale. The seam was a faint scar, as if it had happened a long time ago. She looked up and stared at Tristan, her eyes like small moons in her face. The Prince of Tides smiled.

"What did you want to see me about, if not that?" he asked.

The Roshan lowered her shirt slowly, searching for her voice. "The elves are going to leave the city," she finally said.

"By way of the river?"

The Roshan nodded. "If you think it will be safe."

"It will be," Tristan affirmed immediately. "I will guarantee their safe passage. All the way across the Bay of Ships and to Atlantea if they wish."

"I had not considered that far, and it will be up to the king, I am sure, but I will pass that along. I am told there are rough waters to the south," she said, concerned.

"They will be as calm as a pond," the Prince of Tides assured her. "Ready the boats and bring them here," he instructed. "My men will cover their departure, for we are allowed to defend at all costs, even if forbidden to battle."

The Roshan nodded in understanding and together they

waded from the water to the riverbank, the prince holding her arm to keep her steady in the mild current. Once they were back on solid ground, Ember turned to face him.

"I cannot thank you enough," she said.

A line formed between Tristan's blonde brows. "I am the one," he corrected, "that is indebted to you. I am chagrined that I cannot fight with you, or for you in battle, but I am hesitant to go against the demands of my father."

The Roshan smiled. "I would not have dared go against the demands of my own father either," she told him.

His expression softened at that and he gave her a glimpse of a smile. "Should you come within sight of the water, however, that will change. And," he added, "should you be injured again, come seek me at once."

The Roshan's smile widened and she bowed to him, wondering how many Atlantean women went to sleep every night and dreamed of those blue-green eyes.

Probably all of them, she thought as the prince bowed to her in return, reaching out to run a fingertip gently along her sword arm as she turned away. She strode up the riverbank as the Prince of Atlantea returned to the water.

Traejan watched her with a mixture of concern and curiosity. She swept up her sword belt and buckled it back on, her fingers deft and quick. She moved as if she had not been injured at all.

"Did you hear what he said?" she asked the young prince, as she walked up the gentle slope of sand to where he waited with Coal.

"Of course," he answered. "And I saw what he did." She took the reins from him and stuck a boot into a stirrup. She yanked herself into the saddle and looked down at the elf, waiting for him to join her. He stared at her in wonder before pulling himself up behind her. "I guess I don't need to ask you how you feel," he said, sliding his hands over her hips. Despite what he saw, he was hesitant to move his hands any further.

The Roshan threw him a wicked smile from over her shoulder as Dell mounted his courser. "Feel for yourself," she told him, putting her heels to Coal to get him going.

Traejan slipped his right hand under her shirt and gently moved it up over the side of her ribcage, letting his thumb come down in an arc where she had been cut and burned. The was a ripple there in her skin, so thin that he imagined it would be almost unnoticeable, especially amongst all her other scars.

"By the Gods and the Circles," he whispered.

"You're telling me," Ember answered. "More than just healed – I feel like I have just slept a whole week and had an entire pot of coffee."

The young prince smiled and moved his hand up until it was cupping her breast. He dipped his head until his lips were next to her ear.

"In that case, come and stay with me tonight," he whispered. "Or at least pay me a visit."

The Roshan's smile widened. "Maybe I will," she said. "Maybe I will."

26. RETREAT

Back at camp there was a stunning amount of activity. The cookfires had been stoked and braziers had been brought outside for more light. What was left of the supply building was quickly being dismantled. Men and elves moved everywhere. A few Gnomin moved among them but, tonight, they were mostly attending to their own. All of the Vikemen were out, lending their strength.

"I feel this day has lasted a week," Dell remarked as their horses approached the cabin, "and I have the feeling the night will prove to be equally long." He reined in his courser and dropped from her back, signaling for a groom to come and take her.

"Then I owe the Prince of Tides even more thanks," the Roshan said, reining Coal to a stop as well. "I feel better now than when this war began."

"Save some for me," Traejan said in her ear, pressing his lips ever so slightly against the corner of her jaw before he slipped down from her horse. Despite the height, he landed lightly on his feet. He placed his hand over the toe of her boot and looked up at her. "I will inform the general immediately of the security Tristan Greenwater has offered. Where are you headed?"

"First," Ember replied, looking west, "to see my men. Then I'll find Ryen and meet you at the cabin."

"Give him a kiss for me," Traejan said, smirking.

The Roshan scowled at the young prince. "Do not antagonize him," she scolded. The elf scowled back up at her.

"He's been antagonizing me," he argued, "for weeks!"

Ember looked down at him, a small smile tucked into the corner of her mouth. "Whose place would you rather be in now?" she asked.

"Ugh!" the prince grumbled, pushing on her boot as he turned and strode away, Dell at his elbow.

The Roshan laughed and turned her massive horse towards the red camp. She truly did feel better than she had in a very long time and it showed as she rode up to her tent. Ian, along with Aiden and half of the Wildboys were outside, waiting. Patrek stood in the shadows with his arms crossed over his chest and two pages at his side.

Ian hurried to her as she dismounted, while Patrek grinned and sent one page running. The Wildboys gave a shout of cheer at her return, jumping around like a pack of jackals. Ian, ever concerned, tried to help her walk but she pushed his hands away with a good-natured grin. "Get me a glass of wine," she told him.

"Yes!" Aiden called loudly. "Bring her wine!" He went to her and, though he wanted to embrace her, he had seen the grievous wound she had suffered and clasped her hands instead. "How are you, my lady?" he asked earnestly.

The Roshan gave him a rakish look. "Ready to fight," she told him. The Wildboys let up a howl at this and danced around each other as she turned to the red captain who was grinning at her from ear to ear. He dipped his auburn head respectfully then straightened, his lavender eyes made violet by the night.

"The rest of our injured soldiers have been attended to," he reported. "Gavan and Rhys are in the white cabin. Ryen is inside your tent."

The muscles in the Roshan jaws flexed. "Get Sloan and go to the cabin. I will meet you there in twenty minutes."

He gave her a brisk nod before he dispatched the second

page to fetch the other captain. The Roshan turned and entered her tent. The Vikeman she had known for many years, had fought with and even loved, was seated in one of the chairs by the desk, drinking a cup of wine. She could tell in a single glance – and mostly by his position and his expression – that he had drunk a few cups already.

"Care to join me?" he asked.

Ian handed the Roshan a cup but stayed in front her. His beautiful face was drawn and his dark eyes were full of apprehension, though it had nothing to do with the Vikeman.

"Go ahead," Ember challenged. "Take a look."

Ian held back for a moment, then reached forward and carefully lifted the edge of her black shirt and raised it up. He got one good look at her side before his dark eyes lifted back up to stare into her own. "How?" he asked.

"It seems the Prince of Tides is a bit of a demi-god," Ryen announced rather loudly, tilting his head to the left so that he could see around Ian as the steward lowered the hem of the Roshan's shirt. "But don't worry about losing your job," the Vikeman assured her squire as he leaned back in his chair. "I have the feeling his powers only work while he is in the water." His icy blue eyes went to Ember. "But he's not the prince I need to worry about? Is he? He is not the one I lost you to."

The Roshan pressed her lips together and, glancing at Ian, jerked her chin towards the tent flap. He did not look pleased about having to leave, but he ducked out reluctantly and she sat herself across from the Vikeman.

"How does your boy feel about him?" Ryen asked, watching Ian leave. The Roshan too, watched him go and she sighed.

"You keep calling him a boy and I keep correcting you. But, in a way, you are right. He is still a child in many ways, they all are. Except for Marco, which is perhaps why they look to him as a king, but also like a father. The rest are like children. Children that have been forced to suffer through what no child should have to face, no adult either for that matter." She turned her face and her eyes of amber and green and gold sought out the icy blue gaze of the Vikeman. "I learned a lot, living in Redtown this past year. A lot about myself. And it made me feel small. I always thought I was entitled to know about my family. That I deserved more than what I was given. Living with these people, Ryen, made realize how foolish and selfish such thoughts were. It made me realize that none of us are entitled to anything. We take what is given to us, and what we do with that is what makes us who we are."

Ryen studied her with his glacier blue eyes for moment and a smile so small that it was almost sad played at the corners of his mouth. "I love you, you know."

The Roshan nodded, her crooked smile mirroring the same edge of sadness. "I know. I love you too. Are you angry?"

Ryen was thoughtful for a moment and then shook his head. "No. A little hurt." Ember bit her lip.

"You know it never would have worked for us."

"I know. That doesn't make me love you any less."

Ember took a drink from her cup and rolled it between her palms. "Why hurt?" she asked.

"Because when you finally chose, it wasn't me."

"I did not choose," she said softly. "I was chosen."

Ryen grunted. "In that case, I *am* angry. And jealous."

"Jealous?" Ember asked, surprised. "Your taste for women is more varied than my taste for wine."

That brought a smile to his lips. "That is true. But I like to hoard treasure – it's in my blood. And you are the greatest treasure I have ever found." Ember smiled and took another drink from her cup. "You love him?" he asked, his blue eyes still doubtful as they searched her own. "Truly?"

"More than my own life," she answered without hesitation. Ryen's body jerked slightly, stung, but his face remained expressionless.

"Then I am happy for you," he told her. "I hope you both live long enough to enjoy it."

"So do I," the Roshan agreed, draining her cup. "Let's get to the cabin." The Vikeman drained his cup as well and stood. "Besides," she said, grinning at him as he pulled her to her feet, "if you and I were together, what do you think would happen should your fidelity...slip?"

"I think one of your knives might do the same," he said, pulling her close and kissing the top of her head. "Perhaps you are right," he conceded as followed her from the tent. "Maybe it is better this way."

The Roshan laughed as she turned to make her way to the white cabin. The leader of the Wildboys fell in step on her other side and she smiled. She could not ask for a better honor guard.

At what remained of the supply building, the Norsemen were busy removing sections of walls and organizing them carefully. Ryen motioned at two that were shouting orders at the others.

"Aksel and Birger are both from shipbuilding families," Ryen said. "They are from the borough closest to the sea."

The Roshan nodded and looked at Aiden. "Get your men to help them," she instructed. "They are short-handed tonight."

"Not for long," Aiden assured her before he turned on his heel and ran back in the direction they had come.

Inside the cabin, the captains and the general, along with Otto and Wilhelm, were at a table on the right side of the room, gathered around a map that showed the Elysian Forest and the river.

"Here," Traejan was saying, his finger on the map, "is where we will launch the boats." He glanced up at the approach of the Roshan and the Vikeman and waited for them to join the others at the table. "Our retreat will be as prolonged as possible, falling all the way back to the Great Lawn as our last point of defense, but if we fall back as far as here," the young prince moved his finger northward and stopped, "and our people are still evacuating the city, we have to do everything we can to keep the Crommags from the woods."

"We can rig the treeline with traps," Otto told them.

"And explosives," Wil added.

"I can fill the trees along here," Zephyrn said, tracing an arc on the map, "with archers."

"And I will have an equal amount of Jägers," Dell said, "right underneath them."

Halloran nodded in satisfaction. "It will be up to our army to hold the field of battle for as long as possible so we have time to build what watercraft we can and for our people and allies to get away."

"If we lose the field," Jennings said, his eyes on the map, "we can hold them here, at the slope, for quite some time. Their forces will be bottlenecked and have the disadvantage of fighting uphill."

"I suggest holding the field with our infantry for as long as we can," the Roshan said, "with the elfin infantry protecting the slope."

"My archers will provide support as well," Zephyrn affirmed, "thinning out the enemy ranks as best we can."

Traejan gave a him an approving smile, hardly able to believe this was the same younger brother that had spent a lifetime indulging himself in leisurely pursuits.

All eyes moved then, glancing at one another, waiting to see if there were any more suggestions to be made. Seeing there were none, the general straightened his broad shoulders and gave his captains a quick nod.

"Very well," he announced. "It has been a long day and the dawn will come soon. I will see you all at our normal hour, unless we are alerted of an advance by the enemy."

❧❧

It had been a long day for Ayala as well. By the time the elves and their allies were calling it a night, the leader of the Great Men was finally retiring to his own tent with a horn of grog. His leg was throbbing, his maimed hand was stiffening, and the spot where he had pulled the cagna's knife from his shoulder was aching. Worse, though, was that his head was pounding.

The Great Man took a drink of grog and looked at what remained of his brother's head. The flesh had been boiled away and the empty eye sockets of the skull stared at him from atop an empty barrel. "And I thought your head was small before," he snorted before taking another pull from his grog. He sighed and sat down heavily on the hides that made the end of his bed

"I'd complain to you about my day," he said, "but yours was still probably worse." He took another drink. "Actually," he continued. "Mine was worse, because you didn't have a day at all." He shook his head slowly in disbelief. "Has it really been only one day?" he asked. "Just this morning since they found what was left of you?"

The mountain of a man shifted his weight and winced at the pain. His leg, like his hand, had been bandaged, but both hurt like demons.

"Sclecht and Spate arrived late this afternoon with the rest of Pel's Ice Walkers, which is good. I am quite sure that *cagna in neru* that you called the *Spirit of Death* is either dead or dying, which is also good. I cut her open like a winter goat and now one of the elfish leaders is gone, making them even weaker than before. But what tries me, besides these stupid wounds, is that the little metal men have disappeared. Not died, not escaped, for we would have seen them. They are just…gone."

Ayala licked his lips. "We have plenty of weapons laid by, and the little men were becoming of little use, but the whispers it raises…"

The leader of the Great Men looked at the skull as if waiting for it to answer. He drank and he waited. He needed Noga's opinion, his advice, now as ever. After an hour, and another horn of grog, the skull finally spoke.

An hour before dawn, Ayala dispatched his own tribe to clear the battlefield of the dead. The Crommags, working nervously in the dim gloom of pre-dawn, dragged as many of the bloating corpses as they could and dropped them in the holes that had originally been dug to ensnare them. The huge pits had all been marked by Noga before they had arrived, and carefully uncovered.

The leader of the Great Men told them it was so the bodies would not get in the way, which was true, but he also did not want the incoming tribes to see the losses they had suffered at the hand of the elves. Even at the arrival of the Ice Walkers there was a muttering that did not bode well.

There was a strange river that rose up and swallowed Great Men whole. The elves, though smaller and weaker and horribly outnumbered, had not been driven from the field of battle they were determined to protect. The entire tribe of little metal men, in charge of the weaponry, had suddenly vanished.

Many whispered that the Great Men had ventured too far from the mountains. They were no longer in the domain of the God of Ice, but instead under the rule of foreign deities they did not understand.

As the sky lightened in the east, Ayala climbed atop the rock from where he had commanded the first two days of battle, the skull of his brother strapped across his broad back.

The enemy had already descended from their protected bluffs and had fanned out close to the slope. The leader of the Great Men leaned forward and squinted his eyes, trying better to make out a shadow at the front of their lines, then he straightened. It was no shadow.

It was the cagna.

Ready to fight as if she had not almost been cleaved in two just yesterday.

For the first time, the superstitious whispers began to flutter in Ayala's own mind. But he was a great man among the Great Men, and he shook his narrow head to clear it of the murmurs.

Today the elves would face fresh fighters and the Ice Walkers were eager for battle, awaiting the command to charge. They gnashed their fangs and pounded their chests, clashing their weapons together as they stomped their feet.

Yon, who had clambered up on the rock again with his leader, looked at him, waiting. Ayala, frowning at the enemy, gave a quick nod and Yon blew the horn. The members of the Ice Tribes let out a blood-curdling howl and began to move north across the field, picking up speed as they went.

After crossing the field and closing with the elves and their allies, the first line of warriors from the Ice Walkers was dropped by two companies of crossbowmen. After a single barrage, Sloan and Patrek's men slipped behind the infantry of the red army. The second line of Crommags were feathered by the elfin archers on the slope and the cliffs above. The third line, confused about their brethren falling dead all around them, met the red army and were cut to shreds.

Ayala found himself already used to their tactics and was not bothered in the least. The long-legged Ice Walkers simply stepped over their dead, howling like the winter wind and each swinging a long-handled adz.

The Roshan fought in the midst of them with the elfin prince, Traejanale Royce, at her right hand. The pair was flanked by four Vikemen on each side. As a fighting unit, they were both unreachable and indestructible. The red army was trained for such combat, and the elfin archers continued to pepper the ranks of the Crommags. Still, for every monster they cut down another two would take its place in the ranks, slobbering with bloodlust.

The battle wore on for an hour and then two. In the third hour, the infantry began to tire, and fall. Gavan, watching from his post on the earthen ramp, saw what was happening and charged forth, calling for the cavalry to follow.

The mounted troops spilled into the battlefield, replacing the flagging infantry. Gavan rode along the front towards his commander, cutting down Crommags as he went. Before he could reach her with an update on their movements, he was knocked from his horse by an errant cudgel.

The same second, the Roshan turned to see him go flying. "Gavan!" she shouted, seeing her captain fall. She cut down one Ice Walker and then leapt over another that was falling over with an arrow shaft in its neck.

She fought her way towards the golden-eyed youth as he was moving up slowly to one knee, the breath knocked from his body. A Crommag loomed over him with a five-foot long broadsword raised high above Gavan's unprotected head as he gasped for breath.

A dagger thrown into its neck by the Roshan gave her captain time to roll away and rise, faster this time and ready to fight. Gavan, laboring for breath, finished the beast with his own sword, and then turned to fight two more.

Ember stepped back from the front line, assessing what Gavan did not have the breath to tell her.

Ayala stood on his rock, appraising the heat and the strength of his own men. He hated that the men on horses were now just advancing. It was hot and getting hotter, and his men were slowing. But there were still ranks of Great Men from the Ice Walkers that had not tasted battle. He watched as they pushed their way forward and he waited.

The Roshan saw the fresh ranks moving forward as Gavan's men replaced the field troops. She knew that her own small company would soon begin to fail. Traejan struck down one Crommag and then spun around to cut down another with the momentum of his first swing. Then he dropped back slightly, looking at her for direction.

The Roshan stepped back into the fray and slashed apart two Crommags before turning to Ryen. "Call your men back!" she shouted, throwing a dagger at the nearest beast. "Send in your next group!"

Ryen gave her a nod of assent as he sliced a Crommag from neck to groin and then called to his men as Gavan went down a second time. Ember cursed and leapt in front of his body, stopping an adz with her sword before it was able to split his head. Again she turned to Ryen.

"Get him out of here!" she yelled.

"No!" Gavan shouted in protest even as the Vikeman grabbed him by the back of his collar and began to drag him from the battle.

The Roshan drove her sword into the closest Crommag as she turned to Traejan. "Have the Vikemen on your side fall back!" she shouted. Traejan moved to carry out the command, killing as he went.

Yasgir and Kamut took the field with seven more wild-eyed Vikemen. Yasgir, with his black hair streaming behind him and wielding an enormous battle axe, began felling Crommags left and right.

Ayala, watching from his place on the rock, saw a fresh barrage of the giant northmen join the battle and begin to force a wedge down the center of his army. Even in this battle, fresh Great Men were beginning to flag in the growing heat and the leader motioned for Yon to signal retreat.

The armies slowly pulled away from each other, snapping and howling and taking last jabs where they could.

The Roshan was atop Coal in seconds and rode hard up the earthen ramp, the fight dissipating in her wake. Traejan and Aiden followed, her own Praetorian guard. She reined in the Night Stallion at the top of the slope, her restless eyes searching until they spotted Ryen's khusar outside her own tent. She found the Vikeman inside where Ian was attending to Gavan.

"He has broken ribs," Ian told her after he had bound and wrapped the captain. "He should not ride, much less fight."

Gavan shouted curses at the steward from where he lay on the Roshan's cot. "Faith be damned, and you as well, if you take me from this fight!"

The Roshan grinned at him from around Ian's form. "Trust me, an injury like that will cause you more pain from shouting than fighting. Be still!"

Gavan, grimacing with the pain, relaxed back down as much as he could. He knew she was right, she always was, and hoped that he would have as much time as possible to heal.

He did not.

For the first time since the war began, the Crommags launched a second attack after the heat of the day began to fade. The red troops were the first to respond to the alert with Rhys leading their Second Cavalry and supported by Zephyrn's archers on the bluff. Together, they held the battlefield as the fading afternoon deepened into dusk.

Fortunately for the elves and their allies, as the light faded away, so did the Crommags. They melted back into the forest in a final retreat for the day.

They held the vale for two more days, buying as much time as they could for the boat makers while the elfin people packed as much of their lives as they could into sacks small enough for them to carry on their backs.

Finally, even the red troops began to flag, plagued with fatigue and falling to injuries. The black-haired Yasgir was knocked down by a Crommag mace and killed with another's sword. He was the first Vikeman to die. Rhys lost eighteen of his men. Twelve of Gavan's men were wounded grievously, five died. Patrek and Sloan each lost half a dozen crossbowmen.

The battle of numbers had truly commenced and the tide began to turn for the Crommag army.

That night, a funeral pyre was built for Yasgir. All of the Vikemen and many other soldiers gathered around to say farewell. Before it was lit, Sloan approached the body of Yasgir, laid out upon the wooden planks with his hands clasped over his chest, holding his mighty axe. The white-haired soldier lifted a crossbow and placed it by the Vikeman's side. As he turned to leave, he noticed one of the Vikemen on his knees.

He was one of the youngest of them, his black hair falling from a widow's peak and his black beard short not because it was trimmed, but because it had barely begun to grow. Sloan noted his hooked nose and the tears that slipped from dark blue eyes.

"Ingmar, is it?" Sloan asked. The young Vikeman nodded. "He was your father, wasn't he?" Again the Vikeman nodded. "He was a great man," Sloan told him.

The youth looked up, his dark blue eyes meeting the blue eyes of the silver-haired captain. "He was," he agreed. "And I will avenge him," he promised.

Sloan nodded and stood behind Ingmar as the pyre was lit.

The next day the elfin cavalry took the field as the city of Tuar Ceath made their final preparations for the evacuation.

The day after, the casualties were too great and they had to fall back to their positions on the cliff. The elfin infantry covered their retreat as the battle for the bluff began.

27. HEARTFELT GOODBYES

On the day after the red troops left the blood-soaked Morgan's Vale for the last time, the evacuation of Tuar Ceath began.

With Jennings and Nevin holding the slope with the elfin infantry, Traejan was at the river's edge to bid his family farewell. It was his father that embraced him the longest, releasing him at last to hold him at arm's length by his broad shoulders.

"You hold them off," he instructed, "and then take the pass. The Gnomin have assured me that the way is clear, but will be blocked after you have escaped."

Traejan nodded and smiled at his father. The Gnomin had assured him of the same, but Traejan knew the odds of any of those left behind escaping with their lives. It all depended on how quickly the evacuation went. With as many people as there were, the odds were slim. To none.

His mother gave him a perfunctory kiss on each cheek as if she expected to see him by dinner time. Xander gave him a dutiful hug but parted with a smile and, for that, Traejan was glad beyond measure. The young prince moved to his grandfather last, meaning to embrace him before helping him onto the waiting barge that had been made especially for the royal family and their Praetorian, but the Battle King stepped back quickly with a look of scorn.

"What are you doing?" he demanded of Traejan.

The young prince could only look at him, dumbfounded. "Saying goodbye," he answered honestly. "You have meant a great deal to me. More than you can ever..."

"Bah!" Acqtraejale spat. "Save it for later! I am not leaving."

"Excuse me?" Traejan asked, leaning towards the old elf, thinking he had misspoken or that he had misheard.

"You heard me fine," the Battle King admonished before turning and giving his own farewell embraces to those in his family, along with the Lady Karamine, that waited upon the barge.

Traejan's eyes sought out his father and the king, meeting his gaze, only shrugged in return. "It seems as though I can tell him what to do as well as I can you. All I can ask now is that you keep each other safe. Zephyrn too."

The young prince found himself without words so he smiled, and bowed to his father and watched as the barge was pushed gracefully out into the river. His family and their servants looked like ghosts in their pearly garb. Karamine stood among them like a shining jewel, wrapped in red silks embroidered with gold thread. They raised hands in farewell and Traejan did the same.

The royal barge, and all of the smaller watercraft that had been boarded, drifted off in a smooth current.

Up to his waist in the water, but seemingly dry, stood Tristan Greenwater. He was attended by dozens of water nymphs that helped manage the current and see to it that no one fell out of a boat.

Another group of elves moved down the bank as a group of Gnomin helped push more boats into the water. The elves looked at the watercraft with brave smiles and eyes brimming with terror. They held each other as they waited their turn to board, sharing the fear and the hope alike.

After the royal barge had sailed beyond his sight, Traejan turned to the Roshan, his smile melting into a scowl.

"Go to him," he commanded.

"I am fine," the Roshan argued, her voice low. Her face was pale and haggard. "He cannot heal what ails me."

"Go anyway," the young prince repeated.

Ember sighed and stepped into the water between the departing skiffs and rafts. Tristan spotted her and held up a hand, silently entreating her to stay where she was. The Prince of Tides instead came to her, beaming with that unearthly glow that only he seemed to possess.

"Are you hurt?" he asked, reaching out to touch her arm and hold her steady though only her boots were in the water.

The Roshan shrugged. "A few cuts and bruises, nothing so horrible as last time," she managed with a smile. The smile on Tristan's face, however, melted away.

"But you are hurting," he observed, one hand coming up to cup her face. "Worse than last time, if that is possible."

Ember's gem-like eyes stayed fixed upon his own blue-green gaze for a moment and then she nodded. "I have lost many men, and many more are injured. It is their pain I feel."

Tristan's smile resurfaced and he laid his hands on either side of the Roshan's face. "It is not their pain you feel," he said, "but the responsibility you feel for it. It is often a heavier burden than the pain alone." He gathered the Roshan to his body as if she were a child and she disappeared in the glow from his embrace.

The glow around their bodies intensified and grew brighter for a moment before it shimmered and then died away. "Send me your injured," the water prince whispered into the Roshan's hair as he released her. She stepped back, breathing deeply and standing straighter than she had before. Gone were her bruises and cuts. She felt as if she had awakened from a long and restful sleep.

For a moment she could only stare at him, then she laughed.

"You could make me a dangerous woman," she said.

Tristan smiled. "You are already a dangerous woman. And I believe you are also promised to another prince."

The Roshan laughed again and bowed her head in gratitude. "Thank you," she said. "And not just for me."

The Prince of Tides shook his head, his white-blonde hair shining. "It is nothing compared to our debt. I wish you would hold your battle here on the riverbank. That way I could at least fight unquestionably by your side."

The Roshan gave him a glimmer of a smile. "Maybe next time," she promised, moving up the bank from the shallows. He reached out and touched her hand as she left the river and, as he did, she felt the water being sucked from her boots, leaving them dry.

"Maybe next time," he echoed, walking backward into the current as she smiled at him in wonder and admiration.

From where Traejan kept a steady stance on solid ground, Ember felt him take a firm grasp on her elbow even as she saw Tristan fade away into the waters.

"How do you feel?" the elfin prince asked, remembering the transformation that had happened the last time she had taken to the waters with Prince Tristan.

"Ready to fight," she said.

Traejan's lips pulled down at the corners. "You are always ready to fight."

The Roshan laughed softly and looked up into his eyes. "But part of me feels empty, hollowed out somehow."

Traejan pulled her close and she pressed her face against his chest. "Come stay with me tonight. Perhaps just one good night of rest, with someone watching over you, you will feel whole again."

"You might be right," she agreed, "but that will not be tonight. Tonight I must bring as many of our injured men to the river as I can, so they may receive the same aid. They deserve healing and rest as much as I, and they will be all we have in the coming days to guard the evacuation."

The young prince pressed his lips against the top of her

head, kissing her hair. "You are right, of course. And the sooner we get them taken care of the better."

The Roshan finally sighed in satisfaction and together they turned to where the Battle King was in deep discussion with Duncan, one of his Praetorian guards. Duncan, like Drustin, who was currently reorganizing the elfin cavalry, had been with Acqtraejale Royce for centuries. The old elf was battle-scarred from wars in another galaxy.

"What are you two plotting?" Traejan asked, unable to stifle his smirk.

"Duncan, as you know, has been in charge of the defense of the city," his grandfather told him. "We were discussing the possibility of evacuations at the north bend of the river should we have to fall back."

"We should be able to hold the slope for some time," Traejan informed them. "A few days, at least. The Crommags are bottlenecked and are not able to spread out our lines so thin, plus we have the advantage of the high ground."

Acqtraejale nodded. "Very good. I will be staying at Castle Royce with a minimal staff, but we are planning on posting the last defenses in front of Castle Song. Send a messenger should anything change."

Traejan and the Roshan both bowed to the Battle King who, with Duncan, took their leave amongst the multitude of elfin citizens making their way to the river.

The elfin infantry alone held the slope for two days, while the evacuation steadily progressed. The red troops held it for the third.

On the third day, after the Crommags had finally had enough of the heat, General Halloran and his captains met in the mess pavilion. A map was on the table where they normally ate. The war room, like the supply building, had been dismantled and carted off to make boats and rafts.

As a group, their exhaustion showed as plain as their

physical wounds.

"The enemy has moved their camp here," Halloran informed them, pointing to a spot on the map that indicated the bottom of the bluff. "They have finally decided to spare themselves the morning march to battle and get right to it." He looked up at Prince Traejan, his steely eyes hard with an unspoken question.

The eyes of the elfin prince darted to the Roshan, dirty and bloody from another day of combat, and the muscles in his jaw tightened before his gaze went back to the general. "We can hold the slope for one more day," he informed him. "Two at most."

The Roshan frowned and looked as if she might argue, she certainly wanted to, but kept silent.

Halloran pursed his lips thoughtfully before he spoke. "Or how about none at all?" he asked.

"Excuse me?" Traejan responded.

"If we pack up tonight," the general advised, "and fall back to regroup on the Great Lawn, I am in hopes they will lose a day puzzling over where we went and what is going to happen next. We might even get another day as they move camp. From the way I see it, we can spend a day fighting or a day recovering."

"Though I would normally vote for a day of fighting, a day recovering would serve us well and them ill," Kamut said. The face of the lean Vikeman was tacky with blood that had come from a gash in his forehead. His opinion was met by murmurs of agreement and appreciation.

The general looked next at Zephyrn. "How goes the evacuation?"

"Smoothly," the youngest prince informed him. "Another day, two at the most, and we should have the entire civilian population out of the city."

"Find out if it is one or two. I want numbers – of civilians and soldiers both."

"Yes, sir," the prince acquiesced.

"Can you finish the river evacuation from the north bend?" Halloran asked.

"Absolutely," Zephyrn answered without hesitation. The general's gray eyes lifted and found Traejan's.

"It will allow our military to fall back to the castles," the older prince acquiesced, his brows high with optimism over his soft brown eyes, "we can guard the river from there until everyone is gone, and then slip through the Crook."

The general, his steely eyes full of the same prospect of hope, looked around to see if there was any dissent, but there was none. His gaze fell last upon the Battle King himself who had ridden to the camp for the purpose of this meeting. The white-haired elf only gave him a shrug and smile. The decision was the general's to make.

Halloran stood up straight and brought his big hands together in a single clap. "Very well!" he announced. "Let's get the fuck out of here."

The announcement was met with no small amount of quiet laughter and great relief. Word quickly spread through the mess and then throughout the rest of Kriegslager. It was finally time to pack up and move and all did so with astonishing haste. As the soldiers saw to weapons and horses, the Gnomin assisted in taking down tents and packing up supplies.

The Battle King and Duncan rode for the south bend in the river to start moving the evacuation to the north bend. Zephyrn and his archers went with them, securing their retreat and their new point of egress.

The elves and their allies fell back to the Great Lawn, the expanse of rolling green hills that fronted each of the three castles. Duncan, left in charge of the garrison, had set up a line of defense in a half-circle around Castle Song. Behind it, the tents were reassembled as the separate armies and races finally and truly merged as one. Dusk deepened into twilight and spirits were high once again.

The Gnomin erected a massive tent to serve as the mess hall and cooked an enormous meal for the garrison while the others began a harried dig in the woods, setting what traps and pitfalls they could in what time they had to guard the allies on their eastern flank. As darkness began to consume the diminishing light they worked with makeshift headlamps, just as they would in the mines. It was the final effort the race of miners and builders would accomplish in the war.

It was the wish of every ally that the Gnomin evacuate with the last of the people of Tuar Ceath - but it was surprisingly difficult to get them to do so. The Gnomin that had been rescued had recovered and rebounded with astonishing speed and every one of them wanted to help in any way they were able. Those who had been there since the beginning had made many friends among the elves and the red troops, and a special bond had been formed with all of the Vikemen. There were protests at first, some heated, before there were finally heartfelt goodbyes all around. Only two remained behind: Wilhelm and Otto.

The plan was to evacuate the Gnomin in the morning with the small populace of human farmers that had sought refuge in Tuar Ceath. After them would follow the last of the elfin citizens along with the support staff of the garrison. Once they were gone, the general would call in those defending the river. When the sun set the next day, the day after at the latest, they would all fall back and slip through the mountains. Wilhelm and Otto would trigger the explosives in the Crook to cover the retreating army,

It was a simple plan – almost too simple.

ᛒ

Ayala sat in his tent with Pel and Yon (and Noga's skull), drinking a horn of grog. The day had gone exceedingly well. It had been difficult fighting uphill the past few days, but they knew the elves had been forced to defend the narrow slope because their numbers were steadily dwindling. More importantly, just after the sun had set, their last group began to arrive.

The women and children, led by Gorig of the Cave Bear Tribe, arrived in the vale with the wagons that were laden with fresh supplies, including water and more barrels of grog. The women set to work putting up tents, tending to the wounded, and cooking a feast like the Great Men had not seen in weeks.

The sound of children was now heard, giving every soldier the feeling that they had already won and were in process of settling their new lands.

Gorig, accompanied by a bright-eyed runner, ducked into the leader's tent.

"Great Ayala," Gorig greeted, giving a quick nod to the others in the tent. "This runner has something I think you should hear." Ayala did not recognize the young Crommag and he assumed he must have just arrived. It was obvious the youth was nearly bursting with excitement.

The leader of the Great Men wiped his mouth with the back of his huge hand and nodded at the runner to say his piece.

"Great Leader," the youth said, "I am Rog, of the Cave Bear Tribe." He was broad shouldered, as all Crommags were, but he still lacked the muscle and fat of one full-grown.

"You just arrived?" Ayala asked.

"I did," Rog confirmed, "along with my two brothers." The leader of the Great Men gave him a nod and he continued. "We put up our tent and decided to take a look around. We spoke with the sentries at the base of the slope. They said we had already missed the commotion at the top of the cliffs, and the elves had already gone to sleep. Thinking they were sleeping, my brothers and I crept up to take a closer look."

He stopped, as if his whole story had been told. Ayala scowled at him for wasting time. "And?" he growled.

"And they are gone," Rog told him, glancing at the others who were also now frowning at him. "The elves are gone. The sentry said I should tell you right away."

The leader of the Great Men could only stare at the youth for long moments before turning his narrow head to the others, all of them showing the same amount of surprise. Then his eyes fell upon the skull of his brother.

Why would they leave? Ayala silently asked.

They no longer have the numbers to hold the cliff, Noga answered with equal silence. *I told you it was just a matter of time.*

What should we do? Ayala asked.

What they least expect, Noga advised.

The leader of the Great Men was silent for a few more moments, the others watching him stare at the grinning skull.

"They no longer have the numbers to hold their position," Ayala announced, beady eyes marking the others. "They are running away, scared. We must do something they do not expect."

"What would that be?" Yon asked.

Ayala grinned, showing his ghastly set of fangs. "Hunt them down and kill them."

Everyone in the tent exchanged quick glances. Gorig and Rog were obviously excited at the suggestion. Pel appeared the most doubtful.

As he should, Ayla thought. Of all the Great Men, the Ice Walkers had the poorest eyesight and it was even worse in the dark. The Cave Bear tribe had the best. *And they are fresh and eager for battle,* the Great Leader accurately surmised.

"How well can you see tonight?" he asked Rog.

"Well enough to march and fight," the youth answered with a grin of his own, though it was much less grisly. "The moon is as full and bright as a berg."

The leader of the Great Men looked at Gorig who nodded his assent, his fangs gleaming in the light of the tent. "Assemble your men," Ayala told him. "You may lead an attack on the elves tonight, if you can find them."

"We will find them," Gorig assured the leader of the Great Men before he bowed and left with the young runner.

Ayala drained his grog and laid the empty horn next to his brother's skull. "Come with me," he instructed, looking at Yon before his dark eyes found Pel. "You prepare the camp to be ready to move at first light."

The other Great Men nodded, finished their own grog, and moved to do his bidding. They both knew that his plan was both unexpected and cunning. There would be a great victory before the sun rose again.

Two things saved the elves and their allies that night.

One, was the moon. Though the young Crommag runner had been right, it was as bright as a berg, the moon was already descending by the time the Great Men had made their way up the slope and began their cautious exploration at the top of the bluffs.

They crept slowly over the fields that had been trampled and deserted. Instinctively, they wanted to move through the cover of the forest, something they had grown accustomed to over the past weeks. But there the moon was almost entirely blotted out by the trees and they were as good as blind.

So they went across the open country, feeling exposed but still confident even as the moon slowly sank in the west.

The second thing that saved the elves that night were the Jägers. Able to see in the dark almost as well as the day, their keen eyes spotted the Crommags long before they reached the camp. The alarm went up, spurring the approaching monsters into a flat-out run as the elves and their allies snatched up weapons and ran out to meet them.

They rushed in from every angle it seemed, taking down elves and men at every turn. Then, though they had not planned a defense in case of a night attack, everyone came together quickly. Dell ordered the Jägers to fan out on the sides of the invaders in an effort to contain the beasts, lest their own lines be broken and overrun.

Quickly, everyone came together. It mattered not if they were red army or elf, Vikeman, man, or Gnomin. There was no battle plan. Each one of them seized a weapon and put his back to a fellow comrade.

Once organized, the attack was quickly thrust back, and another one did not come for long moments. When it did, it was brutal. A crushing wall of massive bodies came rolling like a tidal wave and fell upon the allies.

But the Jägers, joined by the Vikemen, drove so relentlessly at the flanks of the Crommags that the monsters were pushed slowly into a box that was collapsing all around them. Then, unbeknownst to the elves, the weapons of the Cave Bear Tribe began to come apart. Swords broke off at the hilt and the heads on every mace and adz were falling away after the first kill.

The moon, sinking behind the mountains, finally winked out and her residual light was no longer enough for the Crommags to see. Weaponless and blind, they broke and ran.

The elves and their allies were too battered to raise a cheer. With hands on knees and heads hung low, they gathered themselves and sought out their dead and injured in the dark.

Among those found were Ingmar, the son of Yasgir, and the redoubtable Kamut.

As well as Sloan, the silver-haired captain of the red troops.

It was a long night. They had hoped for rest and respite, but instead suffered some of their cruelest losses in just over an hour of repelling a single attack.

The Roshan sent everyone from her, to get food and rest,

and sat vigil with her fallen captain all night. An hour before dawn, as the sky began to lighten in the east she rose from the camp chair, her muscles as stiff as her clothes, and knelt by the cot where his body lay with his hands crossed over his sword. She leaned forward and grasped his hands in her own.

"The Vikemen believe in Valhalla," she whispered to the white-haired bowman. "The elves believe in heaven, and the humans believe in the Seven Circles, the highest of those being the First Circle, the Circle of Light. I do not know which of them is right, or if maybe all of them are, but I know you have a soul, and it is where it should be right now, cloaked in glory."

She rose, leaning down to place a kiss on his forehead and then left the tent. Though it was still an hour until the sun would rise in the east, the elfin army was already assembling. The Roshan was greeted by what she fondly thought of as her own Praetorian guard: Traejan, Ryen, Aiden, and Ian. The first thing that caught her eye, however, was that Ian was wearing his sword, his hand resting on the hilt.

"Seven Hells," she muttered.

As she walked towards them they broke apart and turned to follow her as she made her way around the tents so she could get a good look to the south, but her first glimpse stopped her boots in their tracks.

The Crommags were not close, maybe a quarter of a mile away, but their ranks spread across the Great Lawn and far back into Fosse Meadow, their ranks too deep to count. They were but shadows in the predawn light, but they outnumbered the elves and their allies more than they had when the war began.

The Roshan guessed the elves probably had three hundred soldiers at most. She knew her own count to the number – one hundred and eighty-eight. It was going to be a slaughter.

Ember turned and strode for the small pavilion that had been erected to replace the war room of the white cabin. She found the general inside, dispatching orders and cursing with the same effectual calm while soldiers moved all around him. He, too, was wearing a sword.

"I need those numbers!" The general thundered. "Where is Prince Zephyrn?" he asked, his head swiveling around.

"Right here, sir," Zephyrn said, stepping forward. "We have just over two hundred civilians that have stayed until the last, mostly families of the soldiers."

"Get them out of here!"

"And nearly one hundred that have served as staff for either the castles or the camp."

"We can fend for ourselves," the general growled. "Get them on rafts."

Zephyrn's blonde head dipped in acquiescence. "They, with the Gnomin and the last of the human refugees, will take at least a day and a half. Possibly two days." The prince hung his head, as if ashamed to have to deliver such news, but the general placed a large hand upon his narrow shoulder and gave it a squeeze.

"Then we will hold them for two days," he assured the prince. Then he jerked his head towards the entrance of the tent, dismissing the youngest Royce. Zephyrn smiled apprehensively and left quickly.

Halloran's steely eyes fixed on the Roshan and her escort from under his iron gray brows. "This day will test us," he assured them. "Make ready your troops."

28. THE SONG OF WAR

The elves and their allies faced their worst day yet. The Roshan lost forty men, the greatest losses she had sustained in a single day. The elves lost twice that, including Captain Jennings as he rallied his troops to push back a drove of mace-wielding Crommags that were breaking through the battle lines.

The air was filled with the song of war – the clash of steel and the screams of the dying. It was a bitter hymn, full of tragedy and loss.

Ayala sent parties through the forest of great silver trees to see if there was a way to get around the elves and flank them. Most ran afoul of the pits and traps the Gnomin had dug and returned injured, if they came back at all.

The largest party, with no less than fifty Great Men, went far enough east to where the Elysian Forest was cut by the Saranac River, and followed it north.

They pressed through the woods cautiously. The ground rose before it flattened out again. The trees began to thin and the group began to distinguish a muttering of voices that joined with the sound of the river.

The Crommags, seeing only a few small forms through the trees and hearing only a few soft whispers, stepped boldly into the clearing that surrounded the north bend of the river and crouched low, waiting to throwback an attack or launch an attack of their own.

The evacuating Gnomin, so recently freed from the yoke of the great beasts, froze like lambs before the butcher and a hushed silence fell over both the defenders and the attackers as each weighed their options and each other.

The Jägers that had been charged with guarding the evacuation were the first to move, raising the cry of Tuar Ceath as they surged forward, swords high as Zephyrn and his archers launched a barrage of arrows at the Crommags. A dozen armed Atlanteans looked to Tristan to order their next move.

The Prince of Tides knew that the waters were his to command. He could make them rise and swallow the beasts, drowning every last one of them until their bodies were released into the Sabado Sea to feed the fishes and whales. But such an act would surely cause the boats currently on the river to capsize and he had a feeling that Gnomin were not hardy swimmers, most probably barely swimmers, if they could swim at all.

The decision was easy and took less than a second. The Roshan was not the only one to whom he owed a debt and, finally, he had every right to repay this one. The Prince of Tides drew his sword and charged the Crommags with a cry for Atlantea that was echoed by every one of his men as they charged with him.

The Great Men, their first surge thrown back by the archers before being attacked by elfin Jägers, were suddenly set upon by what could only be a ghost - so white was his hair and so gleaming was his sword as he rose up from the waters and came crashing forward over the land. They were stricken with fear and their attack turned quickly into a forced defense before they were all cut down.

⊗

Just before the heat of the day became too overwhelming, the Crommags made a last heave at the elves and their allies, rushing forward and swinging wildly. One of them cut down Haldor as they swarmed towards the Roshan.

The giant Norseman fended off a blow that would have cut another man in half, even as he collapsed to his knees.

"Halvar!" Ember shouted, driving her sword through a Crommag's throat. "Get him out of here!"

Halvar did not need to be told twice. He hooked an enormous arm under his brother's mighty shoulder and dragged him backwards as quickly as he could.

The Roshan moved to guard their retreat and was set upon by a pair of Crommags wielding broadswords.

Ember closed the distance as one raised a five-foot sword over his head. She plunged her own blade into his chest, where it promptly became lodged. The other one howled in rage and swung his sword at her.

Traejan was facing the other way as he fought and did not see. But Dell did. The Praetorian leapt past the prince as the Roshan planted a boot on the dead Crommag's gut and pushed, wrenching her weapon free as five pounds of sharpened steel came rushing through the air at her head.

Dell's sword came up and turned the Crommag's blade from the Roshan, but the momentum of the monster's swing kept it on its course, slicing down into his own shoulder. The dark-haired elf cried out and rolled to the side as the Roshan cut the neck of the beast from one side to the other.

"Traejan!" she shouted. But the elfin prince was already commanding the elves around him as Ian was pulling Dell from of the battle.

The elfin infantry, rallying to their prince, drove forward with resolve.

The Crommags were discouraged by their tenacity and wearying in the growing heat. They backed off, leering at what was left of the elves as they returned to their new residences upon the edge of the Great Lawn to drink grog and cheer their victories.

They knew the end would come soon, and that they would win. It was apparent now to even the simplest Crommag.

The Roshan turned to see Traejan, the tip of his sword resting in the dirt. As bloody as she was, the young prince pulled her close and they held each other tight. They stood that way for long moments, the summer sun pouring down on their battered forms.

Finally, the young prince dipped his head so he could speak into the Roshan's ear. "Come inside," he said, smoothing down her matted hair with his free hand. "A hot bath and a few hours of real sleep will do you a world of good."

"What if there is another attack?" she asked into his shoulder.

"They won't come again tonight," Traejan said. "And we will have plenty of notice if they do, there is no way they can slip through our lines. Come stay with me tonight."

She backed away from him, grasping his waist forcefully, as if afraid to let him go. He cupped her face in his hand. He wanted to tell her that this might be their very last night, the last chance they could spend together. But he saw that she already knew.

They both looked up as Dash arrived, reining in a horse almost as skittish as Ian's roan. The young elf looked as battle weary and dirty as the prince and the Roshan, though certainly not as bloody.

"Prince Traejan," he greeted, bowing in his saddle. "My lady. The general would like to see the Roshan immediately in the war tent."

The Roshan gave the elf a nod of acquiescence and, after another quick bow from his saddle, he spurred his horse and was gone.

Ember and Traejan turned and made their way across the northern part of the battlefield towards the line of tents.

Cookfires were being lit and wounds were being tended.

Silently, the pair found the war tent just as Zephyrn was coming out, his mind already elsewhere. Traejan grasped his brother's elbow, stopping him. The youngest prince glanced up, surprised. Seeing it was his older brother, he embraced him.

"It is good to see you are still alive!" he exclaimed, making Traejan smile.

"You as well," Traejan agreed. He jerked his head towards the flap of the tent. "Want to give a me a prelude?" he asked.

Zephyrn let out a great breath of air and glanced at the Roshan before looking back at his brother. "I was truly hoping that we would get everyone out today. It was completely feasible, but we had a few setbacks. A Crommag attack that we repelled but took precious time. Also, one of the larger rafts sank. In the aftermath of the attack people were scared and too many were trying to get on at once." He held up his hands as he saw the expressions of concern. "No one was hurt," he assured them, "and Prince Greenwater swiftly got everyone on land. But we will need to make a new large raft, or more small ones."

Traejan nodded as he considered the news and how much time they would still need. How much time the last of the diminishing army could give them. Then the brothers looked at each other as the unspoken was realized and they embraced each other.

"Stay safe," Traejan said hoarsely.

"You as well, brother," Zephyrn replied, his voice cracking. They released each other and Zephyrn impulsively embraced the Roshan.

It surprised her, but she knew it was his way of saying goodbye.

"Keep him safe," the youngest prince commanded softly in her ear.

"Until my last breath," she promised.

Zephyrn stood back and, when he did, there was a sly smile on his face. "Today could not have been that bad," he remarked lightly. "You still have three daggers and one short sword."

The Roshan laughed. "I actually have five daggers, and both short swords – one is in my belt."

"Even better!" Zephyrn exclaimed. He gave her a sweeping bow, his light blonde head dipping low. He rose and left, giving his brother a hard squeeze on the shoulder as he passed.

The pair watched him go and then turned and entered the war tent, Traejan holding aside the flap for Ember and then following her through. They were both stunned to see only two people inside – the general, and the Battle King. There were three map tables and the old elves looked lost and abandoned behind them.

The prince and the Roshan approached and bowed to the former king before Ember addressed the general. "You wanted to see me, sir?"

Halloran, more grizzled than ever with a two-day growth of a beard, sighed. "Yes. Do you know what lies in store for us tomorrow?"

The Roshan, her expression forbidding and set, dipped her head. "I do. I think we all do."

Halloran nodded. "Very well, I want to tell you that you are one of the finest soldiers I have ever seen, and I have seen many."

The Roshan frowned. It was certainly not what she was expecting. "Thank you, sir." Her eyes wanted to flick to the Battle King and to Traejan to take a measure of what might be going on, but she kept her gaze fixed upon the general.

"The elfin people owe you a great debt. I want to thank you…"

"Sir?" Ember asked, interrupting. "Please get to the point."

The general chuckled. "Blunt, as ever," he growled. "Very well, then, I will return the courtesy. I want you to take your men and leave."

The Roshan felt her jaw unhinge. It was certainly the last thing she expected. She closed her mouth and now her eyes did travel to the two other elves. Traejan looked as shocked as she felt.

"I am sorry, sir..." Ember began.

"Not as sorry as I am," he said, this time interrupting her. "You did not mishear me and you do not misunderstand. I want you to gather your men tonight and leave through the Crook – through the Mountains of the Sun. You said yourself you know what faces us tomorrow. It is pointless for us all to be slaughtered."

The muscles in Ember's jaw flexed as she shook her head.

"No."

"It was not a question."

"It is still your answer."

The Battle King cleared his throat, drawing every eye. "Young lady..." he began.

Both Traejan and the general closed their eyes, their lips pressed tight as they waited for what was coming. Halloran was the first to open his eyes and saw that though the Roshan was gripping the hilt of her sword so tightly that her fingers were white, she was keeping her composure as best she could.

"Commander," the Battle King said, correcting the way he had addressed her, "go back to Redtown. The elves that have fled Tuar Ceath, along with the other peoples of this world, will still need protection from these beasts. Who will raise the army to protect them, if not you?"

Ember closed her eyes again as she gathered herself. "I see the wisdom of your words and the kindness of your heart," she said, opening her eyes. "We will not return an act of kindness with an act of cowardice."

"It is an act of self-preservation," the Battle King told her.

The Roshan's hand tightened on the hilt of her sword once again and when she spoke it was slowly and carefully. "Your Grace," she began, her tone low and controlled, "with all due respect, that is an argument in semantics – one that I will not honor." She drew a deep breath and pressed on. "They came to this land for the same reason as you. They wanted a land without war, without violence. A land of peace. They want to do what they can to see that peace secured. They will give their lives to do so."

"They should not!" Halloran interjected heatedly.

"Why?" Ember demanded, turning her face to his, her voice rising. "Why should they be treated differently from the elves?"

The general shook his head and looked right and left as if there was something that needed to be said but he did not want to be the one to say it. He blew a burst of air from his nose and his face jerked up. "Because we can always make more," he said, leveling his eyes at her.

The Roshan took a quick step back, startled. The muscles in her jaw worked as if trying to force out her opposition.

She thought of the soldiers she had trained and how hard they had fought, and how many had died. She thought of their determination and their valor. She thought of how badly they had wanted to keep the violence far from their people.

Then she thought of Redtown, a city with no children.

The silence in the tent spun out.

Ember straightened and tugged at the bottom of her tunic. "I'm guessing I have just over a hundred men," she stated. "I'll send home half. More if I can."

The general pressed his lips together and gave her a small nod. The Battle King did the same and she turned and left without another word.

"How many horses are left?" the Roshan asked. "Not counting mine or Ian's."

She sat in her tent with Ryen and her three remaining captains. Outside, the sun was going down, a great blaring ball of fiery gas that looked like an eye, orange and blind. Ian handed her a cup of wine.

Gavan shrugged, his golden eyes glinting in the light of the braziers. "In my cavalry? Twenty-eight?" he guessed. "Maybe a few more."

The Roshan shifted her glittering gaze to Rhys.

"About the same for us. Maybe a handful more."

Ember nodded. "I want you to saddle them and leave, tonight. Along with all of our support force. Take the Crook, through the Mountains of the Sun," she told them, ignoring their shocked expressions. "Watch for Wilhelm and Otto, they are already camped there and waiting for us. Go cautiously, see if the pass is guarded at any point. If so, take cover and send back a rider. If not, ride hard for the Southlon. It will be up to you both to warn the people there, and raise another army."

The tent was quiet as her command sank in, along with the implications. Then Gavan glanced up sharply, his golden eyes narrowed.

"That is not why you are sending us," he said, his voice low.

"It is," the Roshan told him. "Ian too."

"Me?" Ian asked. "What if you are injured tomorrow?"

"It won't matter," Rhys said, his blue eyes shining and his tone as bitter as Gavan's. "She won't stop if she gets hurt, not even if she is maimed. She plans on fighting to the death, her own death."

"No!" Ian shouted.

"There *is* a good chance that we will all fight to our last tomorrow," the Roshan agreed.

"More so if you have sixty less soldiers!" Gavan exclaimed,

angry.

"It is my hope that the evacuation will finish early. When it does, the elfin cavalry will cover our retreat, bombarding them with arrows and then riding like the Seventh Circle through the pass, which will be blown by Otto and Wilhelm, making any chase impossible."

Ryen took a long drink of his wine. He had already spoken with Zephyrn and knew that if the evacuation was not finished by mid-morning, the army certainly would be.

"And Patrek?" Rhys asked.

The auburn-haired archer had remained silent for the entire meeting, hoping he would not be noticed. He finally glanced up at the others, his lavender eyes purple with unspoken defiance in the light of the tent.

"He and his men, along with Sloan's, make up eighty-eight soldiers, many of them good bowmen and all of them good swordsmen. They will stay."

Patrek turned his face away, knowing he could not keep the look of pride and relief from it. Ember rose to her feet and the others stood quickly, their discipline outweighing their feelings.

Rhys was the first to step forward, until he was right before the Roshan. "Thank you," he whispered hoarsely, "for everything you taught me. It was so much more than just to fight." Ember was dipping her head in acknowledgment when he reached out and embraced her. He held her tightly for a few moments, then released her and left the tent without another word.

She looked at Gavan who, though he was still clearly furious, embraced her as well. "I would disobey you," he admitted in her ear as he held her close, "if not for the warrior's responsibility you instilled in me. It does not make me less angry."

"I know," she told him. "But you are my best warrior. You need to train more. Make sure the Southlon is always protected."

He nodded in understanding and kissed her on the temple before letting her go. He gave her one long look with his golden eyes, and then he too was gone.

She turned to Patrek next, but he had already slipped out. No matter, she would see him in the morning. Ian stood, clutching a bundle of clothes and weapons.

"Prince Traejan asked for some things," he said and then ducked out before she could say another word.

The Roshan, alone in her tent with Ryen, dropped back down into a chair. Her shoulders were high and her head hung low. He hated to see her in such a way. Her cup of wine was clutched, but forgotten, in slender fingers that were covered in dirt and blood.

A grunt came from her hunched form that could well have been taken for a sob. He pulled his chair closer to hers and reached out and wrapped a large hand around her shoulder in consolation.

"I have fought so many times, Ryen," she said, her voice breaking. "So many battles. Seen so many die. Been wounded more times than I can count. But this time is different, and I am so scared." She looked up at him and tears spilled from her eyes and ran over her cheeks. "I don't know why."

The Vikeman sighed. "Because this time you care for many," he told her, pushing a clump of red hair from her dirty, sweat-streaked face. "Before, you hardly cared even for yourself."

The Roshan looked at him with a sad smile. "I was a child then, wasn't I? Still believing in dragons and magic."

The Norseman sank to his knees and pulled her from her chair and held her slight form close, his arms engulfing her slim body in an embrace. "There *are* dragons, and there *is* magic," he told her.

"Where?" Ember asked, her voice cracking again as she buried her face in his broad chest, her hands dropping into claws, clutching at his vest. "Where are the dragons? And where is the magic? When does it come?"

He tilted his head down, his lips brushing her ear. "When you least expect it," he whispered. He held her tight for a moment, then kissed the top of her head, took a step back with one knee and brushed the tears from her cheeks. "But enough of this talk! Tonight, you should be with your prince."

Ember gave him a crooked smile. "Is that really what you think?"

"It is," Ryen affirmed. "It is not what I want, but what I want hardly matters now. What I know is how much you will benefit from a full night of sleep, in a place with walls and a roof and with someone you trust standing guard. You will be a new woman in the morning, which is good. The one I am looking at now..." the Vikeman trailed off and shook his head, making a sour face.

"Very well," the Roshan agreed, rising to her feet. "And Sloan?" she asked, her voice breaking once more as she stifled a sob.

The Vikeman rose as well and stood very still, the only motion coming from the swallow in his throat. "His body is being prepared, along with those of the other Vikemen that have fallen. An hour after moonset, three hours before dawn, we will light their pyre."

The Roshan nodded and left her tent with the fair Norseman close by, towering over her as always. Outside, a rosy dusk was seeping into the cooling air. Ember reached out and squeezed his hand, afraid if she put her arms around him she would not let go. Ryen squeezed her hand in return and released it as she turned and walked away. He did not watch her leave.

Instead, the ice-blue eyes of the Vikeman sought out his nearest partner in crime. Though Aiden weighed less than one of Ryen's legs, the boy could hold liquor and tell stories till there was no else standing. Plus, Ryen enjoyed his company.

He trundled up to the leader of the Sprites and leaned down conspiratorially.

"Is it time yet to find a drink?" he asked.

"It is always time!" Aiden informed him with a grin that nearly split his face in two.

Ryen turned and headed towards the mess tent. "You know," he remarked as casually as he could, "that nothing would bring the Lady more happiness than if you and your men were to slip away tonight in the darkness."

The Wildboys were small, but quick and deadly with their spears. They were the first to leap forward and fill any gaps in the line, especially if that gap was close to the Dark Lady. Since doing so, however, their numbers had also decreased by half.

Aiden's face was thoughtful. "I know," he agreed. "But how could I live with myself for the rest of my days if I were to leave her in such a way?"

Ryen sighed, knowing just what he meant. Then the Vikeman straightened and threw out his chest. "Let's see if we can deplete the rest of the cider by half tonight," he suggested.

Aiden looked at him with disappointment. "Why just half?" he asked. "I think we should try to drink it all!"

Ryen laughed and placed a large hand on the Wildboy's thin shoulder. "You are wise beyond your years," he told him, guiding the way through the camp and to the mess.

❧

The doors to Castle Song were open and elfin soldiers were coming and going in the purpling twilight, save for one. Dell was standing outside on guard. The edge of a bandage, wrapped around his shoulder, was visible under his shirt. He smiled at the Roshan as she approached and she was unable to not smile back.

"How are you feeling?" she asked, stopping in front of his slight form.

"It hurts," he answered honestly, "but I will be fine."

The smile slipped from her face and she shook her head slowly from side to side. "Why, Dell?" she asked. "Why did you risk your life for mine? You are sworn to protect Traejan, not me."

The corners of the Praetorian's mouth tightened, making him look like a wistful child. "Traejan has pledged his life to you," he told her. "Which means I will safeguard you as well and as best I can. Besides," he added, brightening, "I can fight with my other arm, same as you."

Ember smiled and glanced at the open doors. Dell smiled, then turned and went inside. The Roshan followed him as he took the corridor to the left and then stopped at the bottom of a winding staircase.

"He's at the top," he informed her.

Ember sighed. "Of course he is. Thank you, Dell."

The Praetorian bowed and left, resuming his post by the open doors. The Roshan turned and glared at the looming stairs and, though she was exhausted, hurried up - taking them two at a time. She noticed, as she climbed, the sounds diminishing behind her until there were none at all, as if the whole world was falling away.

When she reached the polished oak door she raised her hand to knock but she hesitated. Something about the silence of the tower, so close and yet so far from the war outside, seemed precious. She turned the handle and pushed the door open.

Traejan was there waiting, sitting in a chair by the fireplace. A small fire was burning, more for the light than the heat. A pair of electric flambeaux burned in sconces on either side of a giant bed. The bed had been turned down and on a bedtable was a plate of hot meat, cheese, and a bottle of red wine. On the end of the bed, folded neatly, was a clean set of her clothes, including undergarments. She smiled, knowing that Ian must truly have had an appointment with the prince. A copper bath had been brought into the room and waited for her - full of steaming water.

Of all these things, the young prince looked the most inviting to her eyes - with the bed a close second. She could not bear, however, to blemish him or his clean linens with the grime of war.

She tore her gaze from the soft sheets and fluffed pillows and unbuckled her sword belt and pulled it free. She wrapped the leather strap around the sheath, leaned it against the wall, and stripped herself of her remaining weaponry.

She pulled off her boots, and began to peel off her clothes. They were stiff with dirt and sweat and blood. Traejan watched her, silent and unmoving. Naked, she eased herself into the tub, glad with the choice she had made. It was almost painfully hot, but made her forget every other pain she had, at least for the moment. She let herself sink deeper and closed her eyes.

Traejan rose from his seat by the fire. He had sworn to himself that he would not speak to her, nor touch her, while she was there. She needed rest and he meant for her to have it. As always - as with her - his mind, heart, and body all seemed determined to act on their own accord. He walked up behind her and laid a hand upon her head. He pushed the hair out of her eyes and cradled the side of her face with his fingers. She looked up at him, held his gaze for a moment of eternity, and then closed her eyes again.

A table next to the bath was laden with towels, soaps, oils, and pitchers of hot water. He rolled up his sleeves and reached for one of the pitchers. He rinsed her hair and then scrubbed it with lavender soap, and then rinsed it again. He longed to kiss her, to hold her, so much that it made him hurt deep inside. He pushed the things that he wanted from his mind and brought his will to bear on the things that he had. He wrapped a towel around her hair and gently squeezed the water from it.

She scrubbed herself all over with the soap, paying special attention to her hands, making sure to get all of the blood and dirt from her knuckles and from under her fingernails. She stood and used the second pitcher to rinse herself off with clean hot water. Traejan took her hand and helped her step out of the tub before he wrapped her in a warm towel that was as big as a blanket.

The Roshan found a hairbrush on the table and brushed out her damp locks. When she finished, she dropped the towel and wrapped her arms around Traejan, pulling his face down to her own.

"You should eat while your dinner is still warm," he told her, breaking the long silence before their lips could meet.

"Let it get cold," she whispered. She tightened her grip on the base of his neck and pressed her lips against his for a mere second before he pulled away.

"You need food," he said, his voice soft and husky. "And sleep."

"I need you more," she told him, cupping his face in her hands so he could not back away again but, this time, he did not even try.

He kissed her, opening her mouth with his own and losing his hands in her damp hair as she undid the laces on his shirt and his pants. He stopped long enough to pull his tunic off over his head. With her already naked, he felt as if he could not get undressed fast enough.

The Roshan laughed as he hopped from one foot to the other, pulling off his boots, and together they slipped into the bed. The mattress was so soft that it brought tears to her eyes and she closed them, relishing the feel of the crisp clean sheets as her head sank into the pillow. Traejan gently moved his body against hers and, seeing her eyes closed, hesitated.

Despite what she might say, he knew she needed sleep more than anything else.

As if sensing his thoughts, her eyes cracked open and she was up and her body over his before he could voice any protest. They made love as if it were their first time, starving for each other. Afterwards, only partially sated, they made love again as if it were their last time.

"I'm sweaty again," the Roshan said at last, chuckling.

The elfin prince kissed her damp forehead. "It's a clean sweat," he said as she wriggled her form next to his, nestling her head into his shoulder. Traejan smiled and pulled her into the crook of his arm. "You told me once that dusk was a time for magic. It certainly was tonight."

Ember laughed softly. "It was," she agreed and then paused for a moment. "Do you remember the rest of what I said that time?" she asked.

"Yes. You said that dawn was the time for miracles."

"We are going to need one tomorrow."

"Then maybe we will get one," he said.

"Maybe," she sighed.

The prince kissed her head and closed his eyes. He tried not to hold her too tight. "Now go to sleep," he commanded.

But there was no need. She already was.

⚜

Traejan awoke two hours before dawn, as he had grown accustomed to, but Ember was already gone. She had left an hour earlier to watch Sloan and the Norsemen, laid with their weapons on wooden biers stacked with kindling, as they were sent on their way to feast in the halls of their gods. She hoped Sloan would like it there.

As their ashes rose into the still dark sky, she returned to her tent where she found Ian, laying out her weapons by the light of two candles.

The Roshan stared at him. She was too deflated to be angry, yet she could not believe he would disobey an order – especially one from her.

"I'm not a soldier," he explained as if reading her thoughts. He put a plate with a cold breakfast on the table. "You cannot command me like the others."

"A technicality," she said. "Though I appreciate your loyalty."

Ian gave a quick nod as she sat down and, after a moment of indecision, sat with her. Together they shared one last meal, each of them silent. Ian watched her the entire time, wanting to ask her many questions as she went to her bed and refilled her brace and holsters with the weapons he had laid out for her.

In the end there was only one he found the voice for and asked as she stood before him one last time. "Is there anything else I can do for you?" he whispered.

The Roshan smiled and shook her head. Then she grasped the sides of his face and pulled it to hers and kissed him on his full lips. When she let him go his dark eyes were large and round.

"If there is any chance, at any time, you get on Meghan and get the Seventh Circle out of here," she commanded. "Promise me."

"I promise," he said softly. *I also promise that I will take you with me*, he thought, *if there is any chance I can.*

As if reading his thoughts, she sighed and gave him a nod.

Together, they left the tent they had shared, just as everyone else was leaving theirs. The red troops, elves, and the spattering of Vikemen and Sprites, all gathered in a group south of Castle Song, and then spread out to form a line as the sky was brightening in the east.

A quarter of a mile to the south, past the blood soaked and

trampled grass that had once been the Great Lawn, were the Crommags. Their lines were hundreds deep. Ayala stood at the forefront, in the center, waiting for enough light. It was slower to come to this meadow than it was to the vale but he had not figured out why.

He looked to the sky and then looked at the meager line of elves. Among them were a few of the large men from the north, the child-sized waifs with the sticks, and a dark spot that looked like a shadow in the ranks. He was too eager to wait. It was light enough, or would be soon enough. The leader of the Great Men bared his fangs in a grin and raised his mace high above his head.

"Today!" he shouted. "Today, they will all die! Today, we will conquer these people, and today, these lands will be ours!"

A mighty roar burst forth from more than a thousand Crommag throats, and then they surged forward, ready to end their first war, victorious.

The Roshan watched them come. She knew she would kill many of them that day, but there was only one that mattered. She kept her eye on him as the beasts closed the distance between them and the elves.

When they were one hundred yards away, Patrek - and what was left of her army from the Southlon - stepped though the line and let fly a barrage of bolts. They had enough time to reload and loose another torrent before the next rank of enraged Crommags picked up speed, rushing at them. They dropped their crossbows and pulled their swords.

"To the last!" Patrek bellowed, his violet eyes blazing in the light of dawn.

"To the last!" his men echoed before the cry was picked up by every elf and ally, including General Halloran and the Battle King himself as they drew their swords and threw themselves at the enemy.

The Roshan cut down one Crommag, and then another.

She fell one more and then was up against the leader. There was no dance this time. She lunged for his injured leg and he leapt backwards, landing on his good leg and turning quickly to swing his mace at her head. The Roshan ducked it with ease and brought her sword down on him.

Ten Wildboys had spread out like a fan around her, their spears whipping around and stabbing through any beast that came near.

Ayala's other arm was strapped with a shield and he brought it up to block her sword. The Roshan spun around and grinned at him, knowing he had the shield because she had relieved him of two fingers on that hand.

"Having trouble holding a weapon with that one?" she chided.

Ayala did not understand her words, but he knew she was mocking him. He leaned forward and roared at her like a bear, spittle flying from his thick lips.

The Roshan moved in again, quick as a snake, intent upon bringing her sword down upon his outstretched neck. The Great Man dove to the side and swung his mace at her legs, taking a nice chunk from the muscle in her calf just as the body of a Wildboy went flying through the air to land, broken, on the ground.

Ember screamed out in frustration more than pain. She risked a quick glance around and saw that the elves were falling quickly. Much too quickly. Worse, Traejan and Ryen were fighting back to back, and close to being overrun.

The giant Crommag saw her distraction and hurdled at her, bringing his mace around for the killing blow. The Roshan fell to the ground before it could connect, rolled away, and came up with the spear of the fallen Wildboy in her left hand. With a scream of fury she brought it down with all her strength and drove it down through the Crommag's foot. Then she grasped the hilt of her sword with both hands and swung it around, its blade parallel to the ground as she used all the momentum from her center of gravity.

It cut through the Crommag's gut and he howled with pain and rage and tried to spring towards her with his mace, but his foot was pinned to the ground. The Roshan gave him a parting look of disgust and triumph and then was gone in the fray, cutting down Crommags like a reaper in a field of wheat.

It was not enough. The line of elves and their allies was breaking apart and being overrun.

The Roshan put her back to Ryen and Traejan and fought on doggedly, determined to ignore the truth.

It was the end.

And so soon, Ember thought, filled with a sickening feeling of despair. *The sun has hardly risen.*

As if in answer to her thoughts, the sun finished its climb over the Elysian Forest, gold and yellow and glorious, pouring the light of dawn onto the land below.

Then the air was split by a shriek that sounded like a dying horse, but a hundred times louder. It tore the sky apart above their heads before resounding in a crashing boom that threw every fighter down flat on the ground.

Traejan rose to his knees and instinctively moved to cover Ember but she pushed him off as she stared at the sky, breathless. Something was streaking through the air so fast that her eyes could only glimpse flashes of light as the sun glinted off it. Traejan's free arm went around her and together they watched as it turned and headed back towards where a thousand combatants had paused mid-battle and now crouched, a multitude of eyes gaping at the sky.

The object slowed just enough to be seen, a flash of silver trailing green light. It flew past and turned again, slowing further as it came around for another pass over the Great Lawn and now even more visible to those below. It looked like great, winged reptile with smooth silver skin that shimmered green in the sun. Its eyes were large and rectangular, taking up most of the creature's head.

"Seven Circles," Ember said, clutching Traejan's arm, "it's a dragon!"

"No," the Battle King said from behind her, "it is too small. It is a Fledgling."

Ayala was about to shout at the Great Men to fight on, knowing the elves were spent, but he was as mesmerized as the rest of them. The Crommags watched in awe as the thing circled again for another pass, this time coming in low. Then the silver monster dropped, descending with an obvious intent to land and heading directly for the Crommags. The Great Men dispersed, some bellowing in fear, and ran for the cover of the woods. Most kept running south, meaning to duck into their tents and hide from the winged demon.

Ayala wanted to scream at them, that the elves were defeated and scattered just at the moment of victory, but he could see the creature was coming directly at him, growing larger by the second. Cursing in anger and fear, he grasped the spear in both hands and wrenched it free from his foot and ran as fast as his legs would take him. The elves had unleashed some final weapon, or perhaps it was an elfin god that had come at last to protect them. The latter seemed most likely. Ayala knew that if the elves had been harboring such a weapon, they would not have waited so long to use it.

He made it to the safety of the woods and turned in time to see the monster-god push out four legs from its silver belly and land on the beaten and bloody grass. Jaws parted and green fire spurted forth. Seeing that was enough for the Great Men that had run for the woods. They turned and ran again, this time putting as much distance as they could between themselves and the great fiend that had descended on them.

The Wildboys and the Vikemen stared in fear and wonder. The elves, however, seemed no less amazed but not frightened in the least. They were helping each other up from the ground and dusting each other off. None seemed terrified. Most were old enough to recognize an IGC spacecraft, but they watched along with the younger elves, the remaining Vikemen and Sprites, and the Roshan.

Ember stared, mesmerized, as a spot on the side of the creature the Battle King had called a Fledgling began to shimmer. The silver skin seemed to melt like wax held to a flame, but kept the shape of a perfect oval as it opened up and a set of silver stairs formed below it. A small backside poked out, followed by slim shoulders before a pair of boots found the steps, went down a few of them, and then jumped to the ground before turning around.

The newcomer was obviously an elf - with pointed ears and high arched brows - but a small one, like a Sylvan. He had chocolate-colored hair that fell over green eyes that danced with merriment and mischief. He flicked his hair from his face, grinning.

"Looks like I got here just in time," he said cheerfully as the Battle King approached him, unable to restrain a smile.

"You certainly did," Acqtraejale agreed. "And, for that, we cannot thank you enough."

"No thanks necessary," the young elf chirped, looking past the white-haired elf to scan the crowd. His eyes lit on Ember and lingered for a moment before passing on, finally coming back to rest on the Battle King. He gave the older elf a disarming smile. "I don't suppose any of you here are part of the de Rossi family?" he asked. "I was sent here to find Hope."

A silence ensued that resulted in a few eyes darting at one another.

Ember paused for a moment and then stepped forward. "I am Ember L'chiross," she said. She took a deep breath and then continued. "I am Hope's daughter."

The Vikeman Ryen Glace, battle bloodied, looked at her and smiled.

Traejan and Aiden both regarded her with surprise, as if

seeing her for the first time.

The Battle King's eyes went wide and then he hung his white head, shaking it gently and and chuckling softly.

The young elf grinned from ear to ear and took a step towards the Roshan. "Your family has been looking for you for a long time," he said, "and I have crossed more distance than you can imagine to find you. But you are well met, Ember L'chiross. My name is Jade."

AUTHOR'S NOTE

I bet a lot of folks didn't see that one coming. Yet, no one who ever walks by my office noticed that my portrait of Jade was moved from the hallway to the spot next to my desk over a year ago. Jade was not just a *deus ex machina* for this story, though he served splendidly, he has simply been waiting.

I love it when a story comes full circle. There is something very powerful about it. It has a feeling of completion and fulfillment. Maybe, in that way, art imitates life. Or is it the other way around? Or is it something about a light and a way....

Well, all I know is that a lot has happened since Jade made the ultimate sacrifice in an effort to save the ones he loved. I can hardly believe there have been six books (and yes, I have to count them off on my fingers as I write this) since then, and four (including this one) since we left all our heroes and villains suspended in space.

You do remember who the heroes were and who the villains were – right?

I am anxious to get back to Scarlett and Blue, the de Rossi sisters and the ever-so-dashing Chimera. Their tale will continue to unfold in my next book, *Secrets of the Earth*. I seriously doubt, however, that it will be the next one published.

If it is ready, I will certainly serve it up. If not, it stays on the stove. Meanwhile, I will offer an intermezzo – a main course palate cleanser. A trifle old, though not stale in the least.

Early in 2013 my teenage daughter broke her leg bad enough to need surgery, including the installation of a steel plate, three steel screws, and the lugubrious condemnation to the living room couch for what felt like forever. I was working on *Moons of Jupiter* at the time and, in an effort to cheer her, I sidelined my own work for at least an hour a day to write her a story.

It was about her, of course, and whatever boy-band that was currently wooing her along with my itunes account. I didn't know zilch about boy bands, but I did know that the IGC was already starting to looking like a bunch of bad mambajambas and I knew how quirky my daughter was.

Drops of Jupiter turned out to be fun to write (my daughter hounded me for each chapter like no publisher could) and I think the eight-chapter novella turned out to be a good story. Also another link in the chain.

Another circle.

And what do circles look like when they touch?

Like a fat number eight too tired to stand up - so that it lies on its side.

We recognize it as the symbol for infinity.

Forever.